Robin L. Stears/WildAss Productions.ne

About the Author

JUDY REENE SINGER is a dressage competitor, a horse trainer, and an all-around animal lover. She is a frequent contributor to international animal rescues and a foster mother to elephant babies. She has written about the equestrian world for more than a decade and was named a top feature writer by *The Chronicle of the Horse*. She holds degrees in English and psychology, and shares her home with cats and dogs, horses, two African gray parrots, a cockatoo, and sundry other creatures.

An Inconvenient Elephant

Also by Judy Reene Singer

Still Life with Elephant

Horseplay

An Inconvenient Elephant

JUDY REENE SINGER

HARPER

An Imprint of HarperCollins*Publishers*

HARPER

AN INCONVENIENT ELEPHANT. Copyright © 2010 by Judy Reene Singer.
All rights reserved. Printed in the United States of America. No part
of this book may be used or reproduced in any manner whatsoever
without written permission except in the case of brief quotations
embodied in critical articles and reviews. For information address
HarperCollins Publishers, 10 East 53rd Street, New York, NY 10022.

HarperCollins books may be purchased for educational, business, or
sales promotional use. For information please write: Special Markets
Department, HarperCollins Publishers, 10 East 53rd Street, New
York, NY 10022.

FIRST HARPER PAPERBACK PUBLISHED 2010.

Library of Congress Cataloging-in-Publication Data
Singer, Judy Reene.
An inconvenient elephant / Judy Reene Singer.
p. cm.
Sequel to: Still life with elephant.
ISBN 978-0-06-171377-4
1. Americans—Africa—Fiction. 2. Safaris—Africa—Fiction. 3. Elephants—Fiction. I. Title.
PS3619.I5724I63 2010
813'.6—dc22
2009030671

10 11 12 13 14 /RRD 10 9 8 7 6 5 4 3 2 1

To all those little creatures that inhabit my office with me and, by virtue of their unremitting cuteness, make it impossible for me to concentrate on my work.

My little red French poodles, Lola and Flash Gordon; the twin-zues, two little shih tzus named Mimsie and Sadie; my two African Grays, Zodiac and Tallulah; and my salty-mouth cockatoo, Samantha. I love you all.

Acknowledgments

IT'S TRUE THAT WRITERS ARE THE MOST SOLITARY OF people, sitting alone in front of their computer screens waiting for that perfect sentence to put in an appearance, but we do have the never-ending support of wonderful people. I want to thank Jane Gelfman, my agent extraordinaire, who is always encouraging and kind and caring and smart and who always understands what I mean, even when I don't. To my editor, Wendy Lee, excruciatingly thorough and brilliant and always on the money with her great suggestions and exquisite sense of character and plot and timing, and whose requests and suggestions have made me a better writer.

I am really grateful that they have my back.

And thanks, as always, to the Gang of Four, who sit with me every Thursday afternoon to listen and laugh or cry as I read, before we attack some memorable lunches.

Chapter 1

WHEN YOU SPEND A YEAR LIVING IN THE AFRICAN bush with baby elephants, you forget your table manners. Though I wasn't exactly trumpeting through my nose in the restaurant, I suddenly realized I was bolting my dinner and hovering over my plate in a protective hunch, habits I had gotten into so that greedy little trunks didn't pull the food out from underneath me. I thought I might have licked my fingers. More than once. And I might have wiped my mouth on my sleeve. At least I hoped the sleeve belonged to me and not to the new friend I had made, Diamond-Rose Tremaine. Although, truth to tell, Diamond probably wouldn't have cared.

We both had to leave Kenya very quickly. When bullet holes adorn the fine linens in your sleeping bag, it is time to move on. Kenya had fallen into political chaos, and for personal safety, the owner of the sanctuary where I was working immediately ordered me to book a flight home to New York. I did, with great reluctance. I had given up everything to work with the ellies, and having to say good-bye was breaking my heart. I would have stayed with them forever.

I had been standing in a long queue of nervous, impatient people waiting for a *matatu* minibus to take us to the airport just outside of Nairobi when Diamond introduced herself. She had been standing in front of me.

"I'm Diamond-Rose Tremaine," she said just as we finally boarded. She was very tall and slim, with wild-curled chestnut hair and sea green eyes, and wearing rumpled safari clothes—tan shorts and matching shirt and heavy brown boots caked in mud.

I glanced at her and smoothed back my hair and surreptitiously rubbed my boots on the back of my pants leg, then wondered why, at a time like this, I was thinking how my mother would have disapproved of the way I looked.

"I guess we'll be traveling together," Diamond said. "Spent twenty years here in Kenya, but I originally come from New York, so I guess I'm going home."

"Neelie Sterling." I offered my hand. "I'm from New York, too. I just left the Pontwynne Elephant Rescue. Twenty years! What were you doing so long in Kenya?"

"I owned WildTours Horseback Safaris," Diamond returned. "Everything went to hell because of the election. Had my horse shot out from underneath me." She sighed. "I think they ate him."

"That would put a crimp in business."

———

Before long, we were racing through the streets of Nairobi, the minibus practically doing cartwheels as it screeched around the corners of a city under assault. I sat nervously and watched the turmoil through the bus window. My year in Kenya had been filled with the tranquil care of baby elephants, and the upheaval around me was alarming. I hoped we wouldn't get delayed by "the jam," the dense, balled-up traffic that hit twice a day and offered up several nervous prayers that we would make it to Jomo Kenyatta Airport without absorbing a round of ammo.

Diamond yawned.

"How can you be so calm?" I asked her.

She waved a hand. "I've seen it all," she said. "Tribal wars, hungry lions, charging rhinos, droughts, floods, and lightning storms that split trees apart right over your head." She plumped up the rucksack perched in her lap and enfolded her head in her arms. "It all eventually settles down," she said, yawning, and promptly fell asleep.

A crackle of gunfire ominously grazed the rear fenders. Huge rocks, lobbed by mobs of angry Kenyans, bounced off the windshield as the driver, in an effort to avoid them, crunched over broken glass and wove in and out of burning fruit stands, executing a series of maneuvers I thought possible only of movie stunt drivers. The passengers outside on the running boards clung precariously to the top rails, chickens tucked possessively under their arms, faces covered with newspaper in the naive belief it would protect them, and screamed, "*Songasonga mathe, songasonga mathe,*" which meant "Move it, mama, move it!"

The bus tore on, its yellow dome light blinking furiously, the new plasma screen in front ludicrously flashing a hip-hop video whose beat emphasized the ruts in the road. All the while the driver loudly reassured us, "We are secure, *sijambo, sijambo,* everything good." But we knew everything wasn't good—the entire country was in crisis, the city was rupturing, everywhere was turmoil and fury.

Something chunked against a window, and there was a noisy confusion. I screamed and jumped from my seat. Diamond lifted her head and slowly blinked awake.

"They're shooting at us!" I yelled.

"Are you sure?" she asked sleepily.

"No," I had to admit, but another thunk convinced us both, and we immediately ducked under our seat.

"Keep your head down," she shouted directly into my ear. "Sorry I'm taking up so much room, I have legs like a giraffe. But keep *down*!"

"I'm trying," I yelled back, compressing myself into a ball in an effort to accommodate her long frame.

Squealing tires protested another sharp turn. Rioting crowds outside lobbed fruit and garbage at the bus. A large orange splatted against the window across the aisle.

"What a waste of fruit!" Diamond-Rose gestured to the juice dripping down the glass. "Oranges should be floating in a pitcher of sangria."

The bus veered sideways and we tumbled together, grabbing each other for support.

"Well, pour one for me," I shouted as the bus spun off

the main road and bounced down a backstreet into sudden eerie quiet.

"Ladies and gentlemen, you can sit again normally, please, please," the driver announced. "This street is secure. *Sijambo.*"

Diamond peeked out from under her seat. "Well, I believe him." She stood up and stretched, then bent down to offer me a helping hand.

But I was unconvinced. "Never trust anything in Nairobi. You know what the locals call it—Nairobbery!"

"Oh, bollocks!" Diamond dismissed. "I think we're safe."

"Suit yourself," I said. "I'm not coming out until we get to the airport and pull up right next to the plane."

A bullet shattered the window behind us, and Diamond dropped to her knees next to me.

"I guess I'll wait down here," she conceded. "Just in case they shoot the bus out from underneath me."

We got to the airport safely, only to be told that none of the planes had vacancies. At least none of the planes going to New York. Or London or any other place outside of Africa. Every seat on every plane was taken, every flight filled by nervous tourists or businesspeople, all with the same intent. To get out of Kenya alive and as quickly as possible.

Our seats had been given away. Not unusual, said Diamond. Someone had come along before us and bid more money.

"But we had *reservations*," I tried to explain to the indifferent woman behind the desk. She was sipping tea and reading a movie magazine.

"But you did not come earlier," she explained with a shrug, peering over the top of the page and reverting to the usual charming but sometimes infuriating African logic. "You should come here first thing. Now it's first come, first go."

"That's not how reservations are supposed to work," I began, but Diamond tugged at my arm.

"Forget it," she said. "You won't win." She pulled her cell phone from her pocket and stepped away for a moment to enter into a spirited conversation with someone, then returned. "I'm good at fixing things. Let me speak to the reservation clerk."

"Oh, that would be terrific," I said, gratefully letting her take my place at the desk, while I moved a few feet away to a Coke machine to buy something to drink. It was empty but took my money anyway.

Diamond-Rose spoke to the woman at some length. There was much nodding and gesticulating while I watched the population in the airport reach critical mass. Every bus that arrived brought another crowd of people pushing, demanding, looking for a fast way out of danger, and I wondered what Diamond-Rose could possibly accomplish.

After a few minutes, she returned to my side, waving tickets.

"Two tickets on Air Zimbabwe for Harare Airport," she announced triumphantly.

"What?" I gasped. "I don't want to go to Zimbabwe."

She gave me a baleful look. "The problem is that we have to leave Kenya straightaway, yes?"

I nodded.

"And so we go where there is available space."

"But there's available space in Zimbabwe only because it's *worse* than Kenya," I said. "No one wants to go to Zimbabwe."

"Very true," Diamond agreed. "But we do get out of Nairobi. Problem solved." She picked up her rucksack and started walking rapidly toward the terminal.

"But that only gives us another problem," I said, grabbing my suitcase and running after her. "What are we going to do in Zimbabwe?"

She flashed me a beatific smile over her shoulder. "I'll work on that problem after we get there."

Chapter 2

THIS COULD BE THE BIGGEST MISTAKE OF MY LIFE, I thought, when I saw the armed guards rifling through the baggage of the person in line in front of me. We'd had a nine-hour wait in Nairobi in an unbearably packed terminal, and then a two-hour flight into Harare International Airport. Diamond's phone call had been to friends of hers, and they were making special arrangements for us to immediately retreat to a secure area after we arrived in Zimbabwe. All I knew was that they were unable to get us a bus out of the city since the buses had used up their petrol ration. They booked us on a small charter plane owned by friends of theirs to Victoria Falls. After that, we would pick up a transfer van north to Charara Safari Area, as the national park was called. Diamond's friends thought it prudent to get us out of the city as quickly as possible and into a more benign tourist area.

I couldn't wait to leave Harare. It was a hostile city, worse than when I had left it nearly two years before, and after we landed it was taking us nearly three and a half hours to clear customs in an empty airport at four in the morning.

It was finally my turn, and I nervously handed my passport over to the armed customs agent.

"Why you come to Zimbabwe?" he asked.

Why indeed, I thought.

"To see your lovely wildlife," Diamond-Rose said over my shoulder.

The surly agent jerked my suitcase across the table and ripped through it, unrolling my neatly packed undies and shaking them out, looking for contraband petrol or much-revered American money.

"Just keep smiling," Diamond whispered in my ear.

"Can they arrest us for not smiling?" I whispered back.

She nodded in reply. The agent unceremoniously stuffed my clothes back into the suitcase, snapped it shut, and slid it across the table at me, along with my passport.

"Welcome to Zimbabwe," he snarled.

Now we had a six-hour wait for the plane, which, we found, flew on an incomprehensible schedule. But at least there was a proper restaurant on the far side of the airport, and we decided to go for a very late dinner.

We paid the nominal entry fee and were seated with a bow from a deferential waiter.

I looked over the menu. I hadn't eaten anything since the previous day and I was starving. "Everything sounds delicious," I said, then read off the entrees. " 'Chicken francaise with wild rice and grilled vegetables' or 'steak au poivre with new potatoes' or 'broiled prawns in garlic sauce.' And Malva pudding for dessert." I loved Malva pudding. The first time I'd ever eaten it was in Kenya—it was kind of a pudding cake with a toffee-like crust made with apricot jam—and it had become a favorite of mine.

Diamond impatiently grabbed her own menu. "The only food I've eaten in the past three days was a hunk of biltong I took with me before I left the bush, so I'm dying for a good meal."

We eagerly ordered dinner. I wanted the chicken, as far from this past year's daily meals of fried samosas and pea beans as I could get. Diamond chose the seasoned steak, though the waiter was vague as to what kind of steak it actually was—warthog or ostrich or wildebeest—and promised to check.

He returned shortly and gave me a courteous bow. They had run out of chicken, he apologized, about four years previous, as far as he could determine. Would I mind an equal substitution? Of course not, I said graciously.

A few minutes later, I was presented with a large platter. "Cauliflower al dente and mashed pumpkin," he announced with a flourish, "with a complimentary side of fried worms in peanut sauce."

Diamond's steak dinner arrived shortly after mine: a large platter of cauliflower and mashed pumpkin, with a complimentary side of fried worms in peanut sauce.

"Perfect," Diamond said as she dug into the worms with the tip of her knife, then chewed them noisily. "Forgive my manners. I'm usually in the bush when I eat."

I waved my hand. "No problem," I said, rapidly tucking into my mashed pumpkin. "I've been eating with elephants for the past year. You're positively dainty compared to them." I watched her dinner disappear at warp speed, then reflected, "Of course, they ate with their noses."

I was still hungry after the mashed pumpkin and turned my attention to the cauliflower, which was al dente if you had dentes like a crocodile.

I looked around. The restaurant was crowded, and it felt odd to be sitting at a real table after a year squatting next to baby elephants. People were chatting softly, daintily blotting their lips, and using all their utensils. No one got smacked in the head for stealing from another's plate. No one threw their food on their back and shoulders. I was going to have to get used to good manners again.

Diamond and I finished our dinners and still had a long time before our plane left for Victoria Falls. It was scheduled to leave around ten or noon or never. We drank an impressive amount of coffee in order to stay awake and ordered doubles on the Malva pudding, which only engendered another profuse apology from our waiter. Malva pudding was not available for dessert. Nor was anything else.

"Tell me again how this is going to get us to New York?" I asked Diamond-Rose as I downed my fifth cup of coffee.

"It won't *exactly* get us to New York," she admitted. "Americans sometimes have a problem getting out of Zimbabwe, but my friends reassure me there is no problem at all getting out of Zambia. Eventually we can take a plane from Zimbabwe to Zambia. Or Botswana. They like Americans in Botswana."

"It's the word 'eventually' that bothers me," I said. I had visions of spending the rest of my life taking planes from one African country to the next, with my new friend promising how each one would be easier to leave from than the last, while the prospect of getting to New York became more and more remote.

"So, who are these friends of yours?" I asked as we ordered still another cup of coffee. "It was really very nice of them to make all these arrangements."

"Charlotte and Billy Pope," she said. "They run Thula-Thula Safaris in Chizarira, but they had no vacancies, so they booked us for Charara. Once we get settled, they said they would gladly take us on safari. It's a lot more wild than anything you've probably seen."

I supposed that was nice, if I wanted to see more of Zimbabwe. The thing was, I didn't. I had come here almost a year and a half before to help rescue Margo, a badly wounded elephant, and her calf, and the country had broken my heart. I had never seen such hunger, such deprivation, such desperation, such shortages of everything, and all due to a depraved and indifferent government. Families were living in the streets, huddled under tarps for warmth, digging through garbage for scraps of nonexistent food. Dogs and cats and goats and cows dropped in the streets from starvation.

We had managed to save Margo and her baby by capturing them in the Zimbabwe bush and flying them back to a wildlife sanctuary in New York, but I had vowed I would never go back.

"So why don't you stay on in Zimbabwe instead of going

to New York?" I asked Diamond. "Or do you have family waiting for you?"

"No family left," she replied, her face suddenly becoming serious. She scraped her flaming hair back, twisting it into a loose knot, and stared off through the restaurant windows at the black African night. "I was raised in Manhattan by my aunt, but she died," she added. "So I guess I'm returning to my native habitat—getting my bearings, you know—before I push off again. Most animals do that."

"No ex-husband? Ex-boyfriend?"

Diamond's face clouded and she looked down at her fingers. My eyes followed her eyes, and I noticed a pale band of skin where a ring had been. She caught me looking and folded her hands in her lap.

"That's okay," I said quickly. "I have one of each, and it only means you still have no one to come home to." I thought of Tom. We had broken up a year earlier.

"I was married for seven years," Diamond said softly, "but the jungle took him." She gulped the last of her coffee.

"*Took* him?"

Diamond gave me a sad smile. "The jungle takes everything," she said. "Eventually."

I wondered at her words, then thought she was right, in a sense. The jungle had taken my heart. And all the plans I had made for a conventional life.

By mid-morning, we were finally on the charter to Victoria Falls. I peered sleepily from the window of our small plane at the green-and-gold savannahs and blue gorges below. The sky was filled with sponged white clouds, and I could see the shadow of our plane following us across the thick green treetops below like a faithful puppy.

An hour later, we landed in a town churning with tourists and filled with tiny roadside stands selling illegally captured, bedraggled-looking wild parrots and cheap African mementos made in China.

"Now what?" I asked Diamond.

"We could visit the falls," she said. "They're only about eighteen miles away, and we have three hours to kill before the transfer van."

She led me to a waiting taxi bus. "Come on," she said. "We'll keep ourselves busy."

"We don't need to keep ourselves busy," I retorted, following her. "We *are* busy. Busy trying to get home."

Mosi-oa-Tunya, the falls are named.

"The smoke that thunders."

Which perfectly describes the white streaming pillars of water that plunge three hundred feet into an abyss that becomes the Zambezi River, sending up an enormous veil of vaporized, billowing spray. It was a wall of white. A world of white. White sound, white foam, white air from white clouds of water, crashing and hissing on their way to join the river, reverberating with such force that I imagined the sound could reach the floor of heaven. The water was alive, possessed with its own life force, with an energy and animation that was mesmerizing.

I stood enthralled, too overwhelmed to move, the roar thrumming deep into my chest, transforming my pulse into a great matching rush of blood.

We stood on thick, wet gray rocks and let the spray wash over us. Speech was nearly impossible.

"We're getting soaked through," Diamond chortled into my ear, pushing me out from the cove of trees that we had taken refuge under and into the spray.

"I don't care," I yelled back, pulling her with me. The water drenched us both, but we only laughed harder.

I stood there in the splash-up of cold water and raised my arms. It was as though the falls were rearranging my molecules, laying me open, pores, heart, and soul, preparing me so that I could absorb the essence of Africa.

I felt something here summoning me. The wild, uncontained fury beat against a door to my heart and forced it ajar. It was overwhelming, and I stood rooted in the steaming spray, trying to understand what was happening.

I was unraveling, being torn into pieces that didn't fit together anymore. Changing. Everything was joining together here and pulling me into it, the sky and the air and the pure white summoning of holy water. How could I leave?

"Don't change," my mother had said to me before I left for Kenya.

"You're changing," Tom had said to me when we spoke a week after I had left.

Tom.

I loved him so much, I used to dream of him all the time. I used to hear his deep, rich voice in my ear cautioning me, *you're changing, you're changing,* and I wasn't sure what he meant. After a while, I couldn't talk to him.

Then I realized I *had* changed. I couldn't help it. Or maybe I had always been like this, maybe I was just becoming more defined. I had felt something in Kenya, when I sat up nights with infant elephants and caressed their trunks and fed them formula, fighting so hard for their recovery. I remember thinking how I could never go back to an ordinary life again. I had loved Tom, and that was an important part of me, but my life in Kenya had become bigger. The falls were reminding me again how I had changed.

Diamond pulled at my arm and pointed. Arcing across the chasm was a rainbow, the bright colors forming a dazzling, jeweled bridge.

"It's a good sign for our visit," she yelled into my ear. "Eyes that see a rainbow will see good fortune."

I couldn't answer her. There were no words left to me. I had been unfastened somehow, undone, changed all the way through, and I knew there would be no turning away from it.

Chapter 3

"WHEN IS THE BUS LEAVING FOR CHARARA?" I ASKED a large woman in traditional dress and head scarf, who was sitting on the curb, eating pieces of grapefruit. Diamond and I had just returned from Victoria Falls to its namesake town, and were hoping to leave fairly soon for Charara.

Next to the woman was a sign nailed to a tree that read, "*Renkini*."

" 'Bus stop,' " Diamond translated for me. "That means this is the stop for the long-distance bus—the one we want."

I put down my suitcase and sat on the curb next to the woman and sighed. She gave me a shy smile and cupped her hands together, a Zimbabwe greeting. "When the bus is full, it will leave," she replied softly.

I looked up at Diamond, exasperated. "I hate that there's never a schedule."

"That is the African way," she agreed with a shrug. "Things start when they start."

The bus in question was sitting vacant in a sunny spot not far from us, the driver leisurely sipping coffee and eating a hard-boiled egg. It was not really a bus in the conventional sense—it was a *dalla-dalla*, a chicken bus, with some regular seats up front and thick metal bars enclosing the rear.

I watched the woman eat her grapefruit, ripping it apart with her thumbs and slowly sucking on each piece before finally chewing and swallowing it. What was I so impatient for, anyway? There really wasn't anyone waiting for me. Oh, there was my family, of course, and my best friend, Alana, who was a therapist, though she had moved out of New York. "There's a lot more mental agita in Florida," she had explained. I knew she'd want to hear from me. And I still had my little house. But they all had been waiting a whole year; another few days wouldn't matter. Even another few weeks.

"I suppose I'm not in any rush to go home," I admitted. Diamond sat down next to me and stretched her legs over her rucksack.

"Wherever you're going, it will be there when you arrive," she replied.

The bus filled within the hour. With what seemed like a hundred people, along with baskets of fruits and vegetables, a few woven chairs, a goat, a dozen crying babies, and too many makeshift containers filled with live chickens. I found a narrow metal bench against a wall and sat next to an un-friendly rooster, who managed to slip his beak through the slats of his crate and nip me whenever my arm came within an inch of him. Diamond wisely found a spot on the other side of the bus. Another twenty or so people pushed on, and we were finally on our way.

We hurtled along at 120 kilometers an hour, swaying and dipping across the rough dirt roads with such force, I feared the bus would break apart and scatter us all across the countryside like litter. There were a few particularly jarring bounces that seemed to launch us completely off our wheels.

Though the horn blasted incessantly at apathetic pedestrians and indifferent cows that shared the road with us, I leaned my head back against a metal bar and tried to doze. Every time I closed my eyes, I saw the falls. I could still hear them, even a hundred miles away. If I had any misgivings about taking time to return home, they were washed away in the great roar of white steaming mist.

It was unbearably hot. Vendors poked corn through the open windows anytime we stopped, radios played African pop music, and almost all the chickens managed to get loose. We bought a few hard-boiled eggs from a vendor, and I hungrily peeled one, only to reveal a reeking dark green interior. I tried not to gag and fed it to the rooster, who snatched it up without so much as a second's worth of ethical consideration and then ungratefully nipped me again.

We stopped three more times, once for a herd of gazelle that decided to spring across the road in airy leaps, seemingly impervious to the heat and traffic, and once for a herd of buffalo that wandered aimlessly in front of us, not caring in the least that the bus was physically nudging some of them along.

Our last stop was at a checkpoint set up by the Department of Veterinary Services, so that we—bus, passengers, and chickens—could be sprayed with insecticide to repel tsetse flies. A man walked around carrying a black hose and a huge vacuum cleaner canister slung over his shoulder, sending an acrid yellow mist everywhere.

"This is horrible," I complained as the fumes poured through the flapping windows, stinging my eyes and throat.

Diamond coughed. "Sleeping sickness is worse," she rasped. "If you want to go to Charara, you have to get sprayed."

I opened my mouth to remind her that I hadn't wanted to go to Charara at all, but another burning whiff had me gagging uncontrollably. We were finally released to continue our journey and arrived late in the afternoon, smelling like a lab experiment.

"No alcohol in camp," the driver warned us as he drove over the pitted, dusty road that led into the park. "No guns. And no citrus. No citrus. The elephants, they smell the citrus and come to your hut. Make much trouble." The sign on the park gates pretty much repeated the driver's warnings, in addition to mentioning no loud music after nine o'clock and no fireworks.

We promised him we hadn't brought citrus. In fact, we hadn't brought anything edible. The last thing we had tried to eat were the eggs. The bus rolled to a stop at the warden's building, and we gladly climbed out.

"You have a message," the park warden told us once we checked our reservation. He handed Diamond a note, and she made a face as she read it.

"Bollocks!" she exclaimed. "Charlotte can't get petrol to

drive to us. She hopes she can buy some on the black market tomorrow. Apparently, there's a van coming up with supplies from South Africa." She stuffed the note into her pocket.

"Why didn't she just call you?" I asked.

"Typical African phone service," Diamond replied. "She says my phone was out for most of the day."

I nodded. I'd had similar problems in Kenya. The service was erratic to nonexistent.

We were assigned a guide, who drove us to our quarters, a brilliant turquoise hut with a thatched roof and a bright candy-pink wooden door. A small wooden table and two chairs sat in front. He swung open the door and gestured for us to go in ahead of him.

"Very comfortable for you," he commented. "You like elephants? They come here all the time."

"I love elephants," I murmured as we entered the hut, exhausted from our almost two full days of travel.

It was surprisingly cool inside, and it was clean and comfortable. The walls were pale green, a colorful spread was tucked over the neatly made bed, a brightly woven rug covered the floor, and another small wooden table was flanked by two woven chairs. A green tole lamp sat in the center of the table and gave everything a welcoming feel. A bright pink curtain led to a tiny stall behind the hut that housed a real toilet, and though there was no sink, there was a shower that drained right into the floor.

The guide stood at the pink curtain to chat. "I think, maybe elephant even come tonight, very bad elephant. Steal dinner." This greatly amused him. "Steal *your* dinner!" he added in a delighted voice.

He turned on the lamp and left us. Diamond dropped onto the rug in weariness, pushed her rucksack under her head, and stretched out. "I need a nap. Why don't you take one, too? Dinner's not for at least another hour."

"Why don't you use the bed?" I said, dropping my suitcase on the floor and opening it to pull out some fresh clothes. A nice hot shower would be wonderful, I thought.

She yawned. "I'm perfectly fine, I'm used to sleeping on the ground." I laughed but she did look comfortable.

"Do you mind if I take the first shower?" I asked.

"I don't mind," she said, with a wave. "You can take all of them."

I gathered up my clothes and one of the clean but very thin towels that had been left on the bed for us.

The water was ice cold, and there was some kind of white cream that I assumed was soap or shampoo or toothpaste or bug repellant or all four. It barely lathered, but I was glad just to wash. I quickly toweled off and put on fresh jeans and a tee, and returned to the hut to tuck my things away. Diamond was still stretched out on the floor, her flame hair surrounding her face like a sunset.

"Hi," she said as soon as I walked in.

"I thought you might be asleep."

She opened her eyes. "You'll know when I'm asleep—I snore like a rhinoceros."

"I was planning to take a walk."

"Fine," she said, closing her eyes again. I stepped over her motionless body to head for the door.

"I'll be back soon," I said.

There was no reply.

"Diamond?"

"Fine," she mumbled. "Just don't get eaten."

The pale blue sky was fading into soft rose, meeting its reflection in glimmering Lake Kariba as I followed the shoreline away from camp. The lake, a reservoir actually, had been made by the government many years before by damming off part of the Zambezi River. It was serene and beautiful. Large houseboats floated by, and a flock of pink-and-white flamingos looped overhead before landing in the lake on spindly legs to fish.

Beyond the lake, far in the distance, a thin, rolling mountain range of darkening purple was fading from view. The soft, dusky breezes blew fringes of rose lavender swamp grass around my legs, rippling the feathery tops, rippling the water beyond them, making everything flow together, undulating in the shimmering light.

There had to be a reason I was still here, I mused. There had to be a reason why I didn't want to leave. Except to see Margo, the elephant I had helped rescue, there was nothing I wanted to go back to in New York.

I was a trained psychotherapist, and I had once vaguely thought of restarting my practice when I got home, but it was a task more complicated than I wanted to tackle. I was bored with the idea of having to find a nice office and acquiring a few dysfunctional clients that might want to make lifestyle changes within their actual lifetimes.

I was even bored with my long-held passion of retraining problem horses. I needed to do more. Something more significant, more challenging.

I walked along the shore, stepping carefully through the heavily scented heather, thinking. I knew only one thing with any certainty: I needed to take part in something that would put an end to my restlessness. I stood for a moment to lift my face into the dimming sun and closed my eyes and took a long, deep breath.

A sudden loud burst of laughter erupted through the brush, the unexpected human sound violating the wild silence. It was coming from a nearby hut, perhaps from campers, maybe even hunters. I knew that hunting parties from all over the world frequented the area because it was so rich with animal life.

Startled, the pink-and-blue Goliath herons arose in one move, pressing themselves against the pink-and-blue sky, nearly disappearing into it, their deep-throated warnings ringing across the lake.

Their sudden alarm unnerved me, and I turned away from the setting sun to quickly return to the hut. A croc drifted close by through the water like a stealth missile, closing in on a small bird. I shivered at the sight and sped up.

The ground was soft and muddy under my boots, and small puddles filled my footsteps as I followed the shoreline back. It felt like the laughter was pursuing me, harsh and unexpected, and I hurried through the fading day. Behind me, the light was an infinity that reached through the horizon, turning the landscape into a mysterious color-filled world. A world perfect by itself and made treacherous by its human inhabitants, poisoned in ways I had yet to discover.

Chapter 4

DIAMOND WAS SITTING AT THE LITTLE TABLE OUTSIDE our hut and serenely drinking a cup of tea. There was a brown-and-yellow clay pot set on the table along with another cup, a small jar of honey, and a single spoon for us to share.

"Still haven't gotten in touch with Charlotte," she announced as I sat down. "Now that *my* phone's back online, *her* service is out." She shook her head. "You know the old joke, if you're in Zimbabwe and can make a phone call, you're not in Zimbabwe."

I laughed and poured myself a fragrant cup of hot black tea, then mixed in some honey and took a sip.

"Good tea," I said.

"Bush tea."

I'd had it nearly every day in Kenya, and I liked the strong flavor. I took another appreciative sip and stared down at my cup.

"You're being quiet," Diamond said. "Did you enjoy your walk?"

I nodded.

"Missing your man?"

"No," I said. "It's not that."

"Yes it is," she said, a mischievous smile playing on her lips. "What was his name?"

"Tom," I said, then looked back into my cup at the tiny leaves that were clinging to the side. I wished I could read them.

"See?" Diamond said triumphantly. "I knew it was a man. It's always a man." She leaned back in her chair and scrutinized me. "I'm guessing that after your lover broke your heart, you ran off to live with the baby elephants."

I gave a little laugh. "Actually, I met him rescuing an elephant. Then I ran off to live with the baby elephants, and *then* he broke my heart. That's how it all started." I thought for a moment, then corrected myself. "Actually, that's how it all ended." I reconsidered my words again. "Actually, I think that means *I* ended it." I sighed. "I think I broke my own heart."

Dinner was served a while later by a guide who drove up in a jeep and briskly pulled a silver metal food container from the back. He lifted the lid to reveal a series of bowls and dishes, and poured out a small bowl of water, offering it to Diamond with a polite bow. She washed her hands, then passed the bowl to me, and I did the same.

Next the guide took out two plates and with great ceremony set the table for our dinner. He put a bowl of dinner *sadza*, made of cooked ground corn, in the middle of the table, along with a bowl of stewed greens, some cauliflower, and a fresh pot of tea. I looked askance at the cauliflower.

"Give us this day our daily cauliflower," I intoned, holding my hands reverentially over our plates.

The man took out a platter of meat on skewers, put that on the table, bowed, and left.

"No forks?" I said. I'd had forks even at the sanctuary in Kenya, dining with the elephants. Well, technically, it wasn't with the elephants. Dr. Annabelle Pontwynne, who ran the sanctuary, was very genteel and insisted on a proper dinner every night with her staff.

"No," Diamond agreed, looking over the food with satisfaction. "But it's *shasleek*!" She grabbed a skewer and pulled off a piece of meat with her teeth. "I love *shasleek*."

I took a little bite. It was very savory and tender. "What kind of meat do you think it is?"

She peered at the piece left on her skewer. "Ostrich? Springbok? Could even be croc."

I stared at my skewer for a few minutes, then looked at the cauliflower, then back at my skewer. I was hungry. I finished the meat.

We ate our fill, politely leaving a small amount as was custom. An hour later, the jeep returned, and the procedure was reversed. Our guide bowed, rolled out the silver container, loaded our plates, and left. Diamond sighed with satisfaction and pulled what looked like a short, tan cigar from her pocket and lit it, taking a deep, contented puff. It smelled like, well, an overflowed toilet.

"What are you smoking?" I asked.

"It's a *bundu* cheroot," she replied. "I roll them myself. Want one?"

"No thanks." We just sat there, content to watch the heavens turn orange and gold, the sun burn itself down behind the mountains, while the blackest of skies revealed a million stars overhead.

"I have an idea," Diamond said into the deepening night. "If I can't reach Charlotte, we can do our own little walkabout. It'll be a great experience." She took another puff on her cheroot. "I'll get permission from the game warden, I'm sure it won't be a problem. I have a Level Three license, with an Advanced Weapons Certificate. And you can snap some photos like a proper tourist. I even bought a disposable camera at the airport for the bargain price of two hundred thousand Zim dollars." She laughed at this before continuing. "There's really another side to this country, and it's quite beautiful."

"Great," I said. It did sound nice to have a chance to play tourist before I went home.

Diamond stood up and stretched, then opened the door to the hut. The little green lamp was giving off a sweet yellow glow. "I'll talk to the warden at first light," she said, lingering at the door to look up at the stars, "and it comes very early, so you'd better get some sleep."

I followed her in.

"Take the bed," she said, dropping to the floor.

"We can share," I said, trying not to sound as doubtful as I felt.

She just stuffed her rucksack under her head and yawned. "Sweet dreams, Neelie Sterling. Dream of your Tom."

I lay down on the bed and rolled the thin pillow under my head and stretched out on the hard mattress. "I hope I don't," I said truthfully.

I wasn't sure what had awakened me. Several sharp reports, then a great noise, a crash, someone shouting, and the familiar trumpeting of an elephant. I jumped from the bed. Diamond was already out the door, the camera swinging from her wrist.

We followed a rush of campers and guides across the dark compound, toward a path where the lights had been turned on. There was a jumble of loud voices ahead, and my stomach tightened with anticipation. I was certain that an elephant had come into the camp. I missed my elephants, and I was eager to see one. I let myself get carried along in the surge toward a campsite about a quarter of a mile away.

"It's probably Tusker," someone said behind me. "He comes here almost every night."

I turned around to see a thin man running with a camera. "Who?" I asked.

"That big bull elephant," he said. "Breaks into camp here around dinnertime. He's famous for it. Practically a mascot. I've snapped quite a few photos of him."

No one seemed fearful. There was a contagion of high spirits and laughter and several comments about Tusker's frequent visits. Some even proudly mentioned they had old videos of him, as though he were a star.

There was a loud trumpet, and my heart jumped inside my chest. For all the hundreds of elephants I had seen by now, the sight of one still sent a thrill through me.

He was just ahead. I could hear him, smell him.

I ran with the others, anticipating him. Exhilarated. He was here. He was here!

I hadn't known what to expect. A camp attraction? Something to amuse the tourists? Some semicomical version of an elephant, not so very large, certainly not truly as wild as the country around us?

And then suddenly he was right in front of me.

In the night stood a colossus of an animal, thirteen feet at the shoulder, at least. His great gray body swayed as he left the shadows and moved into the light, each step slow and deliberate and majestic, until he stood there, illuminated like a god, the gold light falling upon him like a mantle, his ears held out like great capes, his trunk lifted over our heads like an arm held out to bless us. He stood wild and glorious, the god of wild hearts.

The shadows played against his giant head, his ears seemed to fan away the darkness as he approached the crowd of people playing flashlights on his corrugated face. He stopped walking and stood over us, expectant, yet expecting nothing. It was all contained within him, his own splendor, his own personal dignity. He needed nothing from us to complete him.

I could only stare. I wanted to pay him homage. Drop to my knees in reverence. In an instant, I was utterly his.

His one tusk curved delicately inward toward his uplifted trunk like a musical instrument ready to summon other gods to his side. He looked around, turning his attention from one to the other, and we stood before him, chastened, like subjects to a king, as though waiting to be summoned into his glorious presence for a holy convocation.

A large tent had been knocked over, the refrigerator lying on its side and broken apart, cots and equipment strewn across the ground.

"Get your elephant under control," a British-accented voice angrily rang out at one of the guides who had raced over to help. "The blighter's ruined my party."

The guide slowly approached the huge animal and faced him under the light, standing just a few feet away. He braced his shoulders for courage and stood on his toes to clap his hands in the elephant's face. "Away, away!" he shouted. "Away!"

The elephant calmly backed up, his face composed, blinking his eyes to show he would have a sense of humor about it all. He rolled his head from side to side as though to apologize for the ruckus and any trouble he might have caused, and stepping back, back, disappeared into the night with not even the rustle of a leaf.

"There's your Tusker," the thin man whispered to me. "There's your boy."

I could barely breathe. I had seen something so trans-forming, so transcending that I had no need for air or light or anything else, except for this creature. He had retreated and taken my spirit with him. I had never seen anything more noble, more alien, more splendid. Every cell in my body was filled with him, and I felt adrift after he left.

"Bloody pest," the British accent continued loudly. Its owner was a heavy man with a mustache, dressed in an immaculately starched, stiff new tan safari outfit. His round face was flushed as he kicked at the broken camping equipment. "Bloody beast should be shot."

The game warden, whom we had met earlier, walked into the disarray. He leaned over and pulled something from the broken refrigerator—a bag of lemons.

"Citrus! You were warned about the citrus," he said sternly to the heavy man.

"You can't tell me what to eat," the man retorted. "I use them for my drinks. I like my gin and tonic with a fresh twist of lemon." He swayed drunkenly under the light. "The blighter ruined my party."

"He was throwing firecrackers at the thing," someone called out. "He was throwing firecrackers in the bush."

The heavy man waved them all away, his starched shirt riding up around his stomach. "Just having some fun." A few members of his party laughed at this, but some of the other campers became angry.

"I saw you throw firecrackers at him out in the bush. You sent him this way," one shouted. "We could have been hurt."

"You're the one who should be shot," the thin man yelled.

"Damn you all!" The British man waved his arms at them. "I spent a bloody fortune to come here, and no one tells me what to do."

I made a move to join the other campers to protest, but Diamond pushed me in the direction of our hut, and I moved woodenly, reluctantly.

"Don't fight with him," she said to me. "We need to get some sleep so we can go on safari, first thing in the morning." She looked over at the fat man with disgust. "Remember, one never rubs bottoms with a porcupine."

Chapter 5

MORNING CAME UPON US LIKE A GOOD FRIEND, comforting and warm and ready to please.

Diamond was sitting outside our hut, waiting for me to finish washing. I emerged from the little stall shower and stepped into brilliant sunlight. I threw the thin towel over a post—it would dry in just a few minutes—before sitting down at the table with her.

I hadn't slept well. I had spent most of the night sitting at the edge of my bed and thinking about the elephant I had seen. Tusker, they had called him. Tusker. It was a common enough name—most bull elephants are called tuskers—but the name suddenly took on a certain majesty. Tusker.

"Good morning," Diamond greeted me. She pulled her hair back from her face and secured it with a bolo string.

Then she dug into her bowl of breakfast *sadza*, scooping it up with her fingers.

"So, I spoke to the game warden this morning before you got up," she said, slurping down the white cornmeal gruel. "We needed permission for a walkabout, and at first, he denied it because of safety concerns."

I poured myself a cup of tea. "What do we do now?"

"After I told him that I was licensed and that the Popes in Chizarira would vouch for me, he agreed to assign us a guide." She passed me my own bowl of breakfast *sadza*.

"I have to see him again," I said. "The elephant."

I did. He had taken possession of my soul. I could think of nothing else.

"I fell in love with him, too." Diamond smiled. "The warden said he has another name, Dustbin, because he has a habit of picking through the garbage bins. He's sort of a park favorite."

"Dustbin," I repeated. "I hate that he's named after garbage."

"The warden also told me something else," Diamond said, her face becoming troubled. "They've classified him as a problem elephant, which means he's slated for execution."

I jumped from my chair. "What are you talking about?" I gasped. "What do you mean, 'execution'?"

Diamond looked up at me. "He knows there's food here, and apparently he's already overturned seven cars. They were empty, but he can't just flip cars around at will, looking for snacks."

"But *execution*?" I said, my mouth barely able to form the word.

She nodded. "The warden said the Zimbabwe Conservation Task Force is out of petrol again, but when they get their new requisition, he's as good as dead. They plan to come here and shoot him. They're culling elephants all over the country." She scooped up the rest of her *sadza* and held her hand aloft for a moment. "They use their meat to feed the soldiers of the Zimbabwean army. One more elephant death would mean nothing at all to them."

She licked the food from her fingers. Discussing Tusker's death over breakfast was making me sick. I pushed my food away. The orange sun bloomed over the day-bright lake.

"We don't have many options in saving him," Diamond said, deflating the rapid swirl of ideas and solutions that were racing through my head. "I called my friend Charlotte after I spoke to the game warden. She knows about Tusker, says he's on everyone's rescue list, but she said it's very hard work, and the failure rate for rescues is very high. Plus she mentioned that she'd need a lot of help."

I gave her a wondering look. "Does she mean us? There's no reason why we can't help."

"No reason at all," Diamond agreed, wiping her breakfast bowl clean with her fingers and licking them like a cat. "Charlotte says she'll try to come up with some kind of plan."

"I hope she hurries," I said, then sighed, thinking this Charlotte probably knew every bush, tree, and growl of the countryside, and if she couldn't think of something, then we'd have very little chance of success trying to do it by ourselves.

Diamond grinned. "You look worried. But I bet we can pull it off."

"We'd need a crew and planes and tranquilizers and stuff," I worried. "It's a huge undertaking."

Diamond appeared not to be listening. I followed her gaze to the mountains and wondered if she thought of taking Tusker north since we were at the most northern tip of the country. "Maybe Charlotte could let us borrow some horses. Then we could track Tusker on horseback," she mused out loud. "We could push him to Mozambique—its border covers the whole east of Zimbabwe." She thought it over. "No, Mozambique is hundreds of miles away. It would be too far for horses." She poured us both more tea. "Maybe north across the border to Zambia. Or south to Botswana." She sighed. "Either way, it's very far."

"This is crazy!" I exclaimed. "How do we push him? Besides, we'd need to get through the borders ourselves, and then a plane has to be ready and waiting." I felt a wave of resentment. If only Tom and I were still talking, he would have helped. I knew he would have helped. He had contacts and planes and had spent years orchestrating elephant rescues.

Diamond bent over to lace up her boots, then stood. "Well, I've known Charlotte a long time, and I trust her to think of something that will work." She pushed my bowl of breakfast *sadza* back at me. "You'd better eat, or you're going to be very hungry later. There aren't any vending machines in the bush."

I looked down at my breakfast, cold and unappetizing. "I don't suppose there's a spoon."

She laughed. "You carry your eating implements at the end of your arms. Finish quickly. We've got some tracking to do."

"*Shamwari*, you come here for elephant?" a voice asked from behind Diamond. We both whirled around to see a man dressed in the usual tan safari clothes, carrying a large back-pack and a heavy-duty rifle. It was our guide. "*Shamwari*," he repeated in a lilting accent, clapping his hands together, the traditional male greeting. "I was sent to help you. I have sup-plies." He pointed to the backpack and smiled congenially. "Are you ready, *shamwari*?"

Shamwari meant "friend," and I had found in Kenya that almost everyone was your friend—the people are warm and open, the word is used all the time.

Diamond cupped her hands together and clapped them in response, the traditional female greeting. "Yes, thank you, *shamwari*," she replied. The guide clapped his hands at me, and I followed Diamond's lead.

"Thank you for your help, *shamwari*," I said, then pointed to his rifle. "Please, no shooting the animals. No shooting."

He just patted the rifle and smiled pleasantly. "Until you grow big teeth, we will take this."

We slipped easily through the lavender rushes, hiking along the curvature of Lake Kariba, leaving broken stalks of heather in our wake. From the edges of the lake rose half-submerged pale skeletons of dead trees, arms outstretched like graceful dancers, holding delicate white egrets in their hands as though offering up living ornaments to the azure sky. Beyond the flash of flaming orange bushes lay a back-drop of thick blue-green brush and dark blue mountains.

"We make this lake," the guide said proudly. "Many years ago. We make it from the Zambezi River, oh yes."

Hippos drank nonchalantly at the water's edge, and sev-eral crocodiles floated close, their eyes studying the shoreline, watching the herons, the antelope, the impala that drank there, waiting for a sign of weakness. The guide led us away from the shoreline now, and inward, toward the forest.

The smaller brush was gone, replaced by stands of mahogany trees reaching skyward, like heavenly supports. Animals peeked at us from behind the acacia trees, then fled as our guide led us deeper into the interior.

With every step, every move, every turn of my head, I felt watched. The god of wild hearts was watching us, I knew. He would be cautious, hidden within the trees and thickets. Concealing himself within the deeper mopane woodland, where the trees had leaves like pale green butterfly wings that crushed easily under our feet, leaving behind the unexpected scent of turpentine.

We walked forever. After a while, my legs felt separated from my body, as though they had taken on a career of their own, to walk and walk and walk. We waded over brilliantly clear streams that gurgled all the way down from the mountains, feeding pink hibiscus growing all in rows like schoolgirls in pretty dresses. We stepped across small yellow and purple wildflowers that sprang up in natural bouquets, and we carefully pushed away from the undergrowth that grabbed our arms like beggars, always making sure to turn our faces downward to keep at bay the tiny bees following us with great persistence.

The guide finally stopped for a moment before crossing one of the unpaved roads that wove through the park and was frequently used by tourists packed into safari jeeps. On the other side was a lily pond surrounded by a circle of light that streamed down through a series of short, stubby bushes. When we got closer, I could see it was a clearing of trees that had been broken away, standing in a ring as though they were on their knees in prayer.

"Elephant take up trees," our guide explained, making a pulling motion with his hands. "Yes, *shamwari*, your boy come here." He gave us a big smile and dropped his backpack but kept the rifle on his shoulder. "Eat?"

We gratefully nodded, and he unpacked cheese and fruits and vegetables and flatbread. We ate quickly. A troop of baboons found us and screamed loudly, opening their mouths wide, baring long, sharp teeth and snatching at us with sinewy arms until we threw food into the bushes for them. Our guide found a piece of wood and banged it against a tree while we ate, to keep them from returning. Suddenly he stood still, immobile, listening. I wondered what he was listening for—there was no sound at all except for the droning of the insects near our faces.

For a few minutes, the silence was an oasis in time, in movement, as even the trees stopped their sway. The air filled with an expectancy, and I felt the skin on my arms tingle. Something was there with us, something close, but it was concealed, hidden by the leaves and brush. I looked to the guide, but he hadn't moved at all. Diamond, too, had frozen.

Then I realized *he* was here. I knew it. He had come.

Suddenly, before us stood an elephant. He had slipped through the brush and trees like a stream of light, without bulk or gravity, without disturbing a single leaf. Like a secret revealed, with the hushed heralding of the most extraordinary, suddenly Tusker stood before us.

His amber eyes looked from one to the other, his one tusk glowed pale yellow in the sun, and he stood before us as though he was granting a royal audience. He studied us for a moment, three figures. Were we enough to pay him the respect he deserved? He flapped his ears slowly and reached forward with his trunk. My heart stopped beating in deference to him. I, too, stood frozen.

Diamond threw down her chunk of cheese, then slipped her camera from her pocket and surreptitiously pushed its button. Tusker swung the food into his mouth and reached for more. I threw my food before him, standing very still, not moving my arms, using only my hands. He was wild, we were at his mercy, I knew, and he knew. When he was finished, he waved his head up and down and stepped back, melting away into invisibility.

The guide was immensely pleased. "Dustbin," he announced, then asked Diamond, "*Shamwari*, you get photo?"

Diamond nodded. The guide squatted to close up the backpack. "We go away now, *shamwari*," he said to us. "*Haraka! Haraka!*" Hurry, hurry.

Before he could finish, there was a soft rustling behind us, a flutter of leaves, and we turned our heads. Tusker had returned, materializing again as if he were enchanted.

"Bollocks," Diamond whispered, her eyes wide. She was nervous, and suddenly I was, too, my nerves heightened because of her reaction. I knew she was thinking he had come back for more food, and because we had nearly exhausted our supply, this time he might get aggressive.

The guide slowly reached into his pack and emptied its contents on the ground: a small piece of cheese and avocado and some remaining fruit. He took out a few pieces of flat-bread, looked at it, then smiled up at us. "Not for *tembo*," he said softly, returning the bread to his pack. "For me." We understood. His people were starving and bread was very scarce. To throw it down for an elephant was more than he could bear.

Tusker moved toward the food, and the guide backed us away from him calmly, reverentially as he ate, as though we were like the mythological creatures of the African bush who walked on backward feet to fool those that might bring harm to the jungle. He backed us across the road and into the brush, retreating slowly, carefully, almost reluctantly, until the form of the elephant became part of the trees and the trees became shadows and the shadows became whispers beyond the horizon.

Chapter 6

IT IS A HEARTBREAKING SKY THAT FALLS OVER AFRICA when there is death in the air.

Before I knew of Tusker, I had enjoyed watching the sun nestle itself into crimson clouds for the night, turning the sky rose pink and pale peach before slipping away. Now I sat outside the hut and stared at the sky, at the red streaks streaming across, and could think only of blood.

We had tipped our guide well, and he promised to return soon with our dinner, but I had no appetite. Diamond finished both our portions of *sadza* and greens and roasted squash.

"How can you eat, knowing what's going to happen to that elephant?" I asked her.

She looked surprised that I would even ask. "What does the color of maize have to do with the song of the bulbul?"

I still don't know what she meant.

Tusker didn't come back to camp the next day, and I wasn't sure if I was relieved or worried. I had come to think of him as my elephant and felt very proprietary toward him. I worried if he was eating, if he was frightened, if he was spending his day happily pulling trees out of the ground or making mischief by flipping cars. I was so enamored of his great frame and wise eyes and congenial face, of his splendid majesty, that I would have laid my life down for him.

"What do you think he's doing right now?" I asked Diamond several times throughout the day while she tried to get Charlotte on the phone. "Do you think he's okay?"

She rolled her eyes at me. "Neelie," she said with an exasperated sigh. "He's been coming to this park for more than forty years. He's been finding food, water, whatever he needs. I think he's fine."

I flashed her a dark look. "For now," I said.

She was waiting for a phone call from Charlotte, hoping her friend could offer either advice or manpower or horses. Charlotte's safari business was based in Chizarira, about a day's journey from where we were. If there was a chance she and her husband were able to help us, I was sure we'd have to move Tusker nearer to them. I paced our hut nervously, thinking any moment I would hear a fatal shot ring out and my elephant would be dead, but Diamond was stretched out on the floor to nap, with the phone next to her ear to wake her when it rang.

"But will they be able to help us?" I asked her again. "Do they have Rovers? Do they know anyone with a plane?"

"First of all," Diamond replied testily, "the Zim government listens in on all phone calls, so I can't get the information I want, and secondly, I need a nap." She jumped up to push me out the door. "I'll tell you everything as soon as I find out," she said. "Take a hike."

I did.

I followed the path along Lake Kariba in the opposite direction from the day before, tracing the shoreline toward the other half of the encampment. It was unbearably hot and unbearably dry, and I wished the lake could rise up, breach the atmosphere, dissolve into it, and ease the searing heat. I eyed the water longingly, wondering if its placid blue would be cooling or unpleasantly warm, but I wasn't foolish enough to put even a toe in. Several houseboats floated by. Their occupants, mostly wealthy tourists, were taking dips in the lake inside swimming cages that protected them from the profusion of crocodiles that shared the water. Several gazelles were drinking warily, their delicate faces streaked with black that made a straight line up to their antlers, giving them a sport sneaker look. A herd of zebras fled as I drew closer, cantering away in a flurry of dashing stripes.

The heat was hypnotic. Maybe I was dreaming all of this. Maybe I was still in Kenya with my baby ellies. Maybe I hadn't even left New York. How improbable it was that I was here! The intense blue of the sky reached down, connecting with the intense blue lake. The mountains directly across from me were covered in mist, and a fish eagle screed overhead. I squeezed my eyes shut, wondering if it would all disappear if I clicked my heavy boots together, and I would wake up and be home with Tusker, like Dorothy and Toto. I opened my eyes again. I really was here.

But I didn't have the Wizard of Oz to help me.

There was a commotion ahead. Dreading and yet hoping it was Tusker, I ran to a campsite that was supported by a large, flat, rocky ledge the other campers had called the Chill Spot. It overlooked the water and was used by foreign tourists with less formal equipment who were vacationing on the cheap. Tusker was standing in the middle of a small crowd. They were obviously used to the sight of elephants, since elephants appear out of everywhere in Zimbabwe. Garbage was strewn about his feet, and he was being pelted by glass soda bottles that were breaking into shards around him. A boy, maybe sixteen, had another bottle in his hand, aiming to throw it, and I ran to him and grabbed his hand to divert him from his target. The elephant lifted his trunk over his head, and the gathering crowd moved menacingly close, taunting him and screaming obscenities. He shuffled his feet nervously and trumpeted, and there was a collective gasp.

"Give him room to move," I yelled. "Move back and give him room! Give him a way out."

The crowd parted, still yelling, disrespectful and foolish, deceiving themselves that their trappings of civilization, their bright plastic coolers with matching trash pails and flowered umbrellas and rented drop-sided campers were somehow equal to the elephant's irrevocable rights to this territory. They had forgotten, or never learned, that *he* belonged here, *he* was the native and they were the intruders, in their garishly bright reds and pinks and turquoise tropical clothing.

"Leave him alone!" I screamed, even as the game warden drove up and dispersed them in calm, authoritative tones.

"Leave them to me, mademoiselle," he said, and I politely retreated, still watching Tusker, who sorted through another trash pail before he turned around and casually walked away.

"We have to get him out of here soon," I announced to Diamond.

We were eating dinner: *dovi*—a peanut butter and chicken stew—with greens and cauliflower and dinner *sadza* and tea. Inexpensive native food, unlike the steaks and seafood that the guests in the other huts were receiving, since we weren't paying, courtesy of Charlotte and Billy Pope.

"You had to see the way they were treating him," I added. "Have you heard anything yet?" Tusker was all I could think about.

"I spoke to Charlotte, and she's working on a plan," Diamond replied, quickly finishing her dinner. "She's been trying to pull something together ever since the Conservation Task Force issued the execution order."

Execution. The word again sent a chill through me.

"What kind of plan?" I asked.

Diamond made a face. "She thought a crew could somehow push him to where she is, and then she could make arrangements to have him airlifted out. She's been working with some rescue friends that she's known a long time."

Chizarira National Park was the most remote park in the

country, with fewer tourists, and would give us more privacy and more opportunity, so Charlotte's idea seemed logical. Though there were some driving roads cut throughout Charara, the terrain, according to Diamond, would be mostly uncharted.

"Did you tell her that we want to help?" I asked.

Diamond nodded. "She says that we can be the ones to push him to Chizarira. It would save her a few days. He doesn't have a lot of time."

"But how?" I asked. "We can't do it on foot. Is she sending horses?"

"No," Diamond said, eyeing my plate. "They finally managed to get petrol. She's sending us a Rover. Are you going to finish that *sadza*?"

I pushed my plate at her. "Take whatever you want. I never did figure out what the appeal is with this stuff."

"It's cheap and filling," Diamond said, wiping my plate clean with her fingers. "Charlotte also said they're sending an old friend of theirs who has done like a million rescues. She said he should be a big help."

"That's great," I said. "When does he arrive?"

She burped and checked her watch. "In about another hour."

I thought I would never see him again.

There was a rap at our door and a sharp whiff of cigarette smoke as soon as Diamond opened it. Russian cigarettes. From an old Russian friend who was a major part of the rescue team when Tom rescued Margo.

Grisha.

"Madame Neelie," he said with great surprise, his thick Russian accent as garbled as ever. "My eyes cannot believe my heavy amazement!"

"Me either!" I said. I fought the temptation to look over his shoulder for Tom. We embraced and I stepped back to exult in my good fortune. Grisha had spent most of his life helping Tom with elephant rescues and was considered a world expert. "Please, just call me plain Neelie."

He looked just as I remembered him—pale blue eyes that noticed everything, maybe a little more gray throughout the thatch of light red hair he left uncombed, but still lean and muscular, with the ever-present Stolichnye Light hanging from the corner of his mouth.

"What are you doing here?" I asked him joyfully. "How did you get involved with this?"

He looked perplexed. "Have I committed grave confusion? Grisha is thinking woman peoples would have gladness over his present position."

"Oh, we do, we do," I said, and pulled out a chair for him. "Sit down, we need to talk. You have to tell us everything."

Diamond was still standing by the door, watching us, looking mystified.

"Oh, Diamond," I apologized, "I forgot. This is Grisha, Tom's assistant."

"Diamond-Rose Tremaine," she said, extending her hand to him. Ever courtly, he rose halfway from his chair and kissed the tip of her fingers. "Where are the other men?" she asked. "Surely you brought others."

His eyes widened. "But Grisha can drive only one truck at a time! I was disclosed you have help *here.*"

"But it's just Diamond and me," I protested. "How are we going to be able to move the elephant with only the three of us?"

"This is a tribulation," he agreed, sitting back down. "Now Grisha must make new strategy." He pressed his fingers to his chin. "Since we cannot make heavy spectacle here and we must bring ellie to Chizarira, *da*? And Grisha has only one Grisha and two woman peoples . . ." He closed his eyes to think. "We can make use of same plan. Is good plan. *Da*. I have plan to move elephant. Don't make heavy worry too much."

"We have to use the park roads, not the main roads, or we'll be stopped," Diamond interjected. "We have to transport him somehow—or drive him along the more remote park roads until we get to Charlotte's camp. But then what?"

"Oh, when we make arrivement, Mr. Thomas determines to bring plane in and—shoosh!" Grisha made a swooping motion with his hand, implying that we would just lift the elephant and take him away. "But Mr. Thomas having heavy problems too much getting plane in." He gave me a dark look. "We must keep fingers twisted."

"Mr. *Thomas*?" I repeated breathlessly. "Thomas—Tom Pennington? Tom—is he with you?"

"So." Diamond was piecing it together as fast as I was. "This Tom Pennington, the man with the plane is"—she turned to me—"Thomas Princeton Pennington? I know the name!" Her voice dropped reverentially. "Used to get the newspapers flown in from Nairobi. He was always in the business section. Kind of an entrepreneur. He's *your* Tom?"

I looked at Grisha, but he didn't have to confirm it. He just made a helpless gesture with his hands. "Mr. Thomas is only disclosed last night that he has peoples here to bring ellie to Chizarira. He is not disclosed that it is *you*."

"No," I said. "He didn't know I was coming here." I gave Grisha a rueful smile. "In fact, *I* didn't know I was coming here."

He nodded gravely. "Mr. Thomas will not be joyed-over for this, Plain-Neelie," he replied, wagging his finger at me. "Grisha is seeing heavy agitation ahead." He rolled his blue eyes at me and took a very long drag on his cigarette before expelling a cloud of thick gray smoke. "*Heavy* agitation."

Chapter 7

GRISHA'S PLAN WAS SO LUDICROUSLY SIMPLE, SO laughably naive that for a few minutes I didn't believe it. He had driven a ten-seater safari Rover to us, and the next morning, he said, it would be filled with his secret weapon. He had determined, and correctly so, that we couldn't just lead a wild animal through a jungle and expect him to follow along complacently like someone's pet poodle. Nor could we drive him ahead of us like cattle in a scene out of an old cowboy movie, whoopee ti-yi-ellie. The elephant would have to be *lured*. Grisha's plan was for us to drive ahead of him and lay a sporadic path of oranges.

Oranges.

Elephants cannot resist citrus. They love citrus. They adore it to the point that it had to be banned in all the wilderness parks for fear of attracting them to the campsites.

Grisha's plan would take advantage of this peculiarity of the elephantine palate by having us throw the oranges in a zigzag fashion to keep Tusker from directly following the truck. Hopefully, he would find the oranges, eat them, and keep moving on for more. We would be working a fine line between luring him and preventing him from figuring out we were the source.

In the meantime, Grisha said, Charlotte Pope would be waiting for us just outside of Chizarira, on a savannah that lay between the two parks. Once we met up, she would help drive Tusker deeper into Chizarira, where the appropriate tranquilizer dart guns and Tom leading several helpers would be waiting to load him into a large cargo plane.

Comical as the plan sounded, it was very dangerous. And our part was the most dangerous of all.

"I have citrus," Grisha declared. "Grisha buys many kilos citrus. Enough for several cows of driving."

"Cows?" Diamond repeated.

"Hours," I translated.

"How did you manage to sneak oranges into the park?" Diamond asked.

"Not yet. It comes early in the morning cows." Grisha stood up and stretched. "So we sleep now. Tomorrow citrus comes and we commence."

"Wow," I said. "Like the Pied Piper!"

"No, Plain-Neelie," Grisha replied sternly. "No French champagne for celebration. We will drink only good Russian Sovetskoye Shampanskoye."

We were up before dawn to help unload an outside truck

whose driver first bribed the guards and then drove in with the oranges under cover, in boxes marked as sanitation supplies for the compound. He also delivered several machetes and a few of the elephant guns that I had come to hate. Now we had to work fast before the magical smell of citrus attracted every elephant in the park. We stuffed oranges into every available space the Rover had, and since all the seats except the front ones had been removed, there was plenty of room.

"I feel like the Tropicana Queen," I remarked to Diamond, who only gave me a puzzled look and handed me another carton. Humor is definitely not cross-cultural, I decided.

We packed ourselves in, along with our luggage, some thermoses of water, and a few flashlights. Grisha covered everything with an old tarp and declared us ready. Diamond had road maps of the area, primitive though they were, her GPS, and a compass. Dawn still had not broken, but the air made us feel as though we were walking across the face of the sun.

Grisha crossed himself twice, checked to make sure he had his three cartons of Stolichnye Lights, started the truck, and began driving us out of the camp.

We took the road that passed the lily pond. Diamond tossed several oranges around its rim. A few rolled into the pond itself, as well as under the trees and brush surrounding it. Grisha cut the motor and we waited.

Tusker could be anywhere, but we were hoping that the fruit would cast its spell and bring him safely and quickly to us.

We waited for two hours, and Grisha was getting nervous. I knew he had planned for us to accomplish the drive in daylight, and we were wasting it, just waiting. Getting caught in darkness with a truckload of elephant lure was a recipe for—well, I didn't want to think about it. Human à l'orange might make a great elephant delicacy, but not when you're one of the ingredients.

We waited still.

There wasn't even a rustle of brush when suddenly *he* was next to the pond, no more than fifty feet from us, sniffing at our bait. I thrilled again at his massive body, the huge ears flapping with curiosity, the perfection, the majesty, the incredible hulking mass, noble and exquisite to every cell. He picked up an orange with his trunk and tossed it into his mouth, then waved his head up and down with approval.

But this time he had brought a friend.

It was a young bull. Not as tall as Tusker, but enormous, still. He flapped his ears rapidly, and I noticed that his left ear had an odd notch. He peeked out at us from behind Tusker, impatiently waving his trunk up and down, then shaking his head sideways and grunting. Tusker pushed back against him as if to discipline him, and the bull stopped for a moment and stood respectfully. Then he caught the scent of oranges and swung his trunk back and forth across the ground like a minesweeper, sniffing, until he, too, discovered a prize and ate it.

"Bollocks," Diamond whispered in my ear. "He looks to be a young bachelor. They team up with older bulls and get very attached. We may have two on our hands."

Grisha watched them quietly and agreed with her. "Grisha thinks elephant brings too good friend." He shook his head with a grave expression. "Some of times you cannot make separatement of good elephant friends. It makes us even heavier problem now."

"If he follows Tusker, we might have to take him as well," Diamond agreed. "Or one of them can rampage. Maybe both."

"Let's hope that's all he brings," I whispered back. "Or we're going to have to hire a fleet of planes."

Grisha turned on the motor, and the elephants looked up with only a mild interest, not spooking at all, a tribute to how used they had gotten to trucks in the bush. Diamond rolled a few more oranges at the animals, and Grisha inched forward. The elephants stood for a moment, watching us. Tusker raised his trunk and trumpeted loudly, then held his ears out wide. The situation was tricky, and my heart was pounding. We were taking a terrible chance. We were hoping to strike a balance in his mind, that he would somehow know the oranges came from us and eat what was being cast before him without charging us and overturning the truck.

Diamond threw several more pieces of fruit and we watched. Tusker and the young bull scooped them up greedily, then trotted a few feet forward, reconnoitering the ground for more. They looked at the truck and then at the ground. Then at the truck. Tusker trumpeted and shook his head and wiped his trunk along the ground trying to pick up the scent. They moved toward us again, and Grisha gunned the truck. They followed, trunks extended straight out and pointing to us. Somehow they suddenly understood, and we were on our way. Toss, drive forward, toss, drive forward. Slow enough to get out of their way, fast enough to keep them walking behind us.

It was working.

After two torturously slow hours, we had covered about fifteen miles. Fifteen miles of potholes that could pass for ravines, of washed-out roads that had us scrambling sideways to keep from toppling over, of stopping to let a black rhino and her baby trot by, of watching Tusker casually uproot an acacia tree and eat the bark, of watching him argue with the bull over one particular orange while standing on several others.

The road washed out again, and we had to detour between acacia trees, barely squeaking through overgrown and tangled thornbushes that had stickers like claws. We tried to hurry a small herd of buffalo that strolled casually in front of us and ground us to a halt while the elephants were closing in behind. It was all tricky business, and my nerves were strung tight. I looked over at Diamond, who was checking the maps against her GPS and puffing furiously on her cheroot.

Suddenly she glanced up. "Bollocks!"

"What?" I asked breathlessly. "Is something wrong?"

"I'm hungry," she declared. "Did we pack anything to eat?"

"Citrus," Grisha replied, giving an expansive wave at the contents of the truck.

"Great," I said. "So we eat oranges and baste ourselves from the inside out."

We hit a deep rut and bounced hard, dislodging a box of fruit that tumbled across the road, spilling the contents.

"We can't leave all that fruit behind," Diamond announced as Grisha slowed to a stop, "or we'll be waiting here forever to make sure they finish it. Otherwise, we'll have half a dozen elephants running after us."

"*Da*," Grisha agreed. He jumped from the Rover and ripped the box open, kicking some of the fruit across the road into the brush, and picking up the rest that were remaining, before the elephants caught up to us. "Maybe they won't notarize all of it," he said hopefully.

They did notice them and stopped for a feast. It was afternoon now, and we had another twenty or so miles to go. Grisha was growing impatient. Diamond and I were more worried. We were entering the rim of the park, far from any encampments. If we had problems, we would be totally on our own.

There was a drone from one of the side roads. Diamond and I looked at each other in alarm. It was a motor, to be sure, and I held my breath, hoping our good luck would stay with us. We pushed the remaining fruit under our seats and covered the rest with the tarp.

"I hope they're tourists," Diamond muttered, "and not Mugabe's men."

Grisha pointed under his seat. "Grisha has rifles," he said. "Do you have nerves?"

"I have nerves," Diamond declared grimly. "I have big nerves."

It was the assistant game warden from Charara. He drove toward us in his jeep, then pulled up next to our truck.

"I suggest you turn around," he said. "You're pretty far from camp."

Diamond smiled at him. "I'm a licensed safari leader. I'll bring them back before sundown."

"Do I know you?" He squinted at her.

"You probably know my good friends, the Popes? They run ThulaThula Safaris out of Chizarira." She flashed him a dazzling smile and gave just the slightest toss of her glowing red hair. "They can vouch for me."

He gave her a lingering look, glanced over at me, then at the jeep, then at Grisha.

"I only drive truck," said Grisha, shrugging. "I know nothing."

"Well, be careful," the warden said. "I found oranges along the road. Looks like some tourists sneaked them. Crazy bastards."

"Oranges!" Diamond feigned surprise. "I can't imagine anyone being so stupid," she said. "Your guides need to do a better job. I personally search my clients' luggage." She gestured at my suitcase with a stern face. The warden looked over at my luggage, and I pushed the cartons of oranges even farther back under my seat with my legs.

"We'll be very careful," Diamond added. "I know the rules."

The warden eyed the Rover, then eyed the oranges that had been kicked off the road by Grisha, then looked back at us. "We may have to close the roads down for a few days until it's safe again. We can't take a chance."

"Absolutely," Diamond agreed, while I smiled at him, hoping he couldn't smell our cargo, since we were reeking like a mobile orange grove.

"Well, don't touch them," he said. "If the *tembo*s smell orange on you, they'll tear your truck apart. You can follow me back if you want."

"We want to get just a few more photos," Diamond said. "Then we'll be along straightaway." She motioned to the camera hanging by the front seat.

The warden looked us over one last time. "Right, then." He returned to his jeep and drove away. My arms and legs were shaking. Grisha gunned the Rover forward.

Just in time. The elephants were trotting directly at us, hoping for another snack.

Chapter 8

MY BRAIN WAS COOKING. I COULD SWEAR I COULD hear it sizzle cell by cell, even though I was wearing a hat with vents. We all were. They were supposed to protect us from the outright sun, but the heat that collected underneath was cooking my brain. Or what was left of it.

We ate hot oranges. Juicier than normal because the heat released cascades of liquid down our faces, arms, and clothing. We tried to be careful, but there is no way to neatly eat an orange that is practically bubbling inside.

"Why couldn't we bring real food?" I lamented for the tenth time. "I'm actually wishing for a bowl of *sadza*."

"Food is for woman peoples to pack up," Grisha said sternly. "Grisha only plans for elephants."

"I didn't know we would be doing this today," I retorted. "And it's not like we could have ordered room service."

"No more complaints," said Diamond. "We will cope with what we have."

"Don't have," I mumbled under my breath.

We made a few hygiene stops behind the baobab trees, which was much easier for Grisha, as he pointed out several times, than for me and Diamond, who had to balance precariously in a half squat, watch for snakes and predatory bugs, and pee as fast as we could push our bladders to empty.

It took us another two hours, still rolling slowly along, still waiting for the elephants to catch up, then gunning the motor when Tusker loomed too close to the Rover.

By now, Diamond and I had perfected a certain overhand throw, and managed to cast oranges just enough off the road that the elephants had to pause to find them, eat them, and look for more. The road was growing narrower, the brush denser. Large baobab trees blocked our path. At one point a large pond appeared just ahead.

Diamond made a face. "Up for a swim?" she asked, but laughed when she saw the stricken look on my face. "Don't worry—the maps have this as a shallow." She held up the GPS. "Let's hope they're right because we're going to drive right through it."

"Here we go, we are making water," Grisha announced, rolling the truck forward and down the slight bank. He held his cigarette over his head as though to keep it dry, and we sloshed slowly through the pond and up the other side. I let out a sigh of relief, then worried if Tusker and his friend would know enough to follow us. He did, but not before stopping to douse his back with a good spray.

We passed a solitary leopard feeding on a just-killed springbok, the soft brown fur and white fantail of its prey brilliantly stained in red. The leopard lifted its head to stare at us. Its mouth was also outlined in carmine, like ghoulish lip paint, and I shuddered.

The heat was unendurable. My shirt soaked in sweat, then dried from the lack of humidity, then soaked again, getting stiffer and stiffer with each cycle. We were all streaming perspiration, and several times I thought I saw a pond of water glimmering in the far-reaching, flat, sandy expanses that now lay ahead of us.

The water may have been a mirage, but we drove past a disturbing sight that wasn't. Piles of thick bones like bleaching tree stumps were heavily strewn about, and Grisha called to me as we passed very close to a blanched, dried carcass that was opened like a large cave.

"Do not look, Plain-Neelie."

Of course I looked. I could mentally reconstruct the body that had once held these bones. The massive flat fan of the scapula, the elegantly curved jaw like a huge French horn, the long, thick femurs all reduced to white artifacts.

There are no creatures except one that have skeletons that enormous.

Elephants.

It wasn't a normal kill. There were too many. Yawning, empty ruins. Some half decayed. Some of youngsters. Macabre xylophones of death, the music of their hearts terminated a long time ago.

"Poachers," said Diamond with disgust. "Look at the tusks hacked off."

I covered my eyes—the sight was unbearable. Tusker and the bull stopped their journey to examine the area. Tusker walked over to one pile and touched it gently with his trunk. He stood over it for a long time, sniffing, turning the bones, stroking them, then lifting a large bone and tenderly, tenderly holding it, paying tribute to death with a low rumbling sound, then laying the bone reverentially back into its nest, until finally, reluctantly, he moved on.

Grisha lit another in a chain of cigarettes. "We are near last sexual of park," he declared, pointing to an odd line of baobab trees. "That is beginning of Chizarira Park. We are ending here." He checked his watch. "It is taking us nine cows, Plain-Neelie."

"Charlotte said she would tie something around a tree where we should meet her," Diamond said, pulling binoculars from her pack, along with the compass and the GPS.

"Wow," I said, "you really do know what you're doing."

She gave me an amused look. "Twenty years of running safaris," she replied. "Remember?" She did a few calculations. "We need to drive about five miles east southeast."

"*Da.*" Grisha nodded and turned the Rover. I threw oranges while Diamond navigated. Tusker and his friend followed along, more or less out of curiosity now, because they were stepping over most of the oranges, apparently satiated.

Within ten minutes, Diamond spotted a large red rag that was secured around a baobab tree. As we approached, a group of men carrying rifles appeared on horseback from behind the trees. I held my breath, but a petite woman with cropped brown hair and a very large rifle rode up in front of them.

"Charlotte Pope!" Diamond yelled, jumping to her feet. "If you aren't a sight!"

The woman kicked her horse on and trotted up to us.

"Diamond-Rose!" she exclaimed when she reached the Rover. "Bravo! We never thought you'd pull it off! Tie up your cargo and follow us—we've mapped a route back to camp."

"Is road okay for Rover? This sexual of park?" Grisha asked.

Charlotte Pope threw her head back and gave a deep, hearty laugh. "Grisha, if I didn't know you better, I'd think that was a proposition. But yes, there is a road of sorts, and the Rovers fit. We take them through here for our safaris."

She leaned over from her horse to extend a hand to me. "And you must be Diamond's friend."

"*Da.*" Grisha introduced us. "This is Plain-Neelie."

"Hello, Plain-Neelie," Charlotte said. "Are either of you tired of sitting in the Rover? You can get on some horses. My men can switch with you."

"I'll take a horse," Diamond said, jumping down from our truck. I followed. She mounted a bay horse that one of Charlotte's men handed to her, and I was given a brown-and-white pinto. The men who swapped with us climbed eagerly into the Rover and stretched their legs out with happy groans.

"Oh, how nice to get on a horse again," I enthused, and turned to Charlotte. "And it's *plain* Neelie." Then I realized I had done it to myself again. "I mean, just call me Neelie. *Neelie.*"

"Well, I'm glad to meet you, Neelie-Neelie," Charlotte

replied, then gestured toward our cargo of oranges. "I suggest you wrap the rest of those up really well," she said. "I think Tusker will just follow out of habit. We don't want to leave too much citrus around and risk bringing a herd."

"Actually," said Diamond, "we *are* bringing a herd. Tusker seems to be traveling with a young bull."

Charlotte stopped her horse, looking troubled. "Bollocks! That could be a problem if we have to separate them," she said. "I don't know the capacity of the cargo plane."

"We can't leave one behind," Diamond said. "They're *family*."

The men pulled the tarp around the remaining oranges, while Grisha made a sharp turn with the Rover to follow the path that Charlotte had pointed out.

"We threw some oranges to help lure him to our side," Charlotte called out while we trotted along.

There was a loud trumpeting from behind.

"That must be him," she guessed. "Or his friend."

Grisha interrupted her thoughts. "Grisha makes heavy suggestament that we move quickly," he called over.

"He's right," Charlotte agreed. "We'll get them in position, and then we'll dump all the citrus there and say a prayer."

"A prayer?" Diamond asked.

Charlotte nodded. "I heard from Tom just before I left camp. He's having a hell of a problem getting a plane in. He'll tell you all about it when he comes tonight." She sighed. "If he can get here."

"And if he can't?" Diamond asked.

Charlotte made a face. "We told him that his safety comes first. We don't want anything to happen to him." She glanced at Diamond. "Have you met him yet? He's a terrific guy."

Diamond laughed and gestured to me. "I haven't. But Neelie has. He might be very glad to see *her*."

"*Nyet*," Grisha called over. "Mr. Thomas will not be filled with gladment to see Plain-Neelie." He pulled a cigarette from the pack in his pocket while steering with his other hand, lit it with the smoldering tip of the one still in his mouth, and then gave me a smirky grin. "Grisha decides that he will not tell Mr. Thomas you are here. Mr. Thomas can discover himself after he makes arrivement."

"Really?" Charlotte looked at me with surprise. "Tom is so pleasant. I can't imagine him not being glad to see anyone."

"We were sort of friends," I said, feeling my face grow red.

"Lovers," snickered Diamond-Rose from the back of her horse.

"Well, if you prefer, you don't have to stay in camp. You can always pick up a transfer back to Victoria Falls later on tonight," Charlotte said, kicking her horse on. She added re-assuringly, "I know how it is with ex-lovers."

"I'm staying," I said, gritting my teeth. "I wouldn't miss this for the world."

There was another series of trumpeting from behind us. Tusker and the young bull had picked up speed, apparently annoyed that they had exhausted their supply of fruit.

"Let's go," Charlotte yelled. We moved our horses into a canter while Grisha gunned the engine.

Tusker started to amble after us.

"Let's finish the job!" Charlotte yelled. "Another hour and we're going to have ourselves a flying elephant—or two!"

Chapter 9

———∞∞∞———

TOM NEVER MADE IT.

Grisha dumped the pile of fruit in a large, open clearing. A clearing that was perfect to land a plane in. A clearing that was large enough to save an elephant, even two, with good flat ground and low-lying trees on the periphery, but there was no plane waiting for us there.

Diamond and I watched from horseback for a few minutes, then Charlotte ordered the other horses back to camp while we remained a little longer. "We'd better go," she finally said to us. "The horses have had a long day. They need water and a rubdown and to rest a little before we can give them dinner."

"Please wait another few minutes," I begged.

Tusker and the young bull came into the clearing and played with the oranges. The setup was perfect. A few tranquilizer darts, chains to pull them into the plane, and we would be finished.

But there was no plane.

The sun was beginning to soften into rose-orange. Charlotte checked her phone for the third time, but it was still dead. "We can't stay all night," she said to me. "Let's get back to camp and see what's going on."

"No!" I protested. "We can't leave them here. They won't just hang around."

"What do you suggest we do with them?" Charlotte asked in an exasperated tone. "We can't tie them up."

"But what was the whole point of this?" I said, my voice rising. "They'll wander back! They'll get shot!"

"We don't have the plane," Charlotte said sharply. "Let's get back to camp before it gets dark. Maybe Tom's been able to call Billy."

We walked the horses back, while Grisha followed us in the Rover. I could barely look at him as he nervously lit cigarette after cigarette. All I could think was that Tom just had to come, that Tusker's life depended on him.

ThulaThula Safaris was a set of tidy huts and barns, stone barbecues, and a small private residence, which also served as Charlotte's office. We all rode in, with Grisha close behind. There was a man sitting at a table outside the office, sipping a Zambezi Lager. I hopped off my horse. A worker came with his hand outstretched to take the reins.

"I can take care of him," I protested.

"It's my job, *shamwari*," he said, bowing his head. "I give him good dinner."

I handed him the horse just as Grisha pulled me by the arm to take it upon himself to complete my introduction. "This is Plain-Neelie," he said to the man at the table. "She has produced heavy assistance."

"Ah yes, you must be Diamond's friend. Good to meet you, Plain-Neelie." The man stood up and extended his hand. "Billy Pope, here. You've met Charlotte—I'm her husband." He was barely taller than his wife, also lean, with dark curly hair and dark eyes, like a perfectly matched tea set. I started to speak but was interrupted by Grisha.

"Is plane making arrival?" he asked Billy.

Billy Pope shook his head. "I got off the phone with Tom about two hours ago, just before the service went out. He's stuck in Botswana. He can't even drive in—the roads are filthy with Mugabe's soldiers, and he's a marked man. They know exactly who he is."

"Why can't he fly in?" I demanded.

"The air force is still on full alert after Air Marshal Shiri's near assassination last year." Billy sighed. "Tom's cargo plane is no match for their SF.260s. He can't just invade Zimbabwean air space—they'll shoot him down in a heartbeat." He looked at his growing audience—Grisha, me, Charlotte, and Diamond—and made a helpless gesture with his hands. "It looks like we won't be able to rescue this one."

"But we *have* to," I said, my voice growing urgent. "We have to rescue both of them."

" 'Them'?" Billy repeated.

"Looks like Tusker brought a friend," Charlotte explained. "A young bull."

"Bollocks!" Billy exclaimed. "More trouble!"

"But we can't just leave them," I added.

Billy and Charlotte gave each other looks.

"Well, it's late and we're all pretty beat," Charlotte said soothingly. "Why don't we get some sleep and try to figure something out in the morning."

"*Da*." Grisha sucked on the last bit of cigarette in his mouth, though it was nearly all ash. "Grisha requires adjournment for sleep now," he agreed wearily. "But Grisha is on full notification if you have needs of him." He bowed and left us.

"I'm going to find something to eat and turn in as well," Diamond said. She looked exhausted.

I felt stupid that I had forgotten my manners. These were good people, and they had risked their lives to help save Tusker. I was sure they would think of something by morning.

"Thank you for everything you did," I said to Billy and Charlotte. My stomach growled loudly, and embarrassed, I rubbed it with my hand. Billy Pope heard it and laughed.

"There's food in the office fridge," he said. "Leftover cauliflower and cold *sadza*. Why don't you eat, and then Diamond can show you where to sleep. Good night, Plain-Neelie."

"Good night," I returned.

"I'd better check on the horses," Charlotte said, then yawning, she slipped her arm through her husband's. "I need to get some sleep, too." They strolled away, but not before I heard her explain, "By the way, her name is not Plain-Neelie, it's Neelie-Neelie. You know how Grisha gets everyone's name wrong."

There was nothing we could do.

Nothing.

Tom's plane remained in Botswana, and Tusker and his friend were left in the clearing near Charlotte's camp. We were helpless.

I awoke early the next morning to a flurry of new people arriving for safaris and men cooking breakfast. Someone left bowls of breakfast *sadza* outside the hut I was sharing with Diamond, which was nothing like the one in Charara. It was a plain thatched hut, with a toilet and shower built over a drain and hidden behind a curtain in the corner of the room. A clean cot with a few thin blankets stood against one wall, and a folding table and several chairs filled another. Diamond had again volunteered to sleep on the floor, even though I had guiltily tried to talk her out of it.

"I don't mind," she said. "It's what I've always done."

We finished our breakfast, I showered and changed into my last set of clean clothes, and we looked for someone to talk to.

Charlotte was busy greeting newcomers to the camp, speaking to them in German and Italian, and motioned me to talk to Grisha. Diamond and Billy joined us.

"What are we doing about Tusker?" I asked, trying not to sound demanding.

"We're not going to be able to save this one, Neelie-Neelie," Billy said, dropping his voice. "Sometimes the smartest part of rescue work is knowing when you have to step back."

"We can't do that," I said, fighting to keep myself from crying.

Billy shook his head. "I'm afraid we have no choice," he said. "I've seen enough rescues to know when they're not going to work." Charlotte called him, and he excused himself, leaving me and Grisha alone.

"Grisha!" I cried. "Tell me what to do!"

"Billy has correctament." He put his arm comfortingly around my shoulder. "Sometimes, Plain-Neelie, you have to leave elephant behind."

The image of Tusker flashed in front of my eyes, his enormous body, the intelligence behind his amber eyes, maybe even a certain trust that those who shared the jungle with him would treat him fairly. My king of wild hearts in his empire under the golden African sun. How could I leave him to die?

"I can't," I said, and started to sob. "I can't. How can you be so indifferent?"

"Grisha is not filled with indifferment," he said gently. "Grisha sees elephants he's left behind in his eyes every night."

I looked up into his face. It wasn't filled with indifference at all—it was filled with sorrow.

And that was it.

I thought we were finished. Finished with Tusker and finished with Zimbabwe.

Charlotte Pope arranged for us to take a chicken bus straight to Harare later that morning. She had pulled strings and bribed an official, and even managed to get us seats on a plane out of Zimbabwe. To New York.

"We can't just leave," I protested to Diamond. "We can't leave him out there, just like that."

She took me aside. "Well, I know someone who was made

minister in one of the government agencies in Harare," she said. "Joshua Mukomana. An old friend of my husband's. We hid him in the bush some years ago when he fell out of favor with Mugabe. Then he made Mugabe a lot of money, and they became friends again. I haven't thought about him in years, but I seem to remember he was appointed the minister of something or other. I can give him a ring." She gave me a rueful shrug. "I think it's time to call in a favor."

"You are on a fool's errand," Charlotte told us when Diamond mentioned what we were trying next. "The government is so corrupt, they're impossible to deal with."

We had to agree, but if we were on a fool's errand, then at the very least, we were compassionate fools.

Chapter 10

JOSHUA MUKOMANA HELD THE UNWIELDY TITLE OF Minister of Environment, Tourism, Permissions, Unpaved Roads, and maybe Broken Hearts, and we had a last-minute appointment to see him.

First we had to say good-bye to Charlotte and Billy and Grisha. And leave two elephants, who were blithely unaware that their lives were imperiled. Diamond and I had done everything we could, and I was sick with anguish.

One of Charlotte's guides dropped us at the *dalla-dalla* terminal, and we returned to Harare on a torrid and precipitous ride that entailed several bus changes, a collision with an oxcart, and again, too many chickens. The only good thing about it was that we saved ourselves considerable fare.

"When we see Joshua, I think we should tell him that we're part of a big organization," Diamond suggested as we bounced along the road. "They get quite impressed with complicated administrative titles here."

"What kind of organization?" I asked, thinking Diamond was probably right. An official rescue organization would bestow a certain gravitas upon us and make all the difference in the kind of respect we got.

Diamond grinned and pushed a chicken away from her rucksack. "I'm not all that creative with names," she said. "It took me three years to name my first dog, and all I came up with was Hereboy. You think of something. We should be there in about ten more minutes."

It was late in the afternoon by the time we reached Joshua Mukomana's well-appointed office in a new glass building on Causeway, not far from the gleaming modern offices of the president. The entire complex was patrolled by heavily armed soldiers with machine guns slung over their backs, and they were making me nervous.

Diamond pulled open huge glass doors with curved brass handles. We walked into a huge marble lobby decorated with eight-foot purple palms and six-foot-something soldiers. The palms remained in their pots, but the soldiers stepped in front of us.

"I have an appointment with Minister Mukomana," Diamond announced. The soldiers verified it with a call, and we were sent on our way. I could taste adrenaline.

"Have you thought of a title yet?" Diamond asked as she led me through the lobby to the elevators.

I hadn't. The carved mahogany elevator door opened in front of us, we stepped inside, and were immediately carried up to the twelfth floor. I was straining to think of a good name. The Elephant Club? Too pedantic. The Elephant Girls? Could be taken the wrong way. My mind remained firmly blank. The doors opened to reveal another armed soldier.

"No matter what," Diamond warned me as we followed him down a marble hallway, "be patient."

"What was your friend's title again?" I whispered to her. "Minister of Cold Showers and Stale Cupcakes?"

"Never mind," she whispered back. "He's the only one left who can help us."

A few minutes later, we were being served tea and cornmeal cakes sprinkled with sugar by the soldier, who put aside his Uzi in order to perform the social graces required of a secretary.

I took a sip of tea. "ELLI," I suddenly announced with a flourish.

Diamond shot me a puzzled look. "Ellie? Yes?"

"ELLI," I repeated. "Elephant Liberation League Internationale." I spelled it out. "E-L-L-I. We'll call ourselves ELLI. We tell your friend that we're from ELLI." I stood up and raised my cup and announced in portentous tones, "We will save Tusker in the name of ELLI!"

"Shhh, sit down!" Diamond cautioned, then whispered, "ELLI—I like it."

The minister was a very heavy man in his early sixties, with ebony skin, thick white hair, and steel-rimmed glasses that gave him the air of a college professor.

He clapped his hands. "*Sorida*," he greeted Diamond, "it has been a long time since you have traveled this way."

She cupped her hands to greet him back. "*Sorida*, Excellency," she said.

Mukomana eased himself behind his huge polished mahogany desk and signaled the soldier to leave us alone, then turned his attention back to Diamond.

"I am sorry about Jakob." He frowned for a moment in remembrance. "He was my *shamwari*."

"Thank you," Diamond said.

"How long has it been, now?" he asked. "It seems yesterday."

"Two months," Diamond replied. "It seems yesterday to me, as well."

"I have never forgotten how you put your life at risk for me, *shamwari*," Mukomana said, bowing his head to her.

"We could do no less for such a friend," Diamond replied, bowing her head in reply.

"So, you have fallen in love with one of our elephants?" Mukomana asked teasingly.

"I have," she said, shaking her bright hair from her shoulders and giving him a dazzling smile. He watched her appreciatively.

"I am afraid he is a bad one," the minister said, his mood suddenly turning grave. "You have not chosen well."

"We can take him off your hands," Diamond replied. "We have a place for him."

"I see," he said. "You bring him back to Kenya with you, so you can show your customers what a bad Zimbabwe elephant looks like?" He wiggled his eyebrows at her and giggled at his joke.

"We have enough bad elephants in Kenya," Diamond

said, laughing with him. "But I am leaving for America to-night. I want to show bad elephants to the Americans."

"And you?" he turned to me. "Miss Diamond tells me you are Miss Sterling. A capital name!"

"Thank you," I replied. "I am president of"—I took a deep breath—"ELLI. It's an organization that saves elephants." I hoped I hadn't sounded pretentious.

"So why don't you save a good one?" Joshua Mukomana said, his face serious at first, before he laughed at my perplexed look. He leaned back in his wide leather chair. "I know of this elephant," he said. "I am told when he comes into the campgrounds to steal food, he frightens the campers. We cannot take the risk." He gave a sad sigh. "His disposal is already scheduled."

Diamond leaned forward and pressed her hands against his desk. "Joshua, *shamwari*, that is the ministry speaking. What can *you* do to help us?" He rocked in the leather chair and pondered. He sipped his tea and ate a sugary cornmeal cake and pondered for a long time. I felt impatient, but I remembered Diamond's words and just calmly sipped my tea.

"I can sell him to you," he finally said. "We sell many elephants." He paused. "To hunters. Do Americans like to hunt?" He gestured to me. "Ah! You are too pretty to hunt."

I felt my face flush at his words.

"We don't want to use him for hunting," Diamond said casually. "We just want him. He is of no use to you."

"True." Joshua Mukomana drained his tea, holding the cup daintily, with one pinky extended. He pressed a small buzzer on the front of his desk. The armed soldier returned.

"Tea." Joshua Mukomana held up his cup. "More tea

and more cakes." The soldier saluted and left the room. We waited. Joshua Mukomana studied us. "You came especially to see me because of this elephant?"

"We did," said Diamond.

The soldier returned with a red clay pot filled with more steaming black tea and another tray of little cakes, then poured us each another cup. Joshua Mukomana pressed his thick, cigar fingers together and rocked some more in his chair. "Since we are good friends and I have a debt to you I feel obligated to repay, I will authorize his sale to you. You can have the elephant."

"Thank you, *shamwari*," Diamond said. Her voice was filled with relief.

"Seven hundred and fifty zillion Zim dollars," he said. "A bargain, because we are old friends."

It sounded like a defense budget, and then I felt like giggling. A trillion zillion. A squillion. A bozo-illion, an elephantillion. No one in the whole world spouts numbers like that. I glanced over at Diamond, who just kept sipping her tea. No one except people in Zimbabwe.

"Ten trillion Zim dollars," she said evenly.

"He's a fine, big elephant," Joshua Mukomana argued. He stared at Diamond. She took another sip of tea. "Fifty-five trillion."

"Fifteen," Diamond countered. She looked at her watch. "What time is our flight?" she asked me. "It's nearly five o'clock."

"Six thirty," I choked. How could Diamond be so calm? We didn't have any money at all to buy Tusker, let alone a few bazillion joke-atillion lying around.

Joshua Mukomana rubbed the expanse of stomach that protruded from under his light gray suit. "I am like a cat hungry for dinner. I can think of nothing else. Let's finish this. Forty trillion."

"Thirty-five," Diamond said.

He frowned at her. She ran her hand through her hair and shook it loose.

"Thirty-five trillion five hundred million," he said. "My final offer." He slapped a heavy hand on his mahogany desk, and it sounded like a shot.

Diamond only smiled. "How much is that in United States dollars?" she asked.

Joshua Mukomana pulled out a large, ostentatious gold pen and pressed numbers into the calculator on its side.

"That is about thirty-five thousand American dollars," he replied. "Cheap!" He grunted and stood up. "But you'd better hurry. Or his price will go up again." This made him suddenly giggle.

Diamond stood up, too, and offered her hand. "It's a deal."

They shook hands. "You have one week to pay for him and remove him from the park," Mukomana said.

"Six months," said Diamond.

"Two weeks," he countered.

"Three and a half months, and that is *my* final offer," Diamond said.

He offered his hand and they shook again, and we turned to leave.

"By the way, he has a friend with him," Diamond added. "A young bull. He might cause trouble if we take just the older animal."

Joshua Mukomana waved her away. "Take them both. Tusker and his *shamwari*, but listen, make sure you pay me only. You must send me the check. My name alone must be on it, you understand? You send it by special private messenger. A bank check. An *American* bank check."

Diamond shook her head. She understood very well.

"Pay me and you take them both." He looked at her with a grave expression. "No check and we shoot him, *shamwari*." He made a gun with his fingers and fired. Then he gave a loud, hearty laugh.

Chapter 11

WE WERE FINALLY GOING HOME. I DIDN'T REALLY believe it until the plane raced down the runway and lifted its nose into the clear blue African sky. Until we were weaving in between brilliant white clouds and almost touching the yellow crystal sun. Until we could take off our belts and leave our seats to walk the skies.

I wanted to feel happy and expectant, but I felt an ache for the land I was leaving and horribly defeated over the price we had negotiated for Tusker. And Shamwari, the young bull, inadvertently named by Joshua Mukomana.

I chattered nervously to Diamond about the horse and dog I had left behind in New York, and Alley, my cat, and the house I had bought for myself more than a year earlier. I tried to imagine it, but all I could picture was a hut with a thatched roof.

I babble when I get nervous. I think it's because it saves me from having to listen, which I never did well, anyway. It took me a whole year filled with orphaned baby ellies to learn to listen. I listened for signs of pneumonia, little lungs filling with fluid, little trunks struggling for air. I learned to focus on elephant sounds and noises and eventually, even human conversation.

But none of it mattered. Diamond-Rose dozed through most of my soliloquy except to comment that she didn't care about such mundane things as shelter. I had the feeling she would just as gladly have made camp along some highway and wrung the necks of a few passing sparrows to live on.

"Do you have a place to stay when we arrive?" I worried.

She just shrugged. "Something will show up. It always does. As they say on safari, home is where you gather firewood."

"Well, you can't just land in New York and set up a tent on the tarmac," I said, shocked. "You know, my house has a spare bedroom. Actually, it's my office, and it has a daybed. The room's small, but you're welcome to it."

"Thank you. I don't plan on staying in one spot," Diamond said, giving me a grateful smile. "And everything I own is in my rucksack—a few changes of clothes, my toothbrush, and my lariat." She put her head back against the seat and let out a sad sigh. " 'Course, I'll have to pick up a new safari knife. They confiscated mine just before we boarded. Had a good gut-hook blade, too."

"You won't have much use for one," I reassured her. "Unless, of course, you're going to start dating."

We cleared customs, rented a car, and stopped for our first American meal.

"How's this place for dinner?" I asked, pulling into an in-expensive-looking diner along the interstate. I glanced down at my now dusty jeans and soiled tee, and then at Diamond's outfit. "We're not exactly dressed to kill."

"I think we look fine," she said. "I just want a little snack, anyway."

We lingered over coffee while Diamond scrupulously studied the dessert menu. She signaled the waitress and ordered a double slab of chocolate pie, which inspired me to order a piece of chocolate cake.

"So," Diamond asked, "how much will you charge for me to stay with you?"

"That's okay," I said. "Don't worry about paying me for the room. It's my—"

She held up a finger to interrupt me so she could signal the waitress. "Throw two scoops of ice cream on my pie," she called over, then turned back to me. "That just might do me, though I might want some cherry pie, too. It's been a long time since I've seen American desserts."

The waitress brought the check, and Diamond-Rose snatched it from her hands. "My treat." She dug through her rucksack and pulled out a woven red straw purse. "I may have spent my life in the bush and have to be housebroken again, but as they say in Kenya, only someone else can scratch the middle of your back. So, I sleep at your house and the food is on me."

My house was waiting for me, like a faithful friend.

It was a proper house. Windows, with their eyes shut,

about to be awakened at the touch of a light switch. My green-painted rocking chair was still in the corner of the porch, its yellow floral pillow perched invitingly against the wicker. The porch light, left on for me by my brother after I let him know I was on my way home, made a welcoming yellow splotch in the night. My front door stood ready to let us inside, as though we were any family coming home after an evening out. I had been living in a wooden hut for the past year, and I had almost forgotten what it felt like to have a house. Diamond took in everything with a certain hunger in her eyes before she even got out of the car.

"This is it," I turned around to announce from the top of the porch steps.

Diamond grabbed her rucksack. Her boots made hollow thumps as she climbed up behind me. "I really appreciate the invitation," she said. "You know, I had originally booked my flight without even planning what I was going to do afterward."

I lifted the doormat and picked up the key my brother left, along with a little white card. "From my brother Reese," I explained. "He's kind of a goofball." I opened the card and made a face at its content. "It says welcome home, and then there's the usual elephant joke. He's been obsessed with jokes ever since I got involved with elephants." I scanned the handwritten note and then read it aloud. " 'Where does an elephant with a rash go?' "

Diamond gave me a puzzled look. I turned the card over and upside down to read the answer: " 'To a pachyderma-tologist.' " I sighed and stuffed the card into my pocket and opened the front door. "He hasn't changed one bit."

Diamond followed me in and stood there awkwardly as I put my suitcase down and flicked on a table lamp. Its light looked pallid and sullen, and I crossed the room to turn on another lamp. It did help, the room brightened, but nothing like the open, clear light I had gotten used to in Kenya.

"Now we're home," I said to Diamond. "For what it's worth."

I didn't know what to expect, but the house felt almost unbearably stuffy. How ironic that my little hut in Kenya gave me the feeling that I had all of the outdoors to live in, while this house, so much bigger, felt so much more confining.

The air was oppressive with furniture and drapes and carpeting and locked windows, and I fought off the feeling that I was going to asphyxiate any minute. Diamond apparently felt the same way. She dropped her rucksack and took a few gulps of air.

A desiccated plant stood in a pot in the corner of the living room, but there wasn't a spot of dust anywhere. My mother, I thought. She had probably tidied everything before I got home. The plant had been her housewarming gift when I moved in. I supposed she left it here as a quiet remonstration for my leaving for Kenya. I'd throw it out in the morning.

There was a loud click, then a gentle whir. The sound of it startled Diamond.

"Oil burner," I said.

But it did sound like a thousand bird wings flapping furiously to escape a predator. Warm, dusty air rose from the vents, and I, too, stood in the center of the room, flustered. I had forgotten all these domestic things.

Suddenly the ceiling felt crushingly low. A band of panic closed around my chest, and claustrophobia took over. Could I bear to stay here? Where was the sweeping African sky encrusted with all the stars of the universe? Even the carpeting was wrong. I was so used to the familiar red dust that penetrated everything before it got trod into thick mud by baby elephant feet.

The house didn't feel like mine at all. These walls weren't mine, this wasn't my air. It was all wrong. There were nights in Kenya that I had dreamed of home. I needed to know it was still there for me, that it was still mine. But now I wanted to return to the little hut with the woven mats on the floors and my ellie babies. God, how I was missing them already.

Diamond picked up her rucksack from the floor and slung it across her back. "Civilized," she remarked.

I gave her a sympathetic nod. "I hope you'll be comfortable here," I said doubtfully. She had nineteen years of jungle on me. "I mean, I hope you'll be able to adjust." I stopped before adding ruefully, "I hope I'll be able to adjust, too."

I checked out the rest of the house and returned to find that Diamond had summoned the courage to wander around the living room, touching the television, picking up the phone to listen to the dial tone, running her fingers over the back of the floral printed furniture, her rucksack still slung across her shoulder.

"Odd," she said. "Flowered furniture and tables and lamps. It's the kind of home I had always wished I grew up in."

I wasn't sure what she meant, but it was my home and it was a proper home. The thing was, I thought I'd feel more at ease once I actually walked around a bit.

I hung away my jacket and grabbed my suitcase, gesturing for Diamond to follow me upstairs. "I'll show you your room, but the mattress on the daybed in there might be a little lumpy."

Diamond shrugged. "You know I'm used to sleeping on the ground," she replied. "And I'm used to showering with cold water and peeing behind baobab trees, so nothing fazes me."

I laughed. "You'll scandalize my neighbors if you squat behind the hydrangeas, so please enjoy the indoor plumbing. Except I have to warn you, I seem to remember that the shower was a bit like a water ride. It sprays sideways up your nostrils."

"Don't worry about the loo," Diamond reassured me. "I rarely shower. I mean, what's the point?"

At the top of the steps was a little hallway that turned to the right and brought us to my office. It was a small room lined with bookcases, a daybed, and my desk. "All yours," I said, opening the door and making a sweeping gesture with my hand.

Diamond walked over to the window and pressed her nose against it to look out at the darkness.

"How very strange," she murmured. "It's been a long time since I've had glass between me and the world." She threw the rucksack into a corner and sat down on the daybed, testing its springs, then jumped to her feet to pace, finishing at the window again, where she stopped and touched her fingertips against the panes.

"Will you be okay?" I asked. I felt bad for her. Diamond reminded me of the animals I had seen in zoos, pacing the perimeters of their cages, staring out at the world with bewilderment in their eyes.

Diamond turned around and forced a half smile. "Just throw me a blanket and I'll be fine."

Steaming water, fragrant soap, real shampoo. If manna from heaven could be transmuted into water, I was luxuriating in it. Lavender body wash that my mother had once given to me as a birthday gift insinuated itself into my pores, melting fragrantly as I lathered and lathered and lathered some more. Then I stood, shoulders slumped forward, to let it all run off. It was an exorcism of my sharp longing for Africa and my beloved little ellies. Of Tom, though I wouldn't let myself think of Tom right now. It had been my decision to leave him for Africa, and I was living with the consequences. It was okay, I said to myself, I was strong enough to do that.

I was home. It didn't feel like home yet. I knew I would have to give it time. But it was home. I at least had that.

Dried and fluffed, I passed the office on my way to bed. The light was off, and I could hear Diamond-Rose snoring loudly. At least *she* managed to fall asleep, I thought jealously, without the comforting sway of trees and the night calls of animals in the bush. I wondered if I would be able to do the same. If I would be able to sleep without the deep, gentle rumbling breath of a baby ellie by my side. If I would even be able to sleep alone since it would be the first time in a very long time. Over the years, I'd had my husband, and then we added Grace, our Boston terrier. After the divorce, it was just me and Grace sharing pillows together. And then there was, well, Tom, and then me and the ellies, their wheezes filling the night. Now an empty pillow was waiting.

There was another long, resonating breath from the little room, and I cracked the door open to peek in. The acrid odor of B.O. wafted into the hallway. The blanket I had given Diamond-Rose was rolled under her head, and still dressed in her khakis, she was curled up in a ball, sleeping peacefully on the floor.

Chapter 12

―∞∞∞―

DIAMOND-ROSE HAD BEER FOR BREAKFAST.

She had awakened at first light and found a six-pack in the fridge, a welcome-home gift from my brother. She halved its number before eight in the morning and greeted me with a salutary burp as I walked into the kitchen.

"I couldn't find breakfast *sadza*," she said, holding up a beer can, "but this goes down way better." She flashed me a beatific smile.

I grunted and eyed my houseguest. Jet lag had left me feeling disheveled and out of sorts, but Diamond looked strikingly pretty even this early in the morning, even without makeup, even with her hair tangling luxuriously around her shoulders and her green eyes dreamy from heavy sleep and three beers. She was still wearing her safari clothes, and her rucksack sat on the floor next to her, like a chaperone.

"It's for you," Diamond said, handing me the note that had been taped to the beer. "It's another elephant joke from your brother, but I didn't look at the answer. I didn't want to pry."

I scanned the paper. " 'How do elephants call each other?' " I read aloud.

Diamond shrugged and snapped the cap off another beer.

I turned the paper over. " 'They use the elephone.' "

Diamond giggled. "He sounds like a great kid. How old is he?"

I had to do a quick mental calculation. "Thirty-four?"

"Perfect," Diamond said. "Just perfect."

I scanned the kitchen. It was tidy, almost exactly the way I had left it one year earlier, but vacant looking, which meant my mother had been in to clean it as well. My potted herbs were gone, the outdated cow calendar had been discarded, along with the old sponges for the sink. I take pride in my fastidiousness, but my mother could embarrass Mr. Clean for his lapse in standards. I opened a cabinet and eyed its lack of contents. And not only were the cupboards bare, but the refrigerator was empty as well. Everything perishable, crunchy, or soft had been cleaned away.

"You might want to shower and change your clothes before we shop for supplies," I suggested to Diamond. The reality of being home was slowly returning. Food shopping. Laundry. Cleaning. Even a new cell phone. "You can use my washer for what you're wearing."

Diamond looked down at her outfit. "Already changed my clothes," she said, and crushed the can in one hand. "And you know my policy on showering."

———————

We left by the back door because I was anxious to show Diamond-Rose the five acres of pasture and the horse barn that I owned. I was so inordinately proud of it all, my house, my farm, my every twig and leaf, pebble, blade of grass, because it was something I had given to myself. Getting a divorce had been a little like standing in a tornado. When it was over, everything I owned or believed in had been blown away, my pockets emptied, my shoes sucked off my feet. I think I may have lost my dental fillings as well.

We stepped outside. "This is it!" I announced, making a grand gesture with my arms. I turned to Diamond, eagerly waiting for her reaction.

She studied it all carefully. My azaleas were nearly covering the windows, and the lawn could have been used for hula skirts. She took in the expanse of knee-high grass and weeds that had grown totally out of control, her face betraying her bafflement over what exactly she was supposed to be admiring. She looked at the fences, and there were fences everywhere. She looked at the houses behind us, the houses on the side of us, the houses across the street, their roofs cluttering the horizon like nesting chickens.

"Is that grass?" she asked. "Or are you growing wheat for the hungry?"

"Let's just get some breakfast," I muttered, embarrassed, suddenly seeing what she saw. Compared to the sweeping landscapes of Kenya, I had a small plot of land overgrown with useless vegetation. I led her to the rental car. Once behind the wheel, I explained my plans for the day. "First we'll have breakfast, then we're going to visit my ex-horse, and then I'll take you to see the love of my life."

Diamond's eyes widened with surprise. "Tom? I thought you said it was over."

"Margo. She's an elephant." I pulled into our first stop of the day. "And she's the only reason I'm glad I came home."

McDonald's is not the place to be eating breakfast in safari clothes. Diamond-Rose was asked for her autograph seven times before she took her first bite of food, by people expecting her to be accompanied by a crocodile.

"Next one that stares, I'm going to mash him in the beak," she complained as we opened the wrappings for our egg sandwiches. "You'd think they never saw anyone dressed for work before."

I scanned her appearance. "Maybe you need to reconsider your business outfit, because you should know, the first rule of the jungle is blending in."

Diamond just shrugged and looked around the room at the various customers. "I'd blend in better if I put on about fifty pounds." But she wolfed down two egg sandwiches, then sniffed disdainfully at her coffee before draining her cup. "Is American coffee always this weak?"

I sniffed at my own coffee. "I thought it was too strong."

She got up and returned with two more cups. "Quantity over quality," she said ruefully before settling into her chair. "So why don't you just start things up again?"

"You mean with Tom?" I shook my head and stared into

my coffee. "It ended badly. We weren't even talking. There'd be no reason for me to contact him again."

"Of course you have a reason," Diamond said. "Grisha will have told him by now that you were in Zim. Even a small seed can grow a whole cotton tree, you know."

I gave her a blank look. "Meaning?"

"You may not need more than that to get him interested in you again." She leaned forward and cupped her chin in her hands. "I'm good at fixing things. I would call him straightaway and tell him that you're home and you need to speak to him."

I laughed at the idea of anyone fixing what was broken between Tom and me. I rolled up the wrappings from her breakfast and then mine, then wiped the crumbs away with my napkin, then my little area of the table, then wiped my fingers. I am obsessively neat. When I was growing up, Reese used to call me a neat freak, though after a while, he dropped the word "neat." I made sure everything was in order before I answered Diamond.

"What would I say?" I asked.

"Tell him we're sorry about the planes not working out, but that we've pretty much solved the problem with Tusker all by ourselves."

"But we haven't solved the problem. We've only created another problem—now we need a lot of money." It occurred to me that this was a recurring theme with Diamond, solving problems by creating new ones.

"But he's rich," she said. "Rich men know how to make money. He can give you advice. Rich men love to give advice on making money. Most of it is useless, but you'll have him back in your life before you know it."

I looked up at her. "You really think so?"

"Of course! A man does not wander far from where his corn is roasting!" she said triumphantly. "Once he finds out that all we need to do is raise money to bring the elephants here, he won't be able to resist getting involved!"

I didn't tell Diamond that I was positive Tom wouldn't even take a phone call from me since his last words were "You've made your choice and picked the elephants. Now I make my choice. I pick a life without you."

Thereby adding himself to my ever-increasing collection of exes.

I sighed. There is nothing so pathetic as owning the Complete Anthology of Exes. It might even be a winning poker hand.

Definitely a royal flush.

Of the toilet.

I was driving us to my next stop, when Diamond brought it up again.

"Call him and ask him for advice," she said. "We're going to need all the help we can get."

"Let me think it over," I said. "Maybe there's some way I can get a message to him without actually calling him directly."

"Well, do it straightaway," she urged. "We have less than two months."

"I will," I promised. "But right now, I need to see my ex-horse."

"*Ex*-horse?"

"He's not mine anymore," I said. "I gave him to Reese's wife. He's living in my ex-barn, which is the same old barn he's always lived in. I just don't own it anymore."

"Let me get this straight," she said. "Your ex-horse is living in your ex-barn?"

I nodded. "Yep. Behind my ex-house."

Diamond laughed. "You like to keep things simple, don't you."

A few minutes later I was pulling into the driveway of my old house. I'd had to sell it for the divorce, and luckily my brother was newly married and looking for a place to live, so it sort of stayed in the family. Now it stood, a paragon of suburban tidiness, a product of the painstaking care and attention lavished upon it by Reese and Marielle. There were new shrubs, a new mailbox, a newly blacktopped driveway. Reese's and Marielle's cars were gone. They were obviously both at work, and I was actually relieved that I didn't have to put up with Reese's teasing before I got over my jet lag.

The barn in back had been repainted to match the house, and I could see that the two small back paddocks had been joined to make one comfortably large arena, enclosed with new post-and-rail fencing. In the middle stood Mousi, his face buried in a large pile of hay.

"Wait till Mousi hears me call his name," I predicted as we drew closer to the paddock. "He'll race right over for a kiss. Then he'll put his head on my shoulder. He and I had a special bond, you know? A *mystical* bond."

"Lovely," Diamond murmured. "I've had dozens of

horses over the years. I loved them all well enough, in my own way, but in the end, they were just transportation."

"Ha," I said. "Not Mousi. Mousi is my soul mate."

Mousi was horse nobility. He was a Lipizzaner, descended from a long line of pure white steeds, and his real name was Maestoso Ariela. He was my first rescue, my surrogate child, my confidant, my past and my future, but then the divorce tsunami struck, and he needed a loving owner and a good home. Marielle, a horsewoman herself, happily provided both. But it was like giving your son to the gypsies. At some point you need to peek through the woods to see if he's thriving, if he misses you, or worse, if he is getting along perfectly fine without you. I wasn't sure which I wanted to see.

I stood by the back fence and scrutinized Mousi from ears to tail. The gypsies had done very well by my child. He was in good weight, his coat was brushed, his long mane didn't have one tangle, and though Marielle taught at a nearby university, I could see that she took time in the morning to feed him, clean his stall, and turn him out with fresh hay and water.

I cupped my hands around my mouth and called his name. Mousi picked up his head and gave me a vacant glance before returning to his hay. I called his name again.

"A bond, you say," Diamond said, leaning on the fence next to me.

I rapped on the fence with my knuckles. Mousi took another mouthful of hay. "How long do you think it takes them to forget you?" I finally asked.

"What makes you think they do?" Diamond replied.

"He always came to me before."

"He just needs you to ride him," Diamond said. "Horses remember the way you ride them."

I slipped through the fence and walked over to Mousi. He stopped chewing his hay to sniff my outstretched hand, then dropped his head for another bite. I ran my hands along his neck and over his back, and then, with Diamond giving me a thumbs-up, pulled myself astride, gently easing onto his bare back. Mousi lifted his head and pricked his ears. I touched him with my legs and he walked forward, then halted with just the pressure of my seat. I pushed my left hip forward, and he arched his neck as though he had a bit in his mouth and swung left. My right hip turned him right. Then I sat up and asked for the canter, and in one elegant departure, his body thrust forward into its familiar rolling cadence that took me around the entire pasture. I lifted my face to the sky and closed my eyes. It was here that I knew he remembered me, this giving of his body for me to make use of. Diamond was right: Horses remember the way you ride. The way you sit on them. How you hold your shoulders, the ease that releases your back into theirs. He remembered me, and I was exultant. He remembered my body, how I moved and breathed and placed my weight. I tightened my back against his movement, and he dropped to the walk, moving in measured steps, then halted, square and proud.

"You're lovely together," Diamond called out. "Now I can see it. In both of you. The bond, I mean."

I jumped off and gratefully threw my arms around

Mousi's neck. He nuzzled me for a moment, then pressed his head against my shoulder just the way he always had.

I held on to him for a long time. My sudden tears mixed into his white mane, wetting the coarse, curly ends. I rubbed my face against his neck and breathed in the smell of hay and warm horse, and I didn't care that Diamond was watching. Mousi remembered me. Somewhere in his spirit and mind and body he was still mine. He would always remember me because my riding had left something of me with him.

And, I thought with some satisfaction, maybe, unlike other exes, you never really end it with a horse.

Chapter 13

———⟨∞∞∞⟩———

SOMETIMES YOU CAN GO HOME AGAIN.

But you might have to make some adjustments.

I pulled into the driveway of the house I had grown up in, the house of my childhood, the gathering place for sentimental holidays, Sunday dinners, and even Reese's wedding to Marielle, two falls ago.

At first, it looked disconcertingly unfamiliar, so properly suburban, with its new pale gray siding and freshly painted burgundy shutters, sculpted box hedges, and disciplined rows of white and pink mums presiding over a well-trimmed lawn. Diamond and I got out of the car, and I stayed at the curb for a moment, forcing myself to belong here, to this house and its memories. I had just come in from sweeping, unfiltered blue skies and beckoning openness. It was all still part of my internal landscape—the acacia trees laden with gnarled, thorny brown branches and white star flowers, the red-brown dust and rolling moonscape savannahs covered with rocks and ragged yellow weed, clouds the color of a snow stork in an uncannily lit blue sky. I couldn't yet make peace with suburbia, if I ever had.

"Well, this is where I grew up," I said to Diamond, giving her a self-conscious shrug over the perfectly square stone walls and orderly flowers in military formation. My car stood polished and waiting in the driveway. My father had kept it running for me.

"Civilized," Diamond sniffed, but a look of envy crossed her face. "I'm surprised you didn't come here first. Family completes all the fingers on your hand."

"I suppose," I said vaguely.

"It's perfect," she said, flushing. "I was raised by an alcoholic aunt. I never had anything this nice. I'll wager it's lovely inside, all thick carpeting and fat sofas and gold chandeliers. And none of it held together by duct tape."

The front door swung ajar, and suddenly I was spun back to my childhood. There was my mother, dressed in pristine white slacks and a pale pink sweater, tiny rose quartz earrings, and perfectly lacquered hair still the exact honey color it was when I was growing up. I was home, like the many times I had come in from a day of playing in the yard, or returning from a friend's house, or back from a date. Home. It was comforting.

It was suffocating.

My mother held her arms open, and I stepped forward for a hug and a kiss while she murmured how sunburned I had gotten, how thin, how I needed a good haircut, and *oh my goodness*, my eyebrows needed to be tamed *immediately*.

Suffocating.

"Mom, this is Diamond-Rose Tremaine," I introduced them, studying my mother's face for signs of culture shock. "We met on the bus to Nairobi airport."

Always unfailingly polite, my mother took in Diamond's soiled wardrobe and raised her eyebrows only half a millimeter.

"So glad to meet you," she murmured, offering a manicured hand, then stiffening when she saw the state of Diamond's fingernails.

"And, Diamond, this is my mom, Abbie Davison."

"It's wonderful to meet you, ma'am," Diamond said, impulsively giving my mother a bear hug. "Or shall I call you Mum, as well?"

"Yes, I see." My mother coughed a little. "You come right in and make yourself at home." She led us into the house while wiping her hands with an antibacterial wipe she pulled from her pocket. "After you leave your boots at the front door, of course."

Diamond questioningly looked down at her boots, then at me.

"Boots off," I said. "House rules."

"Okay." Diamond reluctantly kicked them off, but left on her gaiters, the little tent of tan material that fastened around each of her ankles. "In case of scorpions," she explained, quickly scanning the wall-to-wall carpeting.

"It's a remote risk," I said, "now that the snakes ate most of them."

We started for the kitchen, but a pungent waft from Diamond's thick gray socks stopped me in my tracks. "Why don't you put your boots back on," I said to her. "I'm sure my mother won't mind after all."

As Diamond followed me and my mother into the kitchen, I could see she was politely taking in the antique furniture, the cranberry glass lamps, the little tables with their vases and statues as best she could without being obvious.

"I used to dream of a house like this my whole life," she murmured to me. "The kind of home you can bring your friends to, without worrying that your aunt's going to roll out from under the sofa and puke on their shoes."

"There is someone waiting to see you," my mother announced as we entered the kitchen.

"It's my ex-dog," I whispered to Diamond. "She just adores me. It's like we're soul mates."

A streak of black and white leaped across the room, and a small Boston terrier attacked my ankle with a tiny but very penetrating set of white teeth.

"Grace!" I screamed with a mixture of joy and pain as I tried to shake her loose. "You remember me!" She was frantic with excitement, wriggling her fat dumpling body with the three extra love handles from side to side, until the momentum fairly knocked her over. Then, overcome with ecstasy, she threw herself across my shoelaces and ripped them open.

I knelt down to cuddle her, and she nipped my nose. "She still loves me!" I declared happily as I pinched my nostril to stanch the flow of blood.

"She might have put on a pound or two," my mother apologized as she poured us all coffee. "She just adores having breakfast with me every morning. She takes her three eggs coddled, along with her bowl of oatmeal."

We sat at the kitchen table, and Grace jumped into a chair at the table, apparently a well-practiced habit, and glared at Diamond.

"Is she friendly?" Diamond asked, reaching over to pet her.

"No!" my mother and I screamed together, as Grace sank her teeth into Diamond's fingers.

"Bollocks!" Diamond pulled her hand away to examine the minor flesh wound. "She's rather deceiving, isn't she? For something that eats coddled eggs."

"I hope you're not planning to take her home with you," my mother worried as I got up to find Diamond a bandage. "She's so happy here."

I could hear Diamond take a sharp breath. Grace squinted at me and growled.

"No," I reassured my mother. "She's all yours."

Some exes, I decided, are much better off ex.

It was good to see my mother again. The kitchen was filling with the aroma of fresh bread with a hint of dirty socks. The dirty socks were courtesy of Diamond-Rose's unlaced boots, and the bread was courtesy of my mother, whose hobby is baking, though *hobby* is not exactly the right word. She bakes bread as though the grain farmers of America were totally dependent on her output. My mother feels there is no occasion, no illness, no disappointment that can't be cured with a slice of bread. A whole loaf, if it's a real crisis. This little reunion was just crying for a few dozen muffins.

"So, Reese said that you just got in last night." My mother's face was composed, but her nostrils were flaring delicately. She couldn't take her eyes off Diamond's clothing. "I don't suppose you two even had time to . . . shower . . . or anything?"

"First thing I did," I said, knowing what she was referring to and trying to help her. "I even used that lavender body wash you once gave me."

"Because you could always shower here—we have lots of hot water," my mother continued, emphasizing "hot water" while giving Diamond-Rose an encouraging smile. She poured us more coffee. "I'll toss your stuff in the laundry for you. It'll be ready before you even miss it."

Diamond seemed flattered that someone cared. "Thanks, Mum," she said, "but I'll have to pass. You know, one thing I learned from the animals in Africa—it's not good to bathe too frequently. It removes the protective oils from your coat."

"Yes, I see . . ." My mother stood up and unconsciously rubbed another sanitary wipe over her hands, then changed the subject. "Well . . . you're probably starving. Why don't I just get you a little something to go with that coffee?" She fluttered from the refrigerator to the table and back, Grace falling in step next to her, to set out a bowl of fruit salad, a platter of deviled eggs, and five or six varieties of breads, scones, muffins, and brioches.

"Primo!" Diamond-Rose pronounced enthusiastically, putting two big muffins on her plate and scooping up a knifeful of butter the size of a golf ball. "As they say in

Kenya, it makes a family when you gather around to eat the same cornmeal."

My mother shot me a puzzled look. I just shrugged. "Yes, well, you'll find a few corn muffins in there," she said to Diamond. "Neelie just loves my muffins. It brought her right back home because I'm sure that's what she craved the most while she was away."

I would have thought toilets that flush or a good haircut, but apparently my mother was thinking homemade bread. In fact, my mother was watching me with great expectations, and though still full from breakfast, I felt compelled to take a muffin because to do anything else, I knew, would be committing the gravest of offenses.

Diamond was already on her second muffin. "You must get a lot of practice baking," she commented, "because these are the best I've ever eaten."

"Why, thank you!" My mother put her hand to her throat, the way she did when she'd been supremely flattered. "I've been told many times that my bread has moral fiber, and I always appreciate the compliment."

"I think they just meant fiber," I corrected her, "but it's still good."

I slowly nibbled on my muffin, Diamond happily polishing off her own two. I finally finished, gulped the last of my coffee, then stood up to give my mother a quick hug and kiss. "Gotta go, Mom, but thanks for breakfast. I called the car rental, and they'll be by today. I'll talk to you soon."

"We'll have dinner," my mother said. "Soon. With the whole family. Everyone missed you so much. Your father was worried the whole time you were gone."

"Oh, a family dinner would be wonderful," Diamond replied, giving her a peck on the cheek. "I love family gatherings."

My mother opened the front door, and we stepped into the sunlight. Diamond followed us out, but not before I saw her furtively tuck a loaf of pumpkin-raisin bread into her rucksack.

Chapter 14

"YOU!"

The owner of the donut shop recognized me as soon as I gave him an order for four dozen jelly donuts. "I no have four dozen jelly! Long time ago you buy donut, donut, all the time donut, donut, and I make donut, donut like crazy jelly donut factory, but then you no come back. My wife and I eat every night, donut, donut."

"Well, I'm back again," I said. "Today I'll take whatever you have, but tomorrow I'll need all raspberry jelly, please."

"You come every day?" he asked, his black caterpillar eyebrows dancing happily while he emptied his shelves of every variety of donut he had and rapidly boxed them.

"Every day," I promised. "Four dozen jellies."

"Wonderful goodness," he said, mollified, and handed me

the boxes with an ecstatic smile. "I tell my wife everything okay now. Then I surprise myself with new big-screen TV."

"Muffins? Donuts? Bread? Your family have a baked goods fetish?" Diamond asked as I drove us to our next destination. "I suppose your brother is competing in the World Cup for pie throwing?"

"These donuts are for Margo," I replied. "She's the elephant I told you about—the one I helped bring from Zimbabwe. She's at the Wycliff-Pennington sanctuary, and that's where we're going next."

"Pennington?" Diamond caught the name of the farm. "Tom Pennington *again?*"

"Him," I said. "But he doesn't stay there, he only supports it."

"And donuts are on the treat list because you think pastries are a natural diet for elephants?" Diamond asked, reaching into a box and stealing a Boston cream.

I pushed the lid closed. "No, but they'll keep Margo from playing her little jokes," I explained. "She just loves picking people up and throwing them across her enclosure."

"Oh, great," Diamond said, noisily sucking out the filling. "I guess I'm dressed for the occasion after all."

Puffs of dust swirled lazily around the car as we pulled into the parking lot of the sanctuary. I was surprised at how rundown it had gotten. The unpaved driveway looked more rutted than I remembered, and weeds raggedly outlined the buildings, which could have used a few coats of paint.

Diamond-Rose uncurled her long legs from the front seat

of the car to stand next to me in the parking lot. She executed a slow three-sixty to take in the several small barns, the larger elephant barn in front, all the fencing and gates. I knew what she was thinking. Fencing and gates. And more fencing.

"Civilized," she sniffed.

But I was puzzled. Elisabeth Wycliff, the elderly owner of the sanctuary, was almost always to be found driving her vintage '70s Chevy truck across the grounds, its bed filled with buckets of fruit or frozen raw chicken or bales of hay for the animals, but now it was parked next to her house, covered in more dust than usual, with a large crumple in the front fender that pushed the hood up like a metal origami. And the truck belonging to Richie and Jackie Chiger, the farm managers, was parked by their house, though it had been a rule that either Mrs. Wycliff or Richie had to be patrolling the property during the day. I knocked on Richie's door, but there was no answer. This struck me as odd since Jackie usually answered. Mrs. Wycliff's house looked equally quiet. Well, I would find them later. All I really cared about was seeing Margo again. And Abbie.

The doors to the elephant barn were wide open, revealing that it was empty except for the usual large pile of hay stacked in a corner of the huge metal cage inside. Everything looked the same as I remembered except for a few heavy-duty truck tires that were suspended by chains from the ceiling for Margo to play with. The familiar smell of elephant hung in the air, and I sniffed at it as though I were inhaling the scent of fine perfume.

"It's been four days since I've smelled elephant," I exclaimed to Diamond, "and I miss it already. Margo must be down at her pond with her baby. Maybe Richie's out there with them, though he usually takes his truck."

We walked from the barn through the gates that separated the upper part of the sanctuary from the lower elephant field. I led Diamond along a narrow path that started at the top of a rise and traced a dusty line along a grassy hill before finally winding its way down to a meadow and the pond.

There was an elephant next to the water. A monolith in gray, standing on the bank, dozing in the afternoon sun, plump and peaceful, the tip of her trunk resting on the ground, her ears slowly fanning away the flies. My elephant. Stunningly large and real and glorious.

Margo.

I pressed my hands to my mouth as my eyes filled with tears. "I've missed her so much," I whispered.

I had missed sitting in the barn at night and talking to her. I had missed our old games, when Margo would wrap her trunk gently around my waist and lift me a few inches from the ground. I missed how Margo shook her head in rhythm to the music when I turned on the radio, or tossed her big beach ball back to me. For the whole year I had been in Kenya, surrounded by dozens of baby ellies, I longed for Margo.

"And that's Abbie." I pointed to Margo's daughter, a yearling now, up to her knees in the green algae pond, gleefully spraying water into the air. "Oh my God, look at how much she grew!"

"Abbie?" Diamond repeated. "Like your mother?"

I nodded. "Margo was named for Tom's mother. I met her once. She's more of a horse person, but she loved having an elephant named for her."

"I don't blame her," Diamond said. "It's an honor."

"And I named Abbie for my mother." I giggled at the memory. "You'd think she'd have been pleased but, well, that's my mother."

Diamond gave me an affectionate smile. "*Our* mother."

We watched quietly from the top of the knoll.

Before us stood two gray silhouettes against the blue sky, framed by the distant kaleidoscope colors of the Catskill Mountains. A loxodontine study of Madonna and child, with all their strength and magnificence and sad vulnerability, pursued no longer, now secure and serene, standing safely together.

"How sad," murmured Diamond. "Two wild creatures. They don't belong here, locked up like criminals."

Of course I knew that. They belonged to a different world. A world where Margo would be with her herd, her mother, her aunts and cousins, as they made their lumbering treks across the African landscape. I knew Abbie needed an extended family to grow up healthy. If I knew anything about elephants, it was this: family was everything.

"She would have died in Zimbabwe," I replied, a little defensively. How could Diamond ruin the moment by criticizing this place? Margo had not been merely taken, she had been *rescued*. She had been wounded by poachers and left to die with her baby next to her. To not take her, to leave them both to die would have been unforgivable. "Besides, where do you think we'll be bringing Tusker?" I reminded her. "We can't just turn him loose once he gets to the States!"

"He can't live behind fences," she said. "It isn't right. We'll have to find something more suitable."

Abbie diverted our discussion by blowing another spray of water into the air and then nudging her mother with her little trunk and squealing with happiness.

I took a step toward them and gestured for Diamond to follow. "I can't wait for them to see me again," I said. "We have a very unique relationship. We're like soul mates."

It was Abbie who spotted us first. She climbed from the pond with a huge splash, barking and squealing until her mother startled awake and turned around to see what the disturbance was. Margo studied us for a moment, then swung her head and trunk sideways with a deep rumble. I took another impatient step down the slope, but Diamond-Rose grabbed my shoulder.

"One thing I learned in the bush," she said quietly. "It's never a good idea to just pop in on your local wildlife."

"Well, she doesn't have a doorbell," I joked, but in my impatience I was rushing things, and Diamond was right to be concerned. I forced myself to stay on the slope and wait for a friendly sign, but Margo slowly flapped her ears and continued to stare. I knew enough about ears to know leisure flapping was good, that the elephant was thinking things over.

Margo didn't seem concerned as we started down the hill. Diamond and I were almost at the base when Margo suddenly rumbled and held her ears straight out from her head, apparently perceiving us as a threat. She marched forward a few steps for a better look. We froze in our tracks.

"That's not quite the reception I'd expect from a soul mate," Diamond said in a low voice.

"It's been over a year," I replied. "But it should be okay—elephants never forget."

Still, I decided prudence was the better part of safety and waited for a sign that it was okay to proceed. Margo rumbled again and took another step, flapping her ears a bit more vigorously, then raising her trunk over her head and blasting us with a trumpeting roar.

"That looks more like a challenge," Diamond whispered.

I wasn't sure. Though I wanted to rush to Margo's side, she was definitely giving signals of intruder alert. A moment later she was moving toward us in a rapid, undulating walk.

"Bollocks! I believe she's coming right at us," Diamond announced in a tight voice, her years in the bush having taught her not to scream while in the direct path of a charging animal.

We both backed up a few steps. "She'll remember me," I said hopefully.

"Before or after she tramples us?"

It was a good question, because between Margo and Abbie, there was probably close to eight thousand pounds of inquisitive pachyderm bearing down on us. The ground trembled with each step, and I worried that I might have been overconfident. A whole year had passed. I was thinner, tanner, and had even brought a stranger. And I knew there was nothing more furiously protective than a mother elephant, except maybe Richie, who would be livid with me for taking such a risk.

I quickly looked around for options, but trying to return to the top of the hill before Margo reached us was not one of them. Doing so could escalate the elephant into a rage, and she was quite capable of outrunning us. My second choice, dodging around the two elephants was too risky.

"Bollocks!" Diamond declared as the elephants closed in to five hundred feet. "Can't you throw her one of those donuts or something?"

"I left them in the barn."

Three hundred feet.

"Neelie?"

Two hundred feet.

"I'm waiting for her to recognize me," I said with a quaver.

One hundred feet.

"What happens if she's myopic?" Diamond demanded.

Fifty feet and closing in.

Good point.

"Margo!" I screamed. "It's me! Margo! Margo!"

Like a runaway freight train that had just found its brakes, the elephant let out one last glorious trumpet blast and screeched to a halt within several feet of us.

"Fucking soul mates, eh?" Diamond breathed a shaky sigh of relief. "That's the last time I ever want to hear *those* words."

Elephant protocol demanded we remain still as Margo pointed her trunk straight at us, sniffing our hair, our faces, our jeans, our shoes, leaving spirals of wet mud wherever she touched.

"Oh, Margo!" I was almost faint with relief. "Margo!"

I wanted to caress her dear, noble face, but it wasn't until she started purring softly that I knew I had been accepted back into her life. My darling Margo remembered me. How could I have doubted her? Elephants remember just about everything they ever encounter in their lives—of course she would remember me. I pressed against her body, took her trunk gently in my hands and blew softly into the tip, the standard elephant greeting. Margo acknowledged me with an affectionate hug, squeezing her trunk around my waist, purring even louder.

"I love you, too," I murmured, and unwound myself from her strong grip to reach up and caress the leathery face.

Diamond watched us admiringly from a few feet away. "She's a beauty," she said softly. I beckoned her to approach, and she moved carefully. She already knew how to bring Margo's trunk to her lips and blow into the tip.

"Now she'll remember you forever," I said as Margo purred her acceptance.

"Is she rideable?" Diamond asked.

I was shocked that Diamond would even think of such a thing "She's wild!" I gasped. "Whatever gave you the idea she would be rideable!"

Diamond just shrugged. "I've ridden elephants. People all over the world ride elephants."

In the meantime, not to be ignored, Abbie dug furiously in my pockets with her little trunk. I knew what she wanted. I glanced at my watch—it was already two in the afternoon. Lunchtime.

"She's looking for snacks," I said to Diamond. Suddenly it occurred to me that there still had been no sign of Richie.

"We'll feed them ourselves," I said. "And then I'll show you the rest of the sanctuary."

We made a slow procession to the top of the hill and back to the barn, Margo and Abbie walking in single file behind me. Margo's trunk rested on my shoulder, Abbie held onto her mother's tail like a proper baby ellie, and Diamond was in the very rear, playing it safe.

"I'm not lucky enough to have one of your special bonds," she said, grinning.

There should have been the usual bucket of apples and carrots waiting for them inside, but their plastic feed tub was empty.

"That's so odd," I commented. "Richie never misses feeding time." I hand-fed the donuts to Margo, who ate them greedily, then sniffed through the boxes for more. "That's all," I chided. "You have to watch your waistline." Apparently agreeing, Margo turned her attention to the hay stacked in the corner, while Abbie dropped into a sleepy gray heap.

"Speaking of lunch," Diamond added, "I try never to miss mine either."

"You can't be hungry!" I gave her an incredulous look. "How do you eat so much and stay thin?"

"I'm just making up for all the meals I missed as a kid," Diamond said, and then laughed.

The elephants were settled, and I reluctantly decided to leave them. When I reached the barn doors, I turned for one last look. Diamond's words about their confinement were still bothering me. Perhaps there *was* something obscene about an elephant behind bars, the massive gray body locked helplessly inside a steel cage, roomy though this one was.

Abbie, who had been only one or two months old when they were rescued, would probably never remember anything different, but Margo, as far as the other rescuers could tell, had been about seven years old.

Which was better? I wondered. Not to ever know true freedom, or to know it once and never have it again.

Then I took a deep breath and closed the creaking gates and locked them in.

Chapter 15

IT WASN'T REALLY THAT COLD. ESPECIALLY NOT FOR a New Yorker in New York in early fall, but I started shivering as soon as I stepped out of the elephant barn. It was a clear day, the sun was bright, but I felt cold.

There is nothing like the heat of the African sun. Burning down from an oceanic blue sky, it sears your skin and bleaches your soul. Once you feel it, you never forget it. You crave it like opium. The New York sun was cold and pallid by comparison. Only one day back and I was already wondering how I was going to get through the oncoming winter.

A sparrow gave a singular chirp in a nearby bush, and a vee of geese flew overhead, raucously breaking the quiet. They weren't nearly as colorful as the birds in Africa, which were lavender and red and green, like flying stripes of rainbow.

Diamond pulled her jacket around her shoulders and scanned the sky as the birds flew over us. "Wish I could follow them home," she said, then gave me a half grin. "Of course, I don't know where home is anymore."

I checked the bulletin board outside the barn. There were a few cars in the parking lot by now. Volunteers had started to drift in to check their assigned tasks, and some of them recognized me and waved their welcomes. "Have you seen Richie?" I called to one woman, who shrugged her reply. And I thought I caught an odd sympathetic look here and there. Probably everyone knew about me and Tom. Our breakup must have fed the gossip mill for most of the year.

"Richie's truck hasn't moved from its spot all morning," I said to Diamond, puzzled. "And I don't see Mrs. Wycliff's old dogs—they usually follow him around—but he could be anywhere on the farm. We'll have to do some walking."

"I'm always up for a walk."

"How about eight hundred acres?"

"That's just a warm-up," Diamond scoffed. "I could do it in my sleep."

I laughed. I forgot who I was talking to.

There were fences and gates and narrow paths. I was never so aware of fences. A donkey brayed hello, starting a chorus of five or six others. Behind another fence, a black bear lazed at the edge of his pond, one foot dangling in the water. Behind another, a buffalo swung his head up and down in a lazy threat before returning to his hay, and in yet another, two wolves glared at us with gold eyes. Several llamas followed us

AN INCONVENIENT ELEPHANT | *123*

across a rocky field in a dignified march. Nearby, two camels watched passively with sweet, dark eyes double fringed in long tan lashes, while a small herd of alpaca hummed at us like a glee club, but there was still no sign of Richie.

We came up to a large field of horses and Diamond stopped.

"What's wrong?" I asked.

"Ah," she said. "There's nothing like the walk of a good horse." I knew what she meant. Sitting on a horse, feeling the swing of his back, the sound of his hooves tattooing against the hard red pack sand. She was missing it. I was missing it. Very much.

"So, here's an idea." She gestured to the horses grazing peacefully on the thick grass. "Why don't we just grab one of these and look for your friend on horseback?"

"I don't know if they're even broke to ride," I replied. I had once offered my services to Mrs. Wycliff, to climb aboard some of the younger ones to train them, but she had steadfastly refused. She didn't want her animals to ever again be stressed by human touch. It was a thorny subject between the two of us, and I had let it drop.

Diamond followed me past the field. "Pity we can't ride them," she grumbled, pointing to a flashy black horse with white stockings that was near the fence. "That one's a looker."

"Yeah," I said. "That's all he's good for. Looking but no touching."

At the end of the path was a large meadow surrounded by a ten-foot chain link fence.

"These are the cat enclosures," I pointed out. "Two lions,

a couple of Siberian tigers. And a jaguar, too." I opened the combination lock, then pulled on the bolt that held the gates together. "People buy these animals when they're cubs and after they grow up, their owners are totally surprised that they're stuck with wild animals."

Diamond hung back. "I have a policy never to socialize with carnivores," she said.

"It's perfectly safe," I said, laughing at her reluctance. "What are you worried about? You must have seen hundreds of lions on safari."

"Of course," she replied, "as long as I'm guaranteed to see them from the outside in, and not from the inside out."

Two lions lazed in the shadows of large rocks that had been specially purchased by Mrs. Wycliff to give them a more natural environment. One lion stopped licking his paw as soon as he spotted us, the paw remaining frozen upright as he stared with glittering eyes.

"Are you sure it's safe?" Diamond asked, helping me bolt the gates together behind us. The second lion pricked his ears and immediately stood up to sniff the air.

"Oh yeah," I said. "They're used to people. They were trained for some dinky circus, but ended up in a small cage at a gas station, like a sideshow. Mrs. Wycliff couldn't stand to see them like that and bought them. They're probably waiting for their lunch."

Diamond raised her eyebrows. "And would that be us?"

"Yep." I laughed. "Saves on the feed bill. Richie just throws them a visitor every so often."

A loud whistle pierced the air. I spun around to see the farm truck rolling down the road toward us with a man hanging halfway out of the window, his beard flapping in the wind as he steered the truck with one hand and whistled through the fingers of his other.

"Richie!" I yelled happily. The truck clanked to a halt. Its bed held a large plastic tub of frozen raw chicken.

"I wasn't sure I recognized your car," Richie said, jumping out from behind the wheel, "but when I saw the donut box in the barn and no fresh bodies lying around, I knew it had to be you. Margo would have flipped anyone else over the fence."

His curly gray-brown hair was pulled back into a ponytail, and he was wearing a navy suit, red tie, and light blue shirt, which provided a strange contrast to the heavy work boots on his feet. "So good to see you." He wrapped me in a big warm hug and held me for a moment. "Welcome home. How was Kenya?"

"Zimbabwe."

He gave me a puzzled look.

"It's a long story and I'll tell you over a cup of coffee." I introduced Diamond-Rose, expecting one of Richie's usual safety lectures on not bringing strangers without his prior approval, but he seemed oddly preoccupied as he shook her hand.

"Welcome," he said, then did a double take at her outfit. "We don't normally allow visitors." He pointed to her clothing. "Did you think this was a theme park?"

"I'm a safari leader from Kenya," Diamond explained. "Level three license, with advanced weapons certificate." She pointed to his suit. "What about you? You usually dress this formally to feed raw chicken?"

"I just got back from an important meeting and didn't have time to change," he replied, then turned to me. "Lawyers. They even sent a car to get me. For some reason, they didn't want me to bring my truck into their parking lot. I'm thinking maybe it's because I had twenty pounds of chicken thawing in the back. Anyway, it was the meeting that I've been dreading." His face grew serious. "And I have kind of a good news–bad news thing."

"Tell me the good news first," I said as he grabbed a tub of chicken and threw its contents over the fence. The lions trotted up to us and, after giving each other their usual courtesy warning growls, grabbed the food.

Richie leaned against the railing and watched as one of the lions picked up a chicken and carried it off. Its fur looked sleek and it was well fed, and I knew how proud he and Mrs. Wycliff were over the cats' good health.

"Well," he said, "for starters, I was offered my dream job last week. I still can't believe it." His voice filled with excitement. "I was hired to help manage that big elephant rescue in Alabama. And Jackie was asked to do a lot of promotional work for them with her photography. It'll pay well for both of us."

"That's wonderful," I enthused. Richie lived for elephants, working in Alabama had been his dream. And Jackie, his wife, was an amazing wildlife photographer. It was a wonderful opportunity for both of them.

He opened the door to his truck and invited us in with a bow. "Honor me with your presence and come back to the house. I'll fill you in."

"And give me a cup of coffee," I reminded him. "But congratulations on your dream job." The three of us squeezed into the front seat. I took a deep breath. "So what's the bad news?"

"Actually," Richie said, "the bad news is not for me, it's for you."

"For me?" I repeated, surprised. "Oh! I know! Because you and Jackie are moving away! But I can come and visit a lot, right?"

"Yeah, but that's not it either."

"What then?"

We bumped along the road past his house to the main house, where he parked the truck and turned to give me a solemn look. "I'm so sorry, Neelie. The meeting I just came from was with Elisabeth Wycliff's lawyer. The sanctuary is being sold, and the elephant barn is going to be knocked down. Margo and Abbie are being sent to Alabama."

Chapter 16

WHEN I WAS A CHILD, I THOUGHT I WOULD GROW UP to have a lovely house with a horse barn behind it, a lovely husband, one or two lovely daughters, and would live a happy, if conventional, but *lovely* life with a good career and a couple of lovely horses to ride. After I grew up, most of my dreams came true. I had a lovely husband, house, barn, and horse. Not to mention a lovely cat and dog. Okay, maybe the dog wasn't so lovely.

And then the dream started to break apart piece by piece, like peanut brittle.

I tried to stop it. I tried very hard to fix it, but there is only so much nutty stuff one can hold together.

The lovely house was sold after the lovely husband cheated on me with his lovely colleague. I had to give away my lovely horse and my lovely dog. Conventionality disappeared the day I left for Zimbabwe to rescue Margo and Abbie, and though I eventually lived in Kenya with three or four baby ellies at my side, I always considered Margo and Abbie my lovely surrogate children, just waiting for me to return home. And now I was losing them, too. Panic tore through me. Something had happened to me in Africa. I couldn't put my finger on it—maybe it *placed* me, somehow. Maybe it taught me that what I thought I wanted, I didn't want at all.

Except for the elephants. I realized I wanted elephants in my life. I couldn't let Richie take them away.

"How could you do this?" My voice rose in fury, but he just waved for me to follow him as he walked up the path to Elisabeth Wycliff's back door. "It's not fair!" I yelled at him. "We all risked our lives to save them! You can't let them go just like that!"

"It wasn't my decision." Richie paused at the back door. "But Tom feels—and I have to agree—they'll be better off with other elephants."

"No, they won't," I countered. "They have me. And Mrs. Wycliff can supervise the way she's always done. I'll come up and help her. I'll come every day. I once worked here, too, you know. I know the routine. And you have that handyman—Ignacio—and all the volunteers . . ."

"You've been away for a whole year," Richie said wearily. "There are things going on that you don't know about."

"I know this—I can't let you take my elephants." My stomach was churning from anger.

"A place with other elephants sounds much better for them," Diamond interjected. I glared at her.

"Actually, they're Elisabeth's elephants," Richie reminded me. "And Tom's."

Ah yes, Tom.

"Well, I can't imagine Mrs. W. letting the elephants leave," I sputtered. "She loves them."

"She doesn't know yet," Richie replied. "And we're not going to tell her for a while."

"What do you mean she doesn't know yet?"

"It was Tom's idea to protect her. When the time is right, he wants to be the one to tell her."

"He can't just arbitrarily move them," I insisted, but Richie was already opening the back door to Mrs. Wycliff's house.

"We'll discuss the whole thing when we get inside," he said. "But I'll tell you this—Tom's pretty much made up his mind."

Diamond and I followed Richie into the sparsely furnished mudroom. An old dart gun hung on the wall next to a row of pegs that held Mrs. Wycliff's brown corduroy jacket, a green plaid raincoat, and an old pith helmet. A pair of bright red wellies were neatly parked underneath. Oddly, we had to step over a charred hole burned into the floor.

"Was there a fire?" I asked Richie, gesturing to the blackened wood.

"Mrs. Wycliff," he said, leading us into the kitchen. "Her latest hobby."

The kitchen is the soul of the house, and I always liked Mrs. Wycliff's kitchen because it was so unlike my mother's well-controlled and tightly organized one. It was casual and comfortable, with white painted wooden cabinets, pots hanging from a baker's rack over a big old-fashioned stove, and prints of herbs and spice plants framed on the walls. A round oak table stood in the middle surrounded by four blue wooden chairs with plump blue gingham cushions. Diamond pulled out a chair and immediately sprawled into it.

"Anyone else hungry?" she asked. "We missed lunch, you know. Could chew on a good strip of biltong 'round about now."

Richie jumped at the word "biltong." He and Jackie were strict vegetarians, and he gave Diamond a horrified look. "I'll make you coffee," he said. "But don't even mention biltong. It's cured *animal*."

"And ostrich makes the best kind," she blithely replied. "I have a great old recipe. The secret is curing it in a lot of fresh coriander."

"You could cure it in fresh gold," Richie muttered darkly, "and it's still a sacrilege. It's not nice to eat meat."

"It's necessary," Diamond said, with a snort. "You know, there aren't too many salad bars in the jungle."

Richie took an ancient coffee pot off the stove and unproductively tinkered with it for a few minutes before setting it down on the counter. "I don't really know how to do this," he finally admitted with a sheepish grin. "Jackie always makes the coffee, and she's in Alabama, looking for a house for us." He picked up a bag of coffee and peered at the lettering, looking for directions. "There's got to be a recipe somewhere on here."

Diamond-Rose leaped from her chair, grabbed the bag

from him, and then hunted through the cabinets for a saucepan.

"This is the way we do it on safari," she said, dumping the contents of the bag into the pan, filling it with cold water and sloshing it on the stove to boil. "Makes good coffee after you let the grinds settle."

Ten minutes later, we were sipping coffee that bore a strong resemblance to melted asphalt.

"So, what's going on?" I asked, after stirring three or four heaping teaspoons of sugar into my cup, which still didn't help.

Richie brought his finger to his lips. "Elisabeth's upstairs, probably taking a nap," he whispered, then pointed over his head to where the bedrooms were. "I don't want her to wake up yet. It's exhausting to keep up with her."

Diamond got up to pour herself a second cup, offering a refill to Richie. "Another cup of my coffee and you could keep up with a jaguar."

"Actually, your coffee could fly a helicopter," Richie said, quickly putting his hand across the top of his cup to decline, "but that's not what I meant by keeping up."

Diamond wasn't the least insulted. She sat down again and leaned back in her chair. "Mind if I smoke?" She reached into her pants pocket, pulled out one of her cheroots, and chomped it between her lips. Another pocket produced a tin of matches, and after striking a match against the bottom of her boot, she lit the odd-looking object with a deep inhale. The room filled with the scent of fresh dung. I tried not to gag.

Richie watched her with some fascination. "Is that a camel turd?"

"A bundu cheroot," she replied, exhaling with a sigh of satisfaction. "We make them in the bush all the time. Gum tree root. I can give you a couple next time I see you."

"I've smoked a lot of joints in my time"—Richie laughed, waving the smoke away from his face—"but I'll pass. I don't think Elisabeth wants anyone smoking in the—"

"Oh my! Do I smell a cheroot?" Mrs. Wycliff's voice preceded her as she toddled into the room, leaning on her cane. She threw her head back and inhaled deeply. "Mmmm."

She looked just the way I remembered her, gray hair pulled into a utilitarian bun and still wearing the ubiquitous white cable knit sweater and jeans that had been her fashion statement since I had first met her, more than ten years ago. Maybe she moved a little more slowly, and maybe she was a little thinner, but she sounded as strong as she always had, with good color in her face and eyes bright with curiosity. I shot Richie a quizzical look. She looked perfectly fine to me, and with someone else doing the actual physical work, I didn't see why she couldn't stay in charge of her own sanctuary.

"Elisabeth," he said, "you remember Neelie Sterling? She helped Tom bring Margo back last year."

"Hello." I extended my hand.

"Good to see you again, dear." She took my hand in her thin, cool fingers and held onto it while leaning forward to drop into a conspiratorial whisper. "Sorry that I had to fire Margo. She was very sloppy in the kitchen."

Before I could reply, Richie stepped in. "Margo wasn't the housekeeper," he said to her in a gentle voice. "She's the elephant." But Mrs. Wycliff had turned to stare at Diamond-Rose.

"And who is this redhead?"

Diamond stood up and extended her own hand. "Diamond-Rose Tremaine," she said, a delighted look crossing her face. I could see she was taken with Mrs. Wycliff right off.

"Hot damn! I did smell a cheroot!" Mrs. Wycliff pointed at Diamond's cigar. "Do you have any more? It's been a while since I've had one."

"Take mine," Diamond offered generously. "I have plenty."

Mrs. Wycliff took it with a pleased grin, then whispered to me, "But don't tell Harry. He hates when I smoke, so it'll be our little secret." She took a deep puff, then carefully lowered herself into a kitchen chair. "If Harry wasn't such a damn crank about me smoking, I would enjoy one with my Irish coffee every morning."

"I rolled about ten dozen of them before I left Kenya— had to sneak them through customs twice," Diamond said. "I have a few outside in the car, if you want one."

"Speaking of vehicles"—Mrs. Wycliff impatiently looked around the kitchen—"where are the keys to my truck?"

"I have them," Richie said. "Your truck isn't running. It needs repairs."

"Oh, that's right." Mrs. Wycliff exhaled a long, smoky breath across the table. "It got dented when I hit that black rhino last week."

"We don't have any black rhinos, Elisabeth," Richie corrected her. "You hit the side of the garage."

"Whatever it was," Mrs. Wycliff agreed. "Stampeded right into the engine."

———

Mrs. Wycliff was enjoying her coffee and smoke, and sat back in her chair to regale us with stories of her life in the bush. Diamond-Rose was listening with her head resting on one hand, her face a study in adoration, but I was growing more impatient with each passing minute. I wanted to talk about the elephants, not adventures that took place fifty years ago. I wanted to find out how to keep Margo and Abbie at the sanctuary, and ask Richie the best way to contact Tom about Tusker.

"Richie!" I made an eyebrow gesture for us to go into the living room. He nodded and left the table, trying not to disturb Mrs. Wycliff. We left her and Diamond in the kitchen, happily passing the cheroot back and forth and comparing notes about their last safaris.

The spacious living room was furnished with a view toward practicality and comfort. Two black fluffy cats lounged on afghan-covered sofas, while a plump tabby was being accommodated by one of the overstuffed chairs that flanked a bay window. An antique mahogany desk stood against one wall, with a leather chair that hosted yet another sleeping cat, a gray striped, that snored softly. A small table by a side window had a porcelain elephant planter with what looked like the stringy remains of catnip growing from it. In front of the large marble fireplace lay Mrs. Wycliff's two old black Labs, Baako and Dafina. I drew closer to study the pictures hanging above the mantle, stepping over the snoring dogs. Neither of them lifted an ear.

I had seen these pictures before—they were of a young Elisabeth Wycliff in safari clothes and pith helmet, posing with elephants or horses or chimps. In one picture, she was caressing a large Bengal tiger. In another, she was kissing the nose of a down-stretched giraffe. My favorite was the one where she was sitting on a horse and holding a lion cub across her lap. It had been an enviable life, and she had done many good things for wild animals. I stood on my tiptoes for a better look.

"She's always loved animals," Richie said, standing next to me. "I think she was only seventeen in that picture—took a trip with her father and already doing rescue work. Mostly in Kenya, though she was in Botswana and a few other places, too. Of course, all those countries had different names then."

"She's a remarkable woman," I agreed, then turned around to face him. "And that's why it's not Tom's place to take her elephants away from her. She should be respected for everything she's done. Maybe she moves a little slower, but she can still run things."

"No, she can't," Richie said. "She gets confused."

"All she needs is a little help," I argued.

Richie frowned and plucked a cat from the side chair before sitting down. The cat stretched across his lap and purred. "Neelie, you haven't been here for a whole year. She can't run this place anymore."

"Then what about this Harry she mentioned?" I demanded. "What's wrong with him? Why can't he help?"

"Harry was her third husband, and he died thirty years ago," Richie said.

"Then hire someone to take your place," I said. "Another manager." I was getting an idea.

He dropped the cat to the floor and stood up. "Look, I

tried. I found two people that just might have worked out, but"—he made a helpless gesture with his hands—"she thought they were poachers and chased them off with her old dart gun." He shook his head. "She's erratic. Her last housekeeper was so intimidated, she left in the middle of the night."

I stated the obvious. "What about me?"

He put his hand on my arm. "Did you forget who her partner is? Do you think Tom would want you up here?"

Tom again. And I knew the answer.

"Anyway, the elephants are being moved," he said with an air of finality. "We're in the process of making arrangements for them."

My thoughts started whirling like something out of Dr. Seuss. I could not lose my elephants, I would not lose my elephants.

"What about *him*—Tom?" I said. "He can hire just about anybody to help her keep this place running. Even if it's not, you know, me."

Richie ran his hand through his hair. "Last I heard, he was talking about buying Elisabeth out and as I told you, knocking down the elephant barn. You know Tom—he always has some kind of plan going. And you see what the barns and fencing look like. Elisabeth never wanted anything changed, and now things are just falling apart." His voice took on a powerless tone. "It's not up to me. He wants to buy her out, and then her estate could use the money to take care of her. It's really a good idea, Neelie. She has no one." He gave me a final shrug signifying our discussion was closed and got up to return to the kitchen, but I stepped in front of him.

"There must be something I can do," I said urgently. "Maybe Mrs. W. is elderly, but she conceived this whole place and she has to be respected. She's got to have a voice in any decision he makes."

"She can't live alone anymore." Richie was getting impatient. "And she has no one. Jackie's been the one watching over her. After we leave, the power of attorney goes to Tom or her lawyer, and they'll have to hire someone to care for her. That's what today's meeting was about. After Tom buys her out, what happens to this place will be up to him." He dropped his voice because Mrs. Wycliff and Diamond-Rose were just coming in to join us. "You can't fight it, Neelie. Everything's pretty much set."

"But I don't see why she can't oversee her own farm," I insisted. "I'll help. I promise I'll do anything it takes—"

"That's enough blathering," Mrs. Wycliff declared impatiently as she entered the room. "You two have had more than enough time to organize this safari. Summon the dogs. We'll go after that injured rhino first thing in the morning."

Richie gave me a meaningful look as Mrs. Wycliff clapped her hands and turned to Diamond-Rose. "Jackie, get the fire going," she commanded. "We'll be making camp here tonight."

Chapter 17

"WE'RE GOING TO RUN OUT OF TIME," DIAMOND WAS
saying. It was her turn to cook breakfast, and she was leaving
her usual mess of coffee grinds scattered across the stove and
countertops, a puddle of water on the floor, which she was
tromping through to set out the coffee and milk and mugs,
or whatever mugs I had left, as she had a habit of tossing
the dirty dishes into the sink with such force that they usually shattered. A jet of flame rose behind her as the grease
from the bacon she was frying spattered onto the burner.
"I spoke to Charlotte again," she said, casually flipping a lid
over the blazing pan. "I told her that Joshua promised us a
few months, but she says you can't totally trust anyone. You
have to call your man. There's an old saying: You have to get
up before the chickens to gather their eggs."

"He's not my man," I said, watching her nervously. "And

if you get up before the chickens, they wouldn't have had time to lay their eggs."

"Well, the ones that laid these apparently did," she said. "Here's breakfast." She placed two perfectly fried eggs and three strips of crispy bacon in front of me.

I looked at my plate. "How do you do that?" I said. "I mean, you practically burn my kitchen down, but the food comes out great."

"I'm not used to kitchens," Diamond apologized, sitting down with her own plate, "but I am used to cooking over an open flame." She dug into her breakfast, then looked up at me. "So, will you call him?"

"I want to," I began slowly. "It's just that it's going to be so hard after not being in touch with him for a whole year. I don't even know if he'll answer the phone if he sees it's me."

"Did you mention Tusker to your friend Richie? Maybe he could sort of break the ice for you."

I shook my head guiltily. "We got so caught up talking about Margo and Abbie. Besides, we'll just raise the money ourselves. You said you would think of something."

"I did," she said. "I thought of Tom. He has the planes and the expertise."

"That's not a solution," I said testily. "Besides, I can't call."

"Well, it's your pride versus Tusker's life," Diamond pointed out.

My heart sank. "You're right," I agreed glumly, and peered into my coffee cup. "I just wish this was a cup of courage."

It took me four days.

Two days of rehearsing what I was going to say. Two days

of procrastinating, until Diamond took the plastic bulletin board from my office and hung it on the refrigerator, using its red erasable marker to cross off the days left before Tusker was going to be shot. If I were still a practicing therapist, I would have chided my client that not calling was classic avoidance behavior, but I had only me to chide.

"Call Tom," I urged myself. "Tusker needs you."

"*You* call Tom," I argued back. "He's not talking to me."

Another red *X* from Diamond increased my guilt. I finally dialed Tom's cell number with trembling fingers, then hung up, dialed again, rinsed and repeated. Diamond stood over me until I let it ring.

"I'm probably getting upset for nothing," I whispered to Diamond. "We may have had some issues between us, but when it comes to elephants, I know we'll always have a special bond."

"Great," she whispered back. "I *love* your special bonds."

He answered right away, his voice sounding like concern. "*Neelie?*"

"It's me," I said, then thought how presumptuous that sounded. Everyone refers to themselves as "me."

"Are you okay?" he asked, his voice taking on a worried tone. "Where are you calling from?"

"I'm home," I said, and couldn't think of anything else to say. "I'm okay," I finally added, straining to make small talk. "What about you?" I eyed Diamond, who was giving me a thumbs-up.

"Very busy." He sounded mystified that I would care. "I'm very surprised you would call me."

"Well, actually, I called about Tusker," I said, trying to keep my voice from shaking.

"Oh yes," he said, the frost definitely setting in. "I was

waiting for that. Grisha told me you were part of the team in Zim. I am furious that you took such risks. What the hell possessed you to do something stupid like that?"

"What do you mean, 'something stupid'?" I snapped.

There was silence, then, "Did you call me to argue?"

He was right. I changed tactics. "Tom," I said, "Tusker's running out of time."

"Don't you think I know that?" he interrupted me impatiently. "I did everything I could to get a plane in there, but I'm a marked man in Zimbabwe right now. You wouldn't believe the politics involved—"

"What about the sanctuary you were building near Kilimanjaro?"

"There's a problem with the land," he said, getting impatient. "We're still negotiating. Things take time."

"Well, Charara's north," I said. "Can we move him across the border to Zambia or someplace? Maybe they'll let us fly him out of Zambia."

"Us?"

"Us."

He snorted. "Neelie, it's dangerous. You have no clue how dangerous it is. You just need to wait so I can—"

"Are you waiting for the *deadline*?" I snapped.

"I'm trying to get a plane in without causing an international incident," he yelled at me. "Then we have to get him back to Chizarira. I recently spoke to Billy Pope, and he said the elephant has returned to his old haunts. Actually, elephants, since Billy mentioned that you brought two. Did you hear me say that it was dangerous? Stay the hell out of things you don't know anything about—"

"I *do* know!" I returned angrily, but my heart was filling with bitter disappointment. All the work, all the oranges, all the danger. For nothing. "We couldn't separate them," I shouted. "I was there and you weren't! How dare—" But I was talking into a dead phone. He had hung up.

Diamond had been leaning against the kitchen wall, listening. "Shall I cross that special bond off the list, as well?" she asked dryly.

"He didn't even let me finish talking," I said, still quaking with anger.

"I'll call Joshua again," she said. "I'll see if we can get a delay. And maybe someone else with a plane."

"How many people have planes to fly elephants around?" I said glumly.

"I have some ideas," Diamond said. "Don't forget that I'm good at fixing things."

She poured herself yet another cup of coffee and went out on my back porch to think. I peeked through the window and watched as she sat in my old rocking chair, rocking back and forth, sipping her coffee and staring off at my barn, calm and contemplative while I was still boiling over my conversation with Tom.

There was an irony about our lives that I was acutely aware of.

Diamond had come from New York, and so had I, though our backgrounds were entirely different. I had been a child of the suburbs, of swimming pools in the backyard, the cozy nestle of lemonade and snacks on the patio, riding lessons twice a week, and barbecues, oh God, too many barbecues.

The expectations were that I would follow in my mother's footsteps and settle down, live in a nice big house with a neat lawn that sat back on some graciously suburban street somewhere. Expectations that eventually sat on my shoulders like cement blocks.

Diamond had been city bred. A child of subways and fire engine sirens and cramped apartments, of shops on the corner that stayed open until almost morning and an aunt too drunk to notice if her niece ever came home.

Which, I suppose, gave Diamond a certain freedom—the freedom from expectations.

We never would have met in New York. I was towed to the city for ballet performances, semiannual visits to museums, plays, and authentic Chinese food in Chinatown, while Diamond would never have even dreamed of taking an hour's drive to the country just to look at trees. And yet we met. We met on the other side of the world, with the same goals and dreams. I supposed the universe does things in its own convoluted, complicated way.

And I watched her sip her coffee, this woman who was completely opposite of me, who had total confidence in herself that she could, definitely would fix all our problems. She was footloose and unencumbered and free to make any kind of decision for her life that she wanted, and I thought she had to be the luckiest person in the world.

Chapter 18

"HOW DO YOU PAY FOR AN ELEPHANT?" IT WAS SOUNDING more and more like one of Reese's elephant jokes. Except that I didn't have the answer. What kind of job in an uncertain economy would support me and in addition pay for Tusker and Shamwari?

" 'Electrician, engineer, energetic salesperson.' " I read the want ads aloud over breakfast, picking from a box of donuts and once again drinking a cup of deadly cowboy coffee brewed by Diamond-Rose. We had been home almost a week now and looking, first, for ways to support ourselves, and second, to make some inroads toward our future giant purchase.

"Nothing listed for elephant trainer," I joked, trying not to listen to the crunching of coffee grinds under Diamond's boots. Diamond's casual approach to housekeeping was beginning to grate on my nerves.

"There must be a lot of openings for your type of work, at least," Diamond said, accidentally knocking over the sugar bowl while ladling heaping soupspoons of sugar into her coffee. "I mean, you're a licensed psycho?"

"Psychotherapist." I gave an awkward laugh. "You know, couples counseling, life strategies—everything that didn't work for me. But I was always happier training horses. In fact, I always suspected that horse training and psychotherapy are kind of the same thing."

Diamond nodded knowingly. "I'd definitely go with the horses." She paused to brush the spilled sugar from the table onto the floor. "Don't get me wrong—all that brain stuff is good, too. A lot of people are, you know"—she tapped the side of her head—"mental."

I thought about it. I used to love retraining naughty horses, but my growing reluctance to land on my head as a career choice took that option off the table. I sighed and took a big bite of my jelly donut just as Diamond-Rose speared a chocolate cream-filled with a flip of her new safari knife.

I jumped as the knife gleamed past me. "Good God!" I declared. "Do you have to eat everything off a knife?"

Diamond flashed me a grin. "Habit I picked up in the bush," she replied. "My hands were never clean enough to touch food. I have *some* standards, you know." She bit into the donut and noisily sucked out its innards, then rattled her section of the newspaper. "I'm not having any luck either. 'Sanitary engineer, secretary, sewer maintenance.'" She flipped the paper closed in disgust. "Nothing for safari leader."

"I'm shocked," I replied, taking another sip of bitter coffee. "Given how much call there is for safaris in this region."

"If I can't find something soon, we may not be able to save Tusker," Diamond said. "I have some money saved up, but it won't be enough. And if I know Joshua, he'll want every cent of it." She leaned back in her chair. "I don't know what else I can do. Safaris were my whole life." She put her hands behind her head and looked up at the ceiling. "Except, of course, when I was with the circus."

"You were with the circus?" I looked at her in surprise.

"Ran off with some clown when I was sixteen." She rolled her eyes at the memory. "It was after my aunt died. I had no other family. Spent six weeks selling popcorn, then three months cleaning up after the elephants until I graduated to riding them."

"Wow," I said, impressed. "I've always wanted to ride an elephant."

Diamond speared another donut. "Did a little trapeze work, too," she said, delicately chewing it off the tip of her knife blade. "Was asked to leave, though, because I slept with both guys from the trapeze act and they started fighting over me."

"So, why did *you* have to leave?" I asked.

Diamond finished her donut and licked the tip of her knife. "It became a trust issue, when, you know, one guy had to jump from his trapeze and have the other guy catch him? They were never quite sure."

"Good thing you didn't sleep with the knife-throwers," I said, scanning the paper again. "Nevertheless, we have to come up with something creative to make enough money. Thirty-five thousand is not peanuts." I laughed at my inadvertent joke, then realized that having no money was not exactly funny. "We might have to give up eating," I added ominously.

Diamond shrugged and got up to wash out her coffee cup with a swish of cold water and two fingers, apparently ignorant of the existence of dish detergent. "We'll do okay," she said. "I still have that loaf of your mother's bread in my rucksack."

Mothers are a good source of protein.

And sometimes advice.

My mother was brimming with the first two during the welcome-home dinner she had prepared for me and Diamond. The whole family was in attendance, and I wondered how they would react to Diamond's appearance and social graces. Especially my mother, who was meticulous down to the arrangements of the particles in the air, and especially double for my brother Jerome, who was a bit of a stuffed shirt. I had always dreaded Jerome's little flashes of disapproval. In addition, his wife, Kate, had once been a fashion model and always eyed my casual jeans and tees with obvious distaste. I gave my father and Reese and Marielle a free pass, since my father liked anyone who ate his barbecue, Reese was Reese, and Marielle, well, she was married to Reese.

My mother gave me a hug when we arrived, then took a half step back when Diamond, still in her safari clothes, rushed to give her a big embrace as well.

"Now, aren't you just . . . darling," my mother gasped, giving Diamond a little squeeze with the tips of her fingers. "And still dressed in . . . jungle clothes!"

Grace just growled, then spent an inordinately long time sniffing Diamond's boots.

"Haven't had much time to unpack," I offered, not sure if I was embarrassed more by Diamond's hygiene or my mother's thinly disguised repulsion. "We're still a bit jet-lagged."

"I always thought jet lag canceled out when you got back home," my mother replied. She brushed off her sweater as she led us into the kitchen. "I know *I* never had a problem with it."

"Mom, the farthest you've been from home is Maine," I said. "Same time zone."

She flapped a hand at me. "Travel is travel, and besides, it's not the journey, it's the destination, and the destination should always end at home." She introduced Diamond to Jerome and Kate's five-year-old twins, then peeked into the oven. "Well, I hope you're both good and hungry."

"Oh yes, ma'am," Diamond cheerfully declared in front of my wide-eyed nieces. "I could eat a warthog, balls and all."

My father was next to greet us, leaving his usual post at the backyard barbecue, but not before reverentially checking each steak and turning it over with delicate precision. If char-grilling could be a religion, my father would be the high priest and the barbecue pit his altar. Wearing an apron that declared "007—Licensed to Grill," he stepped through the back door to give us both generous hugs.

"Welcome home, Neelie, it's great to have you back," he said, then glanced into the backyard. "But we'll talk later— I've got steaks to watch. Diamond-Rose is it?"

Diamond nodded, entranced with the sight of inch-high meat, aromatically grilling away.

"Well then, Diamond-Rose, prepare yourself for a real treat." He stepped outside again, calling over his shoulder, "I'll bet you two haven't had a dinner cooked over a real open fire in ages."

The house was overflowing with food and family. Not the family that I was longing for, of dusty gray baby ellies tugging at my arms with small, grasping trunks, but my human family of parents, two brothers and their wives, and twin nieces, all tugging at me in a different way. Tugging at me to join them, to fit back in, to remember the old jokes and routines, to fall in line, nose to tail, and walk the path with them. It was disorienting, all the chatting, the jostling, the high trills of conversation between the women cooking food in the kitchen, their voices playing counterpoint to the rumbling bass of the men outside as my father held forth on his favorite topic. "You know, barbecue was the original dinner of early man." He was giving his usual lecture to my two brothers. "That's how they prepared the dinosaurs when they caught them."

I watched from the back door. "I hate barbecues," I said to Diamond. "I grew up smelling like mesquite. I think my lungs have smoke damage." I grimaced. "I don't know why my father couldn't find another hobby. Like making ice cream."

"Then you'd be complaining about your weight," Diamond teased. "A barbecuing father is just perfect! You're so lucky you have family!" I shot her the squint-eye. Friends were supposed to commiserate.

My mother brought over a plate of hors d'oeuvres, and we each took one.

"Well, one thing, you can't get these in Kenya," I said, savoring a warm cheese straw.

"Civilized," Diamond-Rose remarked, but not until after she'd crammed three more into her mouth.

"Steaks are ready," my father announced, proudly bearing a huge platter stacked with sizzling meat and plopping it down on the virginal white tablecloth in the dining room. My mother brought out half a dozen side dishes and a large tray of dinner rolls from the oven, while Reese, who considers himself the Beethoven of raw vegetables since he loves to prepare them but never eats them, carried in an ambitious salad. The wine was decanted, Grace stopped growling and took a spot under the table near Diamond's boots so she could lick them clean, and dinner was served.

"You know, Neelie," my mother started right in dispensing advice while putting shoe-size baked potatoes on each plate, "I think the sooner you get back to work, the better. There's nothing like a job to keep you at home."

"It has to be the right job," I said. "Diamond and I have been checking the papers."

"Have you checked the *Times*?" my sister-in-law Kate suggested. "Everything's listed online." She eyed Diamond. "Of course, you'd have to dress a bit less . . . rustically."

"What about professional journals?" Jerome added. "I certainly hope you're going to resume your profession, instead of wasting all those years you spent in school. Check the university listings, too."

"That's a wonderful idea for me, too," Diamond said. "Schools do go on safaris." Jerome smiled his approval.

"You know, I was downsized from my university job," Marielle joined in. "But there's always tutoring. That's what I'm hoping to do."

"Darling," Kate said to Marielle, "you teach math, so you can tutor math. Neelie is a psychotherapist. You can't *tutor* therapy. You either do it or you"—she searched for a word— "you go crazy."

"Try the zoo papers," Reese added, then looked around with a certain grin that meant he was going to regale us with one of his specialties, an elephant joke. "So, you guys—why did the elephant cross the road?"

"I *have* been checking the papers," I replied testily to Jerome. "Along with the want ads in the back of the professional journals."

"It was the chicken's day off," Reese triumphantly answered. Diamond hooted with laughter, and he gave her an appreciative grin. I just rolled my eyes at him.

"What about bulletin boards in the drugstores?" my mother asked. "Lots of people who take medication might want a therapist."

"Checked everything," I announced, then sighed. "I even called Alana to see if she had spillover. But no one is going to commute from Florida to see me." It certainly wasn't the right time to ask if anyone felt like helping me buy an elephant. I turned to Jerome. "You know, I can do all the job searching in the world, but finding something is just going to take time."

"That's right," Diamond agreed. "As they say in Swahili, It can rain on your head all day but it won't grow a banana tree."

Dinner went on as it always had, with my father insisting everyone take seconds on meat and my mother insisting we finish all seven different vegetables along with the bread. Kate, who counted the calories in a glass of water, helped pass the food around and as usual, raved how delicious it looked but didn't actually take any. And though I had hoped that no one would notice, I caught my family absolutely engrossed as Diamond-Rose plunged her knife into the heart of her baked potato and held it aloft while eating it.

"That's what I like." My father beamed at Diamond, who had by now finished her baked potato and immediately filled the vacancy at the tip of her knife with a piece of steak. "You have a great appetite," he said approvingly, and dropped another steak on her plate. Then he gestured to her uniform. "So, how long you been in the Girl Scouts?"

"Diamond was a safari leader," I explained.

"With a level three license and advanced weapons certificate," Diamond added proudly.

"Better a leader than a follower," my mother chirped, passing Diamond a tray of bread. "Have another dinner roll, and then I hope I can tempt everyone with dessert. It's a coconut cake, with fruit filling, in honor of the jungle!"

"Cauliflower filling would be more appropriate," I muttered.

"It sounds absolutely lovely," Diamond said, grabbing several rolls and dropping them into her lap. "And I'll just pop these into my rucksack for later."

"Neelie, I have a question," Marielle said, while my mother was serving her special jungle cake. "We're on a tight budget now because of my job, so I was wondering if you wanted your horse back?" But I was barely listening. I had been foolish to think my family could help me with Tusker. Maybe it was foolish to think that anyone could. If we were going to buy Tusker and Shamwari, we would need to come up with something quick and practical. Every day was bringing us closer to our deadline.

"Neelie?" Marielle called my name. I tried to remember what she had asked. Something about the safari? Something about horseback? Did she want to know if I had done a lot of horseback riding in Kenya? Yes, that was it.

"No," I replied to Marielle. "Not really. Just no time."

After dessert, Diamond raised her glass for a toast. "You have been very kind to take me into your home," she said in a quavering voice. "You have made me feel like I'm family, and I can't thank you enough for that. I always wished I had family. You know, the word *safari* is Swahili for 'journey.' " She looked around. "So I wish your safari through life may always be a happy and successful one." She held her glass out to me, and I lifted mine and clicked it against hers.

"And a good safari to you, too," I said, then added, "*shamwari.*"

Chapter 19

DIAMOND-ROSE AND I GOT HOME LATE FROM MY parents' dinner party, and I opened the front door to the sound of the phone ringing. It was Richie.

"Listen," he said. "I know it's late, but I just spoke to Tom. He's driving up to the farm tomorrow morning, so if you want to talk to him about Margo and Abbie, you should come by."

I tried to sound calm. "Are you sure?"

"Of course," he said. "I thought you'd want to know."

"Thanks for telling me," I said. "You're right—I have to talk to him." Tom! I would be seeing Tom again. All I had to do was drive to the farm.

"Are you going to be all right with it?" Richie asked.

"Yes, of course," I lied.

"Great," Richie replied. "So, you forgot to tell me about Zimbabwe."

"I'm trying to rescue an elephant," I said. "You have thirty-five thousand dollars lying around?"

"Oh yeah," he replied. "I keep it in a big trunk." He stopped in surprise and gave a sudden laugh. "Hey, get it? Get it? That was my first elephant joke!"

I was going to see Tom tomorrow, and I was determined to repair our relationship. I would be calm and professional and tell him that I understood why he couldn't help us when we were in Zimbabwe and how Diamond had worked things out to save Tusker. That I *did* know what I was doing. And I would ask him if he would be willing to help us raise money for the purchase. I would be strong and dignified. I rethought that. Can you beg for thirty-five thousand dollars and still be dignified?

"Tom is coming up to the sanctuary tomorrow," I announced to Diamond.

"Great," she said. "See? The universe marched him practically to our front door."

But I felt more nervous than I let on. How would I feel when I saw him again? How would he react to me? I spent the remainder of the night in earnest preparation for our meeting by knocking off a whole bottle of Baileys Mint Chocolate Irish Cream with Diamond-Rose.

We were sitting in the kitchen. Diamond had kicked off her boots and propped her feet up on the table. I draped a dishcloth over them as I sat at the table with her.

"It's not really drinking," I explained as I opened the bottle. "It's more like an after-dinner mint, only liquid."

"And you're not really drinking because you're not really in love with this guy, right?" Diamond hooted.

"Absolutely," I replied indignantly. "He had a million faults." I had to pause to think of some. "Right, okay, first of all, he snored. And I was always cold at night because he rolled himself up in all the bedcovers like a taco."

"I was never crazy about Mexican food," Diamond commiserated.

I took a long swallow of my drink. "And he wanted to buy my house so I would have a place to live."

"Terrible," Diamond agreed. "Takes away all your incentive."

"And he ate with his fork in his left hand like they do in Europe, which was very disconcerting," I remembered.

"I have to agree about the forks," Diamond said, polishing off her glass with a huge gulp that left drops trickling down her chin. She wiped her face on her sleeve. "As far as I'm concerned, all you need is a knife." She burped loudly and poured us another round. "But he does rescue elephants."

"He does," I agreed.

"And we need him to rescue another one," Diamond said.

"We do," I agreed. "But it's going to be very hard for me to ask him."

Diamond's face was full of drunken compassion. She refilled our glasses for the last time and tossed the bottle into the sink with a great smash. "So you give him a big kiss and apologize for everything you did and everything you didn't do. Tell him you appreciate how he tried to get a plane in, and that you still care for him and you need him to help us buy Tusker so we can bring him to the States."

"How can I tell him all that if we're not talking," I asked thickly, feeling the Irish cream work itself nicely into my gut. "Actually, we are talking but in very loud voices." I hiccupped.

"True love will find a way." Diamond licked out her glass.

"It's not true love at all," I protested. "And someday I intend to tell him that I'm doing quite well, thank you." I held my head carefully to keep the room from tipping over. "I am very happy without him."

"Oh, bollocks," Diamond replied. "If you're happy, then I'm Sheena, Queen of the Jungle."

After I went to bed, I sorted through all the possibilities that could come up the next morning, which actually amounted to only three. Tom could say no and leave, he could help and leave, or he could help and we could live happily ever after.

Right.

If there was one thing I knew, it was my fairy tale endings. I knew the whole stars-in-the-eyes, bells-are-ringing, birds-are-singing, fireworks-are-zinging thing. I knew how you were supposed to find the man of your dreams, cling to him with heaving bosom, declare your love in passionate whispers, and live happily ever after while romantic music swells to a rapturous crescendo in the background.

I also knew it was all myth and wishful thinking.

It was all bullshit.

I had once loved Thomas Princeton Pennington, even though after my divorce I never thought I could love anyone again.

He was smart and funny and rode horses and rescued ellies. I loved him, he loved me, and I thought that was all we needed. But he had been adamant about me not going back to Kenya to stay with the babies. Commitment had been hard for him, he told me. He had spent a long time avoiding it, but now he was at a stage in his life where he wanted to devote himself to a relationship. With me. He needed to be with me more than the ellies did. He had planned our whole life together. I would travel with him and be his partner in everything he cared about.

Except that I needed to be with things that I cared about as well.

It had been that simple.

It had been that complicated.

Life with Tom meant attending dinners and dances and parties and all manner of social functions where nary a baby ellie would be found. It meant long gowns and small talk with people I didn't know. It meant jetting around the world with little time to ride my horse. It meant giving up the frightened eyes of an orphaned baby ellie rescued from a deep well, or found frantically crying in the bush surrounded by hungry predators.

I hadn't yet had my fill of African light and whispering plains and torrential monsoons that flooded the savannahs and then retreated, leaving them covered in profusions of wildflowers. Hadn't yet had my fill of the dry parch of drought season that burned the bush into russet sculptures and the earth into hard-pack ridges.

We argued a lot.

Until the argument became the relationship, and everything else was lost to it. I started becoming more and more wary of committing myself so soon after my divorce.

It was too soon for me, too soon, and resenting Tom's proscriptions, I chose the ellies. Just for a little while, I promised him, though I didn't, couldn't tell him exactly how long that would be. Feeling wounded, he issued an ultimatum. Feeling trapped, I could do nothing else but flee. And now I needed him to help me buy an elephant.

I sighed and pulled the pillow over my head.

How could I even talk to him about it, after our final words over my trip to Zimbabwe?

But how could I not?

Chapter 20

SOMEONE—MAYBE IT WAS TOM?—HAD ONCE TOLD me that the person who enters the negotiating room first has the strategic advantage over the person who comes later. The first person owns the space. That person can choose where to sit or stand and turn it into a position of power. Since Tom was considered a brilliant negotiator, I decided to follow his advice. Unless I was confusing it with the advice I got from Richie in dealing with lions, in which case you never walk in front of them, and you always let them choose where they want to sit. I wasn't sure which it was. At any rate, Diamond and I left very early the next morning for the sanctuary, hoping it would give me the advantage.

But Tom's car was already there.

A hunter green Bentley was parked next to Richie's battered truck. Tom was somewhere, waiting for me. A hundred feet away, perhaps closer, already waiting for me like a lion waiting in the tall grasses for its prey to arrive.

"I like the wheels," Diamond pronounced as soon as she saw his car. I parked next to it and then sat, rehearsing what I wanted to say to him. I would start with a casual hello, inquire politely about his trip back from Botswana, tell him he looked well, and—

Diamond interrupted my thoughts. "You plan to get out of the car sometime today?"

I smoothed my hair, opened the door, and stood up. Tom would probably be in the elephant barn. No, he'd be checking on the horses—he loved horses. No, he'd be with Richie and Mrs. Wycliff.

"Neelie?"

He was right behind me. His voice, oh, his voice, deep and rich and so sexy that it resonated down into my limbs, the voice that I had heard whispering my name a thousand times in the dark of night. I whirled around. He was a foot away.

He looked the same. The thick silver hair, the odd-shaped scar that violated his handsome face, his eyes the color of reeds and oceans. I had always thought they were such a funny, odd green. He was there, just a few inches from me. Oh God, I thought, it was going to be so hard to speak to him. My heart would drown my tongue in riddles and twist my words and mortify me. But I drew my shoulders back and collected myself. I had risked my life luring Tusker thirty miles through the wildest of Africa—why was I trembling now?

"Hello, Tom," I said.

He looked so tired that I wanted to caress him. Why couldn't I just throw myself into his arms? Why had I argued with him, when clearly we both wanted the same things?

I knew what to say—hadn't I sat up all night rehearsing it?

"Hello, Tom," I said, but it came out sounding too casual, too light. I immediately regretted saying it like that. The words needed more warmth. Not too much, just a little more. And some authority behind it, so he'd know I was capable and strong.

"Maybe we should go inside," he said. He turned away from me and made a gesture with his hand for me and Diamond to follow. "Then we can talk."

I knew from his too-polite smile, from the long, sweeping steps he took until he was leading us from a good distance, that he had taken back all the power. It was the walk of a winning negotiator, and I knew everything was changed between us. If I had any thought there was even a remote chance of resuming things, I now knew it was gone. The chill winter winds that blew across the Kenyan plains had found his heart and frozen it against me.

"He's angry," Diamond whispered to me as we tried to follow him with rushed steps. "That walk tells me you're going to have another battle on your hands."

"Then I will battle," I whispered back, trying to summon my courage. "And you'll help."

I looked at Diamond for support, but Diamond had stopped walking and reached out to put her hand on my arm.

"As they say in the bush, when elephants fight, it is the grass that suffers." She gave me a sympathetic shrug. "I think I'll stay out here."

I had always believed that absence makes the heart grow fonder, that you affectionately remember all the good things about your lover, while everything that had gone wrong fades away like a shadow in the sunlight. I followed Tom through the mudroom, past the red wellies and the charred spot in the floor, over the two black Labs now snoring on the thick Berber carpet, and into the kitchen, where Richie was already sitting with Mrs. Wycliff. I watched Tom move ahead of me, watched the way he strode, the decisive steps that quickly covered the expanse of the mudroom and thought, I was wrong. Absence hadn't made Tom's heart grow fonder—it just hardened it.

"Harry!" Mrs. Wycliff struggled to rise from her chair, but Tom quickly bent over to kiss the top of her head, and she sat again, placated. The black Labs lumbered over to sniff him before dropping down next to Mrs. Wycliff's chair with deep soul-rending sighs.

"I'm glad you made it on time," she said, reaching down to scratch one of the dogs on the head. "We don't want to be late for the party."

"Elisabeth, we all need to talk to you," Tom said gently, taking her hand and sitting down at the table, next to her. I sat myself next to Richie.

"Did you bring my birthday cake?" Mrs. Wycliff asked.

"We came to talk about the sanctuary," Richie said.

"I want cake," Mrs. Wycliff declared. "I've been waiting all year to celebrate my birthday, and I want cake." She pressed against the table to stand up again. Both dogs immediately sat up on full alert. "I'm not doing anything without cake."

"They're making your cake right now," I chimed in. "And they'll bring it in right after our meeting." I patted her hand reassuringly.

"Okay," she said, and relaxed back into her chair, the dogs dropping down again, sighing loudly that they had to move at all. "I hope they won't forget I like mango filling."

Richie cleared his throat and began speaking. "You know, Elisabeth, I have another job waiting for me in Alabama."

"Yes, yes." Tears immediately sprang into her eyes, and she pulled a frizzy tissue from her pocket to wipe them away. "Harry and I are going to miss you so," she said, her voice quavering. "You've been like a son to us."

"And you've been like a mother to me," Richie agreed. "But you know I have to leave."

Mrs. Wyclif gestured to me. "Jackie can stay on. We get along very well."

"I'm Neelie Sterling," I began, then stopped to think. "But of course I wouldn't mind staying here to take care of you." I stole a sideways glance at Tom, but his face was expressionless. "And Margo."

"Neelie, you can stay on with Elisabeth if you want to," Tom interjected solemnly, "but the elephants are not staying. They can't stay."

"I fired Margo," Mrs. Wycliff added.

"Margo is the elephant," Richie and I said together.

Tom looked frustrated. He tried again. "Elisabeth, remember that we talked about me buying this place from you? I had given you a very generous offer and we made a deal."

"Oh yes!" Mrs. Wycliff nodded. "But you said that I can stay here as long as I want."

"That's right, I did," Tom agreed. "But you won't be running the sanctuary."

I knew I had to make my case now. "I can run this place," I said in my most competent therapist take-charge voice. "I understand what the animals need, and I—I even have an assistant! Diamond worked with animals in Kenya. She owned her own business for twenty years. She knows everything about exotic animals. We can run this place together."

"That's all very good," Tom replied, tilting his chair back, a habit of his when he was growing impatient. "But it's not just about throwing a few donuts at your pet elephant. I have plans for this place after the elephants leave." He pursed his lips together before speaking again. "As for running things, you don't really have the right experience. Do you even know how much it costs to feed one elephant?"

I stared at him. I had to admit, I knew the price of a dozen donuts, but I had never thought of how much a bag of elephant chow cost. Did it come in bags? Or did it come in trunks? Now I was getting giddy from nerves.

"I thought so," he said at my silence. "At any rate, Margo can't stay. I'm sorry. And I'm not at liberty right now to discuss my future plans—I don't want them jeopardized. So I guess we're finished here." He stood up and shook Richie's hand and wished him well in Alabama, then smiled at me with his lips curving into a tight smile, his eyes not smiling at all. "Good luck to you, too, Neelie," he said, then added softly, "I wish you every bit of happiness."

I couldn't let it end like this. "Is it money?" I blurted. "Because you have the money to run the sanctuary." Indeed, as a successful entrepreneur, he was amazingly wealthy. "It would be nothing for you. You're . . . just trying to punish me, aren't you!"

"Excuse me." Richie jumped nervously to his feet. "I think I'll take Elisabeth for a walk outside while you two, uh, discuss things." Apparently, he also knew about elephants fighting and the grass suffering. He moved to help Mrs. Wycliff from her chair, but she stood there with her arms folded. The dogs stood at her side and stared up at her, waiting for her next move.

"I want cake," she said. "I'm not going anywhere without cake."

I had to think fast. "Diamond-Rose is waiting outside and has some in her rucksack," I said. "She'll be glad to give you a piece."

Tom and I were alone. It was the first time in a year, and I didn't know what to expect. We were within touching distance, the tension was palpable, yet all I could think was how badly I wanted to touch him. I wanted him to pull me into his arms and kiss me. I never wanted that so much. His arms, his shoulders, I wanted them to envelop me and take away my weariness and my heartache. He took a step toward me, and I lifted my face, half expecting, hoping for a kiss.

He looked so handsome, his lips were half parted, the

scar that ran down his cheek ached for my fingers to trace it. His green eyes studied my face.

"Are you closing the sanctuary?" I asked him bluntly.

He blinked in surprise. "No," he said. "I have no plans to close this place."

"Even after you buy it? You promise?"

He drew himself up and took a deep breath. "Normally, that would offend me," he said. "But I know you mean well."

We stood for a moment. I had something else to ask, something more important, but it was difficult for me. "Tom," I started, "we need to talk about Tusker."

He impatiently brushed it away. "We had to leave him, I already told you that. Let it go." He crossed his arms as though to block any more questions from me.

"I can't just forget about him," I said. "Not after all the work we did getting him to the other camp!"

Tom stared at me for a moment, his lips compressed into a tight line, as if he were struggling with his composure. "I'm trying to stay polite, Neelie," he said, "but what in hell were you doing in Zimbabwe, anyway?" He stepped even closer, and it felt like he was towering over me, even though he was only a few inches taller. His face betrayed his growing rage.

"That part doesn't matter. It was just the way things worked out." I took a deep breath to steady myself. "But Diamond and I are going to save Tusker whether you help or not."

"Are you crazy?" he spat out angrily. "First of all, who came up with that harebrained scheme with the oranges?"

"It worked," I said.

"Until you find out that you have two hundred elephants waiting for breakfast the next morning," he snapped.

"Actually, it was Grisha's idea," I said defensively. "And Charlotte's. And they're the elephant experts. I just followed orders."

He shook his head with exasperation. "I'm not going to discuss rescue strategies with you right now," he said, each word controlled and precise. "You and I just need to attend to the business at hand, which really doesn't concern you, but I am extending the courtesy of an explanation." He paused and took a deep breath. "First of all, Elisabeth is frail and getting, well, getting lost. You can see that for yourself. When she passes, she has no heirs. That's why I'm buying her out."

"But this place is all she has," I protested.

"She's ninety-three, for God's sake," Tom shot back. "I intend to buy the farm from her at a fair price. It's not even in good repair. The money she gets will take care of her very well for the rest of her life. Her lawyer can hire her a private nurse or whatever she'll need."

"But what does that have to do with Margo? Why can't she stay on?"

"She can't, and I won't discuss it any further." His face was impenetrable. There was nothing in his eyes that I was familiar with. "I won't change my mind."

Suddenly it was a year ago and I was back in Nairobi, at Jomo Kenyatta Airport, feeling the biting August winds swirling those very same words into a bitter mix. Nairobi, where I had loved him. Where I had lost him. But we were in New York now. The cold winds might be gone, but the chilling resentment apparently remained inside of him.

"If you won't discuss Margo, then just tell me why we can't bring Tusker here?" I took a deep breath. "We're still planning to get him out of Zimbabwe and—"

"I told you to let it go, didn't I?" he interrupted angrily, his voice cutting my words in half like a knife.

"You don't understand." I shook my head. "After we left the Popes, Diamond and I spoke to someone in the ministry in Harare and"—Tom's face grew more incredulous with each word—"we made arrangements to . . . buy . . . Tusker."

Tom looked at me for one long moment. "You *what?*" His voice rose with anger. "You did *what?*"

"We made a deal."

He ran his hand through his hair and began to pace back and forth, covering the kitchen in great loping strides. "You're a fool! And an idiot!" He spat his words out like bullets. "You did something dangerous and foolish and amazingly stupid! You don't even know what you're getting involved with." He stopped to stare at me in disbelief, his face clouded with fury.

"Please!" I reached out and meant to grab his hand, but caught his sleeve instead. He didn't even look down, just pulled it from my fingers like you would from a street beggar in Nairobi. My cheeks flamed with embarrassment. "Please—just help me bring him here."

A muscle bulged, tightening his cheek, but he didn't reply. Taking his silence as an invitation to continue, I let my words rush out. "It would take nothing from you to fly him back here," I said. "Joshua Mukomana. The minister of mashed potatoes or whatever has promised to release him to us as soon as we pay for him. Please just fly him here. I'm not asking you to buy him, just fly him here. You did it for Margo. I'll pay for the flight if I have to. It'll be on my shoulders alone. I'll find a way to raise the money. You have the equipment—the planes and everything—and Joshua will let you fly safely into Harare and out again. He promised."

He stepped back from me. "*Joshua Mukomana?*"

"Please," I begged. I had never begged anyone before. Not when my ex-husband found a lover and had a child with her and left. Not when he spent every cent we had earned together on his new love. I never begged him to come back. Or to return my share of the money. Even when I was left with nothing, I did not beg. My dignity had meant more to me than repayment or apologies or revenge. It had been the only thing that kept me standing upright. Until now.

"Please," I whispered. "I can't lose these elephants. Any of them. You know how much they mean to me."

Tom's face fell into a weary, hurt look. "I do," he said. And then he said nothing. He was somewhere, I wasn't sure where, but he was staring past me, mulling through something.

"Look, I have plans for this place," he said cautiously. "I know what we all just went through and how hard it'll be to say good-bye to Margo. It's nothing personal, but it's not up for discussion. As for Tusker, you've bumbled into something that you had no right to. I'm warning you, don't go ahead with this crazy idea." I barely heard him through the static of words echoing from our past, could barely see him through a fog of old feelings and newly minted rejection.

He took his jacket from a chair and turned to the back door. "Do not get in touch with Mukomana again. Do you hear me? Do not interfere in things you know nothing about."

He was so brusque, so indifferent to me, so detached. As if our entire relationship was contained in this present conversation. As though all we ever had between us was this polite formality. As though all I had become was just someone seeking alms. I fought back tears. His face was expressionless, and I suddenly understood he didn't love me. His voice was proof of that. He was the perfect businessman, the captain of industry, and he had cut his losses. I kept thinking that as he gave me a brief, courteous nod and walked out the door ahead of me. He had already cut his losses.

That's what good businessmen do.

Chapter 21

"*MAHUMBA NI TOMBO*," DIAMOND SAID AS I DROVE us home. "*Mahumba ni tombo.* 'Love is blind.'"

"Don't be silly," I said. "If you mean me and Tom? There is absolutely no love left between us."

Diamond lit a cheroot and blew the smoke out the car window. Still, the aroma of sewage filled the car. "I saw the color go from your face." She pointed the cheroot at me. "I saw the way he spoke to you, with his jaw all tight. All he wanted was to yank you out of your shoes and throw you in a sleeping bag and climb in with you."

"It's just not true," I said, blinking back tears.

"You are both being foolish," she continued, scolding. "Don't you understand? Only the present matters. Forget the past, take care of the present, and the future will slide in on its coattails. Your future together. But you are both blind to it. *Mahumba ni tombo.*"

I wondered if she was right, that we saw only the past, the transgressions, the demands, the squabbles. "He thinks I'm an idiot," I said.

"He is meant for you." Diamond looked sad. "I see it. You know, it is not so easy to find someone to love. Hearts do not just meet one another like crossroads."

"Well, I guess my heart is stuck in a traffic circle," I said. "And it's not all my fault. He brought me to the jungle, and I fell in love with it. I only wanted to go back for a little while. For the baby elephants. Why couldn't he see that? It was for the babies."

"You lost your heart to the babies." Diamond nodded knowingly. "You needed them not just to love, you needed them to help you find your bearings. Same thing with Tusker. He has become more than a rescue to you. As I said, the jungle takes everyone. In different ways. And I see that it's reaching for you."

It was just past dawn the next morning when I drove back to the sanctuary. Pink feathers of light started breaking through the gray canopy above, and pale, thin clouds struggled to cling together. I parked the car and sat for a moment. The farm lay in a white mist of solitude and seclusion, and I thought about Tom and how much things had changed between us in a year. He was a total stranger to me now. I got out of the car and heard a thunderous bang. The clouds were too tenuous for a storm, the sky was brightening, but there it was again, a loud rolling thump, and I tilted my head to listen, then realized it had a rhythm to it, and it was coming from the elephant barn straight ahead.

I knew Margo occasionally grew impatient for her breakfast. A quick glance told me that Richie's truck was still in front of his house and that he probably wasn't awake yet to feed the animals. I was glad—I had purposefully gotten up very early just to spend some private time with Margo.

I needed time alone with my elephants. Without Richie, without Diamond—just me and Margo and Abbie. The way it used to be.

I rolled the doors open only a crack and slipped between them. The half-light of early morning made Margo an eerie figure, looming black-gray against the dim, grainy shadows. Another loud thump, and I saw that Margo was holding her feed tub in her trunk and banging it hard against the bars of her cage. She stopped when she saw me and dropped the tub, rumbling at me as though she were scolding me.

"Margo." I called softly. She stuck her trunk through the bars and swept it back and forth along the floor to check for treats. I had always thought she was so big, but after Tusker, she seemed daintier, more feminine, if that was possible.

"You're such a girly-girl," I said with a little laugh. "Here's your treat." I held out one of the boxes I had brought with me.

Margo sniffed the offering and gently lifted the lid to remove a donut, then popped it into her mouth. Trying to imitate her mother, Abbie stuck her trunk through the bars, too, and waved it around. I kissed the tip of it before holding a donut out to her. She squashed it against the bars and held her trunk out for a second one. Two dozen jelly donuts were gone in a few minutes.

"Well, you've had your dessert first," I told them, "so I

guess I'll give you breakfast now." Their feed was in a large bin in the corner of the barn, and I measured out their oats, wheat, and corn, watching the grains overflow the scoop and listening to the elephants expectantly sniffing the air.

Margo ate with good manners, curling the tip of her trunk to lift a small pile of food to her mouth, while Abbie played with hers, spilling it across the floor. I watched them, thinking how much I loved them. Could anyone love them more? Well, Richie, of course, and Tom, I was certain, but he kept his passion behind a veil of business.

As soon as Margo finished her breakfast, she slipped her trunk through the bars and swept it along the floor, looking for hay. Richie always gave her three or four squares before she was put outside, so I opened a bale and carried the hay into the enclosure. I had done it so many times before. Haying Margo was the simplest part of our routine.

Not this morning.

Margo spun to face me as soon as I walked through the gate. She gave a low, rumbling growl, and before I could react, raised her trunk and slammed it against me, flipping me hard against the bars of the cage. I tried to call out, but the air was knocked from my lungs. Another blow sent me skidding along the cement floor.

"Margo," I finally managed to gasp. "Margo, stand. Stand!" She flapped her ears at my voice and raised her trunk over her head and trumpeted loudly.

My leg throbbed. "Stand, Margo," I yelled again, and hoping her tantrum was over, crawled along the wall, careful not to look up at her. She was rocking back and forth, from one foot to the other and rumbling, a sign of agitation. And an agitated elephant could be a killer elephant in one move. I grabbed the bars to pull myself upright, hand over hand, careful not to look at Abbie, careful not to move too quickly, though I wasn't sure I could move more than a few painful inches at a time. I was hoping to slide toward the gate. It was within a few feet of me now, and Margo was still rocking behind me. I was dizzy and blinked hard, everything was getting a white haze over it. I stupidly thought I wasn't getting enough air up into my eyes. I was still in the cage. One more pull at the bars and I would be out. Abbie moved between us. She touched my head with her trunk, almost conciliatory, as though she knew what had happened, then stood there, between me and her mother. I pulled myself forward. The gate was right there, a few more inches. I touched the coiled springs and pushed against it. It opened and I rolled outside, kicking it shut behind me.

I sat up a few feet from the cage and gasped air in baby puffs until I was able to breathe normally. It was over. I watched Margo casually eat her hay and wondered what I had done wrong. What movement, what word or gesture had set off the tantrum? I had been careful, I was always careful, and there had been no change in the routine. I rubbed my fingers across my leg, and though it was already sporting a large, painful bump, it was not broken. Shaking, I sat there. Margo shook her head up and down and gave me an affectionate rumble.

It was a conceit, I knew, to think that Margo loved me. I hadn't forgotten that a little more than a year ago she had been totally wild. And Richie had warned me that she was sometimes moody. He even frequently joked how she could pick someone up and throw the person over the wall if she was so inclined. I got to my feet and stood next to the enclosure. I was not going to tell Richie what had happened. He would only tell Tom, and they would be convinced that Margo needed to be moved immediately.

But I knew what I had to do. It was from the same school of philosophy that had me climb back on a horse after a bad fall. That had me beg for Tom's help after a year of not speaking. You have to face your devils.

"Margo, come," I commanded. Margo popped a thatch of hay into her mouth and walked to the bars and put her trunk through. Still trembling, I took the trunk in my arms and held it. Margo purred softly. In a little while, she would expect to go out for the day, but she would have to wait for Richie to take her. I was all out of courage.

Oh, of course I was going to tell Richie about the incident. To do anything less could endanger his life, and I would never do that. In a half hour or so, he rolled apart the great doors to the barn and appeared surprised.

"You're early," he said as he walked in, accompanied by the black Labs. "But thanks for feeding the girls." He looked me up and down, then tilted his head. "Something you want to tell me?"

"She was a little cranky today," I replied. He reached over to touch the sleeve on my sweater.

"I gathered as much," he said, "because you're covered in hay, your leg is bleeding, your sleeve is ripped out, and"—he gingerly touched my eye with a finger—"you're beginning to get a shiner."

I looked at him guiltily and stepped aside as he pulled the gate open, then picked up the pole he used to guide the elephants on their walks. Margo strolled out calmly, and Abbie followed as though nothing had ever happened. I hung back and watched from the hill while Richie led them down to the pond, the dogs trotting ahead of him and barking. I would be fine, I thought. My feelings were more bruised than my leg. Richie returned to the top of the hill and stood next to me.

"So why did she do that?" I asked.

"Hormones, maybe?" he replied. "Elephants have really big hormones."

Margo and Abbie were now spraying each other with water and squealing with mock indignation, their private version of elephant jokes.

Margo and Abbie. I watched Abbie point her trunk filled with water straight at her mother, who curled her trunk around her daughter's and pushed it away, averting a squirt bath.

Margo. Abbie. Tusker.

That these creatures even had been assigned human names seemed a sacrilege, for who knew what names they had taken for themselves before their capture. What subsonic, unrevealed, intimate rumble they reserved for one another, what gesture, what touch, what private glance that deserved to remain secret. Tusker was not really Tusker. The name demeaned him. And to be called Dustbin was even more disrespectful.

"Watch her new trick," Richie said as Abbie trundled deep into the pond until the water covered her head and only her trunk was visible, sticking straight up from the surface, like a periscope. I had seen baby ellies do that in Kenya after the monsoons, and it always amused me how they loved turning themselves into pachyderm submarines.

"You know, there are huge ponds in the other sanctuary," Richie added nonchalantly. "Big enough even for Margo to do that. And there are two baby elephants rescued from a Mexican zoo that was starving them. Abbie could have friends."

I knew that all Richie wanted me to do was to acknowledge this, but I couldn't answer him. I dropped my head and just stared down at my shoes.

"Neelie?" Richie said. "They're going to be happier."

We stood in silence, letting the breeze fill in for conversation while we watched Margo and Abbie spray each other. Abbie finally grew tired of the water and climbed from the pond to explore a large plastic bucket filled with apples and melons that Richie had left nearby. Margo lifted a cantaloupe with her trunk and carefully placed it under her foot, stepping down and breaking it apart. She scooped up a piece and tenderly handed it to Abbie, who took it from her with a happy chirp.

"I know it's not up to me, but I can't let them go," I finally whispered. "Please don't ask me to give them up."

He sighed loudly and put a comforting arm around my shoulder. "But you will," he said. "I know you will. Because in the end, I know you want what's best for them."

I studied the clouds that were closing in on the horizon. They were gray and big and round like elephants, and ambled slowly across the sky, and I couldn't answer him.

Chapter 22

I WASN'T SURE IF THE FULL MOON WAS ALIGNING with the devil and the entire universe was conspiring to break my spirit, but the next three days were a study in domestic and social torture.

Diamond had accidentally started a fire in the toaster oven, trying to dry out the cheroots she had accidentally laundered while she was washing her summer safari outfits before packing them away. Then she accidentally vacuumed up a thick wool sock that had been lost under her bed, thereby clogging up the vacuum hose and causing the motor to whine at a high-pitched strain until it burned out. As an act of contrition, she whipped up a hearty pancake breakfast, which would have actually been successful had she not accidentally dropped the hand mixer and spattered the kitchen ceiling with thick, doughy, blueberry-filled stalactites.

"Forget breakfast. I'm going to the barn," I finally told her. "I'll pick up something on the way."

"I'm coming with you," Diamond volunteered. "I need a break from housework."

Richie was waiting for us in Mrs. Wycliff's kitchen, an array of papers across the kitchen table. Mrs. Wycliff waved cheerfully, then returned to concentrate on her bowl of oatmeal.

"I'll make us coffee," Diamond said, pulling out a saucepan and a bag of ground coffee. She dumped the coffee into the pot, filled it with water, sloshed it onto the stove and set the flame high. Richie watched her with his usual trepidation, then sat down at the table. I passed him the box of donuts after taking one for myself.

"You know, Neelie," he began, "I think you bit off more than you can chew."

I looked down at my donut to protest. "But it was only a small bite."

"I mean Tusker," he said. "I want you to know I'm totally on board with you saving him, but you're talking a lot of money."

I gave a hollow laugh. "You got any loose change?"

Richie put his hand into his pants pocket and pulled it inside out. "Sorry."

Diamond set out four mugs and filled each with slow-moving, tarry black coffee, and sat down to listen.

"You have any whiskey for this coffee?" Mrs. Wycliff asked Diamond, who shook her head. "Try the sideboard in the dining room." Diamond left to check.

"First of all," Richie started, "what did Tom say to you?"

I tried to concentrate on Tom's exact words, but like the donut I was eating, there was a hole somewhere in the middle of the conversation. "He said that he wasn't going to help me," I said. "He told me to stay out of things." I diplomatically left out the part where he called me a fool, an idiot, and stupid. I may have gotten the order wrong.

"Well, he may not want you to stay out of things anymore," Richie said. "I leave in another two weeks, and someone has to manage this place, so I pushed for you and Diamond and salaries for both of you. He finally admitted that it might not be a bad idea. He's just not sure you know what it entails." He pushed a few papers in front of me that were covered in numbers. "So, I'm going to give you a crash course."

"Why didn't he tell me himself?"

"Are you going to say no because he asked me to ask you?" Richie sounded exasperated. "I got the feeling that maybe you and he were having trouble holding a civil conversation."

"Only with each other," I replied, picking up the sheet of paper he pushed at me and glancing at it. It was the budget for the sanctuary.

"The work itself is doable," Richie began explaining. "I ran this place pretty much okay. There's Ignacio—he's been working here for years. And the volunteers, though they can be sporadic."

"This looks so complicated," I whined, looking at columns and rows of numbers. "Budgets and workers and numbers, oh my."

"And you're the one who wants to handle thirty-five thousand dollars?" He slid another set of papers across the table. I sighed and glanced at the lists of animal feed. Diamond returned with a bottle of Tyrconnell and poured a healthy dollop into Mrs. Wycliff's coffee. "Anyone else need a slug?" she asked. I held out my cup.

" 'Two bags of barley,' " I read off as Diamond spiked my coffee. The magnitude of what I wanted to do was beginning to sink in. " 'Seventy-two bags of crimped oats.' "

Mrs. Wycliff reached over and patted my hand. "The oats are for me, dear. I always have oatmeal in the morning."

"Plus 'a hundred and thirty pounds of hay,' " I read. " 'Fifteen bags of corn, fifteen bags of wheat bran.' "

"Forget the Wheatena," Mrs. Wycliff said. "It sticks in my teeth."

" 'Equine sweet feed,' " I continued. " 'Five to ten pounds each horse,' times fifty-seven horses."

"And the big cats go through seven or eight weekly packs of Carnivore Ten," Richie added, "in addition to over a hundred pounds of raw meat every day."

"I don't eat meat, myself," added Mrs. Wycliff. "So that's a savings right there."

Diamond looked over my shoulder at the list. "Check, check, check," she said. "We can order all of this without a problem. I think we're going to have a lot of fun running this place. It'll be like going to the circus every day, except no sex with the acrobats."

I looked at her in surprise. "You never told me about acrobats."

"Yeah, well, they were before the trapeze act." She poured a healthy shot of whiskey into her own coffee, took a sip, and savored it.

"Trapeze act?" I repeated.

But Diamond-Rose was lost in memories. "It was cool," she said. "Three guys, very limber, if you know what I mean."

Evening falls so differently in New York than in Africa. The African sky is a grand, summoning curve of open blue. The sky in New York is so close you can carry it on your back. Dusk falls earlier, grayer, with no prospects, no hope. I sat on the back porch and watched evening drift in sideways, curling around the houses, draping itself over the rooftops, finally obscuring everything beyond. The clouds hovered and then parted, revealing a full moon hanging ripe, like an orange.

It wasn't that I didn't get it. Actually, I have a lot of problems with animal sanctuaries.

Animals shouldn't need them.

Animals shouldn't need to be rescued from their own natural habitat and put in an artificial representation of that very same habitat. Rescuers shouldn't need to pull skeletal horses from knee-deep mud just hours before they die, or help two sad, scrawny, moth-eaten lions with severe dental problems hobble from a nine-by-seven concrete cage because their legs are half paralyzed from the cramped conditions. Or even take a magnificent elephant, humbled by pain and torturous wounds, too weak to care for her infant, and push her into the cargo bay of a plane for an agonizing trip across the globe to a climate and place about as familiar to her as the moon.

Animals just need people to stop blundering around in their world.

I rocked back and forth and thought about my empty barn. How I wished I could move Margo in there. And Abbie. Tusker, even. *Shamwari*. I would tell no one, it would be my secret, my delicious secret. They would be loved and they would be safe. And I would sneak out to the barn every day and talk to them and feed them their fruit and hay and tell them how much I loved them, and it would be perfect until, of course, the first time they trumpeted. Though I had never met my neighbors, they just might have a problem with elephants trumpeting across the lawn to one another. Somehow I didn't think four elephants could pass under the radar.

Diamond opened the back door and came outside to sit in the other chair, pulling it next to mine. She put her stocking feet up on the porch rail and lit a cheroot. That first puff of smoke always makes me gag.

"Sorry about the drapes in the den," she said as I tried to catch my breath. "I was flipping my knife, and it got a bit stuck in them, but actually, I think they look better short."

I sighed. It was just another incident in a long line of domestic catastrophes, but I had a bigger problem on my mind. "How on earth are we going to raise the money we need?" I asked glumly.

"I do have a solution," she said. "All we have to do is hold a proper fund-raiser."

"Fund-raisers don't work," I said. "I held a bake sale for a class trip once, and we made fourteen dollars and thirty-two cents. It was just barely enough for one pizza."

"Well, I'm good at fixing things." Diamond exhaled a long breath. The reeking smoke eddied around her face and lifted away with the breeze. "And I vote for a fund-raiser. You know, I never had a lot of money, so I had to be inventive. Especially after Jake died."

"Jake, who got taken by the jungle?" I asked, then realized how flippant it sounded. "I'm sorry."

Diamond took another puff on her cigar. "Yes, that Jake," she said simply.

"You never told me what happened."

"He followed his grandfather," she said. "That's what they say in Kenya when someone dies. He followed his grandfather."

I didn't ask any more. It was like Tom and me. There are things that are for thinking and things that are for speaking.

Diamond didn't say anything for a long time. "Jakob Tremaine," she said, raising her face to the full moon. "I have finally forgiven you for dying."

"Why would he need to be forgiven?" I asked.

She shrugged and didn't answer, but her face lost its repose for a moment.

I stretched back in my rocker and stared at the moon. A bold cyclopean eye, it hung full over us now, staring down from the heavens. Clouds crossed in front, obscuring it, then scuttled off. "It's okay if you don't want to talk about it."

"AIDS," she finally said.

And that said everything. I knew that Africa had the highest rate of AIDS in the world. And the highest death rate. I supposed that her Jakob had strayed. "I'm sorry," I said.

She didn't hear me. "I was very angry with him," she reflected, picking her words carefully. "He got very sick very suddenly. When he first told me he had AIDS, he was already very sick. He told me he would soon die. One day he came back from safari so sick. He didn't want me to drive him in the Rover to the hospital, and he didn't want to drive himself. The only other option was to take a horse all the way back to Loisaba and pick up a private charter to Nanyuki to see the doctor." Her voice trailed off. "He came back from safari so sick. He didn't want me to know until it was too late." She stood up and pinched out her cheroot and put it in her pocket. "What can I say? I didn't know it was his time until the end. *Mahumba ni tombo*."

"He put you at risk," I said softly. "You couldn't have loved him, I mean, after you found out."

"He didn't put me at risk," Diamond said flatly, then stood for a moment with her eyes closed. "He made sure he didn't. I was more his daughter than his wife. Now I close my eyes and see his face. He had a lovely face." She took a long breath. "My heart doesn't love him anymore, but my eyes do."

Another cloud drifted across the moon, and I waited politely for it to leave before I spoke. "You can find love again," I said.

But Diamond was already someplace else. "Listen," she said. "We will raise money to buy Tusker. We will invite that Tom of yours, and we will invite everyone in New York who loves animals and ask them for a contribution. He must know other people who are into rescues." She jumped, then felt her pocket and slapped it a few times. "Damn, I've set my pants on fire again."

"Tom'll never come," I replied. "And we don't know

anyone in New York. Except my family and his mother. I met her once. I know she is very involved with racehorses and contributes lots of money to horse charities."

Diamond laughed. "There you go! You have to give your man an incentive to attend."

I didn't like where this was leading. "And what would that be? Kidnap his mother and hold her for ransom?"

"The very thing," Diamond said. "Because you must find a way to get a lot of people here. People bring money. You have to use a little jungle strategy. When you invite a gazelle, the lions come to the feast as well."

I snorted. "Yeah, except for one problem," I said. "What happens if I'm the gazelle?"

Chapter 23

IT TOOK DIAMOND ABOUT TWO DAYS TO FIGURE OUT what I already knew—that you need funds to hold a fund-raiser. And we didn't have any.

"I'll think of a way," she promised. "I always come up with something, one way or the other. You know, when the lion cannot find meat, it eats grass."

We had taken over some of Richie's chores by now, in anticipation of his leaving soon for Alabama, and he had given us a long list of cautionary instructions: Don't trust the chimps, always feed the lions together, always walk *next* to Margo, never in front. Count the poultry before you lock them in at night. Nothing about how to be a good negotiator.

Diamond worked hard alongside me. We fed the animals,

cleaned cages, organized the volunteers a little better, and gave Ignacio long lists of chores.

"We could use that truck." Diamond was eyeing Mrs. Wycliff's old truck after we pulled in one morning. She walked over to it, pried open the hood, and began tinkering. Half an hour later, it grumbled to life. "There are no garages in the bush," she remarked to a pleased Richie, "so I learned some basic mechanics."

With two trucks running, we were able to get the work done twice as fast. When it was time to feed the horses, Diamond got behind the wheel and drove one truck through the horse field, while I threw bales of hay from the bed.

"Fifty-seven hay burners," Diamond tsk-tsked, and pointed at the horses as they galloped up for their hay. "They need to get a life."

We were having lunch with Richie later that afternoon, sitting on the elephant hill and watching Margo and Abbie wrestle with each other. Richie dug into a bag he had just brought back from the deli. "Tomato on rye," he announced, and dropped a wrapped sandwich onto his lap. He made a face and handed another sandwich to Diamond, commenting, "And here's your bologna on rye. I personally never eat anything with a face."

She unwrapped her sandwich, lifted the bread, and peered underneath. "Bologna doesn't have a face," she reported.

"And ever the diplomat"—Richie handed me mine—"bologna on rye with tomato."

"I have an idea for the horses," Diamond announced in between bites. "Bring Mrs. Wycliff down to the horse field after we finish eating. I want her to see something."

"Elisabeth doesn't like anyone messing around with her babies," Richie cautioned.

Diamond laughed. "I am going to give Mrs. Wycliff a performance she'll never forget."

We were waiting by the gate in the horse pasture when Richie pulled up in his truck, Mrs. Wycliff sitting next to him, wearing her pith helmet.

"Right on time," Diamond said as they drove up. "Come on."

I followed her over to the truck. Richie helped Mrs. Wycliff to the ground, and she gave us a happy wave.

"How are my babies?" she called to us.

"Ah, yes, your babies," Diamond replied. "I have an idea for your babies." She walked back to Mrs. Wycliff's old truck, reached into the backseat and pulled out a coiled lariat. "Let me show you what I've been thinking."

Climbing into the pasture, Diamond uncoiled the lariat. "I counted fifty-seven horses," she announced as she spun the rope in a hypnotic circle over her head. "And they're all standing around waiting for a job."

"They can't be ridden," Mrs. Wycliff protested. "You don't ride your children."

"If we don't do something, your children are going to be sent away," Diamond replied, still spinning the lariat. "They have to pay for themselves."

"But I made a promise to each of them," Mrs. Wycliff said. "Absolutely no interference with their personal lives."

But Diamond wasn't listening anymore, She pointed at the black horse with the white stockings. "That pretty black one, for starters," she called out, winding her lariat up and down like a yo-yo. "Let me show you what I mean."

She coiled the lariat over her head and rolled it away from her, aiming at the horse. It settled around his neck, and he immediately stiffened against it. Speaking softly, Diamond moved to his side, shortening the slack in the rope as she went. She placed her hands on his back and, in a flash, mounted him.

"I say we turn them into a paying enterprise," Diamond called from atop the horse. "We train them and sell them."

"Absolutely not," Mrs. Wycliff declared. "I promised they would have a good home forever."

"And you would still be keeping your promise," Diamond pointed out. "It's just that the good home won't be with you. There are plenty of people who are looking for a nice horse." She clucked loudly and tapped the black horse in the ribs with her heels. He backed up a few feet and then trotted off.

"Young lady," Mrs. Wycliff called after her, "you step down this minute. I don't want any injuries."

"I'll be fine," Diamond called back. "He likes this."

"I think she's referring to the horse," Richie called out.

They trotted back and forth. Diamond brought the horse to a halt with a pull of the rope, then clambered to her knees and stood upright on his back with her arms outstretched, one hand still holding the lariat. She clucked loudly, and the horse picked up a smooth, rolling canter with Diamond standing balanced on his back. The horse gave a little squeal and a buck as he passed us, but Diamond still managed to stay on. She continued to make a circuit of the field, finally slipping down to a sitting position as she headed toward us.

"My goodness," said Mrs. Wycliff. "I didn't know Jackie could ride like that."

"I didn't either," I said.

"Nice horse, too," said Mrs. Wycliff. "Wonder why she hasn't ridden him before."

"How did you know you weren't going to get killed?" I asked Diamond later as we drove home.

"That's how Jake and I used to find horses for the safaris," she said. "We'd take a day trip in the rover to Borana Lodge. They always had horses for sale. Kept them in a large pen, and Jake and I would just hop on the ones we fancied. We'd find out soon enough if a horse wasn't suitable and just bail off."

"Pretty brave," I said. "That black horse probably hasn't been ridden in years."

"Oh, I know," she said. "Of course, it helped that I found tranquilizers in the barn and shot him up with a couple of cc's of acepromazine first."

The next day was Reese's birthday, and I had invited him and Marielle over for dinner.

"I'll cook dinner," Diamond volunteered. "You can make the cake."

Knowing her culinary skills were limited to bacon and eggs, cowboy coffee, and burned toast, I politely declined her offer.

"Trust me," she said, "I'll make something good. It'll be my contribution to his birthday. He's my brother, too, you know." An hour before Reese and his wife were supposed to arrive, I still didn't notice anything in the kitchen that might indicate the preparation of food.

"Dinner?" I asked. I had already made a cake early in the day to give Diamond full access to the stove without my interference, but she was sitting with her feet propped on the table and reading a newspaper.

"All taken care of," she replied. "So, what are you giving Reese for his birthday?"

I held up a package. "New earbuds for his iPod."

She blinked a few times. "Oh, right," she said. "They're in season now, aren't they?"

My brother and his wife arrived, and Diamond had dinner on the table by the time they took off their coats. She had made a salad, opened a few cans of chili, heated it, and poured it over wedges of Italian bread, which, I knew, was pushing her culinary skills to the limit.

"Voilà," she said, standing back from the dining room table with pride. "And here comes the best part." She plopped a six-pack of Heineken on the table. "International cuisine."

Reese started dinner with his usual opening. "How do you make an elephant float?" He looked around expectantly. When there was no reply, he answered himself. "Two hundred bottles of cream soda, two hundred scoops of ice cream, and an elephant!"

Diamond hooted with laughter, while Marielle gave him an indulgent smile. We started eating.

"Great chili," Reese pronounced. "Marielle hasn't made her special chili in a long time."

"It's because I'm busy—I'm doing a lot of tutoring," Marielle said, then looked at me. "How about you? Have either of you found work?"

"Sort of," Diamond announced. "At the sanctuary, but it's still not enough to buy the elephant."

"Do you really think you're going to raise enough

money?" Marielle laughed as she passed the platter of food to Diamond, who stabbed the bread with her knife, dripping chili across the tablecloth to eat it *en pointe*.

"*Two* elephants," I corrected Marielle. "For the bargain price of a trillion eleventy zillion dollars. We're planning to have a fund-raiser, so if you have any ideas, let us know."

"Sorry." Marielle shook her head. "We had a bake sale when I was in pony club, and we made nine dollars. Everyone had ice cream. I don't think fund-raisers really do much."

We ate dinner and endured several more elephant jokes until it was time for dessert. I stood up to clear the table.

"I'll clear the table," Diamond offered. "You can put the candles on the cake." I looked with apprehension at the dishes. Her gaze followed mine. "Or we can switch, if you want," she added. "And I'll light the cake."

I pondered this for a moment. Which did I want to chance—broken dishes or a fire in the kitchen? The fire seemed more remote.

"You light the cake and bring it in," I said, carrying the dishes to the sink.

Reese followed me into the kitchen. "Who was the most famous female animal jazz singer in the world?"

"Don't you ever run out?" I asked, stacking dishes in the dishwasher. "All right, who?"

"Elephants Gerald!"

Diamond guffawed and dropped the cake she was carrying.

Reese opened his earbuds, we sang two rounds of "Happy Birthday," ate the remains of the cake, and in general had a pleasant evening.

"I've got to be up early," Diamond excused herself as I was saying good night to Reese and Marielle at the front door. "We've got horses to train and sell."

"I don't know that you're going to sell any horses," Marielle said sympathetically. "The economy is scary. Horses are a luxury—there are an awful lot of people in my position who do what I had to do."

"What position?" I asked guiltily, since I had monopolized the evening talking about Tusker and hadn't even bothered to ask Marielle how her tutoring was going.

"Oh, you know," said Marielle. "I'm teaching only two courses now. The tutoring doesn't bring in all that much—half my salary is gone."

"Oh, right," I said. "That must be so hard."

"We've been budgeting like mad." Marielle sighed. "Thank heavens I met that really nice man who took that old horse of yours."

My blood froze. The hairs on my arms stood up, and a cold, sick feeling grabbed my stomach. "What really nice man?" I asked breathlessly. "What are you talking about?"

"Remember? I asked you about it during dinner at your mother's, and you said it was okay. So I put an ad in the paper." Marielle smiled and patted my arm. "And this really nice man with two kids answered the ad. Pulled up with a horse trailer and took Mousi right away." She gave a little giggle. "It's not like I sold him into slavery or anything. The man promised him a good home—going to make him a 4-H project—and he was really nice, so there's nothing to worry about."

Chapter 24

"IT'S A SCAM," RICHIE SAID. I HAD CALLED HIM IN a panic before Reese and Marielle had even gotten into their car to leave. "The really nice man with the two kids, the 4-H project. Sometimes it's a really nice woman. They pick up the horse and sell him the same day to a slaughterhouse dealer. Fast money, no investment."

I knew that he was going to tell me that. I knew it even before I called him, that Mousi had been given away to an unscrupulous slaughterhouse dealer. I was sick. "I have to find him," I cried into the phone. "The phone number he gave Marielle isn't working."

Richie gave a hollow laugh. "Never is," he said. "How long has it been since he's gone?"

"Marielle said it was less than a week ago." I could barely speak the words. "I'm calling all the barns that I know, all my friends that have horses, all the horse vets, all the farriers. I don't know what else to do."

"Let me ask the people that I know," Richie tried to reassure me. "If your horse is still alive, we'll find him."

"*How* will you find him?" I wailed. "How do you even know where to start?"

"Well," Richie said, "I'll start by getting the name of every really nice man in the county."

Aside from a hundred frantic phone calls, there was nothing more I could do until I heard back from Richie. How ironic that I was so preoccupied with rescuing one animal that I lost the one I truly loved. How stupid I had been. How could I have not heard Marielle asking if I wanted my horse back. I wanted to reverse time, turn the week to that day, to that moment when Marielle first asked me, and shout, Yes, I want him back. Yes, yes, yes, yes, yes!

I sat up all night in the rocking chair on the back porch, fighting to keep pictures of Mousi out of my mind. He would be frightened, terrified, maybe injured, maybe being slaughtered this very minute. I pushed my fists against my eyes. I couldn't allow myself to see him like that.

I had to find him. I would search everywhere. Every barn, every farm, call every. . .

I opened my eyes and it was morning. My body felt stiff, and I was chilled through. I had fallen asleep in the rocking chair. It was very early, the beginning of another day. Another day less for Tusker, and another day less for Mousi.

I stood up to stretch. Fall was beginning to conquer the trees, golden leaf by golden leaf. The Catskill Mountains in the distance were a baroque tapestry of russets and maroons and blazing orange, but they held no beauty for me. The skies were a cool gray-blue. New York skies. They held nothing for me either, not a trace of hope. I had gone to Kenya and lost Tom, and gone to Zimbabwe and lost Mousi. Diamond was right. In the end, the jungle takes everything.

I needed someone who would listen to me, someone with a sympathetic ear. In fact, a big, flapping, sympathetic ear. And a long, gentle nose to wipe away my tears.

I needed an elephant.

The sun was strong by the time I got to the barn, melting the dew that had been frozen like so many crystal flowers in the fields below. The chill was melting away, warming into a bright day, but I felt nothing. The chill inside of me remained.

I went into the elephant barn and gave Margo a scoop of elephant chow through the bars.

"It's not that I don't trust you anymore," I told her, "it's just that I don't really trust you anymore."

Margo nodded her head up and down as though she agreed with me, then carefully curled the tip of her trunk around the pellets and scooped them into her mouth.

"It's all my fault," I continued, tears rolling down my face. "I shouldn't have trusted anyone with Mousi. If you love something, you don't just give it up. I was so stupid." I began to weep.

Margo swept hay from the floor and dropped it across Abbie's back like a good mother. It was an ancient elephant ritual to protect their children from the elements. Then she returned her attention to me.

"See?" I said. "No one can take care of something you love like your own self." She lifted her trunk to sniff my face. "Why didn't *I* take care of Mousi?" I cried, pressing my face to the bars. "Why did I even give him away? I could have paid board on him in some barn." The rough edge of Margo's trunk traced a sympathetic path down my face, and I knew I couldn't let her leave, either.

"Richie will be so busy. Who will watch over you?" I sobbed to her.

I couldn't bear it. Who watches over any of them? I left her and walked outside.

Farms are so eerily quiet in the early morning, as though the noises of the day haven't quite found them yet. This was especially true at the sanctuary. The property was so big, it filtered out every sound except that of the animals. But this time I heard voices. Men's voices. Curious, I followed the sound, walking down part of the road that led to the horse pasture.

In the distance, just on the other side of the pasture, was a large blue truck parked next to several men. Hunting is a local pastime, and after a year in Kenya, caring for baby ellies whose mothers had been killed by poachers, my first thought was that the men were trespassing to hunt. Fury swept through me as I thought of the bears, the lions, the wolves, all easy targets, trapped in their enclosures.

It was too far to walk. I ran back for my car and drove madly to the bottom of the road. I knew my car would be able to fit through the gate into the pasture. Diamond and I had driven the old truck through, loaded with hay, all the time, and I knew I could probably drive over the first few acres of the flat pasture, but beyond that was stony terrain that dipped sharply into muddy wetlands, making it impossible to proceed any farther.

I had to protect the animals. I had seen too many sport hunters grow bored tracking the animals they had wounded, leaving them to crawl through the jungle maimed until they died a slow, wretched death. I'd had my fill of death. I was not going to allow even one more animal to suffer.

I stopped the car at the gate and got out. There was only one mode of transportation that could safely navigate the rest of the pasture, and it had four legs. Actually, there were fifty-seven makes and models, with several variations of color—I just needed to find the most suitable one. The black horse that Diamond had ridden was too far away, but there was an overweight, phlegmatic-looking chestnut mare practically standing next to me, her eyes closed in a peaceful doze. She looked like a quarter horse, and I liked quarter horses. They are generally gentle and user friendly and easy to ride. Reassuring the mare in a soft voice, I walked to her side. Her eyes popped open and she looked me over, then dropped her head to graze, a good sign that she was relaxed. I stepped up to her and rubbed her neck for a minute, and she sighed blissfully. Then I pressed both hands against her back and got ready to mount her. She snorted loudly and struck out at me with a front leg.

"So much for introductions," I said, and quickly jumped onto her back, out of striking range. The mare shook her head and pranced around in indignation. I grabbed a shank of her long mane and wrapped it around my hand, then sat back to balance myself. She pawed the ground and spun in a small angry circle. Not quite the way it had gone for Diamond.

"Knock it off," I said in my best Voice of God imitation, but the mare was apparently an atheist and took off at a full gallop across the field. Her plump conformation made her easy to sit, but she was running with an energy born of resentment and overfeeding.

Her canter became a series of springs and leaps, and she was racing toward the fence with more speed than even she knew she possessed. I wrapped my legs tightly around her middle and prayed I would stay on while she incorporated 360-degree pivots on one hoof, along with other amazingly engineered equine movements. She swung her head wildly up and down while I took a stronger grip on her mane and tried to kick her forward. We were turning into a spectacle and out of the corner of my eye, I could see the men in the distance getting interested in our impromptu performance. One man was holding onto something long and linear—a rifle, I thought—and for a moment I entertained the notion that a quick bullet to either me or the horse would almost be welcome.

A few more minutes and the mare was beginning to tire. Her pace slowed, and she was panting from her exertions. I took advantage of her fatigue to kick her on and keep her cantering toward the fence.

As we drew closer I could see two men in jeans holding surveying instruments along with a packet of red flags. Not poachers, I realized with some relief, surveyors. Several other men in a circle of suits were joining them in what was apparently an open-air business meeting.

"Thank you," I heard someone say. "We'll get the proposal to you as soon as we can. We should have the papers signed before the month is out. I guess this fence will be coming down."

They shook hands, apparently making some kind of business deal over the very land I was riding on. So that's why Tom was going to send the elephants away and tear down their barn. It hadn't been for Margo's benefit, after all. It was to snatch all the land in the area!

And to do what? Build another housing development? Another mall? Tom had betrayed me, betrayed Mrs. Wycliff, betrayed the elephants.

Anger tightened the muscles in my throat, and I gave the mare another strong kick toward the men. I wanted to let them know that I *knew*. That they could go back and tell Tom—tell him what? I had to laugh. Tell him that some woman with a black eye came galloping up on them out of the morning mist like a half-crazed Valkyrie and she was very indignant?

The mare was blowing hard by now, and my legs were weakening from the strain of staying on. But at my urging, the horse lowered her head and caught a second wind and plowed on, the only good thing was that we were now both agreeing on the direction of travel. The fence was straight ahead. I pulled back on her mane to stop her, but the mare only bore down and picked up speed. The fence was twenty or so feet in front of us, and I started worrying less about the mare's braking skills and more about how adept she was at jumping. Luckily, she demonstrated a certain dim notion of self-preservation by screeching to a dead halt just before she would have crashed us both through the fence. A scream escaped my lips as I flipped off her back and slid several feet across the slick mud, ending with a perfect forward roll. There were loud gasps followed by uproarious laughter from my audience. Three men, dressed in dark, pristine business suits were staring at me in frank delight. A man pushed through from the back and leaned over the fence to extend a hand and help me to my feet. I couldn't see him for the mud in my eyes, but his voice startled me.

"Why, Neelie," Tom said. "What a surprise! I wasn't expecting you to drop by today."

Chapter 25

<small>⸺ ∞∞∞ ⸺</small>

I HAVE BEEN IN MANY SITUATIONS IN WHICH I fervently wished that the earth would swallow me whole.

On this particular occasion, the earth had made a good attempt by enveloping me almost completely in mud. Unfortunately, I had to reemerge in front of a group of highly entertained and chortling spectators.

As Tom lifted me to my feet, there was a flutter of hooves behind me, and we turned around just in time to see that the mare, finished with the task at hand, was departing for her previous location at warp speed.

"If you wait a moment, I'll give you a ride," Tom said, an amused smile playing across his lips. He wiped his muddy hand on one of the red flags. "It looks like your taxi just left without you."

There was another round of guffaws, followed by a round

of farewell handshakes, and the men got into their cars and departed, leaving me and Tom alone.

"I know what you're doing," I snapped at him.

"Certainly nothing as dramatic as what you've managed," he replied. "A rodeo and a mud slide, all in one morning!" He swung open the door to his Bentley. "Would you care for a lift?"

"Thank you," I said with all the dignity my grubby state would allow. He waited for me to spread his morning copy of the *Wall Street Journal* across the front seat in an effort to keep from soiling the pristine caramel leather upholstery. "I can't promise a ride as exciting as your last one," he said, "but it will certainly be cleaner."

"I know what you're up to," I said, after carefully settling in.

"And what would that be?" he asked in a patient voice.

"You're selling the sanctuary, and it isn't right," I said angrily. "Or you're developing it into something. You forgot to mention that was the reason you wanted all the land!"

"What on earth are you talking about?" he demanded, turning around to stare at me. "Who said I was selling the sanctuary?" His voice rose in anger. "Those men were selling me the land next to it."

"It's probably even a conflict of interest or something," I continued, growing even angrier, my words ending in a near shout. "You lied about keeping the sanctuary open! How *could* you?"

"Don't raise your voice to me. I didn't lie. You're totally misunderstanding what's going on here," he said. "As usual. There are other plans for this place that I'm not at liberty to discuss at the moment because it could sabotage the deal."

"I don't care what plans you have," I snapped. "I'm going to warn Mrs. Wycliff that you're either buying or selling her property for nefarious reasons." We were at the elephant barn by now, but my fury hadn't spent itself. "And I'm going to tell her that you're buying all the other land, too, and planning to build all sorts of . . . commercial . . . things, and that—that—" I was at a loss for words. "And that's why you wanted to get rid of Margo, because she won't fit inside your shopping center or something. Anyway, I'm telling her."

"Yep, you tell her everything," he said cheerily. "Give her all the details."

"That's right," I said. "I'm going to tell her that you're the one who wants to take away all her animals because you're the one who stands to profit from it." I glared at him defiantly as he got out of the car and opened my door, still the gentleman, although I thought it was more because he didn't want me touching the door handle. "It's all about profit, isn't it? I'm going to tell her right now."

"Oh yes, you be sure to let her know," he said, and flashed me a big smile. "But be sure to get your story accurate. I'm *buying* the sanctuary. From her. And I'm buying the land next to it. About six thousand acres. She knows all about it, but make sure you tell her, and mention my name a few times, *Tom Pennington*, because she always gets mad as hell when she thinks Harry has done something behind her back."

Tom left as soon as I slammed out of his car. He gave me a curt salute with his two fingers along with the parting words "I would take a shower if I were you. That horse shit is pretty ripe," before roaring down the driveway. I stood there, defeated. I hadn't really overheard anything, hadn't saved anything, and had mortified myself. There was nothing to tell and no one who was of sound mind to tell it to. Worse than that, I had totally confirmed Tom's earlier notion of me being amazingly stupid, a fool, and an idiot. I may have the order mixed up.

I stood in front of the elephant barn, feeling as though a lifetime had passed since my arrival early that morning. My mud-encrusted jeans were beginning to harden around my legs. Richie's truck was gone from the front of his house, the elephants were already in their field, so there was nothing more for me to do except go home; take a long, hot shower; rub a bottle of liniment into my throbbing leg muscles; and wait for Richie to call me with his list of really nice men. I heard the sound of a car coming back up the driveway and spun around, my heart beating in fast expectancy. Tom was returning! Coming back to apologize, or explain what was going on, or maybe to take my hand and press it to his lips and beg my forgiveness. I would apologize, too, and give him a chance to explain himself, and beg *his* forgiveness and hug him. Okay, given my mud-coated state, maybe postpone the hug. But I didn't recognize the red Subaru that pulled into the parking lot. Diamond-Rose jumped out.

"Hey!" she exclaimed. "I wanted to talk to you."

"Are you crazy?" I asked, gesturing to the car. "You hitched a ride? In New York?"

She flapped a hand at me. "We do it all the time in the bush. Whatever Rover is passing through. I think she's your neighbor. Want me to introduce you?"

"No thanks," I said, thinking, how wonderfully perfect this was. A neighbor. I hadn't really met any of my neighbors yet, and now here was Diamond-Rose dressed in her safari clothes like some early Halloween costume, ready to happily introduce me to my own neighbor, while I was standing around looking like a breaded chicken cutlet. My neighbor eyed my clothes, gave me a wan smile, and left.

"I'm going home," I said to Diamond. "And if I never see another horse—"

"Speaking of horses," she said, "remember my idea about training those horses down in the field?"

I nodded. "I suppose." She pushed me ahead of her, down the path.

"Well," she said, "if we're going to sell those horses to raise money, we've got a lot of riding to do. And we're going to start today."

We rode six horses apiece, each one a mystery followed by a revelation. Some reared, some stiffened their legs as soon as they were mounted and refused to move an inch, one rolled over in protest, one backed up almost the whole length of the field, another whipped his head around to one side and pulled my shoe off with his teeth.

Diamond was sitting on a palomino that was spinning in small circles. "This one isn't so good if you're in a hurry to get somewhere," she called out, but I couldn't answer as the horse I was riding had gotten down on his knees.

"This one might be saying his prayers," I yelled back just before I jumped off.

Diamond had brought a large red felt-tipped marker, a

pencil, and a pad, and after writing a big red number in the middle of each horse's forehead, she wrote the corresponding number on her pad along with a little note about its training and behavior.

"Great system," I said admiringly as I dismounted from my last horse and leaned against his rump to keep from toppling with fatigue.

"Yep," Diamond agreed. "I have to say, I've got it all organized. That's my forte."

Margo was bedded for the night, and I lingered with her in the barn because I really didn't want to go home and face the disarray that Diamond was certain to have left for me. Margo had finished eating and now was reaching down for another trunkful of hay, which she tossed over her back.

"Dinner is not a fashion statement," I chided her, but had to smile at how comical she looked with hay draped across her head. She rumbled contentedly and tossed another trunkful across Abbie's back. Properly covered, Abbie sunk down into the sweet-smelling straw and closed her eyes. I had forgiven Margo her tantrum. How many times had I ridden a horse, only to be bucked off? How many times had I been kicked, stepped on, knocked over, flung across riding rings? Elephants, except for their massive size, were no different in their behavior. A tantrum was a tantrum, but they generally forget about it as soon as it's over. I would just have to be more careful.

"I love you, Margo," I whispered ardently.

Her amber eye scanned my face. She pushed her trunk through the bars, and I let her wrap it gently around me.

Her whiskers prickled through my shirt, and she rumbled very softly. Maybe she was telling me that she was happy here, happy that she had someone to love her and watch over her. Maybe she was apologizing for hurting me. We stood together, and she held me in her great, strong trunk, and we listened to the rain just beginning to fall against the roof. I wondered if she sensed how stressed I'd been? Did she understand, somehow, that there were plans being made to send her away? Had she been trying to tell me that we would have to say good-bye?

Or had she been trying to tell me not to let her go?

I sighed and kissed her good night and walked out of the barn into a light rain. I opened my car door to find Diamond waiting inside.

"Glad we finished riding when we did," Diamond announced, pointing to the rain on the windshield.

I slid behind the wheel of the car. "Yeah, and that was a good idea you had," I agreed. "You know, to mark their heads so we know which ones we rode."

"Yep." Diamond put her head back against the upholstery, exhausted. "It was that marker that I found that gave me the idea."

I paused, car key in hand. "The red marker from my kitchen?"

Diamond nodded. "It's from that shiny white board thing on your fridge, why?"

I started laughing, with tears born of frustration and fatigue. Tears ran down my face. I laughed until I couldn't breathe.

"What?" she asked.

"Marking the horses was a great idea," I gasped, getting more hysterical with each word and stuttering them out between hoots. "Except for . . . one thing . . . that red marker is . . . water soluble!" I took a deep breath and pointed to the rain. "All your hard work is going to . . . wash off."

Chapter 26

HOW MUCH SHOULD YOU CHARGE FOR A LIFE when it's sold into ownership? To whom does it belong? Tusker was going to cost thirty-five thousand dollars. The horses we were selling were worth only eight or nine hundred apiece. Was Mousi being sold to the slaughterhouse for meat this very moment? He was chubby. Do you sell life by the ounce? By the pound? Wasn't there some kind of immutable stewardship that every living creature is entitled to? And despite my ethical reservations, it was up to Diamond and me to set prices on the horses we were selling.

The good thing was that we *were* selling horses. It seemed that we had an edge on the market. Short, calm, overweight, bucket-headed horses were in great demand, and that's exactly what Mrs. Wycliff had accumulated over the years. We managed to sell ten horses in two weeks and now horse number eleven, having met all the prerequisites, with the bonus of being remarkably unattractive, was being loaded into a lovely well-kept trailer to become a gift for a ten-year-old girl.

The horse had been at the sanctuary for two years, having been left behind in someone's backyard after they moved. My guess is that he patiently waited for his owner to remember he was still back there. Waited patiently for his owner to return home and feed him his dinner or to offer him a bucket of water to slake his thirst. Waited patiently, faithfully, quietly for weeks, while his life was being starved away. Until someone noticed, and he was brought to the sanctuary, where Mrs. W. named him Sprinkles, in honor of the black dots that splattered across his white coat, and just like that, his life was restored. Diamond put a price tag on him, someone came to ride him and thought he was wonderful, and now his life would become a gift to someone else.

Of course Diamond and I had made sure to inspect his new home, had the mother sign papers that stated we could drop in unannounced anytime to make sure he was okay and that he was to be returned when he wasn't wanted anymore. That's how it should be done when you sell lives. Too bad Marielle hadn't thought of it.

Now Diamond and I stood together in the parking lot and watched Sprinkles's black-polka-dotted rump wiggle up the trailer ramp and disappear as the tailgate was shut behind him.

"I hate selling animals," I grumbled. "If that was a person, it would be considered immoral."

"If that was a person, we could send him out to get a

job to support himself," Diamond replied. "He isn't and we can't, and we need to make money and room to save more."

"I hope we never have to take him back," I said as the trailer made a track of dusty spirals down the driveway before rounding the corner, out of sight. "Doesn't it bother you that Sprinkles has no say in where he's going to be spending the rest of his life?"

Diamond stepped in front of me. "You know, sometimes we don't either," she said impatiently. "But with his sale, we've made a total of eighty-five hundred dollars, and it's enough money to throw the fund-raiser."

Margo was cranky. Again. She was pacing her stall when I let myself into the barn and even slapped Abbie with her trunk for getting in her way. Abbie squealed a protest and stood chastened in a corner until I quickly brought her mother a tub of grain garnished with sliced carrots, sweet potatoes, and apples, which Margo graciously allowed Abbie to share. When their breakfast was finished, Margo grumbled and threw her tub at the bars, though I suspected that I was the more likely target, standing just outside. The tub hit the bars with a crash, and I shuddered from the memory of having been flung like that not too long ago. I waited until Margo settled and allowed her trunk to be stroked before I gave her the daily donut treat. I didn't want to reinforce the wrong behavior.

"Here's a little mood elevator," I said, handing her a jelly donut through the bars. She popped it into her mouth, then slipped her trunk back through the bars to give me a hard push. I skidded back and lost my balance, landing once again on the floor. Apparently, jellies weren't the drug of choice this morning.

"Good thing you stayed outside the bars," Richie said, entering the barn just as I hit the floor. "She's been a little out of sorts lately."

I righted myself and brushed the hay from my jeans. "Does she hate me?"

"If she hated you, she would have killed you," Richie said, his face serious. "She's had any opportunity to do that." He picked up the long stick he used to guide her down to the bottom field and opened her gate. "Maybe it's the change of seasons." He led her out, then pointedly called over his shoulder, "or maybe she's just plain lonely."

Margo marched through the gate and out the barn doors, with Richie careful to stay at her shoulder, instead of leading in front, the way he used to. Abbie trotted behind them, and I followed Abbie, mulling over the significance of Richie's remarks. Margo had her child and she had us—it seemed to me she had all the companionship she needed. Or did she? Was the need for her own kind so strong that it surpassed her affection for us? It had been little more than a year since she had left her wild family behind, and I knew she remembered them. Elephants remember everything. But surely our love was enough. I stopped at the top of the hill and watched as Margo swung her great body from side to side, marching next to Richie in slow elephant steps. She was going down to the pond. Where she went every day. Elephants in the wild wander hundreds of miles, and Margo was walking the same seven or eight hundred feet to her little pond. Every deadly boring day.

And I suddenly knew Richie was right. Margo shouldn't need to walk next to anyone. She was an elephant, a wild creature, and she deserved her independence. She needed her own kind, her own sovereignty, her own leaders and followers. She needed to walk with them over huge fields and complicated landscape. She had been trying to tell us that there was a void in her life. To keep her here was wrong. To keep her isolated from other elephants was cruel. If I loved her, I had to let her leave. It would be the completion of her rescue.

"Sorry about the microwave," Diamond said to me in a defeated voice when I got home. Apparently it had produced a lightning storm of sparks that eventually burned out the magnetron tube because she had stuck in a can of soup to heat for lunch, forgetting that microwaves hated metal. She was sitting at the kitchen table, fingering the blackened can and drinking a cup of coffee.

"That's okay," I said wearily.

"I'll get you a new one tomorrow," Diamond said. "I promise, first thing."

I knew she didn't mean to destroy anything. She just acted impulsively, drawing from her experience in the bush to sort things out. The trouble was, experience in the bush did not exactly translate to domesticity.

Bedsheets, for instance. They had pockets at the corners to fit the mattress. But after she'd washed the sheets, the art of folding them totally confounded Diamond. She had tried every which way, until one day, exasperated, she just rolled them into lumpy piles and heaped them up like colorful beach balls in the linen closet. From then on, she left her bed tidily made and returned to sleeping on the floor under her heavy safari jacket.

And then there was the remote control to the television in the little den downstairs. Actually, I had two remotes: one was for the satellite television, and one was for the CD player, though Diamond could never quite figure out where the music was coming from.

"Where the hell are the satellites?" she had asked me, peering up at the ceiling. And how could I explain that pushing a button on a rectangle of black plastic made the TV in front of us send beams into the heavens to change the station we were watching. Okay, maybe it didn't quite work like that, but Diamond accidentally deprogrammed each remote at least four or five times a week, sometimes in the middle of whatever we were watching, and the problem was that I had never quite mastered how to fix them.

My computer mystified her, and she regularly tried the TV remote to change an Internet site. She melted plastic containers into colorful puddles in the oven and stood flustered in the supermarket, staring at the skin and hair care products with amazement.

"Why does anyone need anything more than a nice soaking rain?" she would ask. I had no answer for her. Especially since she rarely saw a need for that, either.

I knew Diamond wanted to go home. And home meant sitting on a horse, traveling broken trails, listening to the wind for a certain cry that meant danger, sniffing the air for the telltale scent of a predator coming her way.

In her own way, she, too, was a child of the jungle. It didn't judge her—it had only wrapped itself around her and allowed her to survive.

And now I watched her as she got up to pour herself another cup of what was left of the morning coffee, even stronger for having been fermenting in its grinds all morning, and sit down again at the kitchen table. She looked solemn.

"Doesn't that keep you awake?" I asked her.

"Coffee doesn't bother me. I like to sleep light," she said. "So I can be ready."

I gave a little laugh. "But you're safe here." She nodded and burst into tears.

"You know, I was civilized once," she sniffed. "Honestly. I bet I could fit in again. I'm trying so hard."

I knew she had grown up in the city. That she had done all the things that are part of the civilized world. Opened gifts on Christmas morning, ridden subways and buses, and walked through shops that sold everything. I also knew that she had shoplifted food for dinner when her aunt had spent all their money on bottles of vodka, and that her Christmas gifts ultimately wound up being sold off for the same reason. I knew all those things about her. And I knew she had gladly left them all behind for wide skies and tall, rude trees and nights filled with a meadow of stars.

"What does civilized mean, anyway?" I asked, snapping open the bottle of wine I had brought home and passing it to her to take the first drink. It had been a question long on my mind, the quality of being civilized. "We've both lived civilized, and we've both lived wild." I stopped and took a breath before giving voice to something that had been on my mind since I had come home. "And I think wild was infinitely better."

"Civilized is overrated," Diamond agreed. "You can be civilized in your heart without all the other stuff."

The phone rang behind us, and Diamond-Rose reached for it and handed it to me.

I could see on the caller ID that it was Richie, which struck me as odd, since I had just left the farm.

"Hey," he said after we exchanged hellos, "are you ready for some news?"

"Only if it's good," I said.

"It isn't," he replied. "I just got a phone call. We found that really nice man."

Chapter 27

—∞∞∞—

SOMETIMES FATE MAKES A MISTAKE BECAUSE NO one was listening.

But sometimes, if you try hard enough, move fast enough, engage in a quick sleight of hand, you can convince fate to change its mind and turn everything around.

I was lucky that fate was giving me another chance. I was lucky, too, that the horse world is small but very public and very willing to help one another. The really nice man, traced quickly through Marielle's description of his truck and trailer, coupled with Richie's diligence, was definitely a buyer for the slaughter sales. His name was Lou Dickerson, and that's what he did for a living. He ran a kill pen. He posed as a nice man, promised he would take your free horse home to his children, promised that your horse would have a forever home, and resold it almost immediately to a slaughterhouse in Canada that was near the New York border. He wasn't really a nice man at all.

"Oh God, no," I gasped, when Richie gave me the news. "I have to go right away."

"Be careful" was all Richie could say. "And be prepared for the worst. Your horse may already be gone."

We ate dinner in silence that night. Diamond had made stew by mixing several cans of soup together, cutting up a few potatoes, then heating it all in one big pot. The blending of colors and ingredients looked odd, but I didn't have much of an appetite anyway.

"We're going first thing tomorrow," I said to Diamond, "since we won't be able to see horses in the dark. We'll leave before the sun comes up."

"Where are we going?" Diamond asked, ladling more stew into her bowl. The potatoes hadn't really cooked through, but Diamond said a good stew should have a little crunch to it.

"Lou Dickerson's stable is about two hours from here," I replied. "And he has a horrible reputation." I gulped back tears. "I never thought Mousi—" I couldn't finish my sentence. I put my head down on the table in my arms and wept.

Diamond rose from her chair to put her arms around my shoulders. "Here's one thing I learned a long time ago," she whispered. "Don't cry tomorrow's tears."

There are places on earth that are so wretched, that you would wonder why Providence had turned its back on them. When I helped rescue Margo, I saw poverty in Zimbabwe that shook me to my core—starving children, starving animals, people broken from desperation. When I returned to the States the first time, it was with a certain complacent belief that my own country was above such agony. I was wrong.

Anadilla Horse Sales was a two-hour drive from the sanctuary. Diamond and I made the sanctuary our first stop so that we could borrow Mrs. Wycliff's horse trailer. It was a roomy trailer with four large stalls and a dressing room in front, which meant we also needed to borrow Mrs. W.'s truck to pull it.

I grabbed my checkbook, though my own savings were rapidly shrinking, thinking I would offer everything I had to buy Mousi back, while Diamond, apparently not believing in the easy availability of fast food, filled her rucksack with peanut butter sandwiches, our passports, and a week's supply of cheroots, in case we had to chase Mousi over the Canadian border. Also tucked away in the bottom were her entire life savings from the last twenty years in Kenya. We had no idea how much Mousi's freedom would cost, and she wanted to make sure we had enough.

"I can't believe you'd do this for me," I said, weeping. "But if he costs a lot, I will pay you back. No matter what it takes."

"I'm not worried," Diamond said. "I know you'd do it for me."

She drove as I stared stonily out the window, unable to hold any kind of comprehensible conversation. All the mental images of Mousi that I had forced myself to repress over the past two weeks flooded into my mind. I was picturing the worst beyond the worst.

Diamond was smoking the cheroot clamped between her teeth and ripping along the highway at top speed, though she didn't have a valid New York license.

"You have such great roads here," she enthused. "I bet I could hit a hundred without a problem."

There was no sign outside the place. Just a rutted muddy driveway that wound off the main road and threaded its way through gnarled trees and thick, impenetrable groves of sharp-needled thornbushes.

"Ugly," I spat out.

"They're planted on purpose." Diamond pointed. "See how straight the lines are? They're to keep animals from escaping. They do that in Kenya, too. Almost the same kind of bushes. Only to keep the wild animals from raiding the farms."

One more turn and we found the pens. They were large, three of them, bordered by broken post-and-rail fences strung together with barbed wire and rotted rope. Several broken trucks chocked up on cement blocks littered the landscape, while broken horses stood quietly in the pens, waiting for their last trip. They stood without shelter or food or water or hope.

"It's a holding pen," said Diamond.

"I'm afraid to look around," I gasped. "What if I don't see him?"

"Toughen up," she commanded. "We're on a mission."

We slipped through the broken wire and wandered through reeking pens filled with horses and donkeys, one after the other, standing knee deep in piles of manure. I tried to scan each pen carefully, glad for once that Mousi's white coat, normally a nuisance to keep clean, would stand out against the dark, muddy coats of the other horses. Diamond and I walked through the pens together, gently pushing aside blind horses, injured horses, frightened and trembling animals, their starvation-rough coats plastered against prominent ribs and sharp bony hips. Pushing past horses with deep ragged wounds, horses down, horses nickering to us, begging for a last morsel of food or a sip of water.

"Bollocks! How does he get away with this?" Diamond demanded, gesturing to a small white shack that stood way off in the back of the property and apparently functioned as the office.

"He's been reported dozens of time," I said, "but the authorities don't care. Come on—we need to hurry."

"You're right." Diamond shook her head with disgust. "Let's just find your horse and get out of here. And then we can report him."

We combed through all three pens, but Mousi was not in any. There was another pen on the far side that held a few foals, but he wasn't there either.

"There's nothing else around," I said, sick with disappointment. "Maybe we can drive up to the border and ask if one of his trucks went through recently. Or maybe we can find the slaughterhouse and ask—"

"Shh." Diamond put a finger to her lips. "Listen."

I tilted my head and strained my ears. There was a muffled sound, a low, defeated whinny, but I couldn't place it. "Where is it coming from?"

Diamond climbed through a fence and stood for a

moment to look around before walking to a clearing behind the pens where a large rusted truck stood. A horse nickered softly from inside. I helped Diamond quietly lower the back ramp.

"Stay here," she cautioned me as she climbed up and peered in. "It may be something you don't need to see." She disappeared into its dark interior. "Looks like they were going to take this shipment pretty soon," she called down to me. "Bollocks, it's dark in here. Hey! Here's a white horse." She was quiet for a moment. "Bollocks!" she exclaimed again. "It doesn't look like the horse I saw at your brother's."

"Oh God," I said, holding my stomach. "I have to see for myself." I started up the ramp.

Diamond reappeared at the top. "Know what? I think it might be him. Just don't get upset at the way he looks."

I was up the ramp in a flash, my heart pounding, then taking tenuous steps inside until my eyes adjusted.

"If it's him, you'd better get him off straightaway," she said, throwing me an old frayed rope that she had pulled from somewhere inside the truck. She walked the rest of the way inside with me, then helped me drop a long metal bar that blocked our path to the back of the truck. The floors were slick with manure, and the ammonia smell burned my eyes as I tried to scan through the darkness for a white horse.

"First stall all the way in the back, on the left," Diamond whispered to me.

It was Mousi. He nickered when he saw me, and it was all I could do to keep from screaming out his name.

He had lost a lot of weight, he was filthy, and his mane was matted, but at least he was still alive. He was wedged in between two foals. I slid the rope around his neck and quickly took him from the stall, and walked him down the ramp while Diamond held the foals back.

I led him to the waiting trailer, but Diamond remained behind.

"Oh, Mousi," I whispered to him as I tied him inside, then gave him a long hug. "Mousi!"

I looked over my shoulder for Diamond, but she hadn't followed me. I retraced my steps—she was still in the big truck.

"Let's just pay for Mousi and get out of here," I urged her.

"We can't leave them here," Diamond said, pointing to the foals staring at us with large, frightened eyes. "Get some ropes," she said. "They're coming, too. And so are the others."

I looked back at Mrs. Wycliff's trailer. "How many are there?" I asked.

"It's too dark to count them," she replied, "so let's just unload them. We can't leave them."

Diamond was right. In my impatience to get Mousi home I had forgotten my own heart. We couldn't leave the others to be taken to slaughter. "How many do you think we can squeeze on the trailer?" I asked. "It only has four stalls."

Diamond squinted her eyes and calculated. "They're awfully thin, so I'm figuring two to a stall, Mousi in the aisle stall, and maybe one or two of these foals in the dressing room."

"That makes eleven," I said.

"Eleven sounds about right," Diamond said. "That's always been my lucky number."

There was a thin chestnut mare ready to foal, who had a

sweet face and a huge open gash across her neck and chest; a skeletal brown-and-white pinto gelding, obviously sick, judging by the amount of mucus pouring from his nose; an emaciated black-and-white pinto mare that was trembling violently in a corner—nine in all, not counting the foals.

A dark bay mare hobbled painfully over to the fence as we passed with the last horse and nickered to us before leaning her body against the precarious fencing for support. Diamond looked at me and raised her eyebrows.

"She'll make twelve," I said to Diamond.

"Twelve's always been my lucky number," she said.

We stuffed the mare in the middle next to Mousi and put the foals, who were huddling together and shaking with fear, into the dressing room and locked them in.

We had loaded them as fast as they could walk up the ramp—the pregnant mare, the babies, the geldings—before finally slamming the tailgate shut. Suddenly a loud shout echoed across the pen.

"What the hell you doing out there?" A rough-looking man in a yellow slicker slogged through the mud and manure toward us. He stopped and rapped his knuckles against the trailer. It must be Dickerson, I thought. He stuck his face right into mine, and I tried not to inhale his acrid cigar breath.

"I asked you a question," he snarled.

Diamond dug into her pocket and casually lit a cheroot. The smell resembled the paddocks we had just walked through. "I'm the one you need to be talking to," she said, taking a long drawn-out puff and casually directing it into Dickerson's face. It didn't faze him in the least.

"All right, then, I'll talk to you." He jerked his head toward the trailer. "What you got in there?"

"Twelve horses," I answered him in her place, trying to keep my voice from shaking. It was possible that Dickerson wouldn't even want to sell any. "How much for them?"

He stretched up to peer over the back gate. "Why, they're nothing but skinners," he sneered. "Look how you got them packed in there! Like sardines. Slaughterhouse won't take them in that condition."

Diamond was impatient to leave. "How much for all of them?" she asked, blowing an especially large puff of cheroot smoke in Dickerson's direction. It smelled particularly acrid.

"Are you kidding me?" He took a step back to avoid the smoke. "I can't be bothered. Biggest bunch of miserable shit I ever saw."

"Spare us the lectures," Diamond snapped. "Just give us a price so we can get out of here."

Dickerson flapped a hand at us, his face filled with a well-practiced disgust. "I won't buy a one," he said. "I wouldn't get a penny for any of them at the knacker's. Get them the hell out of here. Get them the hell off my property."

I looked at Diamond. A lightbulb sparked over her head. We were thinking the same thing. Diamond drew another long breath from her cheroot and blew it casually into Dickerson's face. Now he waved it away and gave a little cough.

Diamond gave me a defeated shrug. "You heard what the man said."

"I did," I replied.

"So, we'd better comply."

"We should."

We slammed the trailer doors shut and hurried into the truck.

"That's right," Dickerson called over his shoulder. "You just get them the hell out of here. Take them back home. I won't spend my good money on shit like that."

"Whatever you say, boss," Diamond yelled from the window, and gunned the engine. The truck groaned under the weight, and the front wheels spun as they tried to gain purchase against the mud. Diamond backed up slightly, then touched the gas again. The wheels grabbed and slowly rolled us forward rut by rut, slick mud to hard dirt, and back to slick mud. Diamond pressed the pedal for more gas, the truck heaved, and for one horrible moment, I thought we would get stuck. Finally we were moving from the driveway onto the solid asphalt of the highway.

Two miles away, I started breathing again. I turned to Diamond and gave her a sardonic grin. "I guess this makes us bona fide horse thieves."

Diamond hooted loudly. "Wouldn't be my first time," she said. "Now let's get your boy home."

Chapter 28

⎯⎯⎯⎯ ⦵⦵⦵ ⎯⎯⎯⎯

SHE HAD A TATTOO, THE DARK BAY MARE, WHICH meant she was a thoroughbred, an ex-race horse, bred to run, bred for better things, but there was nothing sleek or shiny about her now. We had saved her life, though there wasn't much of it left. She had to come off the trailer first, because she had been the last to load, and it took four of us—Diamond, me, Ignacio, and Richie—to help walk her down the ramp. She had tufts of dull brown hair that grew between the open sores of her skin. Thickened white scaly patches made an unsightly mosaic across her skeletal frame. One front leg angled sideways, obviously broken; her head hung low; and her sunken, dispirited eyes spoke of unremitting agony. I had never seen a horse look that bad, and I thought I was going to vomit.

"How is she even standing?" I said, and turned my face away. Diamond gave me a sharp jab of elbow.

"That won't help her," she said brusquely. "Let's get her into the barn."

We inched the horse along, encouraging each shaky step with gentle praise. She shuffled past Mrs. Wycliff, who had put on her pith helmet and come from the house to watch. "Get her settled in the isolation barn," she called to us, pointing to a small five-stall barn behind the main house. "Margo"—Mrs. Wycliff nodded her head at me—"get a hot bran mash going. And, Harry," she called over to Richie, "blanket her right away."

"There's a kitchen in the barn," I said to Diamond as we helped the horse into a stall. "It has a microwave and medications and an overnight cot and everything else we'll need."

"I'll call Dr. Harry," Mrs. Wycliff yelled after us. "He's a new vet, but he's good with these rescues. And, Jackie," she called after Diamond, "put extra shavings in the stall. I want it bedded deeply. Have Margo help you."

I was relieved when Mrs. W. mentioned a new vet. Her old vet had been my ex-husband, Matt, and he was the last man in the world I wanted to see.

"Poor Mrs. Wycliff," Diamond muttered as she filled a bucket of water for the horse. "We've all turned into Jackies and Harrys."

"Except for me," I corrected her. "I seem to have become an elephant."

The choreography of chores had everyone working. We got the rest of the horses off the trailer and into the barn, where they were put two to a stall, except for Mousi, who was given the foals for companions. Ignacio had unlocked the dressing room to the trailer and was almost knocked over by the foals, eager for freedom. Volunteers brought buckets of water, hay was thrown, and Mrs. Wycliff called the vet.

I was mixing buckets of warm bran mash for our new guests when the vet arrived. He was an intense, wiry man with dark hair and darker eyes set in a keen face with a thin, high-bridged nose that gave him the look of a raptor.

"This is Dr. Harry." Mrs. Wycliff introduced everyone as he entered the barn. She summoned Diamond-Rose for a handshake. "Harry meet Jackie." Diamond smiled as they shook hands, and he smiled back, his angular face relieved by a pleasant grin.

"And this—" Mrs. Wycliff pointed to me, then grew flustered. "And this is—well, now, you can't both be Jackie, can you?"

"No, ma'am," I said. "I'm Nee—"

"Oh, I remember!" Mrs. Wycliff interrupted. "You're Margo Sterling."

"Margo's the elephant," I said. "I'm—"

But Mrs. Wycliff was impatient. "Oh, you all know who you are, so just sort it out among yourselves." She toddled off toward the entrance to the barn. "I'm going up to the house for my special medicine," she said. "I'll have those horses cured in no time."

Dr. Harry decided that the bay mare was the worst off and immediately began treating her. We helped him sling her up to take the weight off her leg before he could examine her. Everyone stood in a little group outside her stall as he lifted her lip to expose anemic white gums, listened to her heaving chest, examined her eyes and ears, and took a skin scraping. Within minutes, he had drawn several vials of blood, administered antibiotics, and hooked her up to an IV for her severe dehydration. Then he kneeled down and began gently palpating her twisted front leg.

He deftly ran his hands across the deformed limb. "Must have been broken some time ago and never treated," he pronounced softly. "It feels healed over." His face registered disgust as he stood up again. "I won't bother x-raying it until we're sure she's going to survive. Save Elisabeth some money. Besides, I don't think I can fix it anyway."

"Will she live?" Diamond asked, moving next to him. "I've seen horses die in Kenya all the time because we couldn't get them to a vet."

"Well, this one's as bad as they come," Dr. Harry said. "There's not much more we can do except give her supportive therapy and hope she starts healing. But I wouldn't be surprised if she loses her battle before tomorrow morning."

Diamond threw her arms around the mare's bony head. "You leave it to me," she declared. "We're not going to let her die." She looked up at Dr. Harry, her face full of determination.

He smiled at her. "I appreciate your dedication, Jackie. But you have to know the odds are against her."

Diamond laughed and gave her red hair a little toss. "Actually, I'm Diamond-Rose."

"Oh." He looked confused and turned to me. "Then you must be Jackie."

"No, I'm Neelie Sterling."

"I thought I heard a Jackie," he said.

"Jackie's in Alabama," I said.

"I thought Elisabeth mentioned over the phone that *Margo* was in Alabama," he said.

"Margo is supposed to go to Alabama, but we want her to stay here," I tried to explain.

The confusion in his face cleared. "Right," he said. "Margo is going to stay and help run things."

"Margo's the elephant," I said. "Diamond and I are going to run things."

Dr. Harry gave up. "Well, I'm glad to meet you all again." He bent over to pack up his equipment. "I'll drop in tomorrow, but let me know right away if she worsens."

"And what should we call you?" Diamond asked.

"Oh, you can still call me Harry." He smiled back at her. "I'm Dr. Harry Maybern."

"The new horse's name is Black Silk Undies," I read, staring at the computer screen. It was late in the afternoon, and Richie, Diamond, and I were sitting in Elisabeth's office, where I had logged onto a Web site for racehorses to research the bay mare's tattoo. The computer was old, and it practically creaked as it downloaded the information. "And she's still a baby. She's only four years old."

I had gently opened the mare's mouth after Dr. Harry left and copied down the numbers tattooed inside her upper lip. The numbers meant she was a registered racehorse. I tapped a few keys to hunt through the site for more information. A race record came on the screen. "She's a daughter of War Dress out of a Black Kite mare," I read. "Very well bred. She's won more than seventy thousand dollars."

"Seventy thousand dollars!" Diamond gasped behind me. "How could someone let her wind up like this? She's more than paid for her retirement."

Richie leaned forward to study the information. "This happens a lot," he commented. "Some trainers run them until they break down and then just throw them away." He glanced at his wristwatch. "She's going to need her IV changed soon and some more hand feeding."

"Do you mind feeding her, Neelie?" Diamond asked. "I want to pop off to the store and get a camera. We're going to need pictures of this girl."

I looked up, puzzled. "What good are pictures going to do?"

"For the fund-raiser," Diamond replied. "Tusker's going to be our poster boy, and now we've got ourselves a mascot."

Silky was trembling under her blanket, even though the afternoon was fairly temperate. I took a fresh bag of Ringer's lactate solution and microwaved it in the barn kitchen before hooking it up to her IV. Though she was still shivering, I didn't want to load her up with too many blankets because I was afraid they might irritate her thin, hypersensitive skin and break it down even more. It was probably better to warm her up from the inside out with the most tempting mash I could put together, with grated carrots and a large dollop of honey. After I brought it to her, I held a handful against her lips, but she only dropped her head and looked away. I'd never seen horses refuse food like this before, so starved that they were beyond thirst or hunger, so shut down that they were beyond self-preservation.

"You have to eat," I urged her. "Please." The mare's eyes fluttered closed. I ran my finger inside her bottom lip and made a pocket where the bars of her jaws made a natural space, then pressed the mash in and pushed it onto her tongue. She let it stay there, too indifferent to even swallow. I reached in with two fingers and worked the food back toward her throat, but she didn't swallow. I tried to figure out what to do next.

What was the point, I wondered, to force her to eat like this? She was crippled. A racehorse bred for running, every muscle, every bone bred for the purpose of galloping along the ground in great, driving strides. She had given it all away, the gift of her speed and her hot blood and her generous, honest horse heart, all given over for her owner's pleasure and profit, and in return, he had peremptorily discarded her without a shred of regard. If she did survive, what kind of future could we give her? Would her heart break over and over again with each painful, shattered step she took? Would she end up able only to stand and stare across the green fields, knowing that she would never, could never run them again? What would she think about, realizing that her very essence of being a horse had been taken from her? I wiped away my tears with dried-mash fingers.

Suddenly the mare's throat and lips moved, and she swallowed. Joyfully, I pressed in another small mound, and she swallowed again. After a few feeding attempts the animal was exhausted.

"You're such a good girl," I murmured, pressing my face against her bony frame, but I had to look away from the blank eyes and wonder if I was doing her any favors.

"Bollocks! That old gal needs a lot of supervision," Diamond-Rose declared as she came into the barn. I was still in front of Silky's stall, talking softly to her and stroking her muzzle.

"I know," I agreed. "Feeding her takes forever, and Dr. Harry said she could even colic just from finally getting food."

"I mean Mum. You know—Elisabeth," Diamond said. "I would have come out sooner, but she set a small fire in the living room. Wanted to cook up some special mixture. I stopped her, but she insisted I bring this out with me." She held up a bottle of expensive brandy.

"No snifters?" I asked, amused. "Are we supposed to take turns swigging from it?"

"Not for us. This is her special horse medicine," Diamond explained. "She was going to mix it in a mash. Mum said she never lost an animal after pouring in a bottle of good brandy."

" 'Mum'? I've known her ten years, and I never got past Mrs. Wycliff."

Diamond threw her head back and laughed. "I think after you spend an hour fighting a couch fire in someone's living room while getting drunk on alcohol fumes with her, you deserve to be on a more intimate basis. I'm sort of her surrogate daughter now, so you can have your mum back. She'll probably be relieved to get rid of me."

"I think she was getting very fond of you," I protested.

"Thank you," Diamond said, "but I have a new mum. It would get too confusing." She opened the brandy and inhaled its aroma.

"Wonderful! Saint-Rémy Napoleon! Top drawer!" she exclaimed, then looked thoughtful. "Listen, would you mind taking the first shift with the mare tonight? I want to get working on that poster."

I shrugged. "I suppose not," I said. "I want to stay with Mousi anyway. He and I have a lot to talk about. I'll sleep on the cot in the barn kitchen. Just bring me food."

"I'll ask Richie to pick up some pizza," Diamond agreed. "And we'll have a go at this brandy. I'm not about to waste it on a horse."

It was a long, sleepless night. I changed Silky's IV, fed her every two hours, tossed restlessly on the canvas cot, only to jump up again to check on all the rescue horses. Mousi was eating well, but it would take some time to put weight back on him. The others gratefully ate the mash and hay put in front of them. I went from horse to horse, checking water buckets, fluffing hay, and watching for signs of colic.

The barn doors rolled open with the first light of dawn, and Diamond carried in a mug of hot cowboy coffee for me.

"Why don't you take a break?" she said. "I can handle things from here." She picked up the bucket of mash and began feeding tiny amounts to the mare.

"Thanks," I said, stretching my arms and arching my back to get the kinks out. "I just refilled her IV and mixed a new mash."

A car pulled up outside.

"Dr. Harry," we said together.

"She's still alive?" Dr. Harry called out as he strode through the barn doors a moment later.

"Yes, she is," Diamond said. "She ate a little, got her IV changed. She's really trying." She stepped away so that he could examine the horse.

"You did a good job," he said.

"Thank you," she murmured, and gave me a meaningful look. I got the hint.

"I have some work to do," I said. "I want to look through Mrs. Wycliff's files to see what kind of records she kept on the horses."

"Great idea," said Diamond. "There's probably enough stuff to keep you busy all morning." I gave her a grin and left them alone in the barn, wondering if Diamond was ready to take her heart to a crossroad again.

The sun felt warm against my face, although there was an insistent breeze that came up from the fields and penetrated my jacket. Winter would soon be taking its bitter turn, a hostile season that brought its own harvest. I thought with sadness of the weakened, starving animals that wouldn't survive the cold weather, and of Tusker, whose life was shortening with each passing day.

"Hey!" Richie was walking toward me carrying several large bags of apples and carrots. "I plan to look in on the horses after I finish with the other animals," he said. "How's that mare doing?"

I shrugged. "I guess we won't know for a while." We walked silently together until we reached the elephant barn. "I have to talk to Tom again," I said to Richie. He only nodded.

Richie rolled open the doors to the barn, and we were

greeted with a happy duet of trumpeting from Margo and Abbie. We stepped inside, and Margo lifted her trunk expectantly. Richie tossed a bunch of carrots into her open mouth, then caressed her face as she ate them.

"She's a lucky girl," he said.

"I'm thinking of all the ones we can't save," I said miserably. "Please help me convince Tom to save Tusker."

Richie's mouth tilted into a sad line. "You may have to accept that you can't," he said. "And the terrible thing is, after Tusker, there will be more. It's something Tom knows but you haven't learned yet. There are always more elephants."

Chapter 29

"HE WHO WANTS WHAT IS UNDER THE BED, MUST bend over to get it," Diamond announced over dinner.

I was about to drop a slice of pizza onto a paper plate, which we were using now that I was down to one real dinner plate. "The only things under my bed are dust bunnies," I said.

"What I mean is, you have to work hard to get what you want."

"So?"

"So, we made the money to hold the fund-raiser. Now our job is to get people to come to it." She stabbed a slice with her safari knife and ate it as it dangled from the tip.

"I don't know any people," I said.

"Yes, you do," Diamond said between bites, "and stop staring at me. You'd think you'd never seen anyone eat pizza before. You promised you would call Tom when we finished raising the money."

"I can't," I said. "I can't stop staring, and I can't make the call. And besides, we don't have enough money for a big party."

"No, not one of those fancy things that you see given by the queen of England. We'll have a barbecue."

"No barbecues!" I jumped from my chair in protest, dropping my pizza. "I hate barbecues! They're smoky and smelly, and I always had to clean the grill."

"It's the most practical way to do things."

"No barbecue and no Tom," I insisted, then sat down again. "Besides, Tom hates me."

"You have to call him," Diamond said. "He's the key to our success."

"You're wrongly assuming he wants us to succeed." I reached for more pizza.

Diamond flipped her knife across the table, pinning my slice to the cardboard box, then reached behind her head, grabbed the kitchen phone, and tossed it to me. "Call Tom."

I shook my head. "The last time I spoke to him we were in his car and were barely civil to each other, and I'm positive he hates me now."

"Call him and tell him that you're sorry and that you love him," she said, "and that you need him. And maybe his mother, too."

"Are you crazy?" I eyed the knife. It had penetrated the pizza and the box, pinning both to my wooden kitchen table underneath. "I don't love him, I don't love his mother, and I don't want to talk to either one of them."

Diamond folded her arms and gave me a disgusted look. "You know," she said, "he is a fool whose sheep get away twice."

"Would those sheep be under my bed?" I asked sarcastically. "Owned by the man who's bending over?"

"It means you've already made one mistake letting Tom go," Diamond snapped. "How many times do you think that you're going to find true love? Do you know what I'd give—" She stopped herself and plucked her knife from my dinner. "So call him before we run out of time, or I will." She flipped the knife into the air and caught it neatly by the handle. "And I can be very convincing."

"Neelie?" Tom's voice was a mixture of surprise and icy curiosity. "To what do I owe this pleasure?" Though it was a small victory that Tom even answered my call, I thought I detected a note of sarcasm in his last word.

"I need to talk to you?" I said, trying to control my voice, though my nerves were getting the best of me. "I—that is, we—Diamond and I—are holding a fund-raiser? You know? To be able to save that elephant I told you about?" Why was I talking like a fourteen-year-old Valley girl and ending my sentences with interrogatives? "And we need people to attend?"

"Is this a joke?"

"I'm serious?" I had to stop, I had to stop—why was I talking like this? "It's our only chance to save Tusker?"

There was a long pause. "Tom?" I asked miserably.

"I warned you about Tusker, and do you really think I would help you defeat my own plans?"

I mounted my argument. "You didn't have any plans, except to wait until he got shot? We want to *save* him, not stuff him."

"I'm not discussing that elephant with you again. I'm just advising, no, I'm demanding that you not get involved," he said. "And if you weren't so pigheaded, I would—"

" '*Demanding*'?" I shouted. "What makes you think you can demand anything? And how dare you call me pigheaded, when I'm trying to save—"

"I'm not in the mood to argue with you." His tone was that of a parent talking to a recalcitrant child. "In fact, I think you'd—"

"I don't need you!" I interrupted him angrily. "I'll bet your mother would help. In fact, I know her name and her address, and I know she loves animals, and I'm going to call her. I just wanted to give you another chance. I was just hoping you'd have a change of heart."

"My heart never changes," he said quietly.

That caught me off guard. "Yes it does," I said. "Because now you hate me."

"I don't hate you," he said. "I could never hate you."

"Maybe you don't hate me now, but you will after I go ahead with my plans." I stopped myself. I didn't want to bicker—it was so old stuff. "I wish things were different."

Suddenly he laughed. "I have to give you this, you are the most determined woman I have ever met. I forgot how single-minded you can be."

"Then you'll attend? Or ask your mother if she'd be interested?"

"No, I won't," he said firmly. "First of all, I have plans

for the sanctuary, and someday, if you would let me finish a sentence, I'll tell you about them. In the meantime, I am strongly advising you, no, *ordering* you to stay out of the Tusker thing. It's going to create a disaster in ways you can't begin to imagine. Secondly, I don't want my mother involved. She's got too many charities on her plate already."

"Of course I remember you," Mrs. Pennington said after I nervously introduced myself over the phone. "You're the young woman who went to Africa with Tom."

"To rescue Margo," I added. "You know, the elephant that shares her name with you."

"Actually, I share *my* name with her, dear," she corrected me. "And didn't you break things off with my son?"

"I was saving more elephants," I replied.

"How perfectly thoughtful of you," she said. "But I'm wondering why you called."

I took a deep breath to calm myself. "Well, I'm the president of ELLI. It's the Elephant Liberation League Internationale, and we're holding a fund-raiser so we can save another elephant," I explained, helpfully leaving out the part that we were doing it even though her son had explicitly ordered me not to.

"I'm sorry," Mrs. Pennington apologized. "I don't think I can help. I don't know anything about elephants. And besides, I've been donating my time and money to victims of the raging tornadoes they've had in the South."

"Raging tomatoes?"

"Oh my goodness!" exclaimed Margo Pennington. "Who mentioned tomatoes?"

"I thought you did. In any case, we're both trying to save lives," I said. "And it's a good thing to save lives."

"I appreciate what you're doing, my dear," she said, "but the only other charities I care about are the ones that deal with horses."

"Well, we did just rescue a starved race mare."

Margo Pennington sounded surprised. "A race mare?" she repeated. "A *thoroughbred*?"

"Yep. Well bred, too," I replied. "But you know how breeders are. Some of them just don't care what happens after they're done running their horses. I don't know where she'll go if we close down."

"Oh, poo! A good breeder always keeps a spot open for old horses," she countered.

"The *good* breeders do," I agreed. "But they're few and far between. If we run out of funds, we might have to euthanize her."

There was a silence. "You say the sanctuary has been taking in old racehorses?"

"Yes, ma'am," I said, thinking that somewhere out in the pasture of fifty-seven fat, homely, short-strided, lumpy mongrel horses there had to be at least one more thoroughbred.

"But didn't you say your organization was called ELLI— for elephants?"

I thought for a moment. "Did I say 'elephant'?" I gasped. "I must have Margo on my mind. ELLI stands for *Equine* Liberation League Internationale. For the horses. They come from everywhere, you know."

"Well, that certainly sounds like a worthy cause," Mrs. Pennington reflected. "Horses."

"Yes, ma'am. Horses," I agreed, suddenly realizing I was onto a good thing. "Ex-racehorses."

"Well, I'm certain Tom probably won't agree with what I'm doing, and I don't like to contradict his plans," Mrs. Pennington said. "So you'll have to promise me we won't breathe a word of this to him."

"He's not speaking to me," I cheerfully reassured her. "But it's a worthy cause. You have to think of all those horses." I waited for her while she thought of them.

"Okay, I'll come," Margo Pennington announced. "For the horses."

"And an elephant or two," I added quickly. "And we would love for you to bring any friends along."

"I suppose I could," she agreed.

"That's so kind of you," I gushed. "So very kind, and we would be so very grateful. And the ex-racehorses would be so very grateful, all those ex-racehorses just waiting to be rescued would be very grateful. And the elephants, of course. Hugely grateful. Bring everyone you can."

"Thank you, dear," Margo Pennington replied. "If you don't mind, I might even be able to convince Victoria to come. She knows an awful lot of horse lovers in her circle of friends."

"Victoria?"

Yes, Victoria Cremwell, of the Boston Cremwells," Margo Pennington replied. "She's the woman Tom's going to marry."

Chapter 30

I SAT WITH THE PHONE CRADLED IN MY LAP.

"I don't suppose you have a proverb for a fool who never saw this coming," I said to Diamond.

"Only this," said Diamond. "You have to invite the bees to get honey."

I stood up and placed the phone back into its cradle. "Well, I've certainly been stung in the butt."

Diamond gave my shoulder a little squeeze. "Bees bring honey, people bring money. It doesn't matter who they are."

"It does matter," I protested. "I have a strong impulse to call Margo Pennington back and tell her to forget it. I don't think I can stand to meet Tom's fiancée."

"Well, then," said Diamond. "Here's another proverb for you: cutting off your nose to spite your face."

I looked at her in surprise. "Is that Kenyan?"

"No, you idiot," said Diamond. "That's just common sense."

Mrs. Elisabeth Wycliff had a wonderful barbecue planned.

After overhearing me and Diamond arguing over the type of fund-raiser to hold, she made copious lists and hand-wrote the invitations herself, in a fine calligraphy, which stated that Mr. and Mrs. Harold Wycliff were requesting the honor of the presence of their many friends. She had even issued a special invitation to one of Harold's more influential business acquaintances, the president of the United States, Ronald Reagan. There were three major problems, though. One was that the host himself and most of their friends were deceased and wouldn't be able to make it. Secondly, Mrs. W. preempted us by getting the date wrong by several weeks earlier than we had planned, and thirdly, she decided that her living room was the perfect intimate venue, which meant that supplemental guests eventually included several members of the local fire department as well as a few individuals from law enforcement.

Luckily, Richie spotted the smoke early on and pulled Mrs. Wycliff, dressed in her flannel nightgown and pith helmet, to safety before calling the fire department. They had just arrived, sirens wailing and lights flashing, when Diamond and I pulled into the driveway to start our day. We both jumped from the car and raced to Mrs. Wycliff's side.

"There's plenty for everybody," announced a delighted Mrs. Wycliff as the firefighters quickly clambered from their fire trucks and began pulling hoses from the back. "No need to rush."

"Oh, thank heaven! The cats!" Diamond shouted as a man came out of the back door, two cats under each arm. Another fireman led the black Labs.

"They're fine," he reassured her. "I got them all."

"What on earth are those?" I asked the fire chief as his men carried out several lumpy, smoldering objects.

"I believe she was roasting the pillows to her kitchen chairs," he replied. "Luckily there wasn't much actual fire because of the fire retardant in the material, but there's an awful lot of smoke."

"Glad there was no other damage," Richie replied. "Pillows are easy enough to replace."

"I'm afraid you'll have to replace her whole kitchen set," said the fire chief. "She used the chairs for kindling."

Mrs. Wycliff stood on the front lawn, wrapped in a blanket, and watched the proceedings. "I had such a wonderful dessert planned, too," she mourned. "Pity these bush parties break up so early." She coughed hard several times, and a concerned-looking Richie took her hand to lead her to the ambulance.

"I couldn't possibly leave my guests," she protested as they gently lifted her onto a gurney. "I was planning to entertain them with a song. Everyone loves my voice."

"You can sing later," Richie reassured her. "As soon as we know you're okay and they let you come back home."

"But I'm fine," she insisted. "Listen." She cleared her throat and started on a shaky rendition of "Meet Me in St. Louis." As the men lifted her into the ambulance and pulled away, Richie turned to me. "This is just what I've been warning you about. She can't run this place. We could have had a catastrophe. She has no family, you know, and the hospital may not even release her unless there's someone here to watch over her." He ran a hand through his hair and sighed. "I'll have to call Tom to see what we can figure out."

"No! Not Tom!" I grabbed his arm. "Maybe we can help."

"She needs constant supervision," Richie said, running his fingers distractedly through his hair again. "How could you do that?"

"I can watch her," Diamond volunteered. "I don't mind."

"You'd have to move in with her," Richie countered. "She can't be left alone anymore."

Diamond shrugged. "She's like a mum to me, anyway."

Richie considered this. "You'd have to move in right away. How long will it take you to pack?"

"I'm packed," Diamond replied. "I live packed."

The house was empty without Diamond-Rose. There was no one to wake me up at the first light of dawn with a loud rap on my bedroom door followed by a barrage of gorilla hoots. My morning coffee didn't accelerate my heart rate to supersonic speeds. There was no one paring her toenails at the table because the light was better in the kitchen. Or flinging a safari knife across the room to secure the last lamb chop.

And no one to sit with on the back porch during lonely evenings to talk of things wild and domestic, and ponder what it really meant to be civilized.

The day had barely started when my phone rang. I peered out from under my pillow, trying to make sense of the clock on the nightstand. It was almost five.

"You'd better have a good reason for calling me in the middle of the night," I said, annoyed.

"You're wasting the day!" Diamond exclaimed into my ear.

"You know, a person cannot pick up a pebble with one finger."

"Why are you picking up pebbles this early in the morning?"

"It's an old saying," Diamond answered. "It means I need your help."

"Sorry, help doesn't start until after seven a.m.," I said. "Call back later."

"It's about the fund-raiser," Diamond said. "Come for breakfast, and I'll tell you what I came up with."

"I'm not leaving my bed this early."

"Oh, don't be such a baby," Diamond scolded. "I'll make the coffee. Mum is already barbecuing eggs, and you can bring the usual."

There was a bloodcurdling scream in the background.

"Elisabeth just have some of your coffee?" I asked.

"Oh, that's Samantha," Diamond explained. "She's a cockatoo. Brought in late last night. Her owner died and left her to the sanctuary."

"Cup you!" the bird yelled. "Cup you!"

"What?" I asked.

"I'm not sure," Diamond said, "but I think she wants a cup of orange juice."

"Cup you!" the bird repeated. "Cup you! Cup you!"

"It sounds awfully like cursing." I yawned and sat up.

"Yeah," Diamond agreed. "But the poor thing isn't quite getting it." She turned away from the phone. "You're saying it wrong," she corrected the bird. "Listen carefully. It's *fuck* you. Fuck you."

"Don't say another word," I yelled at her. "I'll be right there."

They were sitting at the kitchen table in Elisabeth's new folding chairs, Diamond and Elisabeth Wycliff, along with a large pale pink cockatoo, who sat on the back of a chair, shredding a paper cup. She quickly dropped the cup and turned to me with shining onyx eyes.

"Meet Samantha," Diamond said. "She's very friendly."

I reached over to stroke the soft pink feathers. "Wow," I said, "she's beautiful."

"Cup you!" The orange crest on Samantha's head stood straight up as she opened an amazingly large beak and clamped down on the tip of my finger. "Cup you!" she squawked. "Cup you!"

"I see she's a carnivore," I said, pulling my throbbing finger from the bird's grip.

"Oh, no," said Elisabeth, holding her hand out to the bird, who stepped lightly onto it and cooed. "She's very gentle and sweet. Wouldn't hurt a fly. Isn't that right, Sammy?"

"I love you," Samantha murmured to her, then squinted in my direction. "Cup you."

"Sit down and enjoy breakfast," Diamond said to me, pulling out a folding chair and serving me two char-grilled eggs. "Mum cooked." Diamond had set up a small barbecue in the kitchen to channel Mrs. Wycliff's proclivity toward arson into a more useful skill. A saucepan filled with thick black coffee sat on the coals next to a small frying pan. Diamond gave me a significant raise of the eyebrows. "We want to keep Mum happy," she said, "*don't we?*"

"So what plans have you made for the fund-raiser?" I asked, taking a small taste of blackened eggs before surreptitiously slipping them downward to the black Labs. Diamond poured me a cup of coffee.

"We're going to have food-on-a-stick," she declared.

"Did you say '*food-on-a-stick*'?" I repeated. "That's just

a sneaky way of saying barbecue! I hate barbecues! They're
. . . cheesy."

"Food-on-a-stick is not barbecue, it's a theme," Diamond
said, picking up the list she had made. "And themes are fun."

"Food-on-a-stick is not a theme, it's a *barbecue*," I argued.
"It's where you cook it."

"It doesn't matter *where*," Diamond said, "it's the spirit.
Food-on-a-stick has a fun spirit that will hook people in."

"It's stupid," I said, picturing Tom's elegant mother
waving a barbecue-sauced drumstick between her dainty
fingers and slugging from a can of beer. And I could imagine
Tom's fiancée—*Victoria*—laughing herself silly over our attempts to appear sophisticated. "And besides, how do you
get everything on a stick? Like drinks, for instance? How do
you put drinks on a stick?"

"You make margaritas and piña coladas"—Diamond smiled
triumphantly—"and freeze them with a stick in the middle."

"That solves only drinks," I protested. "The rest is still
just barbecue."

"No, the trick is to have the unusual," Diamond answered. "And since Mum and I figured out the theme, your
contribution is to figure out how to do the soup and salad."

"I even thought of dessert on a stick," Mrs. Wycliff put in
modestly. "Ice cream cake! And I invited a very special guest,
an old friend of mine, and I'm going to donate all my old ball
gowns, just like they do at the Smithsonian. Oh, it's going to
be a grand party."

Chapter 31

⎯⎯⎯⎯⎯⎯⎯⎯⎯⎯

OUR FIRST HORSE RESCUE APPEARED TO BE A SUCCESS.
The pregnant rescue mare foaled a tiny filly, and Mousi made friends with the Gang of Fifty-seven, as I had taken to calling the original horses out in the field, though some of their numbers had been sold. Some of the new rescues were turned out with them.

But mostly Diamond and I were inordinately proud of our success with Silky, because the bay mare was still alive.

We had all taken turns feeding her. Even Mrs. Wycliff helped, though I suspected by the occasional strong smell of brandy on Silky's breath, the mash had been spiked. We were giving her small handfuls of grain now, the IVs were gone, and today Dr. Harry had an appointment to remove the sling that was keeping Silky upright and off the damaged leg. He had strongly suggested that if she failed to stand on

258 | JUDY REENE SINGER

her own, she should be euthanized. She would lose stewardship over her life.

Diamond was waiting impatiently in the barn. She had been
trying to capture Dr. Harry's attention for weeks, offering
him a puff of her cheroot, leaning into him when they worked
on Silky, trying to impress him by double flipping her safari
knife high in the air and ending with his jacket pinned to a
stall door, even though he sometimes was wearing it. Occasionally she would entertain him with a private but earsplit-
ting rendition of the night mating call of the spotted hyena,
always brandishing her chestnut hair like a flag of availability
when he looked her way. She had even offered to lasso and
tie him in under a minute to show him her roping skills,
but I knew none of it was going to work. I knew as soon as I
saw Dr. Harry's neat haircut, the clean oxford shirt and navy
slacks he wore under his coveralls, the way his boots were
always polished, the tidy way he packed up his instruments
when he was finished. I knew as soon as I saw him eye Diamond's crusty safari clothes, her boots that had accumulated
twenty years of exotic grime, the thick gray knee socks, twin
companions to the boots in terms of hygiene. I knew from
the look on his face when she tossed things into a heap in the
aisle, used syringes and cotton wipes, and baling twine and
empty medicine packets, which he promptly retrieved and
threw away.

"You don't need to worry, I got it covered," Diamond
said when I came into the barn that morning. "I've already
planned my day around helping Dr. Harry."

"I know," I reassured her with a smile. "I won't get in your way, I just want to see how the mare does. I'll leave as soon as he checks her over." I walked over to Silky and rubbed my fingers up and down the thin blaze on her face.

"Oh, Neelie," Diamond suddenly said, giving me a mournful look. "Am I trying too hard? You know, with him? Before I was married, I never had any trouble getting a guy in Kenya, but maybe that was because it was me or the monkeys."

"You're very attractive," I reassured her, "but with my two hundred percent failure rate, I'm the last one to give advice. Are you sure you're really ready? I mean, you're the one who talked of hearts and roads and intersections and all that."

"I know." She sighed. "But I'm lonely. And I've decided to put myself officially back on the road map."

Punctual as usual, Dr. Harry arrived a few minutes later, bounding into the barn and bidding us all a friendly good morning before examining the mare.

"Swelling isn't down yet," he said, looking over the leg, "but let's see how she stands." He unhooked Silky from the sling and eased her gently down, onto her feet. She took a wobbly step and collapsed in a heap into the straw bedding.

"Oh no!" Diamond and I exclaimed together.

"Give her a minute," Dr. Harry cautioned.

The mare struggled to regain her footing. She extended her front legs and pressed against them to stand, then groaned from the effort. She fought for a few minutes more, trying to throw her body forward to lift it, but it was too much of an effort and she finally dropped down. Dr. Harry hooked her up to the sling, and we helped him work the winch to lift her again to her feet.

"You're lucky she's tolerating this," he said to us when we were finished. "A lot of horses fight the sling like crazy, but I think it's time we did the right thing by her. Even if we save her, she won't be much use." He waited for our response. Diamond moved to the horse's side.

"What do you think, Neelie?" she asked.

I looked at the mare. Diamond and I had taken turns gently brushing her scrungy hair. Tufts of new growth were beginning to cover her still-bony frame. She had put on a little weight and nickered for her meals now. And her eyes had taken on a cautious interest in her surroundings. Regaining her trust would take a long time, but she was fighting to live, at least that much belonged to her.

"I can't," I said. "At least, not yet." Diamond nodded in agreement.

Dr. Harry shook his head and picked up his medical bag. "I know this farm is on a budget. You'd do better spending your money on horses that can be useful. She needs a humane end. There's nothing wrong in that. My official opinion is why wait for the inevitable."

I saw a look cross Diamond's face. She accompanied Dr. Harry to the front of the barn, where she solemnly shook his hand.

"I guess it's not something you'd understand," she said. "But we're not saving her for us, we're saving her for her."

"So, Margo is leaving right after the party," I said glumly to Diamond as we drove the old pickup down to the lion enclosure to heave yellow basketball-shaped frozen chickens over their fence. "She'll become a corporate elephant, and I won't see her anymore." The truck transmission, having been burdened beyond its capacity when we used it to rescue the twelve horses, was emitting ungodly squeals.

"We're going to need a fund-raiser for a truck, before long," Diamond commented as it shuddered over the rocky field. The lions trotted to the gate and grabbed the chickens in their jaws. "I wonder why it never bothered Richie to toss them chicken," she mused. "Him being a vegetarian, and all."

"Maybe because we have a choice and animals don't. They're kind of hardwired to eat what they have to," I replied. "I always wished I could be a vegetarian. Ethically I am, but stomachly I still crave cheeseburgers."

"I never thought about it," Diamond said, watching one of the lions carry off a chicken. "You're lucky to eat what you can find in Kenya. I think being a vegetarian is an issue for people who aren't starving."

Margo trumpeted from her pen, announcing she was ready for her lunch.

"How am I ever going to be able to say good-bye to her?" I mused aloud.

"It'll be okay," Diamond said, bending over and picking up another raw chicken, then paused. "I wonder if it tastes better underhand or overhand," she said, tossing the chicken to the waiting cat. "Anyway, letting Margo go is the right thing to do. I knew you'd come around."

"How did you know?"

She stood in the bed of the truck and put her hands on her hips. The wind blew her hair around in red swirls, and she looked like a wildflower. "Because it isn't fair to stand in the way of her finding a new family."

I stopped what I was doing to ask something that had been on my mind for a long time. "Family seems to mean so much to you, I wonder why you and Jake never had children."

"Oh," she said sadly, and I was immediately sorry that I had been so intrusive. "You know how we know Joshua Mukomana?"

"No," I said, puzzled at the odd response. "How?"

She gave me a rueful smile. "He and Jakob were roommates at Harvard Law."

"Roommates?" I repeated, surprised. "But Joshua is about—"

"Sixty-seven years old," she said, throwing the last of the chicken to the lions. "And so was Jake. I didn't marry him for romance. Our marriage wasn't like that at all." She stopped. "I guess I married him for family. And I wanted family so bad. He took very good care of me. But he was like a father more than anything. There was never any romance there. Do you know what I mean? He *loved* me. And it was enought for me"

I thought I did understand. "Well," I said, starting the truck up again and waiting for her to climb into the passenger seat. "If we have no one else, we can always make families out of our rescues, right?"

"Of course," Diamond said as we watched the lions trot away with their catch. "A heart that is big enough to hold elephants can hold everything else."

We spent the remaining weeks before the fund-raiser in whirlwind activity, coaxing donations from anyone within a fifty-mile radius, managing to procure food, live music, the free rental of tables and chairs, linens, grills, decorations, fresh flowers, heaters to keep the temperature comfortable, as well as recruiting a faithful coterie of volunteers to help run it all.

"I think it's my clothing," Diamond said modestly, after another successful day of contributions. She had by now changed to more seasonal attire, brown-and-green camouflage slacks with a matching long-sleeved shirt, topped off with her usual red bolo string tie, and in deference to the weather, an all-weather camouflage jacket.

"Wow," I enthused when she showed the list of donors, then added with a sigh, "all I got for a donation was a few dozen donuts. You must be giving them a great speech."

"Yep." Diamond nodded. "I have the whole routine down. First I introduce myself, talk about ELLI, warm up with imitations of some common jungle birds, throw in the call of the howler monkey, and then before I even finish with my specialty hyena screams, they're very eager to help me out."

We had decided to hold the party in the elephant barn. It was the biggest structure on the grounds, although it meant leaving Margo in her paddock under the stars while I spent a few days scrubbing the elephant barn clean, whitewashing the walls, and at the last minute, directing two men who installed a jigsaw puzzle of wooden flooring across the cement.

"I never thought a party would entail so much stuff," I grumbled to Diamond as we watched the men snap the large square pieces together. "We'll never get it all done."

"We will if we keep working," Diamond replied. "As they say in Kenya, you eat an elephant one bite at a time." She clapped her hand to her mouth. "Sorry. No offense meant."

But she was right. We didn't stop for anything, and at last, fresh flowers stood in beautiful arrangements on tables draped in leopard-print tablecloths, ribbon garlands hung across the walls secured to blown-up photos of the animals that lived in the sanctuary, and strings of tiny white lights crisscrossed the ceiling as if it were a runway. Finishing the last job of the day, Diamond hung two huge posters, donated by the local printing shop, of Tusker and Silky to inspire our guests. Silky's picture had been taken the day after we brought her home, and she looked gaunt and disconsolate. Above it hung a photo of Tusker, the sunlight filtering behind him as he reached toward Diamond for the piece of cheese from her lunch. Next to his picture was a large calendar with the days counted off with red crosses.

"If those pictures don't break your heart," I said, standing back to make sure both pictures were straight, "then you have no heart at all."

"They're our real guests of honor," Diamond agreed, stapling the calendar to the wall over her head. "There, it's done."

"Good job," I said gratefully. "I can't believe how fast you pulled this all together."

"It's my safari training," Diamond explained, jumping down from the ladder. "I learned a long time ago, if you dally, you get eaten by lions."

Chapter 32

THE PURPOSE OF A PARTY IS TO BRING PEOPLE together. Sometimes for fun, sometimes for profit, sometimes to meet new people. Diamond was hoping for the first two, I was dreading the last.

In general, I hate parties and would really have preferred to hide in the elephant paddock with Margo and Abbie, away from the chatter and noise. I didn't want to waste one precious second that I could be with Margo, but I had to play hostess, along with Diamond-Rose and Richie and Jackie, who came up from Alabama just for the occasion, and Mrs. Wycliff, who greeted her guests in a cranberry velvet evening gown, pith helmet, and pink cockatoo. And wherever the two of them went, Samantha put her own spin on the social niceties.

"Harold and I are so glad you could make it," Mrs. Wycliff

would murmur, graciously extending her hand to each new arrival. "Please do come in and enjoy one of our lovely drinks. They're on sticks, you know."

"Fuck you!" Samantha would add genially from her shoulder, now having been properly schooled by Diamond. "Fuck you!"

My parents were the first to arrive, both carrying large plastic containers.

"Mom, you didn't have to bring anything!" I exclaimed. "It's a theme party. We wanted everything to be on a stick."

"I know, dear." She held out the container for me to inspect. "That's why I made three hundred breadsticks."

Reese and Marielle arrived soon after, Reese waving a list of elephant jokes he had specially unearthed for the occasion.

" 'What's the similarity between elephants and plums?' " he read off.

It was the last thing I needed to hear. "Come on, Reese, I'm too busy for this."

" 'They're both gray,' " he said. " 'Except, of course, for the plums.' "

I ignored him and busied myself giving the band a place to set up—the only place available was in the elephant cage, which didn't exactly please them—and directing guests to Silky's stall to view the mare, now a hundred pounds heavier than in her picture and meticulously groomed with bows tied into her mane. I also gave a few brief tours to the top of the elephant field, where guests could glimpse Margo and Abbie through the fencing.

But Reese is never discouraged. "Why did Hannibal try to conquer the world on plums?" he asked as I now made my way to the grills.

"Reese, please," I protested.

"Because he was color-blind and couldn't tell them from the elephants," he called after me as I walked away. "Get it? He was riding plums? *Plums!*"

I stood in the doorway of the elephant barn, dressed in a long skirt and velvet blouse and shook hands with 182 people, laughed at 77 inane remarks, explained 100 times about ELLI and how Margo got rescued, and answered yes, Silky had been a racehorse, while thinking at least ten times about the irony of how I had once told Tom how I would hate to stand around in a long gown making small talk.

All the while, I dreaded that Mrs. Pennington was going to bring Miss Victoria Cremwell. Of the Boston Cremwells. I wondered what she would look like. Did Tom have a certain type that he was attracted to? I mean, aside from the obvious of gray, wrinkled, and enormous. I wondered what I would say to her, and if that gnawing sensation in my gut was a craving for something-on-a-stick that was grilling on a corner barbecue or jealousy. In addition, I was trying to keep a watchful eye on Diamond's knife-throwing proclivities and Mrs. Wycliff's feathered shoulder accessory.

Diamond had dressed for the occasion by actually treating herself to a purchase of new safari-brown wool slacks, green silk tank top and matching jacket, and pinning her hair up in big, loose, swirls secured with a skewer, thus launching hair-on-a-stick as a fashion statement. I watched with a sinking heart as she enthusiastically demonstrated her roping skills by hog-tying each guest as they came through the door. Occasionally she would perform her whirling safari knife flip, catching the blade deftly by the handle before it had a chance to behead her captive audience as they cowered in terrorized fascination. On the other side of the room Mrs. Wycliff, encouraging everyone to kiss the lovely pink bird, who, not as socially accomplished as she, responded by nipping the lips of each and every taker.

Mrs. Margo Pennington finally swept through the door, swathed in a full-length black mink coat. Behind her was a beautiful woman with pale blond upswept hair and dark, thick-lashed eyes. She was very petite and dressed in a pale yellow tailored suit with gold jewelry, which gave her the appearance of a fragile but wealthy canary. Mrs. Pennington and her guest stopped near the entrance to look around, obviously seeking out their hostess.

Which would be me.

"Is that animal fur?" Richie hissed indignantly to me as I tried to slip behind him to hide. "Is Tom's mother actually wearing the skin of a deceased animal to an *animal sanctuary?*"

"Please don't make a fuss," I whispered back. "She's our guest of honor. Besides, I'm having enough trouble trying to keep Diamond from stabbing our guests, and Elisabeth and that stupid cockatoo from maiming them. I'm starting to wish that Diamond would solve all my problems and accidentally knife that damn bird."

But Richie wasn't listening. "And it's bad enough you're serving meat," he grumbled, now gesturing to the volunteers circulating with platters of salmon or steak cubes on skewers. "What are you giving out for door prizes? Ivory necklaces?"

"I believe you're the one we're looking for." Mrs. Pennington gave a little wave as she sailed toward me, the gilded Victoria gliding behind her. "Nellie Sterlman, I want you to meet Victoria Cremwell, of the Boston Cremwells."

The sophisticated and lovely Victoria offered her hand. We shook, and the skin of my scratchy, dried hand, chapped from a year of rubbing down baby ellies, caught against her tapered silken fingers. "So glad to meet someone who is doing so much to save our wildlife," she crooned, and flashed me a tooth-perfect smile. "I'm sort of a crusader, myself. I stopped eating Welsh rabbit. Poor little things. So, how long have you known Tom?"

"A little over a year," I said. "I helped him bring back the elephants that are in the pen outside."

She gave me a faint smile. "I never expected someone so, you know, rough-and-tumble. I always thought Tom liked to spend his time with women who can offer a bit of culture, you know? *Refined*. Though I understand your relationship was strictly *jungle*."

Mrs. Pennington put an arm around Victoria's teeny tiny hummingbird shoulders. "Isn't she just darling? Can't you just picture her in a wedding dress?" Victoria blushed and fluttered her eyelashes. "And," Mrs. Pennington continued, "she's just absolutely insisting they take their honeymoon at Tom's place in Bretagne."

"It's because France is so *refined*!" Victoria chirped.

"They treat their animals very well. There's nothing there left to save!"

"Tell that to their ducks," I replied. "You may want to explain why they're being used for foie gras."

There was a stir at the door. A tall, handsome man with sun-bleached hair walked in. As soon as I saw his safari suit, I recognized him as Jungle Johnny of television fame. He had a conservationist-based wildlife show for children that was quite popular, and as soon as he entered the barn, guests circled him like coyotes, shaking his hand and asking questions and pushing napkins at him to autograph.

"JJ!" Mrs. Wycliff called from across the room. "I knew you'd make it! You old dear!" She hobbled over to give him a kiss on each cheek, which he returned. "Neelie!" she waved to me. "Come meet my dearest friend!" I left Mrs. Pennington and the very refined Victoria to meet Jungle Johnny.

He was even more handsome up close. Burning blue eyes in a tanned face and a wide, friendly grin trained on me as he took my hand in his big, gentle one.

"I'm Neelie Sterling," I said. "I appreciate so much that you came."

Jungle Johnny put his arm around Mrs. Wycliff's waist. "Elisabeth and I go back many years—she's a wonderful conservationist. I would do anything for her. You know, as they say in Swahili, old friends are like good cook pots—you use them for the best dinners."

I eyed him. I eyed Diamond-Rose in the corner flipping her safari knife and popping balloons. It was a match made in heaven.

"You really have to meet Diamond-Rose," I said, taking his arm and leading him away. "I think you just might have a few things in common." We crossed the room, and I tapped Diamond on the shoulder. "Diamond-Rose, Jungle Johnny."

He shook her hand warmly and glanced questioningly at her clothes. "Safari colors," he said, smiling.

"I'm a safari leader with a level three license and advanced weapons certificate," she murmured politely, then, to my surprise, excused herself to get a drink.

The food-on-a-stick theme worked out better than I could have imagined. I had managed to devise salad on a stick by skewering cherry tomatoes and decoratively wrapping the stick with frisée. And I had been determined to invent the elusive soup-on-a-stick as well, though it took me more than a week of failed kitchen experiments before I finally thought to run skewers through the rims of small paper cups before filling them. Aside from the dexterous balancing required, they worked rather well, and I was very proud of my clever solution.

The band played through the night from inside the elephant enclosure, the food both entertained and fed our guests, and so far, no one had been accidentally impaled, mauled, hung, poisoned, or insulted, which was a success of sorts.

I danced with Reese, told Marielle that I forgave her for Mousi, how could she have known about the really nice man, though a dash of research just might have helped. I danced with Richie; danced with Jungle Johnny, who was really a good dancer; ardently thanked my mother for the breadsticks, thinking how Margo would enjoy them tomorrow morning; danced with my father while listening to the history of barbecue sauce; and kept an eye on the fluttering, delicate, birdlike Victoria. My fantasies of Tom showing up and dancing with me and changing everything back to the way it was flew out the door after one glance at his Tweetie Pie. I had about as much chance of winning his heart again as I had of dancing around the floor astride Margo.

I watched from across the room as the fluttery Victoria chatted animatedly with her future mother-in-law, and I drowned my heartache by sucking down fourteen frozen piña coladas–on-a-stick. I wasn't sure if frozen alcohol had the same inebriating properties as room temperature alcohol, and I was determined that it was going to be my science project for the night, with the hopeful side effect of getting me totally smashed. I ate nine breadsticks to make my mother happy and ate something unidentifiable–on-a-stick that melted quickly and tasted like soap, which might have been someone's cigarette put out in a soup cup. What did it matter? I felt terrible and looked terrible. Silky had sneezed masticated hay across my hair after I led a few people over to the horse barn to visit her, and the collar of my new velvet blouse had been eaten by Samantha when I took her onto my shoulder so that Mrs. Wycliff could look for Harry.

"I'm so anxious to meet Harry," Mrs. Pennington informed me as we passed each other. She was delicately nibbling ice cream cake–on-a-stick. "We've met Elisabeth a few times socially," she said, "but never met her husband. Victoria and I are going to help her look for him."

Jungle Johnny ran the auction. He was witty and cajoling and doing a wonderful job. Some very nice prizes had been donated, thanks to the generous friends of Margo Pennington: a day at a spa in New York City, dinner at Daniel, fresh flowers every day for a month, a week in Belize; while the less glamorous prizes had been procured by me and Diamond: six months of free lariat lessons, a certificate from Dr. Harry for a free cat neutering, a ten-dollars-off coupon at the local Cut'n'Blow, and a free large pizza from Big Tony's, toppings extra.

It was a lively auction and seemingly successful until I realized that Mrs. Wycliff was one of our most active bidders, blithely outbidding the guests. I marched over to Diamond, who was standing next to her.

"We have to stop her from bidding," I whispered fiercely. "She can't contribute to herself."

"Don't worry," Diamond whispered back. "Everyone knows we're taking the last bid before the lady in the pith helmet."

I looked around at our guests, who were growing more amused with each bid and sighed. I had hoped for a dignified, successful fund-raiser, and instead, we were providing comic relief for the social set.

"I just wish this was over already," I muttered. "It's a disaster."

"No, it isn't," Diamond said. "It's been great fun. And after the auction, Mum is going to sing."

My heart sank. I wondered if there was a limit to our guests' good-natured tolerance. "Please don't let her sing," I pleaded.

"Oh come, it'll be lovely," Diamond replied. "And then I'm planning to give a presentation of my more popular jungle calls. Jungle Johnny said he'd join me—he promised he does an especially good hyena. These things always go over very well. It'll be the perfect way to end the evening."

An hour later, I was listening to Elisabeth Wycliff sing "Meet Me in St. Louis" in her high-pitched, tremulous voice, the lyrics punctuated by Samantha's well-placed curses, and wishing they both were there. I was actually grateful that Tom hadn't come to witness my total humiliation.

Margo Pennington interrupted my thoughts. "What a perfectly amusing evening," she said. "Did you know that Hannibal took plums on his journey through the Alps? What an odd historical fact. At least, I think that's what some young man was telling me."

I gave her a weak smile. Diamond had joined Jungle Johnny at the microphone. Her flame red hair was a perfect foil to his cool blond, and they were both tall and athletic. And practically dressed like the Bobbsey Twins. He should have been the man of her dreams. Was she playing hard to get? I didn't understand it. Diamond announced that she would start her series of imitations with the call of the great Kenyan hadada ibis.

"Hadada! Hadada! Hadada!" her voice rang out. "Hadada, hadada, hadada."

"Fuckyou, fuckyou, fuckyou!" Samantha chimed in from

stage left. Victoria Cremwell was behind me, laughing at how too perfectly *riotous* this all was.

I needed to escape.

I made my way through the guests, dodging wobbly desserts-on-a-stick and melting drinks-on-a-stick, and Reese saying *"Plums*—get it?" to some dignified white-haired gentleman, and Mrs. Pennington clapping her hands for attention and asking for Harry, wherever he was, to *please* step up to the mike and say a few words to the crowd.

"Hadada, hadada, hadada" rang in my ears as I slipped across the room and through the doors and out of the barn. I knew where I needed to go and whom I needed to see. I didn't care anymore about my skirt or my new shoes or whether we had made even one penny.

It was dark out. There was no light except for the glow from the elephant barn and a party of stars above. But it didn't matter. I knew every turn of where I was heading.

I pulled open the gate and made my way down to the elephant pond.

Chapter 33

THERE WAS A SILHOUETTE OF A MAN JUST AHEAD OF me, almost obscured by the night, except for the darker contrast of Margo behind him. He was standing quietly, his head tilted at an expectant angle as I approached, and I cupped my hands over my eyes, trying to capture what little light was coming from the party, hoping the man wasn't one of our guests. It wasn't safe for a stranger to be that close to Margo.

Then I realized who it was.

"Why are you out here?" I called softly, trying not to startle the elephants.

"Do you really have an objection, Neelie?" Tom asked.

"Why didn't you come inside? Your fiancée is already in there," I replied frostily.

He stepped toward me, holding his hand out. Now I could see the silver of his hair, the outline of his chin but not the scar. It was still hidden in the shadowy creases that fell across his face.

"I don't have a fiancée," he said.

"Sure you do," I said. "Miss Victoria Cremwell of the Boston Crème Pies. Why didn't you go inside to be with her?"

"I got here a little while ago," Tom replied. "I didn't want to upset you again, so I thought I'd just wander around a bit without intruding. I figured I'd talk to you after everyone went home." He was within inches of me now. "Neelie, we have to talk about that elephant before you do something foolish."

"You're too late. I'm always doing something foolish," I said. "And the next foolish thing I'm going to do is wish you and Victoria Creamcakes lots of happiness."

"I'm not engaged," he said again firmly. "You must have been talking to my mother." He gave a little laugh. "She thinks I'm engaged. Or rather, I should be engaged. Victoria is the daughter of a good friend of hers. She's been wanting us to hook up for years."

"How wonderful for both of you," I said. "Or should I say, all three of you."

He moved closer. "Oh, come on, Neelie," he said. "She's just . . . someone I—"

"I don't believe you," I said, taking a step back and feeling the heel of my shoe sink into the soft ground.

Tom moved toward me. "You don't understand," he said, his voice filled with exasperation. He reached for my arm. "Can't we talk somewhere?"

"No," I said. "Unless you want to go inside the elephant barn. Oops, I forgot, there's a party in there. With your fiancée. You could give her a little hug. Now, wouldn't that

278 | Judy Reene Singer

be just so *refined*." I turned away from him, pivoting on my muddy heel and accidentally drilling it deeper into the mud.

"Neelie!" He caught my arm with his hand. The warmth of his fingers burned through the sleeve of my blouse. "You should know me better."

"I thought I did," I said. "Now please let go of me." But his grip only tightened.

"I don't know why I owe you any explanations anyway, since you left me," Tom said, "but we need to talk."

"I didn't leave you," I countered, my anger flaring. "You left me. You wouldn't let me have any time to think. I was in the middle of everything going wrong, my life was totally upside down, and I needed time. You had twenty years to sort things out after *your* divorce."

He paused. "You're right."

"And I needed those baby elephants. I *needed* them." He was very quiet as I spoke, and I could feel him staring at me. "I mean, you told me you didn't want children, and I agreed, and you wanted a whole different life, and I was ready to agree"—I stopped to take a breath—"but you didn't give me room for my life, too, and the baby ellies meant everything to me because—well, I just *needed* them."

He was quiet, though he didn't let go of me. His voice was low when he finally spoke. "I'm sorry. I didn't want to lose you."

"Well, how did that work for you?" I said, pulling back. "And please stop apologizing. It'll only make me feel bad, and I've had my fill of feeling bad tonight."

"Can we talk somewhere?" Tom asked, sliding his hand down my arm to hold my fingers. "We need to straighten some things out between us."

"No we don't," I said, tears starting at the feel of his hand against mine. "You need to go back to your . . . future wife. I understand she even has your honeymoon planned."

"Don't be ridiculous," he started, but I didn't want to hear any more. I broke from his grasp and tried to run, but the one shoe stayed behind, stuck in the mud. I didn't care, I teetered away from him as fast as my remaining impractical three-inch heel, bare muddy foot, and foolishly long skirt would allow. Though night had already sealed its own door and the light from the elephant barn was dim and distant, I ran up the path, able to elude him because I was so familiar with the terrain. He stumbled hard behind me, then cursed, but I knew how the little road sloped to the right, how the ground dipped just so, I knew each protruding rock, the muddy hollow, the last curve to the left just before the gate. Hobbling like a car with a flat tire, I passed a loud spill of music and applause, passed the main house, and made it to the isolation barn, where Silky was kept.

Tom was following me—I knew he would—but there was nothing more I wanted to say to him. There could be no reprieve from my complete stupidity, no absolution from my arrogance in believing that even though we were apart, I would always be the love of his life. I hadn't accounted for Miss Victoria Boston Canary. I hadn't accounted for reality.

Well, reality was following close behind me.

Silky nickered as I slid the barn door open and quickly shut it behind me. The first thing I did was kick off my one useless shoe and try to get my bearings. Without light, the barn was black as a closet, and the only sound was the scrambling of my heart and the gentle chew of Silky as she browsed through her hay. I knew the layout of where everything was, even in this darkness. I didn't want to chance climbing into the hay-loft in a floor-length skirt, so I felt my way down the aisle, touching the rough wooden stall doors for markers, counting each metal door latch until I reached the kitchen. I turned the knob and ducked inside. Cabinets on the right, a sink, a small refrigerator, the cot. I continued to feel my way until I reached a small alcove. I pressed myself into the space and waited.

Of course, it was stupid. Tom could just step into the barn and turn the light on, but if I kept my ragged breath and pounding heart at bay, maybe he would just quickly scan the empty aisle and think I had gone back to the elephant barn or up to the main house.

The barn door rolled open, and I heard Tom slip inside and shut it again. Then nothing. He was most likely stand-ing in the aisle, listening for me. I pressed my hand over my mouth to keep my breathing quiet.

"Neelie?" he called softly. "Neelie? We need to talk. Surely you know that." There was a shuffling sound, then "Where is that damn light switch?" It clicked on, and a brilliant streak of light lit the aisle and flashed across the tan tile of the kitchen floor, which made me realize I had forgotten to shut the door behind me. I hoped Tom wouldn't notice it ajar, and I flat-tened even more against the wall, straining to listen.

"Come on, Neelie," he called softly. "I'm not climbing up into the hayloft to look for you. And I'm turning off the light before it attracts everyone from the party like they're a bunch of damn moths." Another click and it was black again.

In a few moments his eyes would adjust to the dark, enabling him to distinguish shadow from shape, and he would find me.

I could almost see him, shifting his weight toward any rustling sound, then making his way down the aisle to the kitchen door. Was it better to be discovered standing here like a quivering mouse, or to announce myself and just wish him well and get all the drama over with? I moved lightly across the kitchen floor and stepped into the aisle. We were now standing just a few feet apart.

"I'm right here," I said. He spun around.

"Neelie," he said, his voice was filled with exasperation. "Why do you have to make everything so damn hard?"

"I don't know." I began to cry. "I never should have told your mother it was okay to bring Miss Victorious Snotwell. I thought I'd be okay, but I'm not okay."

"Didn't you hear what I said?" he asked, reaching out and grabbing my shoulders. "I'm not marrying her. I never proposed to her. I don't love her."

"Well, your mother thinks she's going to look just darling in her wedding dress," I retorted. "And in my opinion, it should be decorated with little yellow canary feathers."

"She won't be wearing it for me," he said.

"And you're having a honeymoon in France," I sniffed.

"No, I'm not," he murmured. He suddenly pulled me to him, then pressed his cheek against my hair and moved his hands across my back. "Oh, Neelie," he said into my ear, "let me hold you. It's been too long."

Oh God, I was in Tom's arms. It was Tom kissing me. It was Tom holding me. I clung to him. It had been a whole year, and suddenly it felt like it had been only one second.

"Neelie? Talk to me," he whispered. But I was afraid that if I spoke even one word, I would awaken, and it would be the middle of the night, and I'd be alone. Alone, without him and without my comforting, snoring baby ellies, without anyone, alone and wavering, like a singular candle flame before it's snuffed. But he held me and stroked my hair, and I felt his breath close to my ear, and I pressed against him.

Silky chewed her hay, shaking it against the stall door to break off pieces. She blew the dust from her nostrils. And I was still in Tom's arms. There was a shout outside. The flame held. He kissed me again, then lifted my chin with his fingers.

"Neelie," he whispered urgently, "we need to go somewhere and talk. I have to tell you something. That's why I came up here."

When someone says they have to tell you something, in that special I-have-to-tell-you-something tone of voice, it means only one thing: bad news. And there is no good place in the world to receive bad news. Not even a sweet hay-smelling barn while you're in the arms of the man you love. I stiffened and pulled away.

"I don't like it," I said.

"I haven't told you anything yet."

"Well, I don't want to hear it. Not now," I said, letting him lead me into the kitchen. "Not yet. Please not yet."

He put his arms around me and rocked me a little. "Let's sit down." He waited for my response.

"All right," I said, stepping away from him. "We can sit here." I led him to the cot and primly sat down and waited for him to speak. He drew in a long breath.

"Listen to me," he finally said. "For once, you have to actually listen to what I'm telling you. It's about that elephant."

I immediately grew angry. "It would have been nothing for you to buy Tusker," I said, my words coming out in a rush. "I guess you'd rather see him shot. Diamond and I are just praying that we raise enough money in time, when you could have easily done it and we could have paid you back. I don't get it." I stopped to catch my breath, and he reached for my hand.

"I know you meant well," he started slowly, "but there's a reason why I never offered to buy him. Think about this—if either one of us bought that elephant, it'd start a horrible new industry for the Zim government."

I jumped from the cot and started to move backward, away from him. "What are you talking about?"

Tom's grip tightened on my hand. "Think about it," he said. "All they would have to do is torture a few elephants, and some idiot will come prancing in, ready to buy them. You would have set a terrible precedent. Can't you see that?"

"First of all, I'm not an idiot," I snapped, "and secondly, I don't believe you. I was there. It's perfectly reasonable for us to remove an animal that no one wants."

"Neelie," Tom's voice rose with exasperation. "Think about the consequences. There's no money in Zimbabwe. They'd do anything to get cash flowing into the country. Poaching, culling, selling elephants for meat—they're desperate."

"But Diamond and I spoke to Joshua!" I protested. "He promised."

"You spoke to him without thinking," he said, his voice growing stern. "I'm surprised you even got out of Zim alive. He wasn't to be trusted."

"You're wrong!" I said loudly. I didn't care there was a

party going on nearby. My party. "I don't want to hear it, you've got it all wrong." I pulled away and put my hands over my ears. "Diamond's husband went to school with Joshua. He wouldn't betray her."

He pulled my hands down. "You're the one who's got it wrong," he said, his voice rising. "I'm really sorry you worked so hard for nothing. I warned you not to go through with this . . . fund-raiser of yours, that it wouldn't change things." He stopped abruptly.

Things are going to end again between us, I thought miserably. He was so close to me, I could hear him breathing. I tried to sort through his words. When he spoke again, his voice was cajoling. "Neelie, you never listen, do you! Please think about what I'm saying. I care about those animals more than anything. It was never about money. You should know me better than that."

I did know him better. I knew him to be a decent man, humane. He had spent a fortune saving elephants, long before he even knew me. Why would he have so abruptly changed?

He hadn't.

"I didn't want to start a cottage industry for them," he said. "Whatever you buy from them, they'll make more of. That's the current mentality of the government."

Suddenly, what he was saying made all the sense in the world. He was right. I never listen. I mishear, misinterpret, mishandle everything. I stood in the dark and tried to think. How could I have gotten so much wrong.

"Oh God, what have I done?" I choked out.

He put his arms around me and held me close to him. I

could feel the warmth of his body through his shirt. "You haven't done anything yet," he said. "I know you meant well. I know that your heart is in the right place."

I couldn't answer him.

"Neelie?"

"I'm just sorry," I finally choked out. "You're right. It would have been a catastrophe. I'm a complete fool."

"No, no," he said, his lips against my face. "We want the same things. We've always wanted the same things. We just have different ideas on how to get them. And I should have explained it to you instead of attacking you."

I looked up at him, and suddenly he pressed his lips hard against mine. The party was breaking up only a few hundred feet away, and I could hear the muted sound of laughter and cars starting. But I was in here, secretly and perfectly in his arms.

"You have to be strong," he whispered into my ear. "I have to tell you something, but you have to be strong."

"What?" I asked, a new panic rising. "What?"

He lifted my chin and held it in his fingers. "Listen to me," he said, then stopped to kiss my forehead, then spoke low, so low I wasn't sure of his words, though I heard them. I did hear them. "Listen to me," he said, "from all the information I've gotten, the word is, Tusker is gone. He hasn't been seen anywhere since the day you left. I'm afraid he's totally disappeared."

Chapter 34

FOR ONE AGONIZING MOMENT, I THOUGHT I HAD been caught in a steel trap and it had ripped me open to my core. Tom's voice sounded metallic, his words were filling me up with an eerie silver light, the taste in my mouth was metallic, everything was gleaming silver, and I realized it was mercury and it was poisonous and I was drowning in its silver viscosity. I struggled to get free, but it was too deep, and I was being poisoned from the words, and dying. I could hear Tom calling my name, feel his arms pull me back, holding me, like a lifeguard, to save me from drowning.

"Neelie, sit down." He helped me, stumbling and light-headed, and sat me back down on the cot.

I heard his words in my head. Or maybe he spoke them aloud again. Tusker was not anywhere. "How can that be?" I choked out. "The minister—Joshua—he promised—"

"A promise in Zimbabwe means nothing. Joshua Muko-mana was assassinated."

"No! No!" I dropped my head into my hands. I could see Joshua Mukomana's face in front of me, round and laughing, then Tusker, his trunk raised above his head, standing so close, good-natured, trusting.

"I'm sorry," Tom said, sitting next to me and stroking my back as if it was going to help. "They said it was a car acci-dent that killed Mukomana, though everyone knows better."

I was broken. The trap had broken me in two. I could do no more, react no more. It was all over.

"Well, I guess we did it for nothing," I finally said, strug-gling not to cry. "Go back to the party. Go back and declare yourself the victor. Ha! A Victor for Victoria."

He held me fast. "We weren't having a contest," he whis-pered fiercely into my ear.

"What did I do wrong?" I whispered.

"You couldn't have helped him, Neelie," Tom said into the dark. "And I couldn't either. Charlotte wanted him to stay in Chizarira, but there is only so much you can do to hold a wild elephant."

"I failed him," I said dully, and suddenly Tusker was in the room with me. His cathedral body, his massive heart and great, good-natured face, his one tusk, which curved so exquisitely inward, as though cradling his soul to his body. He was with me and within me, extending his trunk to me, asking for alms, reaching out to me, asking me to help him. Where had he gone? Taken? Poached? *Eaten?* He was mine. I had been sent to save him. I had been *called*. Oh, what con-ceit to think I had been called.

And I had failed.

I sat in the dark, my eyes open and staring at his image. I didn't hear Tom. There was nothing in the room with me except this elephant, whose only crime was that he had eaten garbage in the presence of humans.

Tom stroked my arm and I let him. I wasn't angry with him. He had tried, we had all tried, all decent people try.

"What about the elephant with him?" I asked softly. "Did you hear anything of him—the other bull elephant?"

"No," Tom replied gently. "But Charlotte Pope stays in touch with me. She promised she would find out and let me know, and I promise I'll tell you."

I don't know how long we sat together in the dark. I was dimly aware that, in another ironic touch, the fund-raiser was still going on. I sat very still, grieving. My tears felt hot against my cheeks, and I didn't wipe them away. I kept seeing the moment Tusker was killed—shot? The surprise in his eyes, the betrayal. When I stopped crying, I could only wonder how things sometimes just don't work out, even when you try as hard as you can.

Tom stayed next to me, saying nothing. He put his arm around my shoulders and drew me close and pressed his lips gently to my ear, but still said nothing.

"Neelie?" he finally asked, then brushed his lips along my face. I pulled away.

"Well, at least you still have your fiancée," I said. "A victory for you."

"You're the victorious one. Neelie, you broke my heart."

Well, that was no victory. It's no victory to break the heart of someone you love, because you break your own heart as well. And if you ever find each other again, all the parts never quite fit back the same way. Tom held me as I sat next to him, trying to find pieces to put back together. There were pieces of our time together and pieces of Tusker and pieces of Joshua Mukomana sipping tea with his pinkie daintily extended, pieces everywhere mixing themselves around in the dark, a thousand-piece jigsaw puzzle that made no sense.

I tried to protest when Tom kissed me again, but he stopped my words with his lips and pulled me against him until I put my arms around him. It was such familiar terrain, the hook of his ribs, the hollow of his collarbone against my cheek. I was barely able to see him in the darkened room, even this close, except the silver of his hair, the cut of his chin, the high slant of his cheeks. I touched his face and knew he belonged to me, that I belonged to him. I could feel him asking me to love him again.

To make love to him.

The darkness made a protective circle around us as we kissed. We kissed again and again. Suddenly he moved away from me and crossed the little room to lock the door.

"You can't be serious," I said, when he returned to the cot.

"I'm not?" he asked, and pulled me down to his side. "It's been hell without you."

Though I only let him hold me, the year washed away, vanquished. Disappearing, collapsing into the night, leaving only this moment, leaving only the feeling of his arms, his body, his mouth. I wanted this. I wanted him more than anything, but I stopped him when he asked for more.

"Do you want to go inside to the party with me?" I asked.

290 | JUDY REENE SINGER

"You mean right now?" he asked.

"Yes. You could hold my hand and dance with me."

He paused. "I think that would hurt a few people," he said.

"I see," I said, my old anger coming back. "So, before we take things any further, I want you to break it off properly with Miss Victoria Cremwell of the Boston Crème de la Crèmes." I jerked away from him and walked out of the kitchen, but not before saying, "And I want you to do this in a thoughtful, *refined* kind of way."

Diamond was calling my name, and I slid open the barn door. Car doors were slamming and motors starting, and party voices spilled into the night, calling farewells. Tom was behind me.

"Neelie," he started.

"I'd better go," I interrupted him. "I have to say good-bye to everyone. Please don't follow me out." I slipped through the doors. "I don't want to add to the evening's embarrassing entertainment."

"Please wait," he said. "I have a business trip, but I'll call you in two days. And I will straighten everything out with both Victoria and my mother by then."

"Swell," I said, and started away from him. It wasn't until a white puff of condensation escaped my lips to join the mist from the cool night that I realized just how much I had been holding my breath.

"There you are!" Diamond exclaimed when she saw me coming up the path. She was standing outside the elephant barn, licking a piña colada–on-a-stick.

"Where's Jungle Johnny?" I asked.

"He asked for my phone number before he left." She shrugged. "But I'm really not interested. No more jungle men for me. I'm done with them. The jungle always takes them back, and I'm not going through that again. Anyway, I have good news."

"What?" I asked as the crowd of happy guests spiraled around us like a centrifuge of party silliness.

"You'll love this," she said, and took a big bite of her piña colada. "We raised almost forty-two thousand dollars. We have more than enough to buy the elephants."

Chapter 35

MY LIFE WAS BEGINNING TO RESEMBLE A PAINTING by Escher. It looked interesting and perfectly logical until you examined it closely, and then you saw a continuous loop of interlocking pieces that twisted and turned on themselves, circling endlessly in curiously repeating patterns that promised resolution but went nowhere.

I would find love, I would lose it, I would find love, I would lose it.

Humans and elephants—everything was linked together, but nothing was permanent. Everything I tried to do slipped through my fingers and disappeared, only to reappear someplace else.

And I had tried. I had tried so hard.

I knew I was meant to rescue animals, I knew that. I knew that as soon as I saw Mousi. And Grace. I knew as soon as I saw Margo. And Tusker. But I couldn't help wonder if I was caught in the middle of some kind of karmic retribution where what I needed to do got all tangled up with my love life, because when I had the ellies, I lost Tom, and now that Tom might be in my life again, I had lost the elephants.

Two days passed, and though I still didn't hear from him, I was determined not to call him. Despite Diamond's best advice that an innocent inquiry whether he had heard anything more about locating Tusker, or maybe even Shamwari, would be very appropriate, I thought better of it.

"I want him to break up with Victoria," I told Diamond. "But I don't want to pressure him. I want him to be totally single before we start again." Then I thought I'd hedge my bet. "If we do start again."

"How will you be sure he's free of her?" Diamond asked. "It's not like she's going to sign a release form for you."

But Tom had said he would call me in two days, and I vowed to wait patiently. By the end of the second night, I was beginning to think karma had abandoned me for someone less complicated. I called Diamond.

"I'm making chocolate chip cookies," I said. "Tuck in Mrs. W., and bring over a bottle of wine."

"A big, cheap bottle or a small, elegant one?"

"Medium," I replied. "He said he would call me by tonight, and I want to be sober if he does."

Barns are meant to be filled. My empty barn looked bleak, sitting across the yard from us. It needed horses and hay and the soft nickering you hear when you tiptoe through the door at 10:00 p.m. to tuck your horses in with night hay. It looked lonely. Or maybe it was me who was lonely. Diamond arrived with a big, cheap bottle of wine, and I was glad to see both of them.

We sat on the back porch, wrapped in itchy wool blankets. Me, rocking back and forth with the phone in my lap, and Diamond in the other chair, hugging her knees to her chest and keeping our glasses filled. I was glad for her company.

"Good cookies," she said, grabbing another handful. "I used to bake when I was a kid. I never quite got the hang of it, though. They always came out so black."

"The trick is to get them out of the oven before they catch fire," I said, grabbing a few more myself.

The phone rang, and I checked the caller ID before I answered. It was Richie, on his new cell phone in Alabama.

"The truck is leaving today and should be up in New York in two or three days," he said. "Then we'll pick up Margo and Abbie and return. I'm flying in tomorrow night to get things ready."

"No," I said.

"Yes," he said, "I'll see you tomorrow," and hung up.

"The elephants are leaving," I announced to Diamond, eyeing my barn and wondering if I could hide them at the last minute.

"New misfortunes erase the old ones," she said wistfully, putting the now-empty bottle next to her chair while I licked the last drop of wine from my glass.

"That's not very comforting," I said. A strong wind whipped around the corner of the porch, sending a chill through me. I pulled my blanket closer. "Why should I get any misfortunes at all?" I was warming up now. "I mean, you create your own karma, right? You get punished for things you did or didn't do. I mean, I never borrowed anything that I didn't return. Not even something blue for my first wedding. So why is everything disappearing from my life?"

"To make room for better things," Diamond replied, but it sounded more like a question.

Tom called me very early the next morning. He told me Charlotte Pope was pretty sure Shamwari had been shipped out of the country. The young bull had gone on a rampage after Tusker disappeared, and the conservation task force had come back for him. Rumor had it that the men were carrying rifles and had herded him away by firing shots over his head, but she didn't know where they took him after that. The only thing she was certain of was that both elephants had disappeared.

I felt sick to my stomach. "I don't want to hear any more," I shouted into the phone. "We raised enough money, I'll find him on my own. I don't care about cottage industries or anything. I'm getting him somehow."

"Calm down and listen to me," Tom said. "Are you going to listen? I need to tell you something about the farm, but you haven't given me a chance."

"Okay," I said resentfully, "I'm listening."

He cleared his throat as though getting ready to present a business proposition. "You know I bought the land next to the sanctuary, but you don't know why. So here's why—I bought it in order to expand the farm. I plan to redo the whole place, make bigger fields. Huge. And build a bigger barn. I want the sanctuary to house bull elephants."

"Why didn't you tell me all this sooner?" I demanded. "Didn't you think you could trust me?"

Tom sighed. "If news of my purchase had gotten out prematurely, I could have wound up in EPA hearings for the next ten years, discussing how to protect the cross-eyed seven-toed night drooler, or something."

I still didn't understand. "But if the sanctuary is going to have elephants, why send Margo and Abbie away?"

"*Bull* elephants," he repeated. "I'm going to take them in, but you can't keep them on the same property as the females. They're too strong and unpredictable, especially when they go into musth. There isn't a sanctuary in the U.S. that wants bull elephants."

I couldn't help myself. "Well, there was one bull elephant you could have helped," I said pointedly.

"I thought we were finished with all that," Tom snapped back. "And I'd like to proceed with my plans without a fight from you."

I was suddenly tired of arguing. "I won't fight," I said.

"You mean for once we have an agreement?" He sounded relieved. "Because it seems like there are always elephants putting up roadblocks between us."

"We're okay," I said. "No elephants between us. And by the way, have you spoken to Victoria?"

"Not yet," he said. "She's an old friend, and I don't want to hurt her feelings."

We didn't need elephants, I thought, because this time the roadblock was being erected by a canary, a certain Miss Victoria Crumb Bum.

The night before the elephants were leaving. I was on a countdown to an empty heart. Richie called to tell me he had arrived and was staying in his old house to get things ready for the next morning, although there really wasn't all that much to do. Shipping an elephant isn't like shipping a horse. Horses need halters and lead lines and blankets and saddles and bridles and leg wraps and coolers and buckets and all manner of equipment. Elephants just have themselves.

"You don't need to come to the barn tomorrow," he said. "It might be easier on you if you stayed home."

"Don't be ridiculous," I said. "Someone has to be there to wave good-bye."

"A quick slash to the heart hurts less than one hundred small wounds," Diamond said. It was early morning, and we were standing in the elephant barn, waiting for Richie to get things ready, waiting for the truck. "So, say good-bye and get it over with."

"I can't," I said. I had already said one million good-byes and kissed the soft spot on Margo's face, near her lips, a bazillion times. But like a bazillion Zim dollars, they had no real value.

Richie was busying himself piling bales of hay, stacking bags of elephant chow, filling buckets of fruit for the ride to Alabama.

I ran my hands over Margo's face, wrapped my arms around her trunk and wept against her shoulder. I stroked the rough skin over and over, wondering, how do you memorize a touch? You can't truly recall it, you have only the

298 | JUDY REENE SINGER

fingertips like vapor. I wanted desperately for my hands to
remember what Margo felt like, but I knew they wouldn't.

"That's it, Neelie," Richie said. He was finished with his
chores and was standing at the entrance to the barn.

It was time to leave her. I stopped, frozen with grief,
unable to take another step away from her. I couldn't let her
go. It had been insane to think I could.

"Neelie," Richie said quietly. "The truck is here."

"No, it's not," I said, even as I could hear the heavy engine
coming up the driveway.

"Neelie," Richie said again.

I took a deep breath and blew Margo a final kiss, though
a thousand kisses wouldn't have been enough. "Be happy,"
I commanded, her last command. I tried to keep my voice
steady. "Be safe, be happy." And then I left her.

Diamond was so wrong. Big slashes and little wounds,
they all hurt like hell.

I waited with Diamond and Mrs. Wycliff in the living room,
peeking out through the bay window because Richie didn't
want us to be a distraction while he put Margo and Abbie
on the truck. Mrs. Wycliff, dressed in her red wellies, jeans,
white knit sweater, and pith helmet, was holding her old
dart gun and grumbling about poachers.

"They're stealing the elephants!" she declared, raising
the dart gun to her shoulder. "I think I can pick them off
from here."

"No," Diamond soothed her, and gently tried to take the
antiquated gun from her hands. "They're just taking them to
another encampment where they'll be safer."

"I can't look," I said.

"She'll be happy," Diamond sternly said to both of us as if we were naughty children. "Think about her being happy."

The silver eighteen-wheeler made a slow circle of the parking area and neatly stopped right outside the doors of the barn. Two caretakers from the sanctuary in Alabama jumped from the cab and went inside. They emerged a few minutes later carrying the bales of hay, kegs of water, the fruit, the last ten bags of pellets, and the two boxes of donuts I had left for Margo.

It was time to load the elephants. The caretakers rolled back the middle trailer doors, revealing an inner cage of thick steel bars, which he swung open. They were ready.

"Oh no!" I grabbed Diamond's arm when I saw Richie lead Margo from the elephant barn to the waiting truck, as though it was going to be just another day in the field. Margo followed calmly, in trusting, measured elephant steps, holding her trunk straight out in front of her like an arm, feeling the air. She had been given a very mild tranquilizer and seemed calm enough, though she flapped her ears at the truck and stopped to cautiously examine the steel bars, the doors, and the straw-covered floor inside. Richie gave her the command to step up. She looked back at him, then, it seemed to me, toward the window where I was standing. I pushed my fist in my mouth to keep from calling out. Margo put one foot up and stopped. I could see Richie coaxing her. She put her second foot in the truck, then lifted herself up and stepped in. Innocent little Abbie followed without hesitation. The men immediately closed the cage and shut the doors with a metallic finality that echoed through the parking lot. They jumped into the cab of the truck, leaving the back passenger door open for Richie to climb aboard.

I couldn't contain myself any longer and rushed from the house with tears streaming down my face.

"Margo!"

Richie put his finger to his lips so that my voice wouldn't carry to the elephants. "We have to go," he said.

Margo was only a few feet from me, hidden inside the steel walls of the truck. I reached out to touch the metal sides with my fingers.

Diamond and Mrs. Wycliff, with the cockatoo on her shoulder, came out of the house together and stopped on the edge of the driveway.

"See?" Diamond said to Mrs. Wycliff. "Margo and Abbie are fine. Come on, Mum, wish them well."

"*Safari njema*," Mrs. Wycliff called out softly, wishing them a good trip.

"*Fika salama*," Diamond added. Arrive safely.

"Fuck you!" called the cockatoo.

Margo heard their voices and trumpeted from inside the trailer. Abbie joined in. Suddenly, it didn't matter how I was losing them. I sat down on the ground and wept. Mrs. Wycliff came over to pat me on the head as though I were an obedient dog.

"Harry and I are breaking camp tonight to track them," she said. "We're leaving as soon as I find my teeth."

Richie leaned from the cab and blew us a kiss while the driver rolled down his window and saluted.

"Thanks for buying us breakfast," he yelled, waving the

box of donuts I had left for Margo. "We'll have them on the road."

If I could stop rain or gravity, if I had that power to summon, I would have summoned it to the full at that moment to keep my elephants.

Gears slid smoothly into other gears, the truck heaved forward like a draft horse trying to gain traction, then rolled down the driveway, rumbling over the potholes, swirling the dust into curls, taking my elephants and my heart away with them.

Chapter 36

THE DAY AFTER THE ELEPHANTS LEFT, A SET OF construction trucks moved in. A large dump truck, two yellow prehistoric-bird backhoes, and a team of men in tight jeans, suggestive tool belts, and hard hats.

They set to work immediately, demolishing the old elephant barn. The roof was pulled off, the wooden walls were splintered, the old giant spiderweb of wiring waved through the air, lifted by a Brachiosaurus-shaped yellow crane, then was dropped into the maw of a huge container.

"Cool," said Diamond appreciatively. "*Safi*! Very cool!"

"The equipment is amazing," I agreed with her, and she rolled her eyes and tossed her red hair.

"I meant the men."

Well, they did work hard, muscles bulging under the warm fall sun, shirts tied around their waists. I could totally agree with the appeal. Diamond spent a large part of the workday standing nearby to watch them, giving little waves and smiles and a few encouraging remarks.

"Be careful with that," she yelled as the crane lifted out the bent, arthritic-looking metal poles that had once been part of the elephant enclosure inside the barn. "Don't want you to drop it."

The man in the crane grinned back, lifted his hard hat to her, and continued working. A few minutes later she was directing the backhoe. "Watch behind you! Not so fast!" The operator gave her a courtesy nod and continued working.

"You know?" Diamond remarked to me when I had to locate her for the fourth time that day for help with the animals. "I think these men take direction very well. I may have a new career if I can't do safaris anymore."

In two days, there was not a scrap of barn left.

On the third day, Genesis-like, a new barn was being created. A cement mixer pulled into the space where the barn had been. It had a rotating red spiral painted on the back, which swirled hypnotically as it disgorged what looked like a ton of oatmeal over the ground. New wood pilings were delivered, stout as an elephant's leg, and shiny silver conduit wiring was heaped like uncooked pasta, along with thick, strong new fencing.

We would all bring out our morning coffee to stand watch. The men in the trucks enthusiastically hooted and whistled at us. Well, maybe just at Diamond.

"We seem to have here several fine examples of the broad-chested, yellow-hatted, American construction male," said

Diamond, after waving and whistling back. "How lovely to be able to study them in their native habitat."

"Observe the multilayered musculature that defines the appendages," I said, getting into the spirit.

"For a thorough study, some fieldwork is called for," Diamond said, leaving my side. "I'll be sure to report back as soon as I have enough data."

Mrs. Wycliff and I watched as Diamond strolled down to introduce herself.

"It's going to be a big building," I commented to Mrs. W.

"Well, I hope it's an indoor pool," she replied. "I was thinking of taking up swimming."

"No, it's a barn," I said. "It's a barn for elephants."

She gave me a beatific smile and clapped her hands. "Oh! Are we going to have elephants again?"

"I think so," I replied.

Except they wouldn't be the right ones.

The men worked for weeks, and Diamond made sure to visit them faithfully every morning. She brought pots of undrinkable coffee, occasionally roped in a few tools, and flirted relentlessly. The payoff was a date with Rocco, who was the general contractor and the man who operated the dinosaur. When she introduced me to him, I could see the basis of their attraction right away, from his mud-encrusted work boots and scruffy dark work pants, to his yellow construction helmet and manly unibrow. He read architect's plans the way she read jungle maps, he offered her rides on the heavy equipment, and he ate her burned cookies with a certain cautious appreciation.

"He's very strong," she enthused as we rode a pair of Appaloosas around the property in an effort to make them trail safe for their new buyers. "And romantic. Yesterday he bought me the most beautiful torch. It has titanium batteries!" She pointed to her belt, where, sure enough, next to her safari knife, a big yellow ProPolymer flashlight with sporty black trim hung from a loop.

"Wow," I said. "That's really thoughtful. He must really like you."

"I know," she crowed. "It's wonderful to have a man in my life again!"

I shook my head. "You know, you had the perfectly gorgeous Jungle Johnny practically drooling all over you."

"And where is he now?" she pointed out. "Back in Tanzania or Rwanda? And I'm here. The jungle always takes them back. I want local love."

So did I. Though I couldn't stop thinking about that night in the barn with Tom, when he held me. I also couldn't stop thinking about Victoria. Apparently, neither could Mrs. Pennington, who called me a few days later.

"I'm very disappointed in you, Nellie," she said. "I tried to help you, and you turned on me. What you did was very underhanded."

"What on earth do you mean, Mrs. Pennington?"

"You're trying to spirit Tom away from the love of his life," she replied. "And I won't let you. He and Victoria were meant for each other."

"I haven't done anything," I replied.

"Victoria told me she saw you coming out of that other

306 | Judy Reene Singer

barn the night of the party. She just happened to be getting into her car, and then Tom came out of the barn a few minutes after you," she said. "She was devastated. Apparently, you two were having a moment."

"I didn't know Tom was going to be there," I said. "And if Victoria meant so much to him, he would have had the moment with her at the party."

"Nevertheless," Mrs. Pennington said, "I gave him my grandmother's pink diamond ring, and I've arranged for a lovely little dinner party, and I promise you, my dear, he'll be engaged before tomorrow night is over."

I called Diamond right away. "What do I do?" I wailed. "I do love him. But now it's too late."

"If you pick the bud you will stop the fruit," Diamond replied. "He hasn't walked down the aisle yet."

"Why can't you just for once, tell me something I can understand," I shot back. "How in hell do you pick someone's bud?"

"You have to find a way to interfere," she said. "You make it your karma to be with him."

I didn't hold much hope that I could interfere with the powerful Mrs. Pennington's plan.

But karma and Mrs. Wycliff had other ideas.

Chapter 37

WEARING HER PITH HELMET AND HER RED WELLIES, and clutching a photo of herself and Harry gaily waving from a vintage jeep deep in the heart of Kenya, Mrs. Wycliff quietly passed away early the very next morning. Diamond found her in the living room slumped in front of the fireplace, near her many treasured pictures of her years in the jungle. Baako and Dafi, her faithful old dogs, were licking her face. Actually, Baako was licking her face. Dafi was finishing her toast.

"She's gone," Diamond cried into the phone to me. "I just called the police, and they sent for the coroner to take her away. What do I do now? I've lost everyone!"

"Wait there for me," I told her, though there really wasn't any other place that made sense for her to go to. *Wait there* is second to that other useless emergency directive to boil water. "You could put on a pot of water to boil," I added, just to make sure.

Of course I called Tom. And Richie and Jackie. Of course Tom drove up immediately from his office in the city.

"Don't worry, I'll make all the arrangements," he reassured a weeping Diamond, cradling her in his arms, his own eyes wet with tears. I felt a touch of jealousy—it should have been my moment with him. I wanted to say, *Hey, I liked her, too, you know,* but that would have been ungracious.

"She left directives," Tom said. "I know what she wants. I'll handle everything."

"Oh, thank you," Diamond whispered up at him, her glorious green eyes moist with grief. "You won't leave me— us—" she amended, generously including me. "We're just gobsmacked."

"I'll stay," said Tom, looking over at me. I gave him a watery smile. She gave me a wink behind his back.

Her plea apparently successful, Diamond left Tom's arms to make us coffee. He walked through the mudroom to the back door and stood there, contemplating the construction site and the fields behind it. I stood in the kitchen doorway and studied him. There was something about him, I always thought, that made him stand out stronger, more compelling, almost formidable, more than anyone I ever knew, and to see him, his eyes red, standing quietly, visibly saddened, touched me. He and Mrs. Wycliff had been partners and friends a very long time.

"I knew she couldn't live forever," he said, without turning, "but she was a very brave woman."

"I know," I said. "I would like a few photos of her. I did admire her very much." He nodded and turned around to walk past me, to wander through the house, picking up pictures and the little mementos she had collected over the years, as if the act of touching them could reconnect him with her. I left him alone. And I left Diamond alone as she wept at the kitchen table over a glass of Irish whiskey, having abandoned the idea of boiling coffee. The cockatoo was sitting on her shoulder, eating a cracker, and the two black Labs were sitting next to them and watching Diamond expectantly, as if she were going to produce their mistress any moment.

I was saddened, of course. I had known Mrs. Wycliff for ten years. My ex-husband had been her veterinarian and had taken care of the animals at the sanctuary, but on those odd occasions that I had accompanied him, I'd had only a few polite conversations with her. It wasn't until recently that I had seen her on a daily basis. Yet I missed her. And admired her. I knew how hard she had fought to rescue the lions, the bears, the others in her odd collections of abused animals. I hoped Diamond and I could carry on her work. Tom came over to me and kissed me on the top of my head.

"She loved the animals so much," I murmured, then reached over to take his arm under mine, curling my fingers around the smooth sleeve of his shirt.

"She put herself on the line, time and time again, to rescue them," he said. "There must be a ton of clippings in the attic about her. She's had shots fired at her and people trying to run her off the road while she drove away with some dying animal in the back of her truck." He pursed his lips at the memory.

"Don't go by what she was like at ninety-three," he said. "She was a hellion in her day."

Diamond was taking it very hard. She sat at the kitchen table and clutched one of Mrs. W.'s fine monogrammed linen table napkins to her nose. "I know she was old," she kept repeating, her grief lubricated by the Tyrconnell, "but she was all I had."

"You have me," I told her. "And I can share my mom with you again." I was sitting with her and Tom. He had found some paperwork in Mrs. W.'s desk and was glancing through it.

"You're a good person, Neelie." Diamond reached over to touch my hand. "A good person, indeed. How many people would have offered their home to a stranger they just met on a bus in Nairobi and then taken them home to become part of the family? And you have the best family." She gave me a blubbery smile and hiccupped loudly. "The best family! Did I ever tell you that? You're all perfect!"

Tyrconnell aside, I hadn't realized how much Diamond thought of my family. She wasn't blood family, of course, but then again, family could be anyone. I reached down to pat one of the Labs on the head and thought how we can all make up a family—dog, cockatoo . . . I eyed the bird, who was shredding another linen table napkin and thought maybe I'd draw the line at cockatoos. My thoughts turned back to Diamond—she was the sister I never had.

"So." Diamond sighed loudly. "Would you mind if I moved back with you?"

Oh no, I thought. I had just managed to replace the few

pots she had scorched and finish scraping the last of the biltong slivers that had been deeply embedded in the rug in my office. Not to mention replacing the microwave, the toaster, the vacuum, and the washing machine, as well as a new remote for the TV.

"No need to move out, Diamond." Tom looked up from his paperwork. "You can stay in this house for as long as you want. It'll be good for the house to have someone in it, and you can treat it like it's yours."

She flushed. "Do you mean it?"

Tom nodded.

"Oh, thank you." Diamond got up to give him a hug. "I've never had a real house before. The one in Kenya had thatched walls and a grass roof and leaked like mad in the rainstorms."

Tom gave Diamond a reassuring smile. "I'll notify Elisabeth's lawyers. There is money left in her estate—I'll see what they plan to do with it." He pushed his chair back from the table and stretched his arms and yawned. "I guess I'll head back to the city. I have some appointments."

Like a dinner party tonight, I thought, then stood up, too. Diamond was right about making your own karma. If I wanted Tom in my life, this was the time to make the move. "Since you'll only have to come back tomorrow to plan the wake," I said to him, "why don't you just stay upstate with us a few days until the funeral?"

His eyes met mine and I smiled at him. "You could stay with me, in fact," I offered, even though the house we were currently in had three other bedrooms besides Diamond's and Mrs. Wycliff's, and Richie and Jackie's former house with its own two bedrooms was perfectly fine and only about one thousand feet away.

"You don't mind?" he asked, with real surprise in his voice. "I'd need to go back to the city first and pick up a few changes of clothes, but I can be back before it gets too late."

"I don't mind at all," I said, thinking of his mother's dinner party. "You just probably need to cancel plans and stuff. Death is certainly a good cause—I mean, to cancel things and stuff."

"I'd better leave now, so I can get everything done," he said, stepping over the old burned hole in the floor as he walked through the mudroom. "Thank you. It'll make things a lot easier."

For me, too, I exulted inwardly. I walked him out to his car. He got in and started the motor, then threw me a kiss. I threw one back, and another one, for his mother. And then a refined one for Miss Victoria Crèmepuff.

"I'll be waiting for you," I called to him. "Hurry back."

Diamond was right. Sometimes you have to grab your karma by the buds.

Chapter 38

⸻❧❧⸻

EINSTEIN'S THEORY OF RELATIVITY WAS PROBABLY not meant to be a personal philosophy, but I was putting it to good use. How odd, I thought, that my year in Kenya had flown by in what felt like a nanosecond, while waiting four hours for Tom to return from the city took an eternity. The whole afternoon seemed filled with opposites that defined each other. Everything was relative to something else.

I went through Mrs. Wycliff's address book to advise those of her friends who were still alive when the service would be held in a local church. There were few phone calls to be made—next to most of the names was a sad notation in Mrs. Wycliff's wavery handwriting: "Deceased." I closed the book and put it back on the desk, and thought of how time had fled from every one of them. Unnoticed and unfelt, one minute just piled itself atop the next, until the day ended, a week rotated, a month, a year dissolved into nothing. And yet, the result of all Mrs. Wycliff's hard work surrounded us. Time leaves us nothing, we leave everything.

I found Jungle Johnny's cell phone number in the back of the book and called him, leaving a message before finally closing the little blue leather book, grateful that there would be enough of us to remember and commemorate Mrs. Wycliff's life.

Diamond-Rose was burning something in the kitchen for a late snack when I sat down at the table to talk with her.

"I'm glad that you'll have a place to stay," I said, waving away the still smoldering cheese sandwich she offered me.

"You really need to develop your palate," she said, taking the sandwich back. "I noticed you're quite the picky eater." She took a big bite. "I'm planning to write something for Elisabeth. From a daughter's perspective."

I smiled at her as she wolfed down her food. "I guess you are the closest relative she had," I said. "And you took good care of her."

"I want it to be the perfect eulogy," Diamond agreed. "To make up for the one I never got to say for my own mother."

She wiped her mouth on her sleeve and got up to retrieve a pad and pencil, and I reflected on how odd it was that Diamond's aunt had treated her so miserably and Elisabeth Wycliff, a perfect stranger, had taken to her. Relatives are where you find them.

Tom arrived carrying boxes of pizza for an early dinner. The Labs immediately perked up and waddled over to sit by the kitchen table and monitor every bite we took.

"I'll pick up Richie and Jackie from the airport tomorrow," he said as we ate. He took a knife from a drawer and cut a slice, feeding little pieces to the Labs. "She loved these two dogs. Now I don't know what we'll do with them."

"They'll stay here, of course," Diamond interjected. "They'll be mine." She paused and gave him a quiet smile. "That is, if it's okay with you."

"Thank you," he said. "And I think Elisabeth would be pleased."

We spent the rest of the day taking care of the animals. Diamond left an announcement on the bulletin board and told the construction men to halt work for a few days. It was growing dark by the time we finished. Diamond left for the house to finish writing the eulogy, and I was closing the hay barn when a light breeze came up from the elephant paddock carrying the familiar smell of elephant with it. I got a sudden lump in my throat. What was Margo doing right now? I could picture her rumbling, purring, and eating hay, maybe tossing a few strands over Abbie to settle her down for the night. The ache was so acute that I sat down on a bank of grass and buried my face in my hands.

There were footsteps behind me. "Come on in, Neelie," Tom called out. "There's a lot to do. Tomorrow I pick up Richie and Jackie, and then we have to meet with the pastor. After that we have to pick out flowers. It's going to be a busy day."

"Give me a minute," I said.

He sat down next to me. "This isn't the right time," he said, "but when things settle down again, I will ask you properly to marry me, and you can say yes, and we can go on and have a great life together."

I looked out over the sanctuary—the grassy fields, the dirt road that led to the paddocks, the nearly completed barn—and didn't reply. "Have you broken things off with Victoria?"

"I haven't had time to talk to her," he said, "but there really is nothing to break off. It was mostly my mother's dreams for me. You didn't give me an answer about my proposing. Would you say yes?"

"I don't know what I want," I said, and it was true. I suddenly realized that I didn't know how I would answer him. "I don't want what my mother has. You know, the house and the lawn, the *barbecue* . . ."

"Do you want me?" His voice sounded plaintive.

"I do love you," I said softly. "But it's all the rest of the stuff that comes with it. Do you understand?"

He sighed. "I'm trying to, Neelie," he said. "I'm really trying to understand what you want. I know how I feel and I thought you wanted to marry me, and it's something I want very much. I love you." He waited another minute or so for me to answer him, but I didn't know what to say.

He stood up and turned to the house, and I followed him, feeling miserable.

We were standing in Mrs. Wycliff's kitchen. Tom took a piece of paper from his pocket. "I spoke with Elisabeth's attorneys and told them to begin probating her will." He looked immutably saddened, and I put my hand on his arm, hoping it was from grief and not my indecision. "Her estate will probably go to Diamond, if there's no objection. I think Diamond was the closest thing to family she's had in the last thirty years of her life. I know she was happy to have Diamond in her life."

"I think that's wonderful," I said.

He nodded and checked his watch. "There's nothing more to be done here. Let's all get some sleep, we have an early day tomorrow."

I gave Diamond a good-bye hug before we left. "Will you be all right?" I asked her.

"I have Baako and Dafi. I'll be fine," she said, pointing to the dogs. "It's not the first time I've lost someone." I kissed her cheek. It was wet with tears.

"You'll never really be alone," I said. "You have me."

She glanced around the kitchen. "I know," she said drolly. "I have you, and I have a life filled with ghosts."

The hunter green Bentley was parked next to my nine-year-old Subaru, and Tom was leaning against it when I came out of the house.

"Do you still want me to come home with you?" he asked me as I approached him.

"Yes," I said. "Of course I do."

"Should we take my car or yours?"

"Hard choice there," I said, laughing and opening the door to his car to get in. There was a brown leather garment bag in the back, and it looked full—packed with what must have been enough clothes for a few days.

"So, was it very hard to get away?" I asked, hoping my curiosity wasn't too obvious. "I know you said you had some kind of important appointment or something?"

"It was nothing pressing," he said. He was concentrating

on the road, his green eyes deepened with the setting sun, his silver gray hair contrasting against the darkening car.

We had been given another chance, it seemed. We could love each other, or we could wound each other. It was entirely up to us.

I knew I loved him—that part was easy. It was getting the rest of it right that was so complicated.

Chapter 39

MY HOUSE WAS WAITING FOR US. AND IT WAS WITH some pride that I unlocked the front door to let us inside. My house. If I had nothing else in the world, I had a place to come home to. Even if things with Tom didn't work out, I wouldn't *need* him, and that gave me a certain independence from my own love for him. Which was very important to me.

Tom pulled the garment bag from his car and draped it over his shoulder to follow me, but stopped at the threshold as though waiting for something. "The last time I was at your house," he said, "I seem to remember being attacked by a four-legged piranha."

"That was at my ex-house with my ex-dog," I said, moving across the living room to turn on a lamp. "They're both gone. Put your stuff down, and I'll make us some tea."

He dropped the garment bag on a sofa and obediently sat down in the kitchen. His eyes were half closed with fatigue.

"Why don't you just get some sleep?" I offered. "My office upstairs has a daybed, and there's also a sofa in the den. It's up to you."

He looked up at me. "I didn't come here to sleep on a sofa," he said flatly, then stood up and held his hands out to me. "Come on, Neelie. Is that what you want?"

"No," I said, and put my hands into his and let him draw me to him. He wrapped his arms around me, and I fell against his body. It was all sweetness, the warmth and pull of him, the fullness of his shoulder against my face, the sound of his breathing against my ear. He bent his head down to find my lips, and we kissed. We were alone now, no horses, no parties, no hard feelings, no interruptions to stop us. It was what I wanted. I knew with certainty that this was what I wanted. It had been so wrong for both of us to give up on each other, a terrible mistake.

He knew it, too. I felt him against me, felt him urgent and hard, and knew he wanted me.

"Why don't we go upstairs," he whispered. "I don't want to waste another minute."

Einstein knew, the movement of bodies is special, that time has no meaning, that energy is all light. That naked singularities create a universe filled with their own heat, and once released, it expands and envelops everything in its path. And I was learning that love could be like that, too.

We were in the bedroom, moving slowly to each other, touching, caressing, erasing time, minute by minute, erasing a year. What is a year? It disappeared when Tom lay down on my bed and held his arms out to me, and I went to him, and he kissed me. Time became irrelevant. There was nothing left but light, the soft glint of touching. He pressed into me, and there was light without the space and time that had driven us apart. It was all undone, redone, completed.

I slept in his arms and heard him breathing. He touched my face a dozen times overnight, asking if that was really me beside him again. We whispered yes to everything, and suddenly time became dawn, and we had more time in front of us than we could ever use up. He finally fell asleep for the last time, and I slipped out of bed and went down into the kitchen to sit at the table and sort it all out.

He had said he loved me—I'd heard it clearly—and I had said I loved him. Everything else needed to be let go. It was serving us no purpose except to anchor us to old wounds.

I made coffee first thing, and he came down into the kitchen and held me and said, "We'll start over again. We can do it," and I gave him a cup of coffee and we kissed.

The rest of the morning was spent with Mrs. Wycliff's pastor, discussing the service for the funeral. Tom picked up Richie and Jackie, and all of us sat together to plan a funeral that was special. Elisabeth Wycliff had been so vital, had spent her life accomplishing so many things, and we wanted that reflected in the service.

It came as no surprise to us that she wanted to be cremated. It seemed a fitting end, considering her latest hobby, but her pith helmet and red wellies were rejected by the mortician. Diamond, insisting that they were an integral part of Mrs. Wycliff, decided they would be put on display next to the flowers we chose for the altar. Diamond picked out sprays of yellow and purple and red, the colors of Kenyan wildflowers. Richie and Jackie chose an elephant made of orchids, its trunk upright, to say good-bye. Jackie wanted nine white doves released to commemorate each decade of Elisabeth's life. Richie wanted a twenty-gun salute.

"That sounds pretty tricky," I commented. "Especially if the guns are fired while the doves are flying around, but maybe we could release Samantha."

This was quickly vetoed, and we moved on to our next task, picking the right music. The pastor suggested "Just a Closer Walk with Thee," and we liked that, until Diamond suggested "Yesu Klisto, Mwiaii," which was "Rock of Ages" sung in Swahili. She sang a few words in a wavery soprano, and it was perfect. Everyone decided it would be the last song in the service.

On the morning of the funeral, the sky was blue and clear and bright, and the sun gave off a welcoming warmth. We were a motley family come together by circumstance but devoted nevertheless, Tom and me and Richie and Jackie and Diamond and Ignacio. Even Mrs. Pennington, Tom's mother, joined us and sat in the back row, dabbing her eyes.

"This was very bad timing when I had an important dinner planned," she whispered to me before the solemnities.

"You think Mrs. W. died just to keep Tom from getting engaged?" I whispered back, shocked.

"Well, I know how tight you all are," she replied. "Friends do things for each other."

To my surprise, the church was filled. Mrs. W.'s friends had come from all over. Volunteers who had worked at the sanctuary through the years, people who had supported her work, vendors who sold her supplies, people who loved animals and appreciated that someone had stepped forward to do the things they couldn't do.

Jungle Johnny arrived early, a rucksack flipped over his shoulder, and I made sure he was seated next to Diamond. I was pleased and surprised to see how crowded the pews were, and what good words everyone had to say.

Richie and Tom and Jackie all gave beautiful eulogies, praising Mrs. Wycliff's bravery, her convictions, her loving heart, her passions for all things living, and her generosity. I briefly thanked her for the opportunity of helping save Margo and Abbie, for inspiring me to do better by the animals, and then just as quickly I sat down.

Diamond was the last to speak. She stood at the altar and fought back tears as she spoke.

She spoke of how loved she felt, how good it had been to have found a mother so late in life, how secure and wanted Mrs. Wycliff had made her feel. She spoke of her admiration for Mrs. Wycliff's life, how she never tired of hearing about the many rescues Mrs. Wycliff had made, how much foresight she had starting the sanctuary, how proud Diamond was to have become her family.

"Elisabeth Wycliff," she ended, "I will never forget you, and I will forever honor you. *Fika salama, mama yangu.* Arrive safely in God's arms."

The organist played a few old gospel songs, but they were quickly overshadowed by the haunting and sweet hymn sung in Swahili that played over the PA system, courtesy of a quick computer download. We each bid her good-bye. I placed a tiny china statue of a baby elephant on the altar, Richie and Jackie placed a small silver Noah's ark, Tom's gift was a white rose, Diamond left a half dozen cheroots tied in a white silk ribbon because she knew Elisabeth would have appreciated them, and Samantha sat on Diamond's shoulder and whispered a tender and heartfelt Fuckyou.

Finally, as the autumn sun rose full into the sky, taking the chill from the air and replacing it with warmth and golden light, Mrs. Elisabeth Jane Hauptmann Wycliff's brave and lovely soul was sent on its ultimate and eternal safari as Diamond and Jungle Johnny gave a duet impression of the farewell call of the white-bellied go-away bird.

Chapter 40

MRS. WYCLIFF WAS QUICKLY CREMATED AND PLACED in a lovely silver-and-maroon urn, which was presented to Diamond for safekeeping.

She moved the ashes from room to room, never quite comfortable with their ultimate placement. She felt the kitchen was too warm—although it was nice for breakfast—the living room too drafty, Mrs. W.'s old bedroom too isolated. It wasn't unusual to see Diamond taking Mrs. W. along on truck rides while she completed her farm chores or accompanied by her as she ran errands into town, Mrs. W. safely ensconced in the front seat, her urn wrapped in the seat belt.

"I feel so responsible for her," Diamond said to me. "At first, I thought it would bother me, but I find her presence comforting. She took me in and gave me a home, and I want to do what's best for her."

"I'm sure she'd be happy just sitting next to her red wellies on the mantelpiece," I replied. "That's kind of traditional, isn't it?"

"But she wasn't a traditional woman," Diamond worried. "Plus, I think getting her outdoors cheers her up. She can't stay cooped up all day in the house."

"I think she needs her rest," I pointed out. "You know, *eternal rest*? She can't be bouncing all over town like this at her age."

But Diamond was insistent. Mrs. W. shared the table for breakfast, lunch, and dinner; sat on the hood of the truck when we worked the horses; and in general, spent more time actively outdoors than she had in the last twenty years of her previous life.

Mrs. W. apparently was sharing Diamond's special moments with Rocco, the construction manager, too. By the time I would arrive at the farm every morning, Diamond was already aboard one of the heavy machines, shrieking with delight as she practiced driving the caterpillar or operating the large claw of the backhoe, lifting beams and huge metal gates, her red hair blowing carefree across her face, with Rocco, always next to her, laughing, his preternaturally white teeth providing a vivid contrast to his florid skin. It would seem they made a perfect pair, each decked out in dark pants, thick boots, yellow helmets, and significant amounts of dust.

"Maybe he is the one," Diamond confided breathlessly to me one morning after hopping down from the cab of the backhoe.

"Honestly," I said as we walked back to the house, "you

had the perfect man in Jungle Johnny. You dress alike. He's handsome. What is *wrong* with you?"

"He isn't local." She shrugged. "I know those types. I lived with one. The jungle is always their first love. I want to be first, just this once."

"Rocco doesn't mind Mrs. W.?" I asked, pointing to the urn she was carrying back with her.

"I told him it was a new kind of thermos," she replied. "He thinks it's very cute."

Diamond planned for Rocco to come for dinner and stay the night.

"Do you think Mrs. W. would mind if I just left her in the mudroom overnight right next to her wellies?" she asked me. "I don't want to spook Rocco."

"I don't think she'd mind at all," I replied. "I think she needs to take a breather."

And so Mrs. W. spent the night sitting on her wellies in the mudroom, her pith helmet parked jauntily atop her urn, allowing Diamond and Rocco a private and romantic evening.

I supposed it was a rousing success because the next day, a blushing Diamond confided that she was ready to give Rocco the ultimate test. If he passed, he would be considered a serious candidate for her heart. She felt that because he had generously taken her for rides in the heavy construction machinery used for the new barn, she would reciprocate. She would open her heart and show him what was dearest to her. Which meant the afternoon on the back of a horse for a thorough tour of the farm.

328 | Judy Reene Singer

Rocco opted out.

The horse traumatized him since it couldn't be influenced by levers or pedals or steering posts. It wasn't mechanical at all. He hated that it was fully autonomous, sometimes cantankerous, and completely independent of its operator. Diamond persisted. Having had years of teaching clients to ride well enough to go on weeklong safaris, she held a strong conviction she could instill enough skill in Rocco for a mere ride around a few hundred acres. Then he would fall in love with riding and horses and Diamond, and it would all be perfect. Plus he couldn't be more local, since he was working in her backyard.

It didn't take.

Rocco mounted the short but sturdy yellow-brown quarter horse and proceeded to freeze into a garden post. Turning a deaf ear to Diamond's remonstrations that he at least breathe, he tipped one way, then the other, before rolling off onto his side and landing next to the horse with a ground-shaking thud.

He stood up and gave the horse an angry slap on its rump for embarrassing him. The horse responded the way horses do when they are suddenly slapped on the derriere by unappreciative riders—with a swift kick out, denting Rocco's rib cage and triggering a giggling fit by Diamond. Rocco stormed off and out of the relationship.

Diamond was heartbroken but philosophical. "Grapes grow on every vine," she said. "There's always another fish in the pond."

"A bit of a mixed bag of metaphors, but you're perfectly right," I said to her.

"Wildflowers fill the hillsides," she went on. "Peanuts grow in every garden."

"That has a nice horticultural ring to it," I admired.

"Yep, I will find love." She patted me on the arm. "One whose seeds have not sprouted yet does not give up planting."

In the meantime, my own garden was getting a rough patch. My phone rang one morning, about a week or so after the funeral, just as I was getting dressed to leave for the farm. It was Mrs. Pennington, Tom's mother, and she had some news to report.

"Tom has broken up with Victoria." she announced. "He told her that his life was taking him in a new direction, but this isn't the end of it, as far as I'm concerned. I hope you're happy now."

My heart jumped at her words. I was the new direction! My buds were blooming! "Actually, I am happy," I replied. I wanted to explain how it was karma and that sometimes karma actually works for you, although it apparently hadn't worked for her, but that was for Mrs. Pennington to delve into her own past to figure out why her buds got nipped.

"Well, Victoria and I have discussed things at some length," she said airily, "and there's no hurry. Make your little plans. We can be very patient because we know who really belongs at his side."

I didn't have little plans, I had big ones, but I still didn't want her to be my enemy. She was Tom's mother and under any other circumstance, really a gracious and good person. I decided to take a different tack to clear the air.

"Have I offended you somehow?" I asked her. "Because if I did, I truly, truly am sorry."

My words must have taken her by surprise. "I'm not of-fended at all," she replied coolly. "You are probably a . . .

decent . . . person in your own right, but you were not meant for my son. Surely you agree. Even Victoria immediately saw that. There's a world of difference between you and my son."

The famous Victoria. Slated by the rigid confines of social snobbery to be Tom's wife, she had probably been writing "Victoria Cremwell Pennington" all over her schoolbooks ever since high school. Maybe even preschool. *Private* preschool. In fact, she probably pooed that name in her diapers.

"But it's up to Tom," I said. "Don't you think? He loves me."

Mrs. Pennington snorted. Not as polite as a horse snort, hers had more indignation and fury behind it, and maybe a tad less mucus. "You know, *any* woman can turn a man's head. You just have to make yourself available in the, er, carnal manner, and they can't think straight."

I was trying not to feel offended, although she was actually insulting her own son by accusing him of thinking with his dick.

"Couldn't Victoria have done that as well?" I asked. "Um, get to, um, know Tom in the biblical sense? I mean, he's sort of open game." This was not where I wanted the conversation to go at all. My romantic life with Tom was special, beautiful, and I didn't want it filleted and dissected and discussed by, of all people, his mother.

"Victoria is a *lady*," she replied. "She won't bring herself down to that level."

"You mean sinking to the level of sleeping with your son?"

She coughed. I had her. And I was irritated enough to make her squirm. "What's wrong with sleeping with your son? Tell Victoria that he's a *very* good lover. She's really missing out."

Now Mrs. Pennington coughed and snorted all at the same time, which sounded impressive over the phone. "That's quite enough," she managed, sparing me the obligation of having to go into descriptions of heaving bosoms and thrusting members.

There was a momentary pause while she regrouped. "You leave me no choice," she finally said, then took a deep breath to deliver her coup de grâce. "I am prepared to make you a very wealthy woman. How much do you want?"

Her words were so ludicrous, so preposterous, so insulting that I was startled by their rancor.

"Mrs. Pennington," I said, then spoke slowly, so she would have the full effect of my answer. "I'll just wait, thank you. When I marry Tom, I plan to become a very wealthy woman in my own right."

Tom was traveling, and I never told him of the words I had with his mother. I was hoping that at some point she would have a change of heart and learn to like me. I didn't want to put Tom in the middle of a girlfriend-and-mother war. His business was requiring him to travel all over the world. It was romantic to get phone calls every night from a different country, and I wasn't going to ruin things with a domestic squabble. His words were always sweet and loving, and he even began sending gifts—CDs from Incan musicians he admired on a street corner in Texas, a knitted shawl from Ireland, a deep pink blown-glass flower from Hungary. I admired them and packed them away. It wasn't trinkets I wanted. I was restless and ached to accomplish something. My house was closing in on me, the sky was closing in on me. And I fretted that each day the money sat in the ELLI account was another animal somewhere that was dying.

Oh, we rescued a few more horses, and two black-and-white female lambs that had been found outside a city apartment house, hog-tied and being used for footballs, a few more alpacas, a sad and tiny donkey that had been tied to a tree and left to die behind an abandoned house. We found a perfect match for Samantha, a local artist who was stone-deaf. The woman's creative eye granted her an appreciation of the bird's beautiful plumage, but she was totally unable to hear the salty vocabulary.

"Maybe we need to get back to Africa," I grumbled to Diamond one morning as we drove the truck down to supervise the sale of another horse. "We raised enough money—what are we waiting for?"

"We'll be faced with the same problems," she said, balancing Mrs. W. on her lap as the truck hit a few potholes. Mrs. W.'s new residence had a few dings in it by now, courtesy of falling off the front seat a few times and rolling into the road. "Tom has the planes, we need planes, we can't afford planes, back to square one."

It was frustrating.

All the while, Tom continued to send gifts. Tea from Japan that opened into tiny pastel-colored lotus buds when you added water, a beautiful silk robe from Thailand with small embroidered elephants, a box of chocolates from Belgium that were silkenly delicious. I packed it all away, except of course, for the latter, which Diamond and I downed in one sitting, along with two bottles of wine.

It was very late one night when Tom called me. I was already in bed and beginning to think that maybe Victoria Cremwell might have a future. Mine was a life in limbo, and I was not going to live it like that anymore. It was time to tell him. If it meant it was over between us, then that was my karma. But I needed to strike out on my own.

"Pack a bag," he said into my ear. "I'm taking you on a special little trip."

"Really?" I asked. "Where?"

"Athens."

"*Opa!*" I said, now thinking of sunny little fishing villages and baklava and the Acropolis.

"Texas," he finished. "Athens, Texas. Diamond's invited, too."

I sat upright. "Why on earth are we all going to Texas?"

"I'm asking you to get married," he replied, and I was puzzled. I hadn't really thought about marrying in Texas, but the Lone Star State suddenly sounded appealing.

"Really, Tom?"

"Really," he replied. "I mean, well, sort of."

"What does 'well, sort of' mean?" I asked suspiciously, wondering if he had been speaking to his mother and somehow found some weird way to make us both happy.

"I'm asking you to get married," he replied, "but I'm asking you to marry Grisha."

Chapter 41

⚬⚬⚬

I LAUGHED FOR TEN WHOLE MINUTES.

Tom laughed, too. "You'll see," he finally said. "It's all part of a plan."

"To ruin my life?"

"To rescue an elephant."

He wouldn't tell me anything else, just sent tickets, and within two days Diamond, Mrs. W., and I were on the next plane to Tyler Pounds Regional Airport, close to Athens.

Texas.

"Did you really have to bring Mrs. W.?" I asked Diamond as we settled into our seats on the plane. She had wrapped Mrs. W., urn and all, in newspaper and tucked her into her ubiquitous rucksack, which was then tucked

inside a suitcase. I was traveling light. I had packed a suitcase, but the clothes I brought with me were decidedly un-
bridal. Tom had mentioned that I would be buying all the
appropriate clothes in Texas. I made a face at Diamond. "I
mean, what happens if they go through your luggage and
find her?"

"There is no law against a girl traveling with her mum,"
she replied.

I cast a baleful eye on her. "There probably is if your
mum is in a jar."

"Besides," said Diamond, "it wouldn't be right for all of us
to be at your wedding while she stays at home."

Tom and Grisha were waiting for us at the airport. Grisha
bowed low, put one cigarette-bearing hand behind his back,
and took my hand to kiss my knuckles in a wet, nicotine-
smelling smack. He actually blushed.

"Plain-Neelie," he said, "it is honorment to make marriage with you."

"Thank you," I said, then turned to Tom. "But you'd
better have a reasonable explanation for playing matchmaker
with people who don't want to be matched up."

"I'll tell you all about it while we drive to the hotel," he
said. "And it won't be forever. You'll only be married for a
few days."

We were going first class. For Athens, at least. Tom had
made the reservations at the Holiday Inn Express, a wide,
pseudo-elegant tan building dressed up with a porte cochere
with pretentious Grecian columns at each corner.

"Dr. and Mrs. Grisha Trotsky," Tom announced grandly to the clerk, pointing to Grisha and me.

"Trotsky?" I shrieked after we were all led up to the room, or rather, suite of rooms.

"Yep," Tom agreed. "We wanted a name that sounded vaguely famous. The people we'll be dealing with are sleazy and clever but not smart."

"Well, Trotsky," I mused. "It does have a nice horsey ring to it."

There was a table in the corner of the room, and the four of us sat ourselves around it. Five, since Mrs. W.'s urn was placed in the middle as if to preside over the meeting.

Tom slid some papers across the table. "Grisha is going to pose as a multimillionaire from Russia. You are his adoring wife. And you are going on a canned hunt."

"Like Campbell soup cans?"

He gave an ironic laugh and said, "I wish," and handed me a sheaf of papers. It was a glossy brochure for a sportsmen's ranch just outside of Athens. Photos of lions and tigers, a bear, a rhino—exotic animals for your hunting pleasure.

"Bollocks!" Diamond exclaimed. "This looks like Kenya."

"Except the animals don't have a chance," Tom said grimly. "It's all fenced in. You ride around in jeeps, they turn on the floodlights, the animals are chased into a narrow chute, right into your gun sight."

I felt my stomach heave. "What's the purpose?" I gasped.

Tom shrugged. "Damned if I know," he said. "There's no sport in it. It's all vanity. They take the head home and hang it up somewhere."

"That's so disgusting," I said, "but you said something about an elephant?"

Tom threw a photo in front of me. It was blurry and taken from a distance, and the angle was funky. But my heart stopped. I pulled the picture close to my face and squinted at it. Could it be? One tusk curling inward, the massive head and body. I wanted to crawl into the picture with him.

"Tusker?" I choked. "He's *here*?"

Grisha took the photo from me and studied it. "*Da*. We have follow elephants out of Zimbabwe. We have obtain the information they make arrivement in Texas. We think it is same elephant that we make lurement with oranges."

I turned to Tom. "Why didn't you tell me?"

"I didn't know for sure. Grisha wasn't certain of his information. I didn't want to get you hopeful and then have to give you bad news again. You don't do well with bad news. And besides, this had to be totally confidential."

"What do you mean?" I felt insulted. "I'm good at keeping secrets."

"You know, there's an old proverb," Diamond interjected. "Three can keep a secret when two are dead."

I gave her the squint-eye, then turned back to Tom. "So, what kind of secrets are we talking about?"

"Please to understand, Mr. Thomas is not blameful," Grisha apologized. "Many enamels ship from Zimbabwe. They go all over world. Big funtime for sheiks in Middle East to hunt trapped enamels."

"You think they're going to hunt Tusker?" I gasped. "Here? In Texas?"

"Texas is the biggest canned hunt location in the world—it's wide open here," Tom said.

"*Da*." Grisha nodded. "Is should be illegalment." He made a face. "In Russia, we do not have illegalments. *Politsiya* everywhere!" He lit another Stolichnye Light from the stub of his last one and breathed in deeply before holding it up to his face to admire. "Grisha is glad of Russian cigarette. American cigarette like smoking empty paper."

"Yes," I said, standing up and walking over to the window to look for a way to open it and let out the quickly accumulating cloud of blue smoke. "Lucky I'm not really your wife, or I'd have you quit smoking those things."

"Grisha never quits!" Then he threw his head back and laughed. "Look at Plain-Neelie! Wife for five minutes and already we fight!"

We had lunch sent to the room—Diamond-Rose; Mrs. W., who was put on the desk and given the job of temporary paperweight; Tom and me and Grisha. Two waiters rolled in a steam table across the floor and lifted the lids to reveal Texas-size steaks, mountains of mashed potatoes that matched Kilimanjaro for altitude, garlic toast, and a salad that could feed an army of vegetarians. And several bottles of good wine.

"I may want to move to Texas," Diamond said, wiping the last dot of au jus from her lips. "That was delicious."

Grisha looked up from his plate. "American steak not as good as Russian steak."

"Yeah," Tom dryly agreed. "One bite of Russian steak is enough to keep you chewing through the entire winter season."

"*Da*!" agreed Grisha. "This is so!" And cut another hearty piece for himself.

Tom checked his watch. "I'm expecting someone to arrive any minute now. He's going to help coordinate things," he said. "He's done rescues and is quite a good animal handler. You met him at the funeral."

Dessert was brought up next, huge slabs of sweet potato pie covered with mounds of whipped cream, and a bottle of Frangelico, courtesy of the hotel. Diamond-Rose dug ferociously into hers, when there was a knock at the door. Tom jumped to his feet and opened it to reveal a familiar figure. Jungle Johnny. He was wearing tan safari shorts, a tan shirt topped with a red bolo, gray socks, heavy boots. Diamond's doppelganger.

Tom made the introductions. "You all remember John Galloway? Jungle Johnny?" We shook hands all around.

"Call me JJ," he said. "Takes less time."

He eased himself into a chair and helped himself to a huge piece of pie. "Love working with you, Tom. You spare no expense," he said.

"We don't normally eat like this," Tom replied, "but Grisha has to look every inch the Russian mafioso, and they like big, heavy meals. I like my details perfect." He turned to JJ. "And I want you in civilian clothes tomorrow."

JJ poured himself a glass of Frangelico, took a sip, and sighed loudly. "Ahhh! The devil is in the details." Then he leaned conspiratorially forward. "Now, let's get to work. Talk about details, we've got to get everything just right." He sat back and gave us a solemn look. "Ladies and gentlemen, I hope you're up to it because tomorrow we're turning into Russians!"

Chapter 42

NOT REALLY RUSSIANS, MORE LIKE RUSSIAN ACCOM-
plices, but it was as though a switch had been thrown. Suddenly my heart felt alive. Suddenly something inside of me
awakened, something I hadn't felt in months. I pulled my
chair closer to the table. I was almost quivering with anticipation. Tom led off.

"Later on today Grisha and Neelie will meet Lance Imperialle of the Circle D Ranch," he said. "Neelie, you will
not look like or act like a horse person or animal bleeding heart or anything of that nature, or they will detect
your cover a mile away. You are merely Grisha's arm
candy."

I looked over at Diamond. Her brilliant red hair was
pulled up into a tangled bun, and her green eyes were bright
with excitement. Jungle Johnny couldn't take his eyes off

her, and I wondered why she couldn't see his enthrallment. My thoughts were interrupted when Tom threw a set of maps on the table.

"The ranch is about three thousand acres," he began. "Diamond knows how to navigate quickly and easily over new territory, so we'll use her when we are actually getting the elephants out of there. Neelie's job is to see if there really are elephants, where they are kept, what kind of security system they have, and how the animals are maneuvered for the hunt. She'll be documenting everything."

JJ whistled. "That's a tall order," he said. Which was just what I was anxiously thinking.

"Neelie's smart, she'll be able to do it," Tom replied confidently, and I shot him a nervous but grateful smile. "They don't allow anybody on the place to just poke around," he continued, "and Grisha will be busy in the office."

"Grisha is making contract with Mr. Lance first things after lunch," Grisha added, alternately smoking and plowing through his dessert. He licked his plate but not before declaring, "American dessert too sweet. You should try good Russian *vareniki*. Not tasty at all."

"So I go with Grisha," I repeated. "How do I document what I see?"

"We'll give you a camera. Try to get some pictures— see what they have. Wander around as much as you can. Even if the elephant isn't Tusker, we're going to take it anyway. A friend of mine thought they might have an old circus elephant that they're planning to shoot. These old animals become big inconveniences when they're done performing. I guess they've found a lucrative way to get rid of them. Try to get a feel of the place while Grisha signs the contracts for the hunt." I gave an involuntary shudder.

Grisha finished his dessert and lit a cigarette. Both Jungle Johnny and Diamond dug into their rucksacks and pulled out cheroots in a simultaneous choreography, then looked at each other and smiled. The room began to fill up with that peculiar cesspool odor that I had never quite adjusted to.

"So, Grisha is millionaire—" Grisha began.

"Billionaire," Tom corrected him. "You are part of the Russian mafia. They have money to burn."

"Much heavier!" Grisha smiled approvingly, taking another puff. "Grisha likes this! Grisha is heavy billionaire and heavy bored with life. Grisha wants to hunt. Big trophy. Maybe two. And Grisha will pay heavy for special considerations." He had learned his part quite well.

Diamond looked over at Tom. "Why can't Neelie pretend to be married to you and then the two of you can go. You really *are* a billionaire, right?"

"Mr. Thomas has face with heavy recognizement," Grisha pointed out correctly. "Mr. Thomas must stay out of lamplight."

Now Tom focused his attention on me. "Do you think you can do it?" he asked.

"Yep," I promised. "I will say nice things and be gracious. I will come off silly and vain and indifferent."

"Perfect," Tom said. "Try to be everything I hate in a woman."

"I thought I already was," I retorted, but he didn't laugh.

Tom did not waste time. He had already arranged for Grisha and me to take a private tour of the Circle D ranch later that afternoon. We arrived in a rented Rolls-Royce Silver Cloud, with a driver—Tom truly was sparing no expense—and were ushered through a pair of tall, garish silver-and-gold gates by a man dressed in a pale blue safari suit with silver trim, who introduced himself as Julian, our safari coordinator. Grisha, dressed in an expensive dark brown business suit and chocolate brown tooled crocodile-skin cowboy boots, puffed on his cigarette and looked imperious. I did my best to function as the trophy wife, Texas style, with stiletto heels, a flouncy miniskirt, and low-cut blouse enhanced by a push-up bra, courtesy of a frantic shopping trip after lunch, as well as a heavy veneer of makeup, courtesy of Miss Stella, the beauty consultant at the Holiday Inn Hair and Beauty Spa. She also sprayed my hair into a two-foot cement block of banana curls.

"Now, don't y'all just look darlin'?" she had drawled, stepping back to admire her work. "Your hubby's mouth is just gonna *water*." I was hoping it wasn't the kind of uncontrolled salivation that comes just before vomiting.

Our Rolls was whisked away, and we waited a moment under a tent-size silver umbrella held by Julian, to protect us from the hot Texas sun.

"Canapés and drinks will be served in the inner sanctum," he informed us, and for a moment, I had the heady feeling that I was royalty going to be locked in a cave. A minute later, a bright gold safari jeep pulled up. We drove along a Belgium-block driveway to a many-columned Georgian mansion with a brass sign outside that declared "A Man's Castle Is His Castle," and whose innards were done up in red velvet and gold trim, an obvious paean to bad taste and conspicuous consumption. Julian led us down a dark-paneled hallway across rugs that ate our ankles to the private office of Lance Imperialle. It was here, Grisha was given to understand, he would sign contracts and pay for his special considerations. I flounced my way down the hall on Grisha's arm, nervously aware of the GPS in my hot pink Marc Jacobs handbag, with the tiny digital surveillance camera tucked into its clasp, a little gift from Tom.

"They'll be looking at your handbag," he had said. "You need a good one." No objection from me. A little arm candy for the arm candy seemed a nice touch.

Lancelot Imperialle, owner of the Circle D Ranch, was, as Tom described, a self-made sleazeball in good standing. He was waiting as though at attention when we were led in. Julian gave a little bow and disappeared. Lance gave us a small nod of his head.

His black hair was pulled back in a greasy ponytail, he wore tight white jeans, white leather boots with fringe, and a white muscle shirt that highlighted bulging workout muscles under artificially tanned orange skin. Every knuckle had a big gold ring. He wore a large gold *L* on a chain around his neck, and he leered at me every time Grisha looked away. He gestured for us to sit down.

"You came highly recommended, Dr. Trotsky," he said to Grisha. "Everyone I've spoken to seems to somehow know your name."

"I am big man in my country of Russia," Grisha grunted, and took a puff on his cigarette.

A man came in carrying a tray of champagne and little crackers with caviar heaped on top. "Iranian caviar," Lance pointed out. On Wheat Thins, I noticed with amusement. I guess the veneer of wealth only goes so deep.

"Needs spoon from mother-of-pearls," said Grisha, helping himself to a handful of crackers.

"So, how can I help you," Lance Imperialle asked, pouring a glass of champagne and offering it to me.

"What kind is it?" I asked, adding just the right amount of petulance in my voice.

He looked at the bottle. " 'Armand de Brignac,' " he read off. I made a face and took the glass from him.

Grisha noisily let his breath out. "I am already bored. You have something interested for me?"

"Yes, of course." Lance Imperialle sat down at a huge Gothic rosewood desk. There were animal heads on every paneled wall. Exquisite lions, and what I recognized as a rare white Bengal tiger, a grizzly, a white rhino, a springbok, a polar bear, all stuffed, glass eyed, jaws lined with perfect teeth and open in a final, soundless protest, all of it soulless and sickening.

"Like my rogues' gallery?" He gestured to the walls.

"You have Masai giraffe?" Grisha pointed to a doe-eyed, beautiful marked creature with velvety dark chocolate patches on rich gold fur that hung behind Lance.

"We have everything," Lance said. "What we don't have, we can order. Takes a while, but we can get anything you want."

"Do I have to sit here for this?" I whined. "I'm boo-rrr-ed, too. I hate business talk."

Grisha jumped to his feet. "My darling, you must not be bored! Grisha will buy you diamonds when we leave here."

"Then let's leave now," I whined again. Grisha bowed and gave Lance Imperialle a helpless shrug.

"Don't worry," Lance said. He pressed a button on the desk. "I can have my personal assistant give your little lady a tour. Would you like a tour?"

"Can I have more champagne?" I asked.

"Of course," Lance Imperialle said soothingly. "I noticed you didn't like this bottle. How about Cristal? You like Cristal?"

I gave a careless shrug. "Louis Roederer?"

"The very one," he said.

Julian came back into the room.

"Take Mrs. Trotsky out for a little tour," Lance said, "while Dr. Trotsky and I sign these boring contracts." He gave me a wink. I wanted to kiss him for playing right into my arm-candy hands.

I wobbled to my feet, balanced on my three-inch spikes, fluffed my skirt and my hair, which I realized was irredeemably unfluffable, before I bent over to give my adoring Grisha a much-lipsticked kiss on the lips and followed Julian out the door. Stumbling across the weedy gravel path, I clutched my handbag, adjusted my décolleté, turned on my GPS, and told Julian I couldn't wait to see all the nasty little beasties.

"Oh, we've got lots of nasty beasties," he said, "ready and waiting for your entertainment pleasure."

Chapter 43

WELL, THE CHAMPAGNE WAS GOOD.

The gold jeep had a wet bar and a snack bar and a television, as if the specter of destroying animals wasn't entertaining enough. Julian was unctuously devoted to my comfort.

He pointed the car to a road behind the mansion and drove. The trappings of the ranch dropped away as if it were a Hollywood set. The Belgium-block road turned to dust, and the lush trees and plantings, the huge swimming pool and cabana were quickly replaced by a landscape that was drearily plain and definitely low budget. Mesquite trees, stunted oaks, and date palms, all draped in Spanish moss; scrub brush; and stalky, tan bromegrass covered the rest of the compound. The humid air filled with dust. Sticker bushes lined the twelve-foot-high chain-link fence that ran along the road. With a little shock, I remembered the sticker bushes at the horse kill pen and how Diamond had remarked how those bushes were frequently used so that the animals couldn't get through without tearing themselves apart. And true enough, the two-inch-long spikes were a treacherous barrier. We drove about a mile, with nothing to be seen. It looked quite banal, except for what I knew took place here.

"Bored," I called from the back, and indeed I was. I took another slug of Cristal.

"Here we go," Julian called out. We came up to a series of cages, dozens, more than dozens, a long line of dirty, rusted metal cages, sitting sullenly in the sun. "There are your nasty beasties."

They were in there. Caged and crouched. Lions, tigers. A grizzly, several gazelle huddled together, all panting heavily from the heat, their eyes clouded with misery. A panther, some pronghorn deer. Small cages set on concrete slabs, some sitting directly out in the hot Texas sun, each a solitary confinement. The smell of ammonia wafted up to the jeep as we drove by. I could see the water buckets were barely filled, with an inch or so of silt at the bottom. I maneuvered my handbag and pressed the clasp, hoping I was getting clear pictures.

"Oh, I can see these in the circus," I sneered, taking another sip from my flute of champagne. I looked away, hoping to feign boredom, hoping to keep the tears from springing into my eyes.

Julian nodded. "Well, I'll take you to see something special. We just got them in. Your husband expressed some interest in them."

He pulled ahead, driving past cages and cages of animals on death row. Some of them were panting ferociously, harrowing looks of fear on their faces. And they were all thin, that seemed to be a given. So thin. Of course, they were thin, I suddenly realized. The sport hunters only cared about the heads.

I took pictures and pressed the buttons on my GPS and hoped that Julian wouldn't notice. I wasn't nervous, more high-strung, my adrenaline pushing my fear aside, making me almost giddy.

"How do you keep them all, you know, from getting stolen?" I asked Julian.

He gave a short laugh. "You think someone is going to break in here and steal a lion?" He whistled at the stupidity of it. "We got four dogs and a security guy. We mostly rely on the dogs. They don't get drunk on Saturday night and forget to show up."

"I like dogs," I said, then poured myself more champagne.

I estimated we drove another mile when I started to smell something, the familiar, warm musky smell that I knew so well. Definitely elephants.

We drew closer. There was a cage behind a large tangle of brushy trees. Julian stopped the jeep, turned off the motor, and helped me out. I still held the champagne glass in my hand and my handbag in the other. "Thank you," I said sweetly, and followed him to the cage.

He stood cuffed in heavy chains around his front legs, immobilized on a small cement pad. It was Tusker. The delicately curved tusk, the great, giant body—it was unmistakably him. He was emaciated. A trembling skeleton. His flesh hung over an arc of ribs, his spine cut a sharp outline down his back, his gaunt face was a mask of misery. And his head was tilted, giving it an almost inquisitive look, as if he were asking me why.

My king of wild hearts had been broken.

I couldn't look and I couldn't look away. I clutched my stupid drink and gave my host a gracious smile.

"Ever see anything that big?" he said.

I tried to answer and stopped for a deep breath. I would not cry. I would not cry.

"Big," I said. His trunk hung limply, his amber eyes stared glassily beyond us, closed down, seeing nothing.

I didn't want to stay there with him another second. I couldn't bear it. The tilt of the head, the golden eyes that had been so filled with good humor and life. I gripped my champagne glass.

"Well, I guess I've seen him," I said. "Anything else?" I hoped my voice hadn't betrayed me.

Julian nodded. "We've got another bull further down the road. Can't keep them together. The other one's younger and smaller. This one's got the bigger head but one shit-ass tusk. The other's got two tusks, but some kind of rip in his ear. If your husband wants both, I'm sure Lance can give him a special rate. He can also arrange for another tusk to be put on this one's head."

I gave him a bright smile. "Oh, wow. How does he do that?"

"Resin, after he's shot, but you wouldn't be able to tell the difference," Julian said proudly.

"Fabulous," I said.

"We do it all the time. Replace teeth, horns, you know, we promise perfect." He waited for my approval. "Probably can fix the ear, too. You know, of the other one."

I nodded. "So, does he just shoot him right in there?" I gestured to the cage, littered with a small pile of dry-looking manure mixed in with a handful of bromegrass, though I was really trying to look for electric fencing, any kind of wiring.

Julian shook his head no. "The back of the pen opens to a chute."

I looked and sure enough, there was a locked gate opposite me. A simple lock hung on a latch.

"We chase him into the chute with an electric prod. The chute's only about thirty feet long, so you're hardly exerting yourself. Most guys like to hunt before dinner, gives them a big appetite." Julian winked at me. "And later, too, if you know what I mean." I giggled. Julian returned to the jeep. I turned my back on Tusker and followed Julian.

I couldn't spend another second looking at the elephant. I felt I had betrayed him. I came from a race of killers and predators of the worst order. I was so ashamed. So ashamed. So ashamed.

We drove on. A few thin horses browsing on bromegrass, another tall, narrow cage full of parrots, sitting listlessly. "We rent them out for parties," said Julian. "You know, theme parties."

We passed still another cage with a black panther sitting in the hot sun next to a tub half filled with water and no shelter, his pink tongue unrolled and quivering like a ribbon of defeat.

"We do safaris on horseback, too," Julian said, gesturing to the horses. "Some guys think they're quite the cowboy. They ride for about fifteen minutes"—he laughed—"then they're ready to call it a day."

"Can I see the other elephant?" I asked. "I want to see the tusks. Dr. Trotsky is very fussy. He saw a nice elephant in"—I had to think—"Budapest! It was perfect."

"Sure." Julian refilled my glass once again and drove us farther into the compound. We were alone, and suddenly all my giddy power from righteous anger melted away and I felt vulnerable. I had nothing to protect me out here but my silly stilettos and a hot pink Marc Jacobs bag. I wished I had a gun, though I realized that I might have used it a little too quickly.

Shamwari was at the very end of the dusty road. I could see his movement before I could get a clear view of him. He was weaving. Rocking back and forth, back and forth, back and forth in a mindless dance of insanity. His eyes were closed, he rocked his head to one side, and then followed through with his thin, freshly scarred body, rocking, rocking, lost to some internal, private hellish rhythm. Back and forth. I slipped my hand in my purse and pressed the buttons on the GPS. They would help the others determine exactly where the elephants were. Then I pressed the clasp of the handbag. Tom said we would need pictures for prosecution. The pictures were vital. I stood at Shamwari's cage and tapped the sides of it lightly with my fingers.

"Hello in there," I called like a fool. "Hello, you big thing."

Julian checked his watch and made an impatient noise.

"I'm done," I said, and finished the champagne. I almost wished it was poison. "It was very awesome."

Julian drove me back. I tried to banter with him, saying how much fun my husband was going to have, how good the trophies—they weren't called heads, I had to remember that—how good the trophies would look in our lodge in Russia.

"I thought your lodge was in Switzerland," Julian countered.

I gave him a drunken wave. "That's the *ski* lodge. Truthfully, I have no idea where he wants to put those dirty things."

Julian laughed and gunned the big engine of the jeep. "You always wanna keep your man happy," he said.

"Oh, I do," I said meaningfully. "I *do.*"

Grisha came out of the office, waving a sheaf of papers. Julian had parked the jeep and was holding the ubiquitous umbrella over my head as we waited a few moments for our Rolls to be brought.

"We are hunting," Grisha said happily. "Tomorrow night!" Lance was next to him, smiling a big, greasy smile. "I like night hunting. Heavy challengement."

"You don't mind he wants to do it at night?" I asked, truly surprised.

"Honey," said Lance, "he could hunt butt naked in the moonlight. I just take the money."

"It is Grisha's pleasure to give you money," Grisha replied. Our Rolls pulled up.

"Well, I want to shop," I said, yawning. "I've had enough of this. Come *on.*"

"Grisha must make marital woman happy," Grisha declared, helping me into the car. I wondered if there were cameras charting our every move because everything seemed so seamless. It was a point I had to bring up when I got back to the hotel.

"You promised me a diamond watch," I whined.

"Make her happy," said Lance, closing the limo door on me. Then he walked to the other side of the Rolls and helped Grisha in. "Tomorrow night, we make *you* happy."

Chapter 44

"IT *IS* TUSKER," I ANNOUNCED AS SOON AS WE GOT
back. I felt disgusted and soiled and was ripping off my
clothes before I made it into the bedroom suite, not even
caring that I had an appreciative audience in the form of
Jungle Johnny, Diamond, Grisha, and Tom.

"I like Plain-Neelie undressing her clothes," Grisha announced gleefully as my miniskirt flipped across the room,
the low-cut blouse and push-up bra following. I threw the
shoes in the garbage and began scrubbing at the mascara
with a sanitary wipe from my handbag while I pulled clothes
together for a shower.

"Not that it matters what elephant it was," I was saying,
grabbing jeans from my suitcase.

Jungle Johnny was sitting at the edge of the sofa and
hanging on my every word. Maybe not hanging on my words

so much as hanging on whatever of mine that was visible. Grisha was searching for another pack of cigarettes, and Tom was racing for a bath towel from the bathroom to wrap around me.

"We have to get those elephants out of there," I said with urgency. "And I don't care how we do it. It's inhumane. It's misery!"

"Grisha liked Plain-Neelie in special makeups. Like beautiful Russian woman," Grisha called after me as I headed for the bathroom. "Don't wash off makeups!"

"Grisha can find himself a beautiful Russian woman," I countered as I ducked inside. "This one is spoken for." I gave Tom a sideways look.

"Is that my cue?" He laughed.

"No," I said, irritated by his laugh. "I didn't mean you, I meant Tusker." I shut the bathroom door behind me and took a shower, ungluing my hair, scrubbing the sadness and grime and rage and cruelty from my skin. When I emerged, half an hour later, Jungle Johnny was napping, Tom was reading at the table, Diamond had left on an errand, and Grisha was happily puffing himself into oblivion.

Diamond returned an hour later with a shopping bag. "Last-minute stuff," she said, and sat down at the table where everyone had gathered.

"Trucks are ready," Jungle Johnny was saying. He had a tiny screwdriver, the kind used for repairing eyeglasses and was prying the camera from my handbag. "We use trucks all the time. They have no lettering on them, plain faded blue trucks. We use them for emergency seizures. People don't remember faded blue, so we can move them around and no one notices. I ordered two of them, one for each elephant."

"Someone has to get in and open the gates to the pens," I said. "They have big padlocks."

"I have men to do that," Tom replied. "They'll carry bolt cutters, check for alarms, monitor our movements, back us up, everything we need."

"And they have security dogs," I said. "I didn't see them, but Julian mentioned them."

"Easy," said Tom. "Sedatives mixed into hamburger meat."

"It has to be perfect timing," said Jungle Johnny. "Grisha has to keep that Lance guy occupied, while we get the elephants out of there. He has to invite Lance and his men to dinner, get them drunk, tell him he wants to hunt *after* dinner. By the time they get back to the ranch, the animals will be gone. Tomorrow night is the only chance we'll get."

"Why tomorrow?" I asked.

"Lance Imperialle has other clients," Tom said. "We made sure Grisha was the first to contact him after the elephants came, but if we don't work fast, someone could move in and outbid us."

We had dinner in the hotel dining room. Our group was loud and happy and boisterous. Diamond and JJ, as he kept insisting to be called, seemed to be hitting it off; Mrs. W. was tucked neatly under Diamond's chair; and I fiddled with the huge shrimp cocktail in front of me, my stomach in knots from what I had seen that day. I finally pushed it away and drank wine while the others ate.

"JJ has a TV show," Tom said.

"For kids," said Jungle Johnny. "Try to teach them conservation."

"I like kids," said Diamond, and they smiled at each other.

After dinner, Tom stood up. "I think we should convene to the honeymoon suite," he said, "and finish our conversation. That is," he gave me a mischievous smile, "if the honeymooners don't mind."

"I don't mind at all," I said to him. "It may be my only chance to use one."

They were refining plans for the next day. Tom and Grisha and Diamond. Apparently my job as wife was done. Grisha's would be wining and dining Lance Imperialle and Julian by himself, while the rest of us worked behind the scenes.

The trucks would be moved to just outside the far end of the ranch. Tom's men would be cutting away a large portion of the chain-link fence earlier in the day, but would roll it back into place so that the breach was not noticeable. JJ and Diamond and I were going to slip inside, release the elephants, and drive them to the end of the property, through the opened fence, and up into the truck. That simple. That crazy.

And everything would depend on the speed of the elephants. We weren't even sure they would leave their cages. And once out, they had to be marched across the property to the waiting trucks.

And the whole time, Grisha would have to keep Lance Imperialle and Julian happily eating and drinking and concentrating on the huge profit they were going to make.

Everyone was on edge—there were variables in every corner of the plan.

"Why can't we just let the authorities take the elephants?" Diamond asked at one point. "We could file a complaint."

"They'll be dead by the time anything gets to court," Tom said. "Let's hope Neelie got some good shots. They'll be used to build a case."

"I've done a lot of seizures," said JJ. "And it's always the same story. The authorities just had no *idea* anything like this was happening right under their noses." He shook his head in disgust.

"We'll all be wired together," Tom announced. "I have enough electronics to launch a rocket. You'll all have mikes and earphones and GPSs. Johnny will carry the bullhooks."

"Bullhooks!" I repeated. "What do you mean, 'bullhooks'?"

Tom made a face. "We are going to have to get those elephants out of their cages fast. We won't have time for civilities. They have to be driven out any way we can."

"Plain-Neelie, we cannot throw oranges this time," Grisha agreed.

"But bullhooks?"

"Well, we don't want to use them, but this is life or death," Tom chided me. "If it's going to be a problem—"

"Bollocks, we'll both be fine," Diamond said firmly, giving me a kick under the table. "A determined woman is the equal of the strongest man."

"Women hold up half the sky," JJ interjected with his peculiar Kenyan homily. I looked at him and I looked at Diamond. They dressed alike, thought alike, both given to

cheesy proverbs—it was too perfect. I wondered if she noticed, too, but Diamond only stood up and yawned.

"I guess I'll get some sleep," she said.

JJ stood up, too. "I can walk you to your room, Diamond,"
he said, then blushed to the roots of his blond hair. "If you
don't mind. Maybe we can have a cup of coffee before we
call it a night."

"I don't mind at all," she said, and gave him a beatific
smile. "You can call room service while I take a nice, hot
shower." She bent over to retrieve Mrs. W. "I don't want to
forget Mum," she added, then explained, "she and I are sharing a room."

"I like a person who honors her elders," JJ replied, taking
the urn from her. They left together.

"If Diamond is even taking a shower," I said to Tom, "this
must be true love."

His eyes met mine, and he gave me half a smile. "Do you
believe in stuff like that, Neelie?" he asked.

"Actually, no," I said. "I don't believe in anything anymore."

Tom and Grisha and I went down to the dimly lit bar where
Tom had a bourbon, Grisha enjoyed a vodka, and I had another glass of wine. They quietly finalized a few more details
for the next day, and I mulled over my change of heart. Had
my heart changed? I stole a glance over at Tom and wondered
what I wanted from him. I loved him, I wanted to spend my
life with him, and he loved me—Diamond was right, I would
be a fool to let him get away twice—yet all the unrest I had
felt from a year before was still with me. I finished my wine.

Maybe he wouldn't mind if we put marriage on the back burner for a while. That would solve everything, I thought.

Grisha yawned. "Grisha is ready for sleeping now," he declared. I looked over at Tom, about to ask him if he had gotten me my own room for the night.

"Go to his room, Neelie," Tom directed me softly. "Go up with him."

I stood up. Grisha gave me a little bow and offered me his arm. I took it, and we walked together to the elevator, Tom watching me until the door closed behind us.

I wasn't worried at all. Grisha had always been a total gentleman. From the first time I met him, spending my first week in Africa, peeing behind baobab trees while he stood guard, he was honorable and good.

"Plain-Neelie," he said, when we reached our room, "you can have bed. Grisha does not mind crouch."

I undressed in the bathroom and came out into a darkening room and sat down on the king-size bed. "Have you ever done anything like this before?" I asked Grisha, who was sitting in a chair near the window, the drape opened just enough for him to see out.

"Marriagement?" he asked. "*Nyet*! Grisha makes many romance, but never marriagement. Too heavy travel! Too heavy risk!"

He lit another cigarette and took a long drag. "Grisha suffers from"—he paused to think of the right words—"wild heart." He thought about his words for a moment and then repeated them. "*Da*. Grisha cannot make explainment to you, but—"

"You don't have to explain," I said to him. "I think I know what you mean."

How odd, I thought. I had actually meant to ask him if he had ever taken elephants under these circumstances, and he had misunderstood, but suddenly his answer set my thinking on another course.

I had been floundering. Fretting. I had come home to New York, to a house that I was so proud to have purchased for myself. And yet I was as uncomfortable in it as a mismatched shoe. It felt tight and rubbed at me in all the wrong spots.

I grew up suburban. And I had always chafed at my childhood. It had been so neat and properly contained, and even though I thought I would grow up to emulate it, I couldn't. Yet I didn't know what else I wanted. Tom had come along and taken me to Zimbabwe, and we rescued Margo, and it was the beginning of even more unrest within me. I had found some answers during the year I spent with the baby ellies, but there was something else. Something I could not or didn't want to define just yet.

I lay back on my pillows and tried to sort it out.

"*Da*," Grisha said into the darkening room, his voice filled with both sadness and acceptance. "Grisha cannot be domestic. Grisha suffers from wild heart."

Chapter 45

SOMETIMES THE WORLD BECOMES MORE THAN A SUM of its parts. Sometimes the cruel part, the viciously indifferent part, the part that is so unspeakably mean overwhelms everything good and humane and forever unbalances the ratio of kindness and goodness. Then the world becomes irredeemably ugly and filled with nothing but darkness.

When we found Margo, she had been wounded. Trying to nurse her calf and unable to keep up with her herd left her vulnerable and starving. When I first saw Tusker, he had been the butt of cruel taunting, even though he had done nothing but innocently seek food. When I saw him again, he was a trembling skeleton. And the worst part was that it hadn't been the lack of rains over the lowland plains of Kenya or the sparse growth of savannah grasses that caused it. It hadn't been natural at all. It had been part of human design, a cruel act that forever disarranged the karma of the human race.

I sat up almost all night, nervously thinking about how we were going to get Tusker off the ranch. About all the things that could go wrong and the danger we would all be in. When I was finished torturing myself with that, I thought of Tom and me and Diamond and JJ and Grisha—who was the happiest out of all of us. I wondered who was the most content with their life, and whether their work or love was the most responsible. By dawn, I hadn't solved anything philosophically, but I did manage to give myself a raging headache.

I slept for about an hour when I heard a rap at the door. Room service. The room suddenly bloomed with the delicious scent of food. By the time I sat up, Grisha was already at the table and digging into a huge American breakfast.

"Grisha likes this room servant," he declared. "Come sit with your husband, Plain-Neelie. We eat before everyone comes."

I joined him at the table. It was set for two. There was a lid over my plate, and I lifted it to reveal eggs Benedict and fresh strawberries.

"Wow," I said, "you nailed my favorite breakfast."

Pleased, he closed his eyes and smiled. "Husband should know how to make pleasure with marital wife."

, I laughed.

He cut into his egg and ate a piece. "Grisha is thinking, Plain-Neelie," he said, "that he gives you wrong information. Grisha is thinking all night. He is thinking maybe wild hearts need—" He looked at me, and his eyes held something, a longing, and for a moment I thought he was going to declare his love for me, and my mind was already racing for a nice way to deflect him. I took his hand, and he continued. "Maybe, Grisha is thinking, maybe sometimes wild hearts need to come home. Grisha thinks you are suffering from this, too."

His last words were almost whispered, an obvious effort for him, and I jumped from my chair and went to him and embraced him. He put his arms around my waist, and we held each other.

I caressed his hair and murmured, "Thank you," and kissed the top of his head before we broke apart.

He rose from his chair and gave me an apologetic smile along with a little bow. "Grisha gets ready now," he said. "Everything moves on Grisha's shoulders."

The day passed quickly enough. Tom informed us to take everything with us when we left the hotel since we wouldn't be coming back to it. He had made reservations in another one across town, in another name, so that we wouldn't be traced.

Grisha dressed in exquisitely bad taste: brand-new starched-looking gold-brown pants, a tan-and-orange plaid shirt, and brand-new boots, ready to hunt. The rifles would be supplied by the ranch and then taken back. His contract, a carefully worded document to protect the ranch from prosecution for illegal hunts, called only for a night of entertainment at a hunting lodge. Two large blue vans rolled past the hotel on their way to the ranch, and just the sight of them made my stomach quake from nerves.

The Rolls came by at precisely four thirty to take Grisha to the ranch and pick up Lance Imperialle and his aides.

The rest of us—Tom, Diamond, JJ, and I—got into another rented car, a simple green sedan not nearly as luxurious as Grisha's. Diamond placed Mrs. W. on her lap.

"Can't you leave that urn in your suitcase?" I hissed at Diamond as she got into the car with us.

"I don't think she'd want to miss out on something like this," Diamond replied.

"The more the merrier," said Jungle Johnny. Diamond flashed him a grateful smile.

The blue trucks were waiting, parked alongside the road that backed the ranch. The men had already done their job, snipping the chain link with bolt cutters and peeling it back like the lid of a tin can. They had lured the dogs, all four of them, and given them the dose of sedatives mixed with hamburger meat, and now the dogs were sleeping peacefully under a nearby tree, in a large mottled heap of black and tan fur.

Diamond, JJ, Tom, and I slipped through the fence. Tom carried a pair of bolt cutters and snipped down the thorn-bushes, clearing a path as we went. Diamond carried the GPS and a compass and the same bag she had brought back from yesterday's errand, though I still didn't know what was in it. Jungle Johnny carried several bullhooks. I could barely look at them. I was assigned to carry two large rifles. For what purpose, I didn't want to know.

"They're loaded" was all Tom said to me.

The air was warm and tacky, like a child's lollipop. My tee stuck to my arms and back, and my jeans hugged my legs. I could feel sweat running down the back of my knees, my hair growing slick, even my feet sweating inside my boots.

Maybe it was nerves, but it seemed that the bushes looked even more oppressively thorny from the ground, thicker and uglier, growing in tight formation, and they snagged at us mercilessly, giving up a hold on our clothing only to bite at our skin and hair.

Diamond was following the compass on her GPS. Her stride was steady and stealthy, and I had to admire how she moved with perfect confidence, slipping this way and that, checking and rechecking her coordinates, as though she had walked the land many times.

"Here," she mumbled, moving to the right, "this way. Now we turn here." Tom followed, snipping down bushes, ripping at the vines, measuring the width of the path we were making.

It was a long walk, and we had to execute each step with precision. There wouldn't be another chance. We were coming from the back side of the ranch, so we wouldn't be passing the other animal cages, and I was glad of it. I couldn't bear to see those faces again.

There was a large enclosure ahead of us. The familiar form of Shamwari, rocking, rocking, rocking filled its entirety.

"We get Tusker first," Diamond said, and Jungle Johnny agreed. "Tusker is the elder. If we move him, Shamwari should follow out of respect."

We pressed on another half mile or so, moving quickly. My breath came hard. It had been so easy to travel these distances in the jeep, and I wasn't that fit to move through the humidity, over the brush, pulling away the low-hanging Spanish moss that wrapped into our hair like moist brown-green spider webs. But it was quiet. We said nothing to each other. Tom made a motion, and we followed the line of his hand.

Suddenly Tusker was straight ahead. Tom moved swiftly to the back gate and clipped the lock off in one neat motion. He pulled at the gate and we stood back. Tusker didn't appear to notice.

"We've got to get him out of there right now," JJ said softly. He slipped inside, behind the elephant. Tusker just stood, his trunk down, his ears close to his head. JJ bent down to examine the leg chains and then held his hand out behind. Tom slipped him the bolt cutters and JJ clipped the chains from Tusker's legs, one, two, three, four. I counted them compulsively, one, two, three, four. Everything seemed to be taking so much time.

"He's emaciated," said Tom. "I hope he has the strength to move."

JJ pushed Tusker lightly on the rump. There was no response at all. He didn't move his head, he didn't take even one step forward. It was as though we were invisible to him.

I was sick. It was as though he had died somewhere between his life in Zimbabwe, the clown of the camps, the majestic plunderer of cars and dustbins and lovely lily ponds, and here, in this dry, soulless, ugly hell, he had died. Only his hulking shell was left, waiting for the rest of him to be called away.

"Move on, move on," JJ said to him, slapping him on one hind leg, but Tusker only backed up a confused step.

"The bullhook," Tom ordered. "We've got to get him out of here."

JJ slapped Tusker on the rear with the bullhook now, the sharp end of it biting into the animal's flank. I turned away, sick.

"Please just move," I prayed. "Please. *Please.*"

Tusker stepped back again. The bullhook had made its mark, and he responded in bewilderment. Tom slipped behind him as well, with a bullhook, to stand on his other side. Diamond and I stepped aside so that Tusker could have a clear view of the open gate.

"Come on, man," JJ said. He looked at Tom, and I knew what they were thinking. If we can't even get him out of the cage, how are we going to move him across the ranch before Grisha returns. The whole prospect suddenly seemed impossible.

Tom lifted the bullhook over his head and gave Tusker a hard whack against his back legs. Tusker's head jerked up from the pain, and he spun around and around in a circle but still made no noise. It was eerie and sickening. The men flattened themselves against the chain link to move out of his way. He circled again. We were tormenting him. He didn't know what else to do.

Diamond opened the bag she was carrying. Oranges. Grisha had laughed at the idea, but she reached in and pulled one out, holding it in front of Tusker's trunk. He was shaking now, his legs shook. He looked at the orange and looked away.

"Give me the bullhook," she called to Tom. He handed it to her, and she sliced the orange in two with the sharp end and rubbed a piece of it on the tip of Tusker's trunk. We waited a minute. Slowly, as though a ghost were whispering in his ear, Tusker lifted his trunk to his mouth and tasted the moisture from the fruit.

"Let's go," Diamond ordered. "JJ, stay in the rear and keep driving him forward." She walked ahead, and I followed her. Tusker took a shaky step, then another, then stopped. Diamond ran back to wipe the fruit again on his trunk. He took another step, another. In a few minutes, he had cleared the cage and was standing outside.

"Bollocks! There's no way we can move him like this," Diamond said. "It'll take all night."

"Fuck," Jungle Johnny snapped. "This is becoming a mess."

Diamond looked around. "You get the other one out," she ordered Jungle Johnny and Tom. "Open the gate and get the other one out. We'll get him moving, I promise. We'll bring this one right past Shamwari."

"You have a magic flute?" Tom asked. "He's not moving."

Sure enough, Tusker was rocking from leg to leg and rumbling to himself.

"Get me up there," said Diamond.

"Up where?" asked Jungle Johnny.

"On his back. Get me up on his back," Diamond ordered. "I'm going to ride him out of here." She handed her bag to me while Jungle Johnny lifted her onto the chain link fence. Pushing the tip of her foot into each link, then grabbing herself up with her hands, climbing like the baboons I had seen in Kenya, lifting up swiftly, gracefully into the canopy of the trees. She managed to climb to the top of the enclosure, where she stood, balanced over Tusker's back. In an instant, she dropped down and scrambled across his back to sit right behind his head. Not used to the strange weight, he shook his head up and down and turned sideways.

It wasn't such a crazy idea.

People ride elephants all over the world. The secret, what they don't tell the rest of the world, is that the elephants are trained from the time they are about four, systematically starved and beaten and tortured into submission. Thailand, India, all of those lovely countries that worship the elephant beat and starve them into submission to ride them. This wasn't so different.

Diamond leaned over and grabbed Tusker's ears. Elephants' ears are exquisitely sensitive. "Get Shamwari out of his cage," she said to Jungle Johnny. "I know I can get Tusker going. Neelie, oranges!"

Tom gave me one of the bullhooks, and I resolved I would use it if there was any chance of Tusker turning back. I walked slowly in front of him, luring him with oranges as he took small, unsteady steps behind me. Diamond pulled his ears, one way, then the other.

"Like a horse," she called down to me. "Sometimes you just have to get on and ride 'em. They do catch on."

We walked. The broken elephant and Diamond and I. Every time he stopped, I rubbed the orange on his lips, his tongue, almost putting my hand into his mouth. "Come on," I urged him, I begged him. "Walk."

He did walk. Mechanically, slowly. Even broken, there was something inside of him that still wanted to live. I smacked him with the handle end of the bullhook when he paused. We had to get out of there. I had to keep him moving.

Tom and JJ were having trouble with Shamwari. His gate was open, his chains were off, but he was still swaying mindlessly from leg to leg.

"Get on him," Diamond called over. JJ quickly scaled the sides of the cage and lowered himself onto Shamwari's back and settled, like Diamond, behind his head.

But Shamwari continued to rock. Back and forth, leg to leg, shaking his head from side to side, his eyes blank and unseeing. I ran over to rub the orange on his trunk, but there was no response. I rubbed it on his lips. Nothing.

I reached into the bag. There were only one or two oranges left and a can of something. I pulled it out. Enamel spray paint. Bright red.

"What the hell is this for?" I called up to Diamond.

"Oh, right," she said. "Spray his head. Now! Spray both their heads." I did, without knowing why. I reached up and sprayed the foul-smelling paint, covering their foreheads with huge red splotches of enamel.

Tom came up behind Shamwari and slapped him hard again and again. The elephant lifted his trunk and screamed. A long, heart-rending trumpeting, filled with rage and pain and torment and protest.

"Let's go," Diamond said. "He's come back to life."

She kicked at Tusker. I squeezed oranges until my fingers burned. Tom ran behind the animals, pushing and slapping at them. It was a slow procession, but we moved.

One step to the next.

Across the dust, through the date palms, stumbling over the twisted, dried bromegrass, Shamwari followed his old friend, slowly, painfully, trusting that the old elephant would lead him somewhere safe, and Tusker moved forward, almost as if he understood that every step was a step to life. We got them to the gates. It was nearly dusk, and Grisha would be returning soon. We had to move them faster.

The blue trucks were ready. The back panels were open, the ramps were down. Diamond slid down the side of Tusker and onto the ground, and we pushed and prodded him up the ramp and into the truck. Immediately, the doors were slammed behind him.

Shamwari was next. He balked and screamed as soon as Tusker disappeared from view. JJ was on the ground now, and he and Tom pushed Shamwari up the ramp, sweating and grunting from the effort.

Shamwari fought. He swung his head back and forth, as if to comfort himself. He moved backward, stepping off the ramp, and he trumpeted. His calls were answered by Tusker.

"Hey!" someone screamed from inside the compound. "Hey! What the hell are you doing there? Hey!" It was the security guard. He was running toward us, waving his arms.

We had run out of time.

Chapter 46

SHAMWARI WAS IN NO HURRY. HE RAISED HIS TRUNK and pulled the orange from my hand while Tom and JJ frantically pushed against him. He ate the orange, chewing it slowly. The men pushed some more.

There was a loud rustling sound, and a man screaming in the woods. The date palms swayed like ladies with big hats, disturbed by the grunting efforts of the security guard, who was running between them, tripping over the dried grass and knots of thornbushes. He was overweight, his belly flopped with every lumbering stride, and he ran clutching at his chest and screaming for us to stop.

Shamwari savored the orange, his mouth open, his tongue rolling it around, chewing, chewing, then swallowing it. He took another step, then reached his trunk out to me to ask for more. Tom's two men and JJ pulled on chains that raised the ramp while Tom called Grisha on the cell phone.

"Just get the hell out of the restaurant," he was saying. "Leave the limo and get a cab back to the hotel. The second hotel."

Shamwari wanted more orange. He swept his trunk against me, but I had nothing. He swept the bag, and I threw it up the ramp, inside the truck, hoping he would follow it in, but he stood resolutely waiting for more. One of Tom's men revved up the motor that lifted the ramp. The angle of the ramp was getting higher, forcing Shamwari to slide part way down the ramp. Tom's two drivers each jumped behind the wheel of a truck and started the engines. Finally, Shamwari moved off the ramp and into the back of the truck. We were almost free, but now the security guard was climbing through the cut chain link. Tom and JJ were trapped inside the blue truck with Shamwari. Tom's men gunned the engines, and both trucks rolled safely away.

I ran to the green rented car and turned on the engine. Diamond was just climbing into the passenger seat when the security guard lunged at her and caught her by the leg. They struggled as he tried to pull her out. She fought him, elbowing him, kicking at him, but he hung fast onto her leg, trying to pull her out into the road. I was sitting behind the wheel with the motor running and couldn't reach Diamond to help her. She stretched across the seat and grabbed at the urn, pulling it open with one hand and throwing the contents into the guard's face. He clawed at his mouth and nose, now covered in two inches of thick gray ashes, courtesy of Mrs. Wycliff. Blinded and coughing, he fell back into the road,

Diamond slammed the door shut, and I gunned the motor. The guard sat in the road, wiping at his eyes and nose with the sleeve of his shirt and retching.

Tom paced the hotel room nervously. He and JJ had been dropped off on the side of the road by the blue trucks and had called a taxi to the new hotel, where Diamond and I were waiting. It wasn't nearly as fine as the Holiday Inn, but the plan had been to disappear from view, more or less. We were registered under another false name, Vasya Pupkin, that Grisha had insisted was the simple and forgettable Russian version of John Doe.

It had been nearly three hours since we had taken the elephants, and they were already on their way to a sanctuary in Tennessee, to be checked by a vet, put on IVs, and in general, gotten ready for their long trip to New York. That part had worked, but Grisha hadn't yet returned. He hadn't called any of us and didn't answer his cell phone. The limo driver called Tom to tell him he had dropped off four men at the Circle D ranch, that Grisha had not been with them, and was he finished for the day?

"How hard can it be to get a cab in Texas?" Tom kept asking us. But we knew what he was worried about. Anything could have happened to Grisha—the ranch was big enough to hide anything.

Diamond and JJ were playing cards. I sat by the window to watch anxiously for Grisha's return, when suddenly I remembered something.

"Diamond," I asked, "why did we spray the elephants' heads?"

"Oh, right! I learned my lesson with those horses at the farm," she replied. "When I accidentally used the red marker that washed off."

"But why do it at all?"

She looked over at me. "Trophy hunters? What do they want? Heads! I thought, if we couldn't get the elephants out of there, we could at least paint their heads. Who'd want a trophy with a big red blotch on it that won't come off for years?" She gave a triumphant laugh. "Just wish I'd had the time to spray paint all the other animals."

"The authorities will seize them," Tom said. "Neelie took enough photos—"

The door flew open.

"Is Grisha returned!" Grisha burst into the room, carrying several shopping bags. I jumped up from my chair and ran over to give him a big hug.

"Why didn't you answer your cell phone?" Tom asked.

"Grisha forgets to electrocute it," he replied, then looked around the room, hands on hips. "Where are elephants?"

"On their way to Tennessee," said Tom. "We actually pulled it off."

Grisha nodded and sat down in a chair. "Was sheiks with me at dinner. Was making more bids! Two more men, trying to make heavy bid! I tell them I am Russian mafia. No one makes heavy bid more than Grisha. Then you call. I make excuse myself for toilette and leave through kitchen." He pointed to the bags. "But I stop in kitchen to bring treat. I am told this is famous Texas specialness. Fried prairie oysters!"

"But even with that, what took you so long?" Tom asked. "You should have been back hours ago."

Grisha smiled and shrugged. "Grisha does not remember Athens, Texas. Grisha only remembers Greece city. Grisha tells driver to go to Cypress."

The owner of the sanctuary called late that night to tell us that the elephants had arrived safely. They were weak and injured and were being cared for, and she reassured Tom that they would be ready to undertake their last journey in about a week. It wouldn't be long before they would be in New York, but she wondered why they were both marked in red paint.

"Some kind of ritualistic killing?" she asked.

"Sort of," said Tom. "American ritualistic killing."

The next afternoon, we were having our last meal together before we would fly our separate ways. Grisha had requested real Texas barbecuement for our farewell dinner, since the prairie oysters did not engender much enthusiasm. Diamond looked up a few restaurants in the motel directory and actually found about 162 places, but we let proximity be the determining factor, and we wound up at Bob's BBQ Shack around the corner from the motel.

We toasted one another with beer and ate fiery beef brisket and coleslaw sandwiches, and wished one another happiness and good luck. Grisha announced he was planning for a much-needed vacation before buying a small second home for himself in Rwanda.

"Grisha is thinking, he needs vacationment. Grisha cannot romp the world forever," he declared.

"Rwanda is quite a beautiful country now," Tom agreed. "It has found peace." He saluted Grisha with a glass of beer. "And I wish you peace as well."

"Rwanda," I mused. "I guess a wild heart needs a wild home." Grisha bowed his head to me.

Diamond and I were planning to fly back to New York together, sans the corporeal Mrs. W., though Diamond reverentially wrapped up the urn and packed it into her suitcase.

"I'm glad she came with us," she declared. "Though I'm sorry I have to leave her in Texas. It was her very last rescue, you know."

"But not yours," said JJ, "I'm hoping."

Diamond laughed. "Probably not," she said. "I will always be ready. Just give me enough time to buy the oranges."

Tom stood up and took my hand. I looked up at him, puzzled. I was still holding part of my sandwich in it.

"I would like to make an announcement!" he proclaimed.

"No, you don't," I said, pulling my hand away. "We have to talk first."

"Excuse us," he said, giving a little bow to the group around the table, then helping me from my chair. He led me behind the restaurant, where there were huge pits smoldering with charcoal and half steers spinning on skewers the size of ski poles. I had brought my sandwich with me and took a bite.

"This isn't the most romantic of places," Tom started, "but I'm asking you to marry me."

I looked at him and took a bite of sandwich. His green eyes were dark and earnest, his silver hair curled just a bit over his ears, his shirt was rumpled, his jeans were tight.

"I have to divorce my Russian husband," I joked.

"I'm serious, Neelie," he said. "I love you and I want to marry you."

The men tending the barbecue pit suddenly stood at attention to earnestly eavesdrop.

I took a deep breath. "I don't think I'm what you want," I started. "I mean, I'm not . . . normal."

He gave me a bemused look. "I sort of figured that out."

But I was thinking of how I felt as I stood at the thundering falls watching the water trying to reach heaven, how uncontained it was. How free from encumbrances and expectations. And then I thought of Grisha's words about having a wild heart.

"I can't be home," I said. "I don't want to . . . live . . . in a house . . . all the time."

He nodded. "I know."

"And I may need to leave from time to time," I added.

He nodded. "I know."

"Even if I don't quite know where I'm going," I added. "And I might have to sleep with an elephant once in a while." I took another bite of my sandwich.

He took the sandwich from me and threw it away, then took my hand in his. "I know all that."

"I suffer from . . . a wild heart," I said.

"I have a place just for it," he said, and kissed me to the sound of barbecue forks clacking approvingly in the background. "Next to mine."

We drank the local brew the whole day, toasting and saluting one another, and celebrating a successful rescue and our engagement.

"To the happy couple," said Jungle Johnny.

"To your happiness, always," said Diamond-Rose.

Grisha stood up and gestured with his beer. "Grisha is never so happy to make divorcement," he announced. "Grisha is *filled* with joyness to give wife away to best friend."

Chapter 47

OF COURSE, MY MOTHER MADE THE WEDDING CAKE.

It was in the shape of a huge peanut because she couldn't find a pan that resembled an elephant. It was five layers and covered in chocolate frosting because she thought gray frosting would give it the appearance of being a big boulder. Too impatient to wait for our reception, she proudly showed it off to the family as soon as she and my father arrived. We crowded around the center table for the big reveal.

"That's the oddest-looking cake you ever made!" my father exclaimed when he saw it. "It looks like a big pile of elephant poo."

"Dung," I corrected him.

"Speaking of elephants," Reese interrupted, "why don't elephants like to play cards in the jungle?"

I turned to him. "You know, a nice wedding gift would be a day without stupid jokes."

"Because of all the cheetahs," he finished triumphantly, and kissed me on the cheek. "And that'll be it for the day." I gave him a grateful hug in return.

"You never did appreciate my baking," my mother said.

"Mom, I love your baking!" I protested. "I don't think anyone in the world has a wedding cake that looks like this!"

"I must admit," my mother modestly replied, "I was inspired."

"We can cover it in ice cream," said Marielle. "Ice cream fixes everything."

Tom and I got married at the sanctuary under a big white tent with heaters blasting and a million flowers hanging from everywhere. A flutist, a guitarist, and someone playing the thumb piano performed softly in the background.

I didn't want a big wedding or a fancy wedding or a domesticated wedding of any kind. I wore a simple yellow dress, for spite; Tom wore jeans because I love the way he looks in jeans; and we invited only family, if you follow Diamond-Rose's reasoning that everyone you love is family. My parents attended, along with Jerome and Kate; the twins, Reese and Marielle; Tom's mother, who dressed in enough black lace to look like a Goya painting, but I got the point; Tom's son and his two sisters; Grisha and Richie and Ignacio and Alana, who flew up from Florida; and Jackie and Diamond-Rose and Jungle Johnny and Mrs. W.'s urn, to which Diamond festively attached a sprig of lilies of the valley. I rode down the aisle on Mousi, sitting sideways on his bare back. He was scrubbed white and braided up with yellow roses, and seemed to understand the importance of the occasion, because he did a dignified march right up to Tom and the minister, and held his bowels the whole time.

We had a barbecue, which made my father very happy. And we made sure there were plenty of barbecued portabello mushrooms, which made Richie and Jackie very happy.

"JJ and I are going to travel a bit together," Diamond confided to me while we ate. She had apparently showered for the occasion, the second time in my recent memory, and looked beautiful in a deep green pants suit and a large yellow flower tucked into her flaming hair. She glanced adoringly over at Jungle Johnny. "We leave tomorrow morning for Johannesburg."

"I thought you'd had it with men like that," I teased her. "You know—the jungle takes them?"

"Well, I think this time, the jungle will take both of us," she said, then pulled a cheroot from her pocket. I tried not to choke as the familiar putrefied scent filled the air.

"I just hate to leave you with all the work," she added.

"No problem," I reassured her. "Tom is hiring professional animal caretakers to help run things. And we'll be fixing up the main house so that you'll always have a place to come back to."

She gave me a hug along with another whiff of her cheroot.

There was a sudden barrage of spoons tapping glasses, and Tom leaned over to kiss me.

"I am the happiest man in the world," he whispered.

"Me, too," I whispered back. "I mean, I would be if I were a man, but since I'm a woman, I'm definitely the—"

"Oh, Neelie." He sighed. "Shut up."

My parents strolled over to chat.

"So, where are you going for a honeymoon?" my father asked.

"That's up to Neelie," Tom replied, putting his arm around my waist and pulling me close.

"Well, I hope it's not anyplace exotic," my mother interjected. "I'm certainly glad that her last trip with you was only to Texas. You can't get much safer than the good old U.S.A."

Jerome came over to give me a hug and kiss and advice on prenups, though it was about two hours after the fact, while Kate helpfully whispered, "Don't eat too much wedding cake if you want to wear this dress again."

"I have a question for the new bride and groom," Reese announced. "Why were the elephants thrown out of the hotel swimming pool?"

"Oh, Reese," I said. "You promised!"

"Okay, this is really the last one. Because they couldn't keep their trunks up."

We ate the elephant peanut dung cake with chocolate ice cream, which only made it look worse, and I drank more champagne than I thought I could hold.

The sun was melting away, leaving traces of rose and gold in the sky. Our guests were murmuring with contentment, and I took Tom's hand and led him down to the elephant barn, where our special guests, two elephants from Zimbabwe, were recuperating nicely in their big new stalls.

Brass nameplates on the front of their stalls read, "Tusker" and "Shamwari."

Still brightly marked with huge red spray paint stains in the middle of their foreheads, the elephants were very timid around people. Shamwari comforted himself every night by rocking, and Tusker still hadn't regained his outgoing good nature. His eyes looked haunted, saddened with a new knowledge of humans he'd never had before, but I knew we would fix that.

We stood in front of them, and I pulled Tom close to me. "This is the best wedding gift you could have given me," I said.

"I'm glad you sort of forced me into saving them," he replied.

And it was, as Diamond liked to say, perfect.

We had all done good. We had saved a world.

Actually, two worlds, because it has been said that those who save a life, save a world, and I guess my karma knew a thing or two about what I needed to complete, because I hadn't been allowed to come home from Africa until I put it all together. I'd had things taken from me and given back to me, and I had been given a wild heart so that my unrest would drive me to do what my destiny required.

Tom and I and Grisha and Diamond and JJ, and even Mrs. W. in her own peculiar, deceased way, had all helped restore some balance to what was maybe not such a good world, maybe a sad and broken world, but as I watched the two noble elephants in front of me, I thought, to do anything less was unimaginable.

And I learned something about being civilized. When someone aspires to make the world better for another creature—any creature—then that is truly being civilized.

And that's what it's really all about.

Tom pulled me close. "We'd better get back to our guests, Ms. Neelie Davison-who-won't-take-a-married-name-ever-again," he whispered into my ear. "Or they'll be wondering where we got off to."

I looked up at him. "No, they won't," I said, laughing. "No, they'll know exactly where we are."

Author's Note

THE MOST VULNERABLE CREATURES ON THE PLANET are animals. Routinely hunted, tortured, maimed, and made victim to mankind's most despicable behavior, they have no real power to defend themselves.

On the other hand, the most blessed of humans are those who spend their lives rescuing animals from desperate circumstances. Neelie and Diamond-Rose would want me to dedicate this book to all those people who have carried dogs and cats out of filthy hoarder homes or puppy mills, from floods and catastrophes or abandonment. To those who have picked animals off the streets, taken them from dungeons, removed their chains, given them their first taste of food or water in far too long. To my friends who rescue birds from cramped cages in dark and cold garages and basements. From boxes, where chickens are warehoused for cockfighting.

Thank you to my horse-rescue friends who literally risk life and limb bringing horses and donkeys and mules to safety, and then spend countless hours and money from their own pockets to bring them back from starvation and heal their bodies and hearts.

And to my dear elephants-rescue friends.

There are good, wonderful elephant sanctuaries in the world—I mention them on my website—and they have my total support, gratitude, and admiration for the difficult, grueling, never-ending work they are committed to.

I hope you will find it in your heart to help any one of these creatures. In any way you can. The motivation is to be found in your soul, the reward is to be found in the eyes of your rescue.

Look deep.

ALSO BY
JUDY REENE SINGER

STILL LIFE WITH ELEPHANT
A Novel

ISBN 978-0-06-171375-0 (paperback)

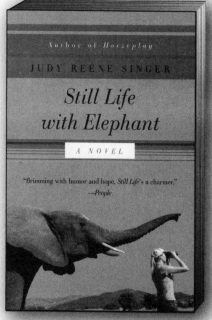

Neelie Sterling never did listen well to the conversation around her. Always preoccupied with an inner monologue, she sometimes misses things. Including the fact that her veterinarian husband, Matt, is having an affair with his colleague, who is now pregnant.

Sent into a tailspin, Neelie throws herself into her horse-training business, until she discovers that Matt is part of a group planning to go to Zimbabwe to rescue a badly injured elephant. Thinking she can repair her relationship with her estranged husband, Neelie manages to get included on the trip. But she never expected that Africa—and a very special animal— could teach her how to love again.

"Brimming with humor and hope, *Still Life*'s a charmer." — *People*

"What sets this story apart from others in the she-finds-herself genre: Neelie doesn't hear well due to her emotional angst. . . . It's an amusing touch in this modern fairy tale." —*USA Today*